MORENGA

Also by Uwe Timm

HEADHUNTER

THE INVENTION OF CURRIED SAUSAGE

MIDSUMMER NIGHT

THE SNAKE TREE

MORENGA

UWE TIMM

Translated from the German by
BREON MITCHELL

A NEW DIRECTIONS BOOK

Design by Semadar Megged
Manufactured in the United States of America
New Directions Books are printed on acid-free paper.
First published clothbound by New Directions in 2003
Published simultaneously in Canada by Penguin Canada Books, Ltd.

Library of Congress Cataloguing-in-Publication Data
Timm, Uwe, 1940–
  [Morenga. English]
  Morenga / Uwe Timm ; translated from the German by Breon Mitchell.
     p. cm.
  ISBN 0-8112-1514-8 (alk. paper)
  1. Morenga, Jakob, d. 1907.—Fiction. I. Mitchell, Breon. II. Title.
  PT2682.I39 M613 2003
  833'.914—dc21   2002015248

New Directions Books are published for James Laughlin
by New Directions Publishing Corporation
80 Eighth Avenue, New York 10011

MORENGA

WARNING SIGNS

On an afternoon in 1904, Farmer Kaempffer sends his houseboy Jakobus, a Hottentot who's been with him for two years, to fetch his youngest son Klaus to do his schoolwork. The faithful Jakobus trots off at once. But neither he nor his son return. Kaempffer finally tires of waiting. He leaves the house to look for them. He finds his son quickly enough, playing near the kraal. But Jakobus has disappeared. Kaempffer searches, calls out, asks the other native workers. They claim they haven't seen him. Kaempffer goes back to the house and returns to his desk. As he sits down, he has the strange feeling that something has changed. He's about to start working on his accounts again when he glances up at the photograph of himself as a lieutenant in the Reserves and discovers a small cross in ink directly above his head.

Farmer Kruse steps from his farmhouse near Warmbad to assign daily chores to the natives as usual.

There's not a man in sight.

He strides over to the native compound. All the pondoks have been taken down over night. A fire still smolders. Suddenly a flight of crowned lapwings whirrs up from a stand of white thorn bushes. Kruse returns quickly to the house, bars the doors and windows, takes his gun from the wall, loads it, and places the remaining shells within easy reach on the table.

On the farm "German Soil," a black worker snatches the whip from Farmer Strohmeier, who uses it to make the men work faster. The native threatens Strohmeier with the whip. The farmer saddles his horse and rides off at once to the nearest police station.

A young Nama woman tells Frau Krabbenhöft: If there's a tap at your window in the night, it will be me, but then you must run fast.

In early June 1904 a telegram arrives at the Imperial Government headquarters in Windhoek: A band of armed Hottentots have attacked isolated farms in the southwestern part of the country, stealing cattle and weapons from white farmers. None of the farmers have been killed. The leader of the band is a man named Morenga.

Who is Morenga?

Information provided by the District Officer in Gibeon: A Hottentot Bastard (father: Herero, mother: Hottentot). Took part in the Bondelswart Rebellion in 1903. Said to have been reared in a missionary school. The name of school is unknown. Last employed in the copper mines of O'okiep in the northern part of Cape Colony.

Morenga rides a white horse that can go four days without water. Only a glass bullet polished by an African can kill him. He can see in the dark. He can shoot a hen's egg from a man's hand at a hundred meters. He wants to drive the Germans out. He can make rain. He turns into a zebra finch and spies on German soldiers.

Telegram: 30 August skirmish between Stempel's patrol and Morenga's band on Sjambok Mountain, Lieutenant Baron von Stempel and four men killed, four men wounded, one missing.

Von Burgsdorff, District Officer in Gibeon, tells Kries, a merchant: We've got to keep the Hottentots from rebelling until the Hereros are completely subdued.

The date is 1 October 1904.

On the afternoon of 3 October, two Witbooi Hottentots, Samuel Isaak and Petrus Jod, approach District Officer von Burgsdorff with a letter from their captain, Hendrik Witboois, declaring war on the Germans.

Burgsdorff decides to ride at once to see Hendrik Witbooi. He's known him for ten years and hopes to change the man's mind. He tells his wife he'll be back tomorrow. Unarmed, he rides off toward Rietmont, accompanied by both Witbooi chiefs.

When he arrives in Mariental the following day, the assembled natives ask him if he received the captain's letter, and when he says yes, a Hottentot Bastard named Salomon Stahl shoots him in the back, killing him. (*The Battles of the German Colonial Guard in South West Africa*, ed. by the Office of the General Staff, Berlin, 1907, vol. 2, p. 13).

On 4 October 1904, the Hottentot (Nama) revolt breaks out in the German Protectorate in South West Africa, almost exactly eight months after the Herero uprising. Now the entire country is at war. The German general staff has to keep sending reinforcements.

BEYOND THE SURF

Veterinary Lieutenant Gottschalk was carried to shore by a black. In the distance, before the surf, the *Gertrud Woermann* lay at anchor. Black crew members paddled the soldiers through the surf. On the beach stood curious onlookers, among them several soldiers, as well as a few women holding parasols. It reminded Gottschalk of a beach resort named Norderney where he had once vacationed. Only the white bandages of the wounded disturbed the impression. When the boat ran aground in shallow water, Gottschalk mounted the shoulders of one of the waiting natives. The man wore nothing but a pair of ragged trousers. Gottschalk felt the perspiring black skin, smelled the sour sweat. He felt sick. With a gentle rotation he was deposited on the beach.

Gottschalk now stood on African soil. It seemed to sway beneath his feet.

Gottschalk had boarded the *Gertrud Woermann* almost three weeks earlier in Hamburg. On the afternoon of 28 September 1904, a fine drizzle set in. The horses had been brought aboard and were now sheltered in the forward hold. Crates of ammunition, guns and provisions were still disappearing aft into the ship. At 6:30 p.m. the steam whistle wailed, releasing a white plume. It was time for visitors to return to shore. The hatches were closed and covered with tarps. On the dock below stood hundreds of people: relatives, friends, and curious onlookers; from the deck of the ship nothing could be seen but their black umbrellas. Gottschalk's parents had written to say they would stand on the dike at Glückstadt and wave, and that he should wave back from the ship, preferably with a white tablecloth. A military band from the 76th Regiment had assembled on the dock and was playing marches. The ship's pilot came on board. The gangway was drawn up and the ship was suddenly filled with a steady, throbbing drone that was to last almost three weeks; the deck planks vibrated gently, somewhere a flange banged. Black clouds billowed from the smokestack and, with no wind and the ship still docked, fell back to the deck beneath the rain. Small greasy coal smuts settled on Gottschalk's gray regimental cloak, leaving dark streaks when he tried to brush them away. Only now, with the hawsers cast off, did the band begin to play: *Muß i denn, muß i denn, zum Städtele hinaus*— faced with the black plume of smoke slowly rolling its sooty way across the ship, Gottschalk suddenly wished he could return to shore. He had no deep feelings about the war that was underway. How had he come up with the crazy idea of volunteering? On the other hand he'd been looking forward to being in South West Africa for the past few days. Summer was setting in there, while in Germany the days were growing shorter and colder. Gottschalk had been having a recurrent dream since childhood: there was no summer. Either he had slept through it, or for some unexplained reason it had never arrived. The officers and troops on board gave three cheers for the Kaiser. Gottschalk heard his own three hurrahs.

Two tugboats towed the steamer away from the dock and out into the river. The lights on the shore road to Ovelgönne were barely visible through the rainy gray twilight. Then the tugs cast off their lines and gave a farewell wail on their sirens.

Around ten the ship passed Glückstadt. Gottschalk stood alone on deck. The rain was falling more heavily now, and a gentle northwest wind had risen. The only thing Gottschalk could make out in the rain-drenched darkness was the navigational light at Glückstadt. Somewhere across the way his parents were standing on the dike with white bedsheets. They probably couldn't even see the lights of the steamer.

• • •

During the crossing Gottschalk shared a cabin with Medical Lieutenant Haring and an N.C.O. veterinarian named Wenstrup. The moment the steward showed Lieutenant Haring his bed, he placed a picture on the only table in the cabin. It was a photo, he told Gottschalk, of his wife and daughter, Lisa and Amelie. That very day Gottschalk discovered how complicated relationships were in the Haring family. Haring had married his cousin, although strictly speaking she wasn't really a cousin, since his uncle had adopted the girl. When Haring asked why Gottschalk wasn't married yet, he said he still hadn't found the right woman.

Wenstrup took no part in these conversations, even when Haring tried to involve him on one occasion by remarking that one could easily ruin one's eyes given the poor light in the cabin. Wenstrup spent most of his time reading in bed.

Gottschalk would have liked to know what book Wenstrup was reading. But it was covered in a snakeskin dust jacket, and he didn't want to ask.

He'd brought along three books for the crossing himself. A textbook on immunology, a South African botany, and a novel by Fontane, *Die Stechlin*.

A few officers in his former regiment had teased Gottschalk at first about his reading habits. Once they even found him on maneuvers sitting in the shade of a wagon wheel with a book in his hand. What kept him from being known as an odd duck was his tendency to downplay his reading, referring to it as a necessary evil to keep up his medical knowledge. But there was no hiding the fact that he also read novels, and contemporary ones at that. Gottschalk had a reputation for getting badly hobbled horses quickly back on their legs. Regimental officers who thought they could wipe their boots on the horse doctor were in for an unpleasant surprise. Major von Consbruch chewed Gottschalk out on imperial maneuvers for advising the major to go easy on his horse, which was going lame. Later, when the troops broke into a gallop, the major had to switch to a side mount in the midst of the action. The battalion commander made a poor impression galloping along behind his troops. He received a personal reprimand from the commanding general. Such incidents became common knowledge, although Gottschalk never bragged about them.

> Regulations for Saluting:
>
> On ships a superior officer is saluted once a day, the first time he is encountered. A Veterinary N.C.O. salutes a Veterinary Lieutenant by touching the brim of his cap or hat. The Lieutenant gives an identical salute to a Medical Lieutenant. All three ranks, N.C.O., Veterinary Lieutenant, and Medical Lieutenant, must salute first, as indicated above, when meeting a Second Lieutenant.

The *Gertrud Woermann* had already passed through the English Channel before Gottschalk and Wenstrup began discussing personal matters.

The wind had risen and men were starting to get seasick. Wenstrup offered Gottschalk an anti-nausea pill. Gottschalk said he had been raised in Glückstadt, with ships practically at his doorstep. His father owned a store for colonial goods and his grandfather on his mother's side owned a herring lugger. He had sailed along to the Dogger Bank a few times during school holidays.

God save us from fire on the high seas was one of the inane phrases Gottschalk's grandfather repeated at every opportunity in his awkward High German.

Wenstrup said he was a landlubber from Berlin, so he'd made a point of bringing the pills along.

It was only later that Gottschalk recalled something strange: Wenstrup offered the pills to him, but not to Second Lieutenant von Schwanebach, who was suffering mightily, nor to the chief supply officer, Captain von Tresckow.

At breakfast von Tresckow maintained that cavalry men didn't get seasick all that easily, there were too many parallels

between horses and ships. He skipped the noon meal. By afternoon he was standing on deck, clutching the railing and staring
off into the distance, which one of the crewmen had told him
would help. His monocle dangled on its cord, clinking against
the steel railing with each roll of the ship. Shortly before supper
Wenstrup entered the cabin and told Gottschalk to visit the
head and check the battle readiness of the Cavalry Guard.

Gottschalk found Captain von Tresckow on the floor, em-
bracing the toilet stool, his green face propped on the white
porcelain rim. When Gottschalk asked if he could help,
Tresckow said, thanks, comrade, without lifting his head.

Gottschalk's diary during the crossing consists almost entirely
of daily notes on longitude and latitude, along with standard references to the weather: dull, overcast, sunny, rainy. Only three
days show somewhat more extensive entries:

Gottschalk's diary,
8 October 1904

Tropic of Cancer. Awnings unfurled on deck. Horsehair everywhere.
The animals are shedding their winter coats with the change in climate.

10 October 1904

At night just above the horizon, the Southern Cross. Longing to be
alone; instead, desultory conversations in the mess. A feeling of inner
tension. W. keeps his distance.

13 October 1904

The ship crossed the equator. At twelve noon, standing upright, you
could cover your shadow with a cap.

Wenstrup, who was growing a beard, let himself be shaved with a
huge wooden knife by one of Neptune's minions (played by Sergeant
Ro., a veteran of the Colonial Guard) as part of the crossing-the-line
ceremony.

Wenstrup maintained a deadly serious expression throughout, as if
he were about to be decapitated. Everyone laughed. Including me.

* * *

Once Wenstrup asked Gottschalk why he had volunteered for South West Africa. Gottschalk's reply: various reasons.

A photograph: Gottschalk is sitting beside a supply wagon in a worn khaki uniform, a peaked cap on his head. Four spokes of the six-foot-high wooden wheel are visible to the right. Gottschalk's left arm rests on a wooden table. On this table lie a field canteen, sheets of paper, pencils, a pocketknife and an oil-cloth notebook (his diary). Dark eyes, a dark beard that he has apparently left untouched for the past few days, a softly curved mouth. A keepsake photo for folks back home in Glückstadt, that's the pose he's assumed. He gives the impression, gazing into the camera, that he's holding his breath.

By the way, what does your father do, Lieutenant von Schwane-bach asks him at supper.

Sells colonial goods.

The table erupts in laughter. They think Gottschalk has allowed himself a little joke.

The scales dangled from the ceiling above the shop counter. When his father weighed out 100 grams of saffron, he used copper weights of various sizes that nestled inside one another like small pots. What little Gottschalk could never understand was why he couldn't eat all the dates, figs, dried bananas and almonds he wanted. (His playmates at school couldn't believe it either). His mother had to negotiate with his father for her cooking needs, and whatever she used was entered into the accounts. There was an invisible border between the shop and the apartment on the first floor, which could only be reached by a narrow staircase from the shop itself. The rules below were different and stricter than those above, and they were sharply drummed into little Gottschalk when he once took a handful of almonds from a glass jar on the shelf. Everything in the shop waited in glass jars, sacks, and boxes to be weighed out at some point, but only in exchange for money; then it was transferred to a new owner. The family seemed to live in a state of waiting.

On 11 October the *Gertrud Woermann* dropped anchor in Monrovia. A diplomatic secretary came on board with news that a Hottentot rebellion had broken out in South West Africa. Then we can kill two birds with one stone, said a lieutenant.

Fifteen black crew were taken on board. They were supposed to paddle the soldiers to land when the steamer reached Swakopmund. Dr. Haring was ordered to examine the natives, who were kept in the forward area of the ship.

Strictly speaking, that's a task for our two veterinarians, said Second Lieutenant Schwanebach. Everyone laughed, except Wenstrup. (Dr. Haring's reaction: the man has no sense of humor). Gottschalk felt he had laughed far too loudly. Strictly speaking, he hadn't felt like laughing at all.

Six days later the steamer reached Swakopmund. That night Gottschalk heard a loud splash and then the rattle of the anchor chain. But something else had awakened him. It took a moment to realize what it was: the steady, throbbing drone had ceased, along with the gentle vibration of the planks, cabin walls and bedstead. Gottschalk thought about going outside and taking a look at the coastline, but hearing voices on deck and seeing that Dr. Haring was already there, he stayed in bed.

When he emerged the next morning, he was astonished to find everything wrapped in a thick milky fog. He couldn't even make out the stern of the ship. Only the steady, recurrent boom and roar of the surf on the shore indicated the direction of the coast. Around eleven the fog began to disperse. A gray-brown desert landscape came into view.

On the coast lay a few scattered brick houses, shacks, corrugated tin huts, tents. No palms, no trees, not a speck of green. Although Gottschalk already knew what to expect from the landscape, he was still disappointed.

* * *

After the black crew paddled the soldiers to shore in the landing boats, the horses were unloaded. They were hoisted from the hold with a deck winch one by one in leather girths and then lowered onto flat wooden rafts. The rafts were towed to the surf by steam launch, where whip-cracking crew members drove the horses into the water. They swam to shore in small clusters.

Wenstrup arrived in the last boat. He had stayed on board to supervise the loading of the horses. When the boat ran aground in shallow water it could be seen he was barefoot. He declined to be carried ashore by a native. With boots, sword, and socks in hand, he waded onto land.

Captain von Tresckow, who stood beside Gottschalk watching the horses thrash wildly as men from the cavalry depot slowly herded them together, said dryly: Those nags can kick and bite all they want, they'll wind up pulling a wagon again, with a coachman or rider holding the reins and a whip.

In Swakopmund Gottschalk discovered he was not to proceed as expected to the Northern Division in Hereroland, but had been assigned instead to the 8th Regiment in the south.

Things are looking pretty bad down there, Lieutenant Ahrens said.

Two locomotives pulled the narrow-gauge train through the desert. Gottschalk could have easily trotted along beside the train, except for the extreme heat. He sat on bags of oats like the others. Tarps had been spread over the open boxcars to protect the men from the sun.

Captain Tresckow was the only one still wearing his uniform jacket with his pistol strapped on.

Is he going to mount the train and ride it, Wenstrup asked Gottschalk as they pulled out, pointing to the cavalry officer's riding crop. Gottschalk pretended not to understand. Later, with the train on its way, they learned he had a small gold cigarette lighter set in the handle of his riding crop, made to order by a whip factory in Allgäu.

Very handy, said Tresckow, the exact words a Hottentot was to say five months later, when he found the crop after a skirmish with a patrol.

Handy because you could light a cigarette before an attack without having to rummage around in your pockets. Gottschalk was sitting in the open door of the boxcar. He hoped the airstream would cool him a little, but it was like sitting in front of an open stove. Outside in the flickering heat lay a dreary, barren landscape from which fissured rocks rose now and again, with occasional immense gravel screes seemingly dumped at random.

Twice a year Gottschalk's father packed a sailcloth bag and took the train to Hamburg. Business trips he called them. In the sailcloth bag was his order book, in which he noted what and how much he needed to reorder from the colonial goods importer.

Little Gottschalk looked forward to these occasions, to these five or six days a year when he could play in the store. His mother would take the glass tops off the fat-bellied jars on the shelves and let him reach in: cinnamon, pieces of brown bark from Ceylon; vanilla, shriveled brownish-black pods from Guatemala; nutmeg, fluted gray kernels from Cameroon; the sweet, heavy fragrance of cloves, thick-stemmed buds from the Spice Islands in the Molucca Sea.

Those words: Spice Islands.

What do you think of when you hear the words Spice Islands, Gottschalk asked Wenstrup once during the crossing. Wenstrup ruminated a moment, as if savoring something, then said: Mulled wine, and to Gottschalk: I think it was the great Moltke who once said: the Prussian army has no room for Jews or dreamers.

The train stopped in the night at a small corrugated tin hut barricaded behind a wall of sandbags. Beside it stood a water tank, a mound of coal and a wooden cross. The station master had been shot by Hereros at the outbreak of hostilities. The station was now manned by six soldiers from the Railway Detachment. Sentries were posted. Gottschalk slept in the open for the first time, and had difficulty getting to sleep. They were awakened at five, coffee was poured, and there was zwieback from the ship. Around six the train pulled out again. They couldn't travel at night, the engineer said, scattered bands of Hereros still threatened the region.

Four hours into the journey the landscape changed: now it was hilly with a few dry bushes.

Dr. Haring and Lieutenant Ahrens discussed how one might go about cultivating the land some day.

Not long afterward the train stopped. The tracks were covered by sand drifts. A troop of Herero prisoners cleared them with shovels. They were chained together in pairs. Two sentries stood by. One was smoking a pipe.

One of the captive Hereros wore a tattered stiff collar—presumably to keep his neck from being chafed by the iron.

Near Karibib the stands of trees and bushes grew denser. Between them, in depressions and swales where water had accumulated, islands of green emerged. The blades of grass had turned to standing hay over the long dry months. Gottschalk saw that livestock could be raised here, but it would require large-scale farming. Finally even Lieutenant von Schwanebach noticed how carefully Gottschalk was studying the landscape, and asked if he was afraid of the blacks or just keeping an eye out for baboons.

Gottschalk's diary contains numerous entries on the flora and soil conditions in the regions through which he passed. There are also sketches of farmhouses, most with six to eight rooms. The floor plans are precise, even if amateurish from an architectural point of view. For example, in one sketch the kitchen door can't possibly be opened, since it's blocked by a water tank.

•   •   •

Gottschalk was looking for farmland where, in a few years, he could raise cattle and horses with the money he saved. More often than not, drifting off to sleep at night, he was already furnishing a farmhouse. There was a library, a living room with a piano (one of the sketches actually included an upright piano in the front room), although Gottschalk himself played only the flute. But his wife, and later his children, would play the piano. We should add that at the time (Gottschalk was thirty-four years old) he didn't know any woman who might potentially be his wife. In Hamburg he had been involved in what was known as a relationship, with the wife of a district court judge.

Low-interest loans were available to members of the Colonial Guard who wished to buy land in South West Africa. On a warm evening, the family would gather in the living room for chamber music, listening in the peace and quiet of the countryside to Johann Heinrich Schmelzer's sonata *La Buscha*. This was one of those scenarios Gottschalk always envisioned; he watched himself playing, but at the same time he could see the house with its glowing windows in the distance, and hear through the stillness of the night the sound of the harpsichord. Whether he would buy a piano or a harpsichord depended on what he was envisioning at that moment, as did the arrangement of the room, and in turn the house (thus the wide range of floor plans in the sketches), and even the number of his children. For certain compositions three would do, in others four, now and then six might be needed, and later, when the farm and livestock were flourishing, he might have to hire a governess, possibly even a tutor, rendering other even larger concerts possible. Applicants would be required to play some particular instrument, for example a baroque bassoon or a natural horn in E flat minor, so that they could also perform Telemann's *Ouverture avec la suite, à sept instruments.*

The train arrived at Waldau, the station in ruins. On the pale brown façade, above the empty windows, sooty traces of fire were visible. Next to the ruins three wooden crosses were stuck in the ground.

Gottschalk had never spoken with anyone about his plans, and certainly not about what one might describe as his fantasies. Gottschalk knew very well what Wenstrup meant when he quoted Moltke: The Prussian army has no room for Jews or dreamers. But there was nothing brooding or odd in Gottschalk's conduct. His manners were, as Lieutenant von Tresckow indicated in his official assessment, tactful, smooth, and extremely polite.

The fishy smell was the worst. In spite of laundry soap and vigorous scrubbing it clung to his hands. Little Gottschalk had to transfer the salted herring from the smaller barrels rolled from the fishing boats to his father's shop, into one large barrel that stood at the door, covered with a lid. The other goods in the shop mustn't absorb the fish smell. Repacking the herring was Gottschalk's job all the way through high school.

He buried his hands in his pockets. Hands on the desk, the teacher ordered. Harry Herring, his schoolmates teased.

Some nights, when he knew the barrels would arrive before school the next morning, he cried.

As von Tresckow observed, Gottschalk had adopted one of Wenstrup's characteristic gestures during the three-week voyage. When asking a question or offering a criticism, Wenstrup had a habit of grimacing and running a finger around inside his collar, as if he were having trouble breathing. One day Gottschalk began tugging at his own collar.

Gottschalk was well aware, by the way, that he tended to pick up certain turns of phrase, intonations, and gestures from others, possibly even personality traits, and he did so unwillingly, for he considered it a sign of immaturity, a weakness of character. He too noticed that he was running his finger inside his collar like Wenstrup, and stranger still, that this gesture immediately put him in a critical frame of mind; inserting his finger in such a way seemed to make him want to raise objections. It all struck Gottschalk as odd, but that didn't keep it from happening.

Although he was already thirty-four years old, Gottschalk still had no fixed physical traits, except for the way he walked, a rapid, jerky gait he'd developed even before joining the military, totally unlike the limping slouch of his father, which even as a boy on their Sunday strolls through Glückstadt he found unbearable.

Gottschalk's diary,
21 October 1904
(in the evening, on the troop train to Windhoek)

A herd of startled antelope raced along beside the train for a moment, then disappeared into the bush.

Tr. says that the entire Herero region will be annexed by the crown, i.e.—opened for settlement. The best land in South West Africa supposedly, good pastures and relatively abundant water. It's a fine thought that at some point there will be eyes in this wilderness reading Goethe, ears listening to Mozart. They call the streams *rivier.*

23 October 1904 (Windhoek)

Windhoek, the colonial capital: a military barrack with a small village attached. General Trotha on horseback. Line of command field officers. The fortress on the hill was supposedly built with bare hands by Captain von Françoise's troopers. The natives, black (Hereros) and brown (Hottentots), as well as numerous half-breeds, called Bastards, look like short, ragged Europeans, only black.

The next day Gottschalk reported to headquarters. Below the fort, near the soldiers' barracks, painted Hottentot women gestured to Gottschalk as he passed: poking a finger in their fists, or sticking out their tongues, trilling, and swaying their startlingly large hips.

The women are fantastic, said Captain Moll, the staff veterinarian, as he outlined Gottschalk's duties, completely immoral, total animals, but unfortunately syphilitic for the most part. Over twenty percent of the men were already infected.

The livestock were kept in large kraals on the outskirts of the village. Cattle, sheep and goats, taken from conquered Hereros. Unfortunately most of them died of thirst in the desert. They couldn't seize them from the Hereros without driving them out onto the sand flats. Now the cattle had to be inspected and checked for infectious diseases.

New animals were being brought in daily.

When Gottschalk asked how the livestock was used, Moll said it provided meat for the troops. The rest simply died. The German settlers protested of course, but those were the General's orders.

The cattle were a pitiful sight, totally emaciated, many injured by thorns or bullets, with festering wounds. Bodies of dead animals lay scattered everywhere. The stench of carrion filled the air.

A large area next to the kraal had been enclosed with barbed wire. Sentries were posted in front with fixed bayonets. Beyond the fence Gottschalk could see people, or rather skeletons, squatting—no, something halfway between humans and skeletons. They huddled together, mostly naked, in the piercingly hot sun.

What a sight, said Gottschalk, gazing at them.

That's our concentration camp, Moll explained, a new innovation based on the English experience in the Boer War.

But those are women and children, said Gottschalk.

Yes, they'd finally started separating the men from the women. Of course there weren't many men anyway. They were constantly coupling in broad daylight, though they received almost nothing to eat An insatiable urge to procreate. But now the death rate far exceeded new births.

The Spice Islands. They lie on the equator, at 130° longitude, in the Molucca Sea. Cloves grow there, blossoming with heavy, sweet fragrance in the fields of the interior, birds of paradise swirling about, the buds plucked by Malays, dried and carried by lines of native bearers through the screaming jungle, escorted at night by the velvet tread of the tiger. From the coast they are paddled rapidly by boat to a ship anchored beyond the reefs. White sails ascend the masts, billow out in the trade winds, drive the ship through the ocean, droop limply for weeks in the doldrums, explode like cannon in the Biscay. New sails propel the ship through the English Channel to the Elbe, past Glückstadt, on to Hamburg. The cloves, sewn up in sacks, are stacked in warehouses, until two are carried to Hannes Christiansen's barge and sail back to Glückstadt, where they fill the large glass jar on the shelf, are gradually weighed out into paper packets hand-twisted by his mother, and then delivered to homes, a task that falls mostly to little Gottschalk. There they are added to the gravy and the mulled wine, releasing at last upon the palate of Doctor Hinrichsen a flavor and fragrance that once merely drifted in the air on distant Spice Islands.

They die, Gottschalk later said to Wenstrup, from dysentery, typhus, and undernourishment. They starve to death.

No, said Wenstrup, they let them starve to death. That's a subtle but crucial distinction.

Gottschalk thought it was simply an administrative oversight on the part of lower-level bureaucrats.

Wenstrup on the contrary seriously maintained it was part of a systematic plan.

What plan?

The extermination of the natives. They want the land for settlement.

As Gottschalk rode out to the kraal the next day and passed by the camp, he saw hands stretched out toward him through the barbed wire.

Someone had lettered a sign and hung it on the fence: Please don't feed the animals.

• • •

Gottschalk had been ordered by Moll, the Chief Veterinarian, to find out why cattle were dying. He took blood samples, dissected a few of the dead bodies, and examined tissue samples under a microscope. The suspicion of rinderpest proved unfounded. A large number of Herero cattle had been immunized against the disease, as could be seen by checking their tails. A surprisingly simple but effective method had been employed, as one of the captured Hereros working for the Germans explained to Gottschalk. A strong thread was dipped in mucous from a cow that had died of the lung disease and then drawn through the skin of the tail with a needle. The thread was knotted and snipped off, so that part of it remained in the tail.

Gottschalk's report reached a simple conclusion: most of the cattle had starved to death.

Gottschalk's diary,
23 October 1904

Walking past the camp I saw white maggots as thick as my finger, as if they had mutated.

Yesterday in the officers' mess Haring said: Civilization is unthinkable without sacrifices.

That evening, Gottschalk told Wenstrup he was going to submit a petition to Colonial Guard headquarters requesting that the dead cattle be given to the starving prisoners.

Wenstrup said it wouldn't hurt to try, but he didn't see much likelihood of success.

Gottschalk expected Wenstrup to say just hide behind your pipe smoke instead. Gottschalk knew it wasn't smart to get mixed up in something that was already up and running, whether or not it was based on a specific order. The military bureaucracy was always temperamental when questions were raised, when someone asked why something already in place was being done that way. The only spot from which you can see everything is the top, Gottschalk's former regimental commander said, a military academy man: the front line soldier is blind precisely because he sees the whites of the enemy's eyes.

What upset Gottschalk was the absurd fact that human beings were starving to death while a few meters away cattle dropped to the ground and rotted away. He was convinced that the order to deny meat to the Hereros was meant to prevent cattle from being slaughtered for the prisoners and based on insufficient knowledge of the actual situation. In fact the animals were dying of starvation by the hundreds. They fell to the flat sandy plain and couldn't get up.

That night Gottschalk composed his petition.

He had two main points:

1. If used for food, the dead animals would not rot, thereby reducing the risk of plague for the Colonial Guard and the prisoners. 2. The lives of women and children would be saved.

Gottschalk couldn't get to sleep. Outside it was pouring rain.

The next morning Gottschalk reported to the office of Chief Veterinarian Moll. He was determined to follow official channels, going first through the Chief Veterinarian and then to headquarters. Gottschalk hoped Moll wouldn't start extolling the virtues of Hottentot women again.

What Gottschalk couldn't foresee was that Moll would be sitting at his desk in silent fury after a nasty dressing-down, a fury he hadn't been able to take out yet on his office orderly, a sergeant who simply hadn't given him an opportunity. Early that morning, Moll had been ordered to report to the base commander, Major von Redern, who normally spoke an easygoing Swabian dialect, but on this occasion chewed him out like a top-sergeant. Most of the oats, which had been stored in the open, had been soaked in last night's storm. No one had thought it would rain, nor were there any tarps to cover the sacks. Wet

oats, possibly even fermented, Moll surely realized as a veterinarian, could disable an entire cavalry detachment. Colic turned
even well-trained steeds into wildly thrashing mustangs. Moll
had to face the worst of all reproaches: he was a dilettante, a
bungler. It bordered on an insult to his honor. The Major
shouted (what was humiliating was that Moll realized Redner
had planned in advance to insult him by shouting). The Major
said it smacked of sabotage, perhaps even collaboration. The in-
sinuation that Moll might be in league with the kaffirs was the
most outrageous insult of all. Moll tried to defend himself, but
each time he tried to reply the Major cut him off: Keep your
mouth shut! Don't say a word unless I say so. Then he dismissed
Moll. On the way back to his office, Moll considered resigning.
Collaboration. Moll chewed his lip as he read the petition, a
fairly narrow lower lip on the thick peasant head so often found
in North Germany: a broad jaw, with slightly protruding ears.
Gottschalk, who had remained standing before Moll (Major von
Redner kept Moll standing at noon too), watched those ears start
to redden. While he read, Moll buttoned and unbuttoned his
right breast pocket with a strange nervous twitch at odds with
his massive body, then looked up at Gottschalk. Meanwhile his
face took on the color of his ears. He stared at Gottschalk, and
then a single phrase emerged from that hinged jaw: Jungle fever!
At last Moll could shout.

That evening Wenstrup asked Gottschalk if denying food to prisoners had merely been a low-level bureaucratic oversight.

Gottschalk said those were the orders.

Wenstrup didn't ask Gottschalk if he had gone ahead with his
petition.

On 3 November, Lieutenant Gottschalk received orders to proceed to Keetmanshoop, in the southern part of the Protectorate.
He was to join the 5th Battery on its way toward Rehoboth. The
route led through rebel Hottentot territory.

TWO POSITIONS

F rom General von Trotha's proclamation of 2 October 1904, to the Hereros: Within the German frontier every Herero with or without a rifle, with or without cattle, will be shot. I will not take over any more women or children. But I will either drive them back to your people or have them fired on. These are my words to the Herero people. The great General of the mighty German Kaiser. (Conrad R. Rust, *War and Peace*, Leipzig, 1965, p. 385)

Governor Colonel Leutwein is said to have worked for a negotiated peace even after the change of command, and described the Herero nation as a "necessary labor force." (German Colonial Archives 2089)

Imperial Chancellor von Bülow: The total, planned extermination of the Hereros would exceed any reasonable measure for the restoration of peace in South West Africa and of punishment. The natives are essential for farming, for raising livestock, and for mining. (German Colonial Archives 2089)

General von Trotha: I totally disagree. I believe the nation as such must be destroyed. (12 December 1904, GCA 2089)

Chief of the General Staff, Colonel-General Count Schlieffen: His assertion that the entire nation must be destroyed or driven from the country makes sense. After what has happened, it will be very difficult for blacks and whites to live together, unless the former are held in an extended state of forced labor, that is, a sort of slavery. The racial struggle that has erupted can only be brought to a close by the destruction of one side. (Schlieffen to the Colonial Office, 23 November 1904, GCA 2089)

Consequences: "Closing off of the sand flats with iron rigor for months," reports another combatant, "completed the task of destruction. The military dispatches of General von Trotha from that period include no reports of any special note. The drama took place on the darkened stage of the sand flats. But when the rainy season arrived, as the stage gradually brightened and our patrols pressed forward to the borders of Betschuanaland, the horrific image of troops who had died of thirst appeared before their eyes.

"The death rattles of the dying and the frenzied cries of those gone mad . . . faded into the exalted silence of infinity." (*The Battles of the German Colonial Guard in South West Africa*, edited by the Office of the General Staff, vol. I, p. 218)

Of approximately 80,000 Hereros, 15,130 survived.

GENERAL SITUATION

October 1904:

Governor Leutwein's awkward position

Immediately following the outbreak of hostilities in Namaland, Governor Colonel Leutwein receives orders from General Trotha to attack the rebel Hottentots and to relieve the encircled villages. Leutwein is Governor and as such would normally be General Trotha's superior, but since he is only a Colonel he is outranked by General Trotha and bound to obey him. An awkward position.

Colonel Leutwein is to press ahead toward Gibeon by way of Rehoboth with the 7th Field Company, consisting of rested and experienced troops from Windhoek. This Company is then taken from the Colonel and he is assigned the 3rd Depot Company instead. The Depot Company is hastily filled out with secretaries, military bakers, and staff trumpeters. Many of these have never been on a horse before. On 7 October the Company saddles up. On 10 October Governor Colonel Leutwein follows. Three days out a military baker accidentally shoots off two of his own fingers. On the same day Seaman Gu. is kicked by his horse while trying to stroke it, shattering his right kneecap. Colonel Leutwein is convinced he can't risk a foray into rebel territory with these people. He stops in Rehoboth. Leutwein again attempts to end the uprising by negotiating with Hendrik Witbooi. Hendrik Witbooi refuses to meet. Governor Leutwein's notion of peaceful colonization, envisioning the spatially segregated development of whites and blacks (on reserves), is shattered once and for all. The entire country was at war. Governor

Leutwein resigned. He had been placed in an increasingly awkward position: first with regard to General Trotha, who considered Leutwein a weak-willed compromiser who, as Governor, stood in the way of his own radical pacification program. Secondly with regard to Trotha's superior officer, Colonel-General Count Schlieffen, Chief of the General Staff, who also considered Leutwein overly inclined toward compromise, and in addition found the ambiguity in the order of command between General Trotha and Governor Colonel Leutwein militarily unacceptable. Thirdly with regard to His Majesty, the Kaiser, who also considered the Colonel relatively weak-willed because he constantly wanted to negotiate, and even worse, at the outbreak of the Herero uprising, finding himself in the extreme southern part of the Protectorate, rather than riding north through the German area, had chosen the quicker course of taking an English steamer to Swakopmund from the English harbor, Port Nolloth. Everyone knew how the Kaiser felt about England. So Leutwein was in an extremely awkward position.

November 1904:
The White Snake

Nor did General Trotha spare the Governor the following: He was stripped of his command of the Southern Detachment, the 3rd Depot Company that had been left standing in Rehoboth. Colonel Deimling replaced him. Deimling and his detachment had delivered the decisive thrust against the encircled Hereros at Waterberg. Deimling received substantial reinforcements from General Trotha: two companies and two batteries. While Colonel Deimling was riding toward Rehoboth, Governor Leutwein prepared to return home, supposedly for health reasons.

All is quiet in the insurgent area. The encircled villages are not attacked. During a patrol skirmish near Kub, seven men are killed and five are wounded. Sergeant Cza. runs for his life. By the time he reaches the German lines, he has two holes in his hat, one in his jacket, two in his trousers, and one bullet has struck the butt of his rifle. He himself is unscathed.

The first task of the Southern Division under Colonel Deimling, was to create some breathing room. Deimling was thought to be the right man for the job: he was energetic, someone who knew how to get things done, a daredevil of sorts. The Witboois called him The White Snake. While Colonel Leutwein, a rotund man from Baden with pince-nez and a highly praised wine cellar in Windhoek, was generally found riding along behind his men, Deimling was usually out in front of his, or at the least at the head of the column. One must lead from the front. And at the same time he was working out a strategy. He didn't intend just to free the encircled villages, he would surround the Witboois and annihilate them.

Deimling's typical vocabulary for skirmishes and battles: crush, shatter, smash.

Colonel Deimling's plan: to smash the Witboois. Then to march south and smash Morenga and his men too.

In the south, Morenga was laying siege to the village of Warmbad.

December 1904:
Deimling advances

General Trotha and his staff felt that any major offensive against the Witboois should be postponed until reinforcements reached the Protectorate.

From 12 November 1904 to 18 January 1905, 198 officers, doctors, and military officials, 4094 men, and 2812 horses were dispatched in six detachments.

Trotha's staff had in mind only minor attacks to relieve pressure elsewhere. But on 30 November, Colonel Deimling decided to take the offensive. The troops were to advance on Rietmont, where Hendrik Witbooi had his headquarters, in three detachments: the main unit from Kub, and two smaller units from Lidfontein and Jackelsfontein.

On 4 December the main detachment launches a surprise attack near Nari, around three o'clock in the afternoon. The artillery fires on the Witboois, who have dug in among black rock formations. They are overrun in a bayonet charge. The Witboois flee. The planned encirclement fails. The pondoks are rifled for anything of use. In Witbooi's house steam still rises from the coffee. They find his silver watch, reading glasses, pen and paper. But Hendrik Witbooi has escaped with almost all his men. The pondoks are set ablaze and the cattle are driven off, together with a few captive women and children.

With the victory over Hendrik Witbooi, Deimling has created the preconditions for all-out guerilla warfare by the Hottentots, who can now operate more freely without worrying about villages, farms, and cattle.

We've shot ourselves in the foot, says Captain i. G. v. Ha.

Deimling advances on Gibeon and installs his staff there.

The entire supply line is threatened by the Witboois. Ahead, in the Karas Mountains, sit Morenga and his men, whom Colonel Deimling and his staff consider their most dangerous opponent.

Von Trotha's staff shares this opinion.

Concept of the Enemy

1.

Making the rounds in staff meetings toward the end of 1904 and passed on with some bitterness are stories of petty insolence on the part of the rebels. Morenga, for example, after driving off all of Captain Wehle's horses and mules, wrote him a letter asking him to feed his animals better in the future, so that next time he wouldn't have to make do with old nags.

2.

Jakob Morenga, a Herero Bastard from a small tribe living in the midst of the Hottentots by the Gainab River (east of Great Karas Mountains), worked in the English mines of South Africa, earned some money and attained a not inconsiderable education for a black. He speaks both English and Dutch, understands German, and over the course of the war has proved a most unusual figure among the natives in general, both in terms of the prudence and energy with which he has conducted his campaigns, and in particular by how, when whites have fallen into his hands, he has abstained from the usual bestial atrocities practiced by his northern tribesmen, even demonstrating a certain magnanimity from time to time. In diverse negotiations, he has proved to be relatively reliable. His unusual importance can be seen in the very fact that although he is a black man, he plays a leading role among the lighter-skinned Hottentots.

(*The Battles of the German Colonial Guard in South West Africa*, ed. by the General Staff, vol. 2, p. 5)

3.

Cavalry Colonial Guard Schmodginsky: The Hottentots are naturally warlike and have developed a great facility for guerilla warfare. It's true that their most important general—Morenga—was black. Basically they are all bandits and cattle thieves. Like the Hereros, they too demonstrated outstanding soldierly qualities when it came to protecting their cattle and water-holes.

Both tribes were armed with modern breech-loaders, model 88, or with good firearms, and handled even those of inferior quality with skill. Their discipline under fire and thrift with ammunition must be fully acknowledged. The weapons of savages, bows and spears, are no longer known in South West Africa. However the *kirri*, a heavy, three-foot-long cudgel made of the hardest wood, serves as a hand weapon.

Several men from both tribes wore uniforms taken from fallen German soldiers, or seized in raids on troop trains. They even carried German flags and used German passwords. Accustomed from childhood to privation, they were far superior to German troops in their ability to endure hunger and thirst. Almost all the officers on our side removed their medals, because the keen-eyed enemy took sharp aim at the leaders. Even a forward motion of the hand was a gesture sufficient to identify the officers.

4.

Captain of the General Staff v. Le.: We grope about like blind men in this land, feeling our way from water-hole to water-hole, seeking an enemy who always has us in his sights. What these blacks are showing us is a new method of waging war. It's a subject our military academy forgot to teach us.

5.

Interview with Jakob Morenga on May 9, 1906, in the *Cape Times*: When the reporter asks if he realizes Germany is one of the most powerful nations in the world, Morenga replies: "Yes, I'm perfectly aware of that, but the Germans don't know how to fight in our land. They don't know where to get water, and they know nothing about guerilla warfare."

Supply lines and other logistical problems

One of the major problems on the stretch between Lüderitz Bay and Kubub is crossing the shifting dunes that lie at some distance from the coast in a belt approximately 5 kilometers wide, where the sand makes every step difficult. Add to that the poor quality of the bay road itself, which consists only of wagon ruts; the base, wherever it has proved possible to clear the road of rocks, consists in many places of deep sand, in which the animals sink up to their fetlocks, and they drag their loads forward only with the greatest difficulty. Now and then the road passes over gravel and along cliffs, through deeply cut rivers and over large rocks, so that demands are placed on a wagon's durability that even the best equipment can't stand up to over time. Not only do supply columns advance extremely slowly under such conditions, taking almost twenty-five days to travel from Lüderitz Bay to Keetmanshoop, but the animals suffer severely, and the losses of the columns constantly coming and going on the bay road steadily mount. Each ox-wagon has a team of three drivers and two guards. These five men live for ten days on the supplies carried by the wagon. A similar quantity of provisions has to be provided for the return journey. The ration of oats for each horse in the column must also be added, as well as provisions provided to way stations, patrols, and telegraph and heliograph posts along the way. Thus the usable payload that finally arrives for the troops in Keetmanshoop is substantially reduced. The supply trains consume themselves in a sense, and are thus quite costly.

(*The Battles of the German Colonial Guard in South West Africa*, ed. by the Office of the General Staff, vol. 2, p. 34)

Commercial world

Taxes

The war in South West Africa cost the German taxpayers 584.78 million marks.

(Helmut Bley, *Colonial Governance and Social Structure in German South West Africa 1894–1914,* Hamburg, 1968, p. 193)

German Colonial Company for South West Africa

In the fiscal year 1904/1905 the Company sold 830,000 marks worth of goods, which yielded them a profit of 230,000 marks. The Company, which had not paid a dividend since its inception, decided not to declare one for the fiscal year 1904/1905 either, since "the general attacks on the major land companies make it appear inadvisable to pay a dividend this year . . . especially taking into account that the present fiscal year promises profits similar to the past one."

The available capital of the German Colonial Company for South West Africa, which as recently as 31 March 1902 had amounted only to 165,000 marks, shot up by 3 October 1906 to 1,981,000 marks. In the fiscal year 1905/1906 the German Colonial Company for South West Africa had already cleared a net profit of 752,000 marks. These realized profits placed the German Colonial Company for South West Africa in a position to distribute 20 percent dividends in each of the fiscal years 1905/1906, 1906/1907 and 1907/1908.

The Woermann Line

Practically speaking, the shipping company held a monopoly on all transportation to South West Africa.

Representative Erzberger pointed out in a speech before the Reichstag on 24 March 1906 that the Woermann Line had wrongfully pocketed 3 million marks in inflated freight costs and a further 3 million marks in demurrage.

On 1 August 1906, in a letter to Imperial Chancellor v. Bülow, Erzberger gave more precise figures on the basis of new evidence. These figures revealed that the Woermann Line "receives 185 marks per ton while another steamer receives around 20 marks for the same service."

The Tippelskirch Firm

Partners in the Tippelskirch firm included among others the Prussian Minister of Agriculture Podbielski, as well as several counselors to the legation of the Colonial Office. As a result of these connections the firm held a monopoly on outfitting the colonial troops. The quality of the goods provided by the Tippelskirch firm was considered inferior and the prices inflated. Protests from the troops had no effect. Only later, in the course of a bribery scandal, did it become apparent that Major Fischer, who had been responsible for the purchase and delivery of the equipment, had received large sums of money from the firm.

The turnover for the Tippelskirch firm amounted to around 2 million marks a year from 1899 to 1903; dividends paid averaged 10.7 percent a year.

As a result of the war, the turnover increased to 11 million a year in both 1904 and 1905. The Tippelskirch firm declared dividends of 65 percent each year.

(Details from: Horst Drechsler: *South West Africa under German Rule*, Berlin, 1966, p. 257 ff.)

WENSTRUP'S DISAPPEARANCE

Early in January 1905, Wenstrup disappeared. Later on no one could give the exact date of his disappearance. They knew only that he rode out of Keetmanshoop heading southwest on 2 January, along with his bambuse, a Hottentot boy named Jakobus.

Sergeant Wenstrup had been ordered to proceed to Uchanaris, a small military station manned by just a few soldiers, where cattle were said to be dying of anthrax. Wenstrup was sent to investigate, and if it was actually anthrax, take appropriate measures. Since they were draft oxen, there was some danger the disease had been transmitted to Keetmanshoop. He was warned not to travel alone.

True, the Hottentots who lived in Keetmanshoop hadn't joined the revolt, but there were constant rebel ambushes in that area, and one could never trust a Hottentot.

But rather than wait for a patrol to leave for Uchanaris, Wenstrup chose to ride off at once. Gottschalk wasn't alone in being struck by such unusual zeal. On the other hand Wenstrup had not volunteered.

Three weeks earlier, shortly before Christmas, a medical officer accompanied only by his boy had left for Uchanaris to remove a sergeant's ruptured appendix. Wenstrup left the village wearing a chapeau claque in place of his military cap, and a bright red scarf under his gray uniform. There was nothing unusual about this attire. Most soldiers rode around Keetmanshoop as if they were dressed for a beggars' ball. A few wore straw boaters, others shabby paletots. The external distinction between soldiers and rebels was beginning to blur.

Supplies are desperately low, said a paymaster in a loden jacket.

In Keetmanshoop Gottschalk felt comfortable for the first time since leaving Hamburg. This was what he thought the war in South West Africa would be like, not easy, but tranquil yet varied. A little later he would begin to view events the way he subsequently described them to friends and acquaintances.

This is evident in his diary entries as well. Gottschalk records some of the tales of grizzled troopers: a lion, already old and gouty, drags a sleeping soldier off from the campfire then flees in fright when his prey wakes up; a giant barrel is towed across the frontier by a crazy man; a lieutenant wakes up to find a sand viper in his breast pocket. There are also mood studies detailing the monotony of camp life in the village.

Gottschalk could arrange his duties as he wished. Military regulations and the elaborate rituals of saluting had worn away in the isolated village, and an almost comradely atmosphere prevailed that even included the officers. No one ruled out the possibility that the rebels might lay siege to the village, or even storm it. Yet all was calm, and Gottschalk ventured out from time to time to hunt. Of course he never went so far into the countryside that he lost sight of the flag, which was to be lowered at the approach of the enemy. The natives were friendly, if somewhat reserved. Their chief had persuaded them not to join the uprising against the Germans. This farsighted man saw opportunities for good business when German reinforcements arrived. Knowledgeable guides and drivers would be needed. Fortunately, headquarters had delivered the entire ration of rum and arrack for the fiscal year 1905 shortly before the outbreak of hostilities. In the cool of the evening the men would sit around with their glasses of rum, while a band consisting of two trumpets, a drummer and two accordions played waltzes and marches in turn. A merry time, until the relief party arrived from Uchanaris.

They had neither seen nor heard from the veterinarian Wenstrup. A delay of two or three days wasn't all that unusual in this country, a sergeant said, all it took was a wrong turn somewhere along the way.

Gottschalk had never really understood why Wenstrup volunteered for the southern front in the first place. As a specialist in immunology, Wenstrup was assigned to the newly founded Institute of Veterinary Medicine in Windhoek. Instead he practically laid siege to headquarters, saying he hadn't come to all the way to Africa to stare through a microscope. He wanted to smell gunpowder. Wenstrup discussed this himself, without saying why he was pressing the issue. In the end, impressed by his stubbornness, the Major issued his marching orders. The man practically glows with enthusiasm at the thought of risking his life for Kaiser, Volk, and Vaterland, wrote the Major in his assessment, and recommended Wenstrup's promotion to lieutenant, which had twice been denied by his former regimental commander. Here in the field, wrote the Major, we often see for the first time the true inner core of a man whose rough outer shell seems grating in the peaceful everyday life of the garrison.

On 14 November, the detachment to which Wenstrup and Gottschalk had been assigned set out from Windhoek in the direction of Rehoboth. Wenstrup maintained that only karstic minds could feel at home in this landscape of karst. A land just made for the dimwitted, for lamps with short wicks.

Gottschalk's diary,
15 November 1904

The landscape: like the Harz Mountains, but totally denuded and wrung dry. Coming over the pass, the mountains slope gently southward toward a plain we enter slowly through the shimmering heat. All about us the sky arches down to the tips of the yellow blades of grass. The scattered shrubs and bushes are so dry they rattle. The landscape lies open to our gaze. Everything that crowds upon our senses in the city is here a broad expanse at rest. But not for W., who leafs through a pamphlet even as we ride.

During the second bivouac, Gottschalk asked Wenstrup what he had been reading the past few days. (Gottschalk hesitated for some time before asking, since he didn't appreciate such questions himself). The thin frayed volume turned out not to be the inflammatory pamphlet for Social Democrats that Gottschalk had expected, but a pyrotechnics manual for detonators. Wenstrup silently handed the book to Gottschalk, who leafed through it confusedly, staring at the drawings and data. What was this?

In battle, one needs all sorts of knowledge. Think, for example, of a grenade fired at a native compound that explodes just as it's launched. The detonator has been mistimed, going off in the faces of the crew and anyone else nearby. One has to be sure not to stand too close.

Gottschalk rode with Wenstrup for a good part of the march to Rehoboth simply because Gottschalk had been assigned to the 5th Battery, and Wenstrup had been ordered to travel with them until he reached the supply squad to which he had been assigned in Keetmanshoop.

By the third day Wenstrup was wearing that red scarf. Nothing was said to him about it, although between his gray uniform and the equally gray landscape the scarf stood out like a signal lantern.

If properly conducted, war grants our sort a certain freedom too, said Wenstrup. Our leaders always keep a sharp eye out because they're zealous and also afraid, but we're their blind spot.

The detachment was protected by an advance and a rear guard. Patrols flanked both sides of the column, and the officers kept constant watch on the shrub-studded countryside through field glasses. Particularly Schwanebach, whose field glasses seemed glued in place.

A lieutenant with six years' experience in Africa told Schwanebach that staring at the countryside was a total waste of time. If the Hottentots ambushed them, they'd know it when the first man fell from his saddle; they would never attack in open country. The Hottentots were much more dangerous than

the Hereros. They let themselves be slaughtered in battle, but
they had few scruples when it came to prisoners. They stuffed a
dead man's mouth with his own severed genitals.

Animals, Schwanebach said, keeping the glasses tightly
clamped to his eyes.

Wenstrup asked if that was some sort of battle ritual. The
lieutenant said no, it was probably because the German troops
had raped and mistreated the Herero women during their advance. The *furor teutonicus* so to speak, Wenstrup remarked.

On 17 November 1904 the detachment reached Rehoboth, a village consisting of several whitewashed buildings and a few clay
huts.

Smelling water, the oxen leaned eagerly into the harness,
their throats rattling, over the last few kilometers. Now they
were gulping it down, pumping themselves so full they lum-
bered away slobbering, their bellies like barrels. Gottschalk reminded the soldiers, many of whom were riding this far on
horseback for the first time, to be careful watering their mounts,
so they wouldn't develop colic.

The commander of the Southern detachment, Colonel Deimling, wanted to push on from Rehoboth toward Rietmont, where
Hendrik Witbooi and his men were encamped.

Wenstrup was still missing. Even after a week there was no sign
of life. Those who knew the countryside said that he couldn't
have lost his way, since he had the Hottentot boy with him.
Jakobus was a Witbooi and came from Gibeon, but Wenstrup
had been assured that any Hottentot, no matter his village,
could find his way through the countryside. Gottschalk was
suddenly struck by the thought that Jakobus might have murdered Wenstrup. But that would require some motive, some particular hate for Wenstrup beyond the quite understandable general hatred toward Germans. But when he thought about it,
Gottschalk always came back to the absence of such a motive,
at least any he could remember. Locals to whom he voiced his

suspicion claimed Hottentots were capable of anything. A servant who had been faithful for decades would suddenly slit his sleeping master's throat at night if it were in the tribal interest. No whites had been warned prior to the uprising. Hottentots had no concept of loyalty, at least with regard to the white man. Only the missionary who convinced the elder chief of the Gochha Hottentots not to join the uprising claimed to know of cases where Hottentots had remained loyal to their masters throughout their lives.

The strange thing was that when Gottschalk tried to recall in detail all he knew about Jakobus, he kept coming back to an event that had nothing at all to do with the boy:

In early December of 1904, the detachment moved out from Rehoboth toward Rietmont. Colonel Deimling intended to surround and attack the village, which was the tribal seat of the Witboois, and to destroy the assembled Hottentots with their leader Hendrik Witbooi. The surprise attack took place at Naris, but the Witboois escaped.

During the battle two prisoners were taken. Small fellows with brown skins. The hands and feet of both men were bound in such a way that they could move forward only in small jerky steps, or by hopping. One of the two prisoners, a young man, wore a Colonial Guard uniform, apparently stripped from a fallen soldier, torn in front by two bullet holes and caked with dark brown blood.

The arms and legs, which were much too long, were rolled up. Apart from a contusion on the left side of his face, the man was unhurt. Lieutenant Ahrens, who was now Colonel Deimling's adjutant, attempted to interrogate the man. Ahrens wanted to know where his countrymen were headed. (Lieutenant Ahrens actually used the phrase: your countrymen). The man just shook his head in reply to each question. Apparently he wanted to show that he understood the lieutenant, but wasn't going to give him any information. Nevertheless, Ahrens sent for an interpreter. A corporal in the reserves appeared. He'd been living in the country eleven years, having served as a cavalryman in the lansquenet troops of the Second Imperial Commissioner under Captain von Françoise. Then he bought a place near Hochanas that he farmed until the outbreak of hostilities. The corporal spoke to the prisoner in melodic phrases interspersed with soft clicks. The man stood silently, calmly chewing his plug of tobacco. Da bugger won talk, Lieutenant, the corporal reported in his Mecklenburg dialect. Ahrens ordered him to continue the interrogation, otherwise they would simply shoot him. The corporal translated the death sentence for the prisoner, and his lumbering Mecklenburg tongue was transformed once more into a circus rider, leaping easily and lightly over hurdles and fences with soft clicks and clacks. The sound of a loud thwack startled Gottschalk. A trooper had struck the prisoner, who jerked back and fell comically to the ground, entangled in his shackles (those standing around him broke out in laughter). He rose to his feet again without being told, having obvious difficulty with the shackles. Why doesn't he just stay down, thought Gottschalk. When the man was back on his feet, he seemed to smile contemptuously. But it was just the right side of his face, slowly starting to swell. The trooper, a former waiter and specialist at interrogation called Old Shatterhand, was left-handed.

Since the prisoner was now standing there without moving his jaw, Gottschalk thought the force of the blow must have made him swallow his tobacco. But then, after a moment, as his grin grew increasingly lopsided, he started to chew again.

It's hopeless, Lieutenant Ahrens said, and ordered Second Lieutenant von Schwanebach to have the man shot, then added, when he saw that Schwanebach had detailed six men, that's too much trouble. Have him shot from a closer distance. Even one bullet's wasted on his kind.

Chewing his tobacco and grinning, the man stared at the gun of the corporal who had attempted to question him in Nama. The corporal had volunteered without hesitation. The prisoner stood there in the open countryside, free, even in shackles.

That really isn't an execution, Gottschalk said to himself, having always imagined that the prisoner had to be bound to a

stake or at least stood up against a wall. Lieutenant Schwanebach ordered the corporal, who had already taken aim, to lower
his weapon, since the man they were about to shoot was still
wearing a German uniform.

What should they do? The lieutenant decided that the prisoner should remove the uniform before they shot him, since
even if it had been desecrated, it was still the Kaiser's jacket, and
remained military property.

They severed the ropes binding the man and ordered him to
remove the uniform. Now the man was standing there naked,
his face still in a swollen grin, chewing his tobacco. Gottschalk
wondered why no one was upset by this complacent chewing,
which seemed contemptuous in the face of the raised gun, the
lieutenant, and those standing curiously about.

When the rebel was lying on the ground, Schwanebach ordered the veterinarian to make sure the baboon was dead.
Gottschalk bent over the body. A trickle of blood flowed from
the mouth like a red thread. In the other corner of his mouth
stood a brownish rivulet. Apparently the man had not swallowed his tobacco even when the bullet pierced his heart.

Gottschalk had started to leave before they shot the man. But
the lieutenant called him back and ordered him to stay, so that
he could declare the prisoner dead according to regulations. At
first Gottschalk was tempted to say that wasn't his responsibility, he was only a veterinarian. But he stayed and said nothing, afraid that Schwanebach might reply, exactly, that's just the
point. The prisoner's face still bore that broad grin. For a moment, Gottschalk thought the man was only playing dead. He
lifted the eyelid carefully, a brown fold of skin that gave the face
its strangely Asiatic look. The pupil showed no reflex.

Gottschalk's diary,
5 December 1904 (at night)
Hyenas escort us. Well-fed vultures dot the evening sky (*Aegypius
monachus* and *Neophoron percnopterus*). Bivouac on a riverbed, a few scattered puddles from the last rain. Otherwise all sand and stones, the

trees and bushes on the bank dry and without song. Yet they say water flows beneath this sandy riverbed. Water, like joy, recedes to greater depths. They should build subterranean dams, create artificial lakes protected from evaporation, force the water slowly upward again, prevent it from flowing uselessly into the sea after sudden downpours, and this land could be the Garden of Eden. W. says we're standing on the wrong side.

Addendum: We were standing behind the corporal.

Three Colonial Guards had their picture taken with the second prisoner (presumably they were the ones who had taken him captive). They've put him in the middle (two on his right, one on his left), but leave a clear gap: a boy dressed in European rags. (They said he was carrying a flintlock when they caught him.) All three lean on their rifles, one clearly grinning beneath the brim of his hat. They must have told the boy to stand still, even with ropes cutting into his arms and legs. A photo for the folks back home.

Then they cut the ropes and yelled, Run! But he didn't move. When they laughed and waved at him to go ahead and run off he took a few tentative steps, looked back at them once, then started to run, and kept going until he was struck by three bullets and fell. Someone said later that he crawled on a few feet.

Captain von Tresckow lost his horse in the battle at Naris, when it was shot twice. In its place he selected a somewhat bony but well-built black horse that had arrived with a supply convoy from the Cape Colony at the outbreak of hostilities. A well-trained horse, the cavalry sergeant assured him.

The captain's boy fetches the horse and von Tresckow immediately tries to mount it, but the horse rears up and kicks wildly. The captain falls to the ground and loses the reins, something a cavalry man must never do. But then the horse tamely allows itself to be caught by a trooper and led back. Several other troopers hold the horse while Tresckow tries a second time. He makes it safely into the saddle and manages to remain there a few minutes before the horse throws itself to the ground in a fit. Tresckow barely makes it out of the saddle. Meanwhile a large crowd of curious onlookers had gathered to witness the battle between captain and horse. The horse has regained its feet, flecks of foam at its mouth, and when Tresckow holds the reins and cautiously tries to stroke it, it rears back with a terrified whinny.

The whole matter would have elicited no further notice if it weren't for the fact that the horse tamely allowed any other rider to approach and mount it, just not Captain Tresckow.

Gottschalk, who was ordered by Tresckow to examine the horse, could find nothing unusual beyond the fact that the animal was highly agitated. Finally he asked if he might be permitted to smell the captain's hand. Tresckow extended it hesitantly and somewhat stiffly. Gottschalk sniffed. The onlookers grinned. Tresckow wanted to know what that was all about. Gottschalk's diagnosis: the captain wore a strong cologne to which the horse was no doubt allergic. There had been a similar case in his former regiment, where a horse couldn't stand a major who used strong aftershave lotion.

Tresckow had the horse shot, as unfit for duty. Too bad about the horse, Gottschalk said later.

A medical team searching the battleground at Naris found fifty dead Hottentots. Their losses were assumed higher, since Hottentots unfailingly carried off their dead and wounded. The report by the Office of the General Staff doesn't break down the dead by gender. The artillery must have been extremely effective in bombarding the village and those fleeing from it.

Three men died on the German side; an officer and eight men were wounded.

Announcement (circular)

A few young Hottentots and Damara are available as bambuses for officers and N.C.O.s. They may be assigned to private use upon application. Their upkeep must be provided from available company left-

overs. Since for the most part they were raised in missionary schools
they offer little danger.
Applications should be submitted in writing to Battalion Headquarters.
Signed: (illegible).

Gottschalk was surprised that Wenstrup was among the first to
apply for a bambuse. Soon thereafter Wenstrup was assigned a
Hottentot boy. Few officers had an interest in taking one of the
prisoners. (Schwanebach: I'd wake up some day with my throat
slit. Ha, ha.) When Gottschalk asked why he of all people had
asked for a boy to work for him, Wenstrup replied, because the
dominion of man over man must be abolished. When Gottschalk said that was surely a contradiction, Wenstrup elucidated:
If a person stands by passively while an entire nation is being
slaughtered, you see, and yet keeps a bambuse, it's only a marginal contradiction, a private paradox if you will, one that will
eventually be resolved in praxis. The whole thing struck
Gottschalk as extremely nebulous.

It turned out, however, that Wenstrup didn't use the Hottentot
boy, whose name was Jakobus, to shine his shoes, but gave him
room and board and took language lessons from him instead.
Wenstrup learned Nama by pointing at various objects the boy
would then name: Tree, bush, sun, cloud, path, and Wenstrup
would stammer them out in turn. Within two days Gottschalk
joined in these language lessons, and soon the two veterinarians
could be heard each evening after the camp meal, practicing
their tongue clicks. The tongue really has to relax, Gottschalk
told Schmidt, the company chaplain. And in his diary we find
the following: Nama, a language that can only be spoken with a
relaxed tongue.

Gottschalk allowed these strange sounds to dissolve pleasantly on his tongue. Once they were both seen inserting their
forefingers in turn in the boy's mouth, which for a time exposed
them to suspicions of pederasty. They were in fact only trying to
determine where in the mouth and with what tongue move-

ments the various clicks were being produced. Riding through flat boring countryside on the way to Gibeon, Gottschalk practiced the four basic clicks, pressing the tip of his tongue against the alveolus then letting his tongue drop sharply, which produced a sound like snapping his fingers, or flattening the front half of his tongue so that its edges touched the teeth on both sides, then lifting the back of his tongue, pressing it against the gums and releasing it again slowly, which always encouraged his horse into a sharp trot.

Does your horse have bees in its butt, asked Tresckow, you're throwing off the whole column.

Gottschalk made slow progress at best with his vocabulary, but he did perfect his accent. He sought words and phrases rich in tonal modulation, where the various clicks followed one another like little hurdles, sentences unlikely, however, to occur in real conversation, such as, the midnight mouse flies through the fitful forest of tea roses. Meanwhile Wenstrup devoted himself to the practical side, wanting to learn as quickly as possible how to make himself understood. His progress matched his efforts, and he was soon able to ask and answer simple questions, even though he blurted them out in awkward gutturals: Where does this road go? Where is the next water-hole? Where can I find something to eat?

The Mecklenburg corporal who sensed that his previously unchallenged position as interpreter was endangered, followed the language lessons of the two veterinarians with suspicion. Nor did he advise them or attempt to answer their complicated questions, the solutions to which both veterinarians were forced to seek by means of gestures and complex sketches in the sand. Meanwhile it was clear the Hottentot boy was learning German more quickly than the men were learning Nama. It must also be said that neither Gottschalk nor Wenstrup ever turned to the corporal for help, although they had made no agreement not to do so.

It became clear after five days, however, that although they rode together, the interests of the two pupils had diverged so widely that the boy was forced to jog back and forth between their horses, hanging onto the stirrups, repeating the required words or sentences, and correcting their pronunciation. (Lieutenant Ahrens had issued a special directive, the so-called Jakobus Order, specifically forbidding a bambuse from using any form of military transportation. It seems a stunned Ahrens had come upon the Hottentot whelp riding behind Wenstrup on horseback—I thought my horse had kicked me, he said.)

Thus, on the way to Gibeon, while Gottschalk, enveloped in the dust of the marching column, worked on the phrase a groundhog slurps donkey milk with a vulture, Wenstrup practiced the proper click for asking the whereabouts of the nearest military post.

And what did the officers have to say about the linguistic exercises of the two veterinarians, which could hardly go unnoticed with their Nama teacher constantly running back and forth between their horses.

They christened them our two horse-witchdoctors, while the foot soldiers called them the click-Kaffir boys. But the major thought the two veterinarians were setting a good example, since the Colonial Guard would need more interpreters in the future. Tresckow even asked Wenstrup the meaning of a few Nama words and had him produce a few clicks, adding that he never would have thought Wenstrup had the energy and ambition to learn such a complicated language, one that would be completely useless in a few years. But it was good to do something just for its own sake.

On the seventh day of Wenstrup's disappearance, the term used in the files, a patrol led by a sergeant familiar with the territory was assembled to search for the veterinarian, although there were no great hopes of finding him alive at that point. Gottschalk's diary entry for 10 January 1905 reads as follows: They're making jokes about Wenstrup: Wenstrup meets a groundhog on the prairie and asks the way to, etc.

Gottschalk enquired quietly among a few veteran troopers whether there had been any desertions. They confirmed there had been, now and again, but rarely, and to their knowledge, never during a native uprising, aside from those missing in action. Rebel natives didn't generally distinguish between deserters and non-deserters in the case of German soldiers, and having never heard of the Geneva Convention they finished them both off. The troopers laughed and asked Gottschalk if he was thinking of joining the enemy. Gottschalk had been puzzled when Wenstrup volunteered for a patrol headed for Keetmanshoop commanded by Second Lieutenant Schwanebach. Gottschalk had been added to this patrol to bring it to full strength. But Wenstrup had volunteered, pointing out that supply trains were the alpha and omega of every offensive and they needed veterinarians. Tresckow shook hands with Wenstrup and acknowledged that one could certainly make a mistake about a man.

Early on the morning of 13 December, at 5 o'clock, Schwanebach's patrol left Gibeon for Keetmanshoop intending to cover one hundred and sixty kilometers in three days. The Hottentot boy Jakobus rode along at Wenstrup's suggestion. Lieutenant Ahrens was hesitant at first, but Wenstrup vouched for the boy. A corporal who knew the way was also riding along.

The rascal could still lead us into a trap, said Schwanebach.

Amazing what reserves of intelligence this Schwinebelly can come up with when it's a matter of saving his own bacon, said Wenstrup. They were riding through a flat, almost treeless prairie. While Wenstrup was perfecting his pronunciation of such boring Nama words as fork in the road, stretch of the road, left and right, avoid, steer clear of, and go around, Gottschalk was concentrating entirely on bushes, rock formations, and slight elevations in the landscape.

Around eight that evening, Schwanebach finally let the patrol stop and dismount. The corporal who knew the territory, a Bavarian from Plattling by the name of Rattenhuber, advised against making a fire, and told them to make as little noise as possible, since every word could be heard for kilometers in the flat treeless countryside. As Gottschalk chewed on some ship zwieback, the snapping and crunching suddenly seemed frighteningly loud. He'd never realized how much noise a zwieback could make. He took a drink of water, walked over to the grazing chestnut gelding he'd named Sumatra, and held out a handful of corn that he had added to his saddlebag. On trips like these, your life could depend on how well you fed and watered your horse. Later on, Wenstrup came over and sat beside Gottschalk. He pulled a silver flask from his uniform pocket. Iron rations. A good strong French cognac. They sat there drinking while Wenstrup smoked. Even the military is more tolerable when there's action and danger, Wenstrup said, that's what's so terrible. In his former regiment, he once watched from a window as the recruits drilled in the barracks courtyard. Everything seemed immersed in an icy light as they goose-stepped and swung their arms. He stood at the window as if turned to stone. It wasn't the absurdity of soldiers practicing a step that they would never use, it was the monotony, the mechanical nature of their movements. It all seemed senseless, and suddenly even the most ordinary of everyday things seemed equally senseless, the eternal dressing and undressing, the stupidity of buttoning and unbuttoning shirts and jackets morning and night. It was like awakening from a daze. He began to question why he shaved every day, and not wanting a beard didn't seem reason enough. A crucial insight dawned on him at that point. When, after a pause, Gottschalk asked what that was, Wenstrup replied, a man who can't freely develop a sense of things makes no sense. That's why the rebels seem to have so much sense on their side.

Wenstrup left for guard duty and Gottschalk cleared the stones from the spot where he was going to sleep, then wrapped himself in his blanket. He gazed up into the starry heavens. As a boy he loved to sail across the Elbe to sand-drift islands covered with willows.

He must have been asleep for a while when he was awakened by music. They all came to their feet. The sound of a harmonica:

Heil dir im Siegerkranz. Schwanebach shouted out orders, his pistol drawn. After a quick search they found Wenstrup sitting on a rock off to one side, his rifle between his knees, playing his harmonica. Beside him, Jakobus, clapping his hands to the halting rhythm.

A damn silly tune, Wenstrup said to Schwanebach, knocking out the spit from the harmonica as he did so. The man is insane, said Schwanebach.

Report of Second Lieutenant v. Schwanebach regarding dereliction of duty and several acts of insubordination on the march from Gibeon to Keetmanshoop.

On the evening of 13 December Veterinary Sergeant Wenstrup was guilty of dereliction of duty by playing a harmonica while on guard. When called to account he replied that he played the harmonica with his mouth, not his eyes.

On the following day as we rode along he suddenly began to yodel. When asked if he were trying to give the patrol away by signaling the enemy (the veterinarian is learning Nama!), he replied it was just an excess of high spirits. I specifically ordered him to stop, yet that evening he yodeled a second time. During bivouac he made seditious remarks that could be heard by soldiers sitting nearby, although he addressed himself solely to Lieutenant Gottschalk. He compared discipline to a trained animal act, and claimed such discipline produced only dancing bears. Obedience was the eagle on the Garde de Corps helmet: made of lead and incapable of flight. When I asked if this applied to the Kaiser too, he replied evasively: Of course. The Kaiser obviously can't fly. If I understood him correctly, the veterinarian regards imagination and spontaneity as positive values. He compared German civilization to a clubfoot, adding, And we think we can teach these people (he meant the Hottentots) how to walk. The following were characterized as equivalent to the Spanish shoe, an instrument of torture: the state, the army, the police, the bureaucracy (particularly the Prussian), chaplains, park wardens, and all head schoolteachers. His Majesty was not personally insulted. Signed: v. Schwanebach

On the ride to Keetmanshoop, Gottschalk saw for himself that Wenstrup, though a native of Berlin, could yodel. Wenstrup claimed that yodeling made the landscape bearable. For a moment Gottschalk questioned the man's sanity. But then he wondered if Wenstrup might be trying to get himself certified. But why would he seek to shirk his duties; after all, he had volunteered when he could be sitting in front of a microscope in Windhoek. And the things Wenstrup said during evening bivouacs might have been a little eccentric and extreme, but they were certainly worth thinking about. When Wenstrup maintained that the state was a Spanish shoe squeezing the individual, Gottschalk quickly asked how he envisioned a social democratic state. No, he had no desire to replace a monarchial state with a social democracy, in which there might be a president, instead of a crowned head, but where the state would remain, quite possibly with the very same bailiffs, railway directors, police commissioners, and ecclesiastical senates. In order to walk upright, you had to shake off whatever was clinging to your back.

This declaration may be found in Gottschalk's diary; some of the pages for preceding days have unfortunately been tornout.

It must have dawned on Gottschalk for the first time on this trek that Wenstrup was not, as he had thought, a partisan of the Social Democrats, but instead something truly unusual—probably the sole anarchist veterinarian in the German army.

Gottschalk was so surprised by this insight (and worried, given those sitting nearby) that he steered the conversation abruptly toward the weather, praising the healthy climate of the highlands, raving about the clarity of the air, in which you could see so far that distant objects appeared closer than they really were. To which Wenstrup merely replied that whenever he was out of doors, particularly around trees, he was constantly reminded that his breath was being absorbed by the leaves as carbon dioxide and transformed by assimilation into oxygen, which he then unhesitatingly breathed in again. Thus they were soon discussing photosynthesis (which made Schwinebelly, who understood nothing, even more suspicious), something that occurred seldom enough in this country, given the scarcity of trees. All the while there was so much Gottschalk wanted to ask Wenstrup. He would have liked to know how he envisioned the transition to an anarchist society. Had anarchists really thrown a bomb into the crowd in Haymarket Square, just like that? And what would such a society look like? Who would organize the trash pickup? He resolved to continue this conversation another time. But that wasn't to be, for the following day they arrived at Keetmanshoop without having encountered the enemy, in spite of Wenstrup's yodeling.

Gottschalk's diary,
14 December 1904

In this dry air the stars seem closer and brighter than they do at home. You think you see a fire on the crest of a dune, until it lifts from the earth and slides slowly up into the sky: a rising star. Orion, his belt a strand of three large stars, burns with the fire of diamonds. Before us the Southern Cross, and below it, standing out from the night sky, a deep black patch, the "Cape Town Coffee Sack." Now and then a shooting star flares up and arcs like a rocket with a fiery tail, so seemingly near that one wonders why one didn't hear its detonation or hiss. What lies beyond the stars? Jakobus translated the word infinite as cloud. But that was quite likely a misunderstanding.

15 December 1904 (Keetmanshoop)

Even the vultures seem to avoid this city. Jakobus showed us the Half-Men, a peculiar variety of trees that, in the right light, do indeed seem to stand like mournful figures. They can be freed some day, but how and when it will happen he does not reveal.

He says that then this land will belong to the right people.

Contrary to Gottschalk's expectations, Wenstrup was not arrested in Keetmanshoop. Lieutenant von Schwanebach submitted his report the day after he arrived, and the local commander interrogated Wenstrup. Wenstrup was able to refute the accusation that he was trying to betray the patrol to the enemy by pointing out that one could see further by day than one could hear, and it made no sense anyway, since he would be giving himself away too. He wasn't a candidate for suicide. Asked why he had yodeled in the first place, he replied: to put people in a good mood. There remained the charge of dereliction of duty and insubordination. But the major didn't want to get into that. There were more important matters to attend to in the surrounded city. The case was forwarded to the appropriate military court in Windhoek. After Wenstrup's disappearance, the matter was dropped.

On 12 January 1905, a search patrol for Wenstrup left Keetmanshoop. Gottschalk had volunteered to go along. They asked about Wenstrup at various Hottentot kraals in the area. It's only pro forma, said the captain leading the patrol. The Hottentots around here haven't joined the revolt, but that's no reason to trust them. When it comes down to it, they stick together like pitch and brimstone.

The station commander at Ucharnaris, a sergeant, could add nothing beyond what was already known. Wenstrup had never arrived at his intended destination. None of the Hottentots living there had seen him. The Hottentots in the region remained peaceable. But the sergeant reported that something unusual had happened: he found one of the Hottentots with a pyrotechnics manual. Of course the fellow was incapable of understanding it. He'd been using pages from it to light fires. He'd already ripped out a few of them. When asked about it, the Hottentot said he'd found the book a few kilometers outside the village. A lie of course, and he had given the man twenty hard lashes.

Gottschalk asked to see the frayed pamphlet. There was no doubt: it was the same book Wenstrup had been reading on the trek. Gottschalk merely shrugged and returned it to the captain.

Gottschalk's diary,
13 January 1905

Memories of W. The way he struck a match. The color of mourning is black or white (India), you no longer see anything. A person should be able to say he likes someone. Open up, open up, open up.

The patrol rode out to four other kraals, all of them near Keetmanshoop. The captain questioned the Hottentots in a mixed jargon composed of German, Afrikaans, and Nama. But those asked, removing their hats politely, maintained they hadn't seen any whites in the last few weeks. The earth seemed to have swallowed Wenstrup just beyond Keetmanshoop.

Gottschalk had seen Wenstrup only from time to time before he disappeared, by the way. They were lodged in quarters far removed from each other in Keetmanshoop, Wenstrup in a tent with three noncommissioned medics, Gottschalk with two medical officers in the warehouse of a former store. Gottschalk was responsible in no small part for the fact that they didn't talk much. Although he didn't avoid Wenstrup, he spent most evenings in what the officers called their tobacco club, a gathering devoted to smoking, drinking, and telling tales. (It was here that Gottschalk first got used to smoking). Wenstrup, on the other hand, avoided this circle. It wasn't until Christmas Eve that Gottschalk exchanged a few words with Wenstrup.

Early that morning a heavy rain set in, falling from the heavens like a warm shower. Gottschalk ran out of the warehouse naked and stood in the rain with the other men. Schwinebelly was seen bare for the first time. They stared at him in shock. He was incredibly hairy, like a black monkey.

•   •   •

That afternoon preparations began for the Christmas party. The rain ceased, leaving behind a landscape of sludge. A Christmas tree was placed outside headquarters, a propped-up tamarisk.

There won't be a dry eye tonight, said a lieutenant. He had already pinned on every medal and ribbon he had.

The standard-bearers of German culture, said Wenstrup, who surprised everyone by sporting a gray chapeau claque with a sprig of tamarisk. He was gradually coming to resemble those he had been sent to fight.

A lance corporal began sobbing that his wife in Kiel was pregnant again and it was all the Hottentots' fault. The corporal named Rattenhuber talked at length about his plan to settle down here when he got out of the service, three months from now, not to farm, as so many former troopers did, but to build an ice-skating rink. Ice hockey could also be introduced, a sport Rattenhuber had started up in his hometown of Prattling. He wanted to be to South West Africa what Klopstock, who first introduced ice skating to his native land, had been to Germany. Rattenhuber was well aware that the conditions in Africa were considerably less favorable than those in Germany, but he was convinced he could overcome these difficulties with the technical knowledge he had acquired in the meantime plus his own energy. The fact that it's still not possible to skate in that country today may be due to the fact that two months later Corporal Rattenhuber was killed in a battle with Morris's men.

That evening, after the camp service, a new joke was making the rounds in the officers' mess, attributed by some to Gottschalk, by others to Wenstrup: Schwanebach, who had been married for five years to a Baroness von Behr, no brighter an intellectual light than himself, had three children, all daughters. Shortly before his departure for South West Africa, his wife gives birth to their fourth child, not the hoped-for son and heir, but yet another girl. The child is to be baptized at home, and the proud parents enter the hallway to greet the pastor. When they return to the baptismal chamber, the child has disappeared from the cradle. The mother hunts, the father hunts, the godparents hunt, even the pastor kneels down and peers under the table. All in vain. Everyone stands around at a loss until someone happens to look up, and points in horror at the curtain rod. There sits the little one, black and hairy as a monkey. And she has prehensile feet.

During the gift exchange the officers receive small presents from the enlisted men, most of them handmade: a cannon carved from camelthorn wood, a pyramid of Hottentot bullets soldered together as a paperweight, a tie pin made from a cactus thorn, an ashtray fashioned from the skull of a Hottentot.

Gottschalk was the only one to receive two gifts, which immediately drew attention to him. First a small Vietnamese pot-bellied pig that Corporal Rattenhuber had carved from a rifle butt splintered by a Herero bullet. Rattenhuber, who had fought in the Boxer Rebellion in China, where he first saw a potbellied pig, was devoting all his energy and dialect-hampered powers of oral persuasion to seeing this enormously fleshy animal domesticated in South West Africa too. Gottschalk didn't know why he had been singled out for this gift. Perhaps in thanks for the fact that Gottschalk had lanced a boil on Rattenhuber's neck while on patrol and listened patiently to the corporal's ice-hockey plans. Or Rattenhuber may simply have wished to win over the veterinarian for his plan to introduce the potbellied pig to Africa.

The other gift was a book wrapped in blue paper that Wenstrup handed to Gottschalk with the dark remark: Not because it's Christmas, but because it's time.

Gottschalk unthinkingly unwrapped the book in the officers' mess, where, in spite of the ominous state of their provisions, champagne had been served, and was shocked to read the author and title: Peter Kropotkin, *Mutual Aid: A Factor of Evolution.*

He shoved the book under one of the sprigs of tamarisk the orderlies had placed on the table as Christmas decorations.

Schmidt, the district officer, gave a speech shortly before the pea-sausage soup with an appeal to all officers. Should they die a hero's death, he asked that they not allow their bodies to be cremated or strewn with unslaked lime. This latter practice generally applied to those who died in an epidemic. He urged them to make the same appeal to their men.

Schmidt was a member of the International League for Humicification. If cremation were widely accepted, Schmidt claimed, the balance of nature could be seriously upset (Schmidt also rejected all forms of artificial fertilizer). It should surely be a consolation to anyone giving his life in the good fight to know that new life would arise from the decomposition of his body. It was well known that decomposition contributed significantly to the formation of humus. It was important to keep that in mind, particularly in a sandy, karstic land like South West Africa, which lacked any effective sort of humus formation. Those who put their lives on the line for German soil must also contribute to a fruitful future with their bodies. Hundreds of thousands of Germans could escape the crushing confines of their native country and find a new German home, if this land could only be cultivated. He would like to offer a toast to this future, and to the German Kaiser.

Although Gottschalk was slightly drunk by the time he left the officers' mess that evening, he still managed to leave unnoticed with the book under his jacket. The next day he wondered if he should bury it. He hid it in an ammunition box.

It was in Keetmanshoop that Gottschalk first heard the name Morenga. People were afraid he might approach the city and lay siege to it, as he had tried to do at Warmbad. A lance corporal reported that Morenga did not execute his prisoners. He had taken part in the skirmish with Baron von Stempel and had seen with his own eyes a trooper reported missing in action reappear two days later, carefully bandaged and provided with ample supplies. He even claimed to have spoken with Morenga. The commander expressly forbade the man, or any other eyewitness, to talk about the matter.

On 15 January, Windhoek was informed that the veterinarian Wenstrup had been officially declared missing in action.

THE PROPHET

Near midnight, in early March of 1904, a man is sneaking around the native compound in Windhoek. After the bloodhounds have cornered him, he is arrested by native policemen. The following morning he is brought to the Windhoek jail, where he is interrogated by a German police sergeant.

When asked where he comes from, the man, a Nama, replies in Cape Dutch that he has been sent by God, and says he has come to Windhoek to preach the word of God. He refuses to answer any more questions, even when the sergeant threatens him with ten strokes of the rod. He'll talk only with his own kind, he insists, which the sergeant thinks must mean in his own language, since even though it's clear he understands Cape Dutch and English, he suddenly speaks nothing but Nama.

The sergeant sends to the compound for the church elder, Daniel Vries, a Nama from Bethany. When Vries asks who he is, the prisoner replies, I am God's prophet. His name is Klaas Shepperd and he comes from Port Elizabeth in the Cape Colony. When asked why he's in the German protectorate he answers that he's trying to reach Samuel Maharero, the leader of the Hereros.

He claims not to know about the war between the Hereros and the Germans. The sergeant, who suspects him of being a Herero spy, has him searched. In his pockets they find a crust of bread, *duba*, *schefel*, and *duivelsdreck*: *asa foetida* as the captain refers to it in his report, after consultation with the missionary. Shepperd is jailed on suspicion of spying. But after a month they have to release him, since they can't prove he's committed any crime, and he's a British subject. During his stay in the Windhoek jail a strange unrest quickly spread among the normally apathetic inmates. The guards encountered repeated acts of insubordination, including two men who refused to work and were punished with twenty-five strokes of the rod. Shepperd, called Stürmann by his fellow prisoners, held a prayer service each morning for the inmates that he called the Sermon on the Mount. The words were indeed taken from the New Testament, but not the Sermon on the Mount, being drawn instead, said missionary Wandres, from the letter of Jakobus, the Book of James.

Hearken, my beloved brethren! Hath not God chosen the poor of this world rich in faith, and heirs of the kingdom which he hath promised to them that love him?

But you have despised the poor.

Do not rich men oppress you, and draw you before the judgment seats? Father Wandres, of the Rhenish Mission, who had been informed by the church elder Daniel Vries the following day of the nighttime capture of the prophet, wished to speak with Shepperd Stürmann at once, for he feared he might represent the Ethiopian Church, whose influence was widespread among the natives in the British Cape Colony and which was opposing the European missionaries. No preacher from this religious movement had turned up in the northern part of the German protectorate yet, and Father Wandres, active for twenty years in Africa and a declared opponent of this militant sect, as he called it, wanted to take this opportunity to find out who was hiding behind it, pulling the strings and providing the money. Since he had to take a short trip for the Rhenish Mission first, however, this conversation didn't take place until the following week, and then not in jail (Shepperd having already been released), but in the mission house. Wandres invited Shepperd for a talk, and the latter in fact showed up, in rags, but not the least shy. His behavior struck Wandres as arrogant, which probably resulted from his religious mania. Once Wandres had settled into his armchair, Shepperd Stürmann did not wait, as good manners demanded, to be asked to sit down, but pulled up a chair and seated himself at almost the same moment. Stürmann replied with frank self-confidence to the questions Wandres put to him as a colleague and brother in Christ so to speak. (The conversation was passed on by Wandres to the imperial government in a confidential report of 6 December 1904). When asked at whose behest he had undertaken this missionary journey and who was paying for it, Stürmann replied that he lived entirely on gifts from the natives, fruit, millet, now and then some meat. I was a stable boy in Kimberley. As I was cleaning the stable one day, I suddenly saw a flame of fire in the midst of a pile of straw, and in the flame a figure whose gaze transfixed me. I realized it was Christ. Beside the figure were black people. The Lord within the flame charged me to go west and preach the word of God to the blacks. Wandres pointed out, as noted in his report, that Stürmann was way off course, heading north instead. To which Shepperd Stürmann simply replied, that's where the path led. Finally, Wandres pointed out to Stürmann that he wouldn't be able to make himself understood where he was going, since he didn't speak the Herero language. To which Stürmann replied, God will give me that gift in good time.

A few days later, Stürmann traveled south by ox-wagon, at the invitation of the Bastard driver. He told Father Wandres that he was trying to reach Hendrik Witbooi, the famous captain of the Hottentots.

During a later inspection of the jail in Windhoek, an inscription was found carved in the wooden doorpost of a cell: The day of salvation is at hand.

Asked about it, Missionary Wandres told the lieutenant conducting the inspection, That's just the problem: the New Testament is so ambiguous.

A photo from the year 1894 shows Father Wandres in Warmbad. He's standing on an animal skin rug outside a round hut, a pondok made of bast matting. Before him, on a bench draped with three leopard skins, sits his wife, between two men. To her left is a bearded man with short (probably reddish-blond) hair, who has placed his pith helmet on the ground beside him. He's the son-in-law of Doctor Schreiber, the Chief of Staff of the Rhenish Mission, who sits to her right in a black suit, his pith helmet cradled in his arm, with the pale, serious face of an academic. Quite different from Wandres, who with his tan and his long black beard and broad shoulders, looks more like a big-boned farmer or woodcutter dressed in his Sunday best. Frau Wandres has her hands folded in her lap on her white frilled pinafore and has donned, presumably just for this picture, a hat decorated with artificial flowers. Her faced is pinched, she stares sternly, almost brutally, at the camera. Two Hottentots stand in the background, ragged, but dressed European-style. (German churches of all denominations collect old clothes for natives in the colonies. They want them to be decently clothed.)

A native teacher by the name of Johannes Dausab claimed he met Stürmann in March on his way to Rehoboth and spent a few days traveling with him. He was struck by the fact that he ended almost every conversation with the same sentence: The day of salvation is at hand.

When Dausab, who was trained in a missionary school, replied he knew of only one salvation, that offered through Jesus Christ, Shepperd Stürmann replied, No, I mean the salvation of the Nama people.

Dausab, who remained loyal to his German masters even during the uprising, found his traveling companion increasingly disturbing, for whenever they came across Hottentots he would immediately start to preach as if a fire had been built under him, crowds would gather about as he spoke of the injustice of this world, and how most whites misused the church, as the usurers and moneychangers misused the Temple from which Christ drove them. The law of the Lord is holy, and the Bible proclaims that in the final days a King will be born, sent by the Lord to rule over the world; God therefore uses him to destroy an empire; thus has the Lord of Hosts resolved.

Dausab left Stürmann shortly before Rehoboth.

• • •

The primary cause of the revolt is undoubtedly a religious mania induced by the Cape Colony prophet, who considers himself a member of the Ethiopian Church. (Governor Leutwein to the Imperial Chancellor, 10 November 1904, ICFile No. 2133, f. 132)

Shepperd Stürmann is said to have contacted Hendrik Witbooi in Rietmont and then gone from house to house and from tribe to tribe. That must have been toward the end of July 1904.

During the interrogation following his capture, the former Witbooi captain Isaak Witbooi stated it was Stürmann who constantly urged his father to rebel, and when the latter objected that conquering the Germans and driving them out of his country was beyond the power of his small tribe, Stürmann replied that God had chosen him to free the country from the Germans, and God had sent him to Hendrik Witbooi that His will might be fulfilled. With God on his side the Germans could be driven out, just as David had defeated Goliath.

Letter from Shepperd Stürmann to District Officer Schmidt in Keetmanshoop, received 27 July 1905

In the beginning was the Word, and the Word was in God, and the Word was God.

Thus these things I now make known to you are from God, the King of heaven and earth. That same Lord has sent with Shepperd Stürmann the knowledge of God. Through me, Israel is delivered by God the Creator. The law of the Lord is holy, and the Bible proclaims that in the final days a King will be born, sent by the Lord to rule over the world; God therefore uses him to destroy a kingdom; thus has Lord of Hosts resolved.

Thus I was born beneath the heavens and was God, to begin this work; thus is the beginning of the Lord and also the ending of the Lord.

Thus I proclaim to you in the name of the Lord, for His name's

sake, that His will may be done; he is not yet born, await him in fear
and trembling, he will soon appear.

Thus when day breaks I will send you a herald. Thus I admonish
you, that you might know before all the nation, because I have this
knowledge from God; I have seen it. This much for now and we close
in the name of the Lord. Amen.

This proclamation comes from the Lord's hand, I am but a fellow
traveler, I write to the name of the Magistrate. (From the government
files for German South West Africa)

Customs and District Officer Schmidt considers Stürmann a religious fanatic, as does former Governor Leutwein, but a dangerous one. Stürmann is said to have coined the slogan, Africa for
the Africans.

At the outbreak of hostilities, Stürmann received thirty spe-
cially-selected soldiers from Hendrik Witbooi. These were later
known as God's Soldiers, a small elite troop sent to the focal
point of any battle.

After the initial losses of the Witboois there were apparently
several confrontations between Samuel Isaak and the prophet.
Samuel Isaak opposed the revolt and was pressing for a negotiated surrender. According to the interrogation of Isaak Witbooi,
Stürmann replied that the losses were the result of a lack of religious conviction on the part of the soldiers. Hendrik Witbooi
followed these exchanges in silence.

The statements of Isaak Witbooi, who placed major blame for
the outbreak of hostilities on the prophet, must be seen in light
of his own situation. At that time he and his people were in concentration camps, and shortly thereafter interned on Shark Island, where they perished by the hundreds. It's conceivable that
Isaak Witbooi, who succeeded his fallen father as captain, may
have wanted to shift the blame for the revolt onto someone who
had disappeared in the meantime. Perhaps he hoped to negotiate
better conditions for his tribe by presenting them and himself as
having fallen prey to a delusion.

• • •

Following the battle of Kowes, on 17 August 1905, Stürmann left the tribe, according to Isaak Witbooi. That was at a time when the Germans were chasing the tribe from water-hole to water-hole across the steppes.

The prophet had vanished, and in spite of an intensive search by the Germans, he could not be found.

It was two years before a rumor came from the Cape Colony that the leader of the revolt, the prophet Stürmann, had been hanged there.

The German government made immediate inquiries by telegraph to the General Consulate in Cape Town.

Cape Town, 10 May 1907

According to information received from the local Commander of the Cape Mounted Police, a native named Hendrik Becker was sentenced to death by the courts and hanged accordingly for having murdered two white workers in the asbestos mines near Hopefield north of Griquatown (Hay District, Cape Colony).

Becker was reportedly one of the ringleaders of the most recent Witbooi uprising. Pursued by German troops, he is said to have fled to the Cape Colony. Once here, he was active as a religious prophet and agitator, trying to stir up the natives against the whites, which led to the murder mentioned above, reported in detail in the *Cape Times* as the "Hopefield Murder."

My source doesn't know if Becker is identical with Stürmann, but has indicated he will make inquiries and communicate his findings. I therefore respectfully reserve the right to make a further report at that time.

I respectfully request you to convey the above information to the Imperial Staff of the Colonial Guard at your discretion.

The Imperial General Consul

By order: (Signed)

Cape Town, 24 July 1907

Pursuant to my letter of the 10th instant—no. 3056—re: Stürmann.

Based on further communication from the Commander of the Cape Mounted Police Becker and Stürmann were indeed one and the same man.

The Imperial General Consul

(Signed)

BATTLE REPORT 1
GREAT NABAS

The major offensive against the Witbooi Hottentots in the Auob region began in early January 1905.

Colonel Deimling hoped to destroy (smash) the Witboois in a focused operation using newly-arrived reinforcements. March separately, attack in unison.

Colonel Deimling's report:

Given the nature of things, it was not possible to determine in advance at what points along the length of the Auob Valley and in what groupings the enemy would gather to meet my attacks. Even scout patrols would have fallen prey to enemy bullets or, since the enemy controlled all the water-holes, died of thirst. No spies were available.

Battle formation:

1. Meister's detachment, consisting of the 4th, 5th, three-fourths of the 7th company of the 2nd field regiment, as well as the 5th field battery, totaling 223 men, including officers, advancing from Kalkfontein (south of Hochanas) out of Auob.

2. Ritter's detachment: 2nd company of the 1st field regiment, Stuhlmann's half-battery, approximately 110 men, coming from Gibeon by way of Gamus-Aukam.

3. Lengerke's detachment: 8th company of the 2nd field regiment, half of the 3rd depot company, 8th battery, one-third of the 9th mountain battery, approximately 300 men, marching north by way of Koes-Persip.

Colonel Deimling selected Gochas as the meeting place for the troops and 4 January 1905 as the date.

He issued an additional order: the strongest of the three detachments, Meister's, was to arrive early at Gochas on 3 January and continue its advance. Deimling was operating on the assumption that the Hottentots, who generally had first-class enemy reconnaissance at their disposal, would take their stand against the smallest detachment, that is, Ritter's column. This assumption was mistaken. He had failed to realize that Hendrik Witbooi might have taken the assumption into account in formulating his own plan. In fact Witbooi attacked the strongest detachment, Meister's, with his own strongest force, while the weakest, Ritter's detachment, was offered only token resistance.

The commander, Colonel Deimling, joined Ritter's detachment, since he thought it faced the greatest danger.

Deimling liked to ride Hanoverians, particularly black ones.

Notes of Division Chaplain, Lic. Max Schmidt:

For camp service, begin with God's words reminding us of peace, and thus reassuring our hearts even in the storm of battle: "Peace I leave with you, my peace I give unto you . . . Let not your heart be troubled, neither let it be afraid" (John 14, 27).

Then more generally: the homeland is watching each of us. The Kaiser. The Reich. The duty of every Christian. Standard-bearers of culture and civilization.

Conclusion: final preparation for battle: "Finally, my brethren, be strong in the Lord . . . take the shield of faith . . . take the helmet of salvation, and the sword of the Spirit!" (Ephesians 6, 10.16.17.)

31 December 1904

Meister's detachment departs at 4:30 in the afternoon. Not a cloud in the sky, a light breeze, very hot. They march along the riverbank of the Auob. A scant two hours later, around 6:30, the head of the column encounters enemy fire from the slopes on both sides. Major Meister issues orders to storm the heights. Captain Krüger is shot through the chest as he reaches the top of the hill. The Hottentots withdraw, but remain firmly entrenched among the cliffs. Meister orders this position stormed as well. The attack founders halfway up the height, two officers lie wounded, three horsemen are dead, four others wounded. The detachment can advance no further.

A thunderstorm breaks over them. The temperature drops. The troops pass the night on alert. Everything is soaked, freezing. Around midnight someone calls out Happy New Year.

1 January 1905

Ritter's detachment moves out from Gibeon.

Lengerke's unit is on the way to Persip. Neither encounters the enemy.

Major Meister calls for reconnaissance. The Hottentots have abandoned their position. No one is in sight. Meister is surprised. Is that it? He doesn't set out again until 9 o'clock. The advance proves difficult. The wagons constantly stuck, cannons mired in river sand. By early afternoon the troops, horses, and draft animals are so exhausted that Meister stops around 5. He plans to make better headway the next day.

He sends out patrols. They return with reports of 400 to 500 Hottentots to the south. Once more, the troops spend the night on alert.

2 January 1905

Lengerke's detachment marches toward Persip. Nothing of note to report.

Ritter's unit reaches Aukam without encountering the enemy. Deimling tells his assistant adjutant Kirsten that things are going smooth as silk.

Meister's detachment sets out again at 5:30 in the morning. Meister says, We have to pull out all the stops today. He has the water wagons, water bags, and field canteens filled. He wants to make up for lost time, but it's already clear they won't make it to Gochas by 3 January.

The countryside south of Witkrans is partially covered with thick brush; numerous folds of terrain intersect the line of march; cre-vices with steep chalk slopes extend from the dunes to the river valley.

Around 6:30 the head of the column is fired on from one of the rough chalk slopes running at an angle to the river. When Major Meister sends men to both flanks, they encounter fire from the rebels, who have also occupied the dunes. Once again the unit is able to advance. Lines of soldiers are deployed, the guns are brought into position, but the enemy is nowhere in sight.

Hendrik Witbooi has selected his position the previous night and deployed his men. The prophet Stürmann forms the front line with God's Soldiers. Witbooi has occupied the dunes. Meister estimates there are 500 Hottentots. Deimling later maintains there were at least 1000. There were probably fewer than 400.

It is a cloudless day. In the sack-like valley not a breeze stirs. The sand glows. In spite of their corduroy uniforms, the horsemen develop blisters on their knees and elbows. They must stand to fire their weapons, while the rebels fire from well-concealed positions above them.

Medical Lieutenant Weltz treats seriously wounded men shot diagonally through the thorax. The wagons have been drawn into a protective circle with the field hospital inside. All three doctors are operating.

Lance Corporal Nägele is raving deliriously about white ravens.

The morphine runs out. Around 5 o'clock the last of the water is distributed.

Why didn't Meister retreat?

He hoped the other detachments would hear the gunfire. But he must have realized they couldn't have reached Gochas yet. The decisive factor was that Major Meister had been ordered by Deimling to move with full strength against any force he encountered. The detachment had to make it through, or at least hold its ground. Retreat would have meant the end of his career.

With the onset of darkness the gunfire becomes increasingly

sporadic, flaring up only when movement is spotted on either side. But not much can be seen of the rebels.

Around 10 o'clock that night heavy dark clouds suddenly appear in the west. It looks like a thunderstorm. Tarpaulins are spread out to catch the rainwater. Second Lieutenant Frhr. v. Seu. kneels in front of his line and prays for rain.

Soon thereafter a tempestuous wind scatters the clouds.

Bread is passed along the lines, but no one can eat it, their tongues swell up immediately.

Nothing can be heard that night but the cries and moans of the wounded. The slopes where the rebels are entrenched are quiet. A solitary stone rattles its way down and is answered immediately by savage gunfire from the German side. Major Meister orders the men to save their ammunition.

The troops spend the night on the lines, rifles cradled in their arms. Only every second man is allowed to sleep.

Lance Corporal Sa. sneaks the last swallow of water from his sleeping comrade's field canteen. Someone sees him and reports it. Meister has him chained to a wagon wheel for stealing from a comrade. When Lieutenant Grü., the company commander, points out that every man is needed now, Meister replies, no, not a man without honor.

3 January 1905

Lengerke's detachment continues to advance toward Gochas. No enemy contact. Around 2 in the afternoon they are involved in a skirmish. The small advance unit, which includes Deimling and his staff, is surrounded, as are the troops with Second Lieutenant Müller v. Berneck. Deimling takes command personally. The situation is precarious. He issues orders to storm a small sand dune from which the rebels are firing on the unit. Assistant Adjutant Kirsten and Deimling's adjutant, Ahrens, try to make their way up the hill with a few of the staff. Lieutenant Ahrens is killed, a man is wounded, the others forced to retreat. The situation is now desperate. Deimling maintains his composure. In such confused circumstances a leader must radiate absolute calm, a calm transferred to the officers, then to their subordinates, and finally to the riflemen themselves. Not an easy optimism, but a serious, stead-fast calm, which alone ensures that orders will be carried out. Someone has to go back to bring up the artillery, which has lagged behind. Colonel Deimling doesn't ask for volunteers, but simply orders Corporal Brehm of the Field Signal unit to ride through the Hottentot lines and deliver instructions to Stuhlmann's battery to enter the fray at once. Brehm rides directly into enemy fire. He gallops through the low brush. He makes it. As he reaches the battery, his horse collapses beneath him. They count seven bullet wounds. Brehm sits down and cries. He's ridden this horse since the revolt began. The battery blasts the way clear for Ritter's unit, led by Colonel Deimling. Deimling is noticeably upset by the death of his adjutant, and hardly speaks to those around him for the rest of the day. The Assistant Adjutant says the commander is upset.

In the Great Nabas valley basin the temperature climbs to over 105 degrees Fahrenheit by noon. The air registers only 15% humidity. By late morning there are already cases of heat prostration and fainting spells. The soldiers are totally enervated. A few grow delirious.

Second Lieutenant v. Kleist is shot in the knee. He will not be able to bend his leg again and will resign from the service. A trooper, babbling incoherently, suddenly stands and theatrically grabs his throat. When the captain looks up, he sees that the man's throat has been ripped away by a bullet.

Two men guarding the horses shoot one and drink its blood.

Several troopers have been drinking their own urine for the past day.

Major Meister has an officer smash the remaining bottles of rum. Soldiers secretly drinking rum have thrown themselves into enemy fire with hoarse moans, their throats dried by alcohol. Their bullet-riddled bodies can't be recovered until the following day.

The stench of corruption spreads through the valley, since they have managed to cover only a few of the dead with a little sand.

The screams of Major v. Nauendorff can be heard over the sounds of battle, even on the front lines.

He was shot in the stomach yesterday and has lived for 24 hours.

He first offers 1000 marks for a drink of water, then 10,000. Yet when Sergeant Wehinger, himself wounded, offers him the last swallow of red wine from his canteen, the major changes his mind: You drink it, comrade, you'll be back at your gun soon, but I'm about done for.

Field Chaplain Lic. Schmidt comforts the wounded and dying. He repeats the story of Job several times. He takes up arms himself to help ward off a Hottentot attack, for example when they try to seize a German cannon on the left flank. They defend it with cold steel. Semper, a second lieutenant in the reserves, has just ordered his men to load their weapons with case shot when he is struck in the stomach by a bullet. He falls across the recoil channel of the cannon. The corporal hesitates to pull the release. Semper says: Fire! The corporal discharges the cannon. The barrel recoils and crushes Semper's pelvis. Not long after he dies in the first-aid post.

Didn't anyone try to desert?

Yes. Even one company commander fled, Second Lieutenant v. Vollard-Bockelberg. Semi-delirious, he must have tried to reach a water-hole behind Hottentot lines. The rebels held up their bulging water bags and called out: German man thirsty—good water here.

This wasn't a psychological ploy to convince the Germans to desert, but a way to lure already delirious soldiers into the line of fire. And in fact several men dashed forward before their comrades could stop them. They were shot down. Three remained missing in action.

Why didn't the rebels try to convince the Germans to surrender?

At the outbreak of the war, Isaak Witbooi offered safe passage out of the country to all German women and children, as well as any man who would tie a white scarf, the Witboois' badge, in plain sight on his hat.

When Major Maercker interrogated Hendrik Witbooi's son Isaak, the question never arose. The German expected no mercy from the rebels.

And the rebels?

What were they supposed to do with prisoners? In guerilla warfare it was impossible to set up prisoner-of-war camps, and prisoners could not be taken along in mobile combat. One could spare their lives as Morenga did, but then they would soon be back fighting the rebels. The problem appears to have been solved by Hendrik Witbooi as follows: the Germans take no prisoners. We will take no prisoners.

4 January 1905

On this day Ritter and Lengerke's units meet in the morning near Haruchas. They stop to await Meister's detachment, which should already be there. As evening approaches, Colonel Deimling voices the suspicion that Major Meister may have dawdled along the way. Or he's stuck somewhere and can't advance.

That morning Meister decides to storm the occupied heights so they can press ahead to the water-hole. By this time the troops can no longer retreat. The soldiers and animals are listless.

Hendrik Witbooi and the prophet Stürmann meet during the night. Stürmann claims that many Germans have already retreated, and that before long all of them will flee. He suggests that Hendrik withdraw from the dunes and move into positions further back to cut off their retreat.

Hendrik hesitates, but in the end he withdraws for reasons unknown even to his son, Isaak Witbooi, who is second in command. The rebels can see that the German detachment was almost entirely surrounded. Perhaps Hendrik Witbooi still believed in the visionary powers of the prophet.

Initially there had been a disagreement about who should go to whom: the captain Hendrik Witbooi to the prophet Stürmann, or the prophet to the captain. Since Hendrik didn't go, the prophet came to Hendrik.

Around 9 in the morning, Major Meister called a general meeting of all officers. A few had to be carried in by their men. Meister gave orders to storm the Hottentot position. When ordered to carry out this mission with the freshest men available, Second Lieutenant Klewitz passed out. Second Lieutenant Zwicke tried to shoot the major, and had to be restrained by four men.

The officers' morale was so low by this time that Meister thought that of the soldiers was better.

At 11 the bayonet charge begins, under the command of Captain Richard. The Hottentots abandon their position. Stürmann's troop of God's Soldiers put up stiff resistance, then they too withdraw. The Germans reach the water-hole at noon. Stürmann joins Hendrik Witbooi, who has taken his main force downstream to hinder the German's retreat, and reports that the Germans have broken through.

Why did the rebels flee when the Germans staged a bayonet charge?

They were not trained in hand-to-hand combat. They were unfamiliar with the tactical response to an attack by storm, which in their eyes appeared insane, crazy, suicidal. They didn't know the rule of thumb: if the enemy attacks by storm, let them come at you, breath deeply, aim calmly and carefully, if the enemy reaches your line, jump up and engage them in hand-to-hand combat. But how do you parry a bayonet thrust?

Notes of the armed forces pastor, Division Chaplain Lic. Max Schmidt (Great Nabas, 4 January 1905)

It was a anxious hour, one we lived through with pounding yet exalted hearts. The two cannons for which there were still shells and soldiers lifted once more their long-missed brazen voices and aided the assault's success with a few direct hits in the enemy's midst. The Hottentots who first replied with stubborn and heavy fire flew screaming before our flashing bayonets, and both cannons and our assault columns pressed through successfully. The water-hole at Great Nabas was taken by storm, the dark and dreadful rock fortress of the enemy was in our hands!

The rebels withdrew to Swartfontein.

Meister's unit withdrew to Stamprietfontein. On 7 January a patrol from Deimling's detachment managed to establish contact with Meister's. On 10 January all the columns were united, seven days later than planned.

None of this could be considered a victory, although Deimling did manage to burn to the ground all the pondoks of the Kopper Hottentots in Gochas. Colonel Deimling waited for reinforcements, in the meantime occupying all the water-holes in the direction of the Great Karas Mountains in hopes of preventing the rebels from uniting there under Hendrik Witbooi and Morenga.

Otto Pahl: "Orlog in South West Africa"

Now with the turning of the year
Came new unrest and newfound fear,
For this time New Year's Eve came in
With a tremendous frightful din.
Above the thundering cannon's roar
A voice was raised to cry once more
What every soldier longed to hear:
All the best in this New Year!
How can anyone not recall
The mud we sat in one and all.
No punch, no grog, no beer!
Bullets rained around us there.

The nearest water-hole was taken then
By Hendrik Witbooi and his men.
At Nabas patiently he waited
Until we came and as if fated
After blows and bullets fell
Around us all, blood flowed as well.
The third day saw at last the sight
Of Hendrik and his men in flight.
Now the battle had been won
And our suffering was done.
The water-hole—our thirst was fleeting.
The blacks had taken quite a beating.

Of enemies is Auob freed.
Still Hendrik finds himself in need
It's said. Because he led his men

Into defeat's uncertain end,

the Hottentots have lost respect.

He may yet see a rope around his neck.

Five thousand marks are offered for his head

And he appears as good as dead.

Hendrik himself must know it's true,

And well the Seventh knows it too.

Our brave lads expect to be

The ones who will divide that fee.

A letter from Hendrik Witbooi, written in Tsumis, delivered in Keetmanshoop on 27 July 1905.

To my honored friend and District Officer.

It is true and I agree with what you say about your might and abundance in all things and I also agree that I am very weak. But you did not write in your answer what I should give you, you just boasted of your might, which I know well. Also you tell me of the price placed on my head, so that I am now an outlaw. As for the troubles you have with my nation, they are not mine, for I have not created anyone, nor have you, but God alone. So I sit now in your hands and peace means death for me and for my nation. For I know there is no refuge for me among your people. And what you say about peace, I say that you are lecturing to me like a schoolboy about your peace. For as you well know, you used me so many times as a pack animal when there was peace, and what can I see in your peace but the destruction of us and all our people, for you have come to know me, and I have come to know you over the length of our lives; thus far for now I close.

I am Captain

Hendrik Witbooi

BATTLE REPORT 2
THE SIEGE OF WARMBAD

R egarding the situation in Warmbad at the end of November
1904.
(*The Battles of the German Colonial Guard in South West Africa*,
ed. by the Office of the General Staff, vol. 2, p. 28 ff.)

Morenga planned to exploit the German weakness at Warmbad and
take the village by storm. He had accurately assessed the town's importance, with its extensive supplies and large prisoner-of-war camp,
and as a base for communication with the Cape Colony. As always, he
set his plan in motion with remarkable speed, energy, and stealth.

On 20 November a relatively small patrol led by a volunteer
named Mostert had managed not only to relieve a band of Hottentots
of the cattle they had stolen at Alurisfontein, but to trail them to
Umeis and kill five and wound two others while suffering no casualties. At that time the region remained free of larger rebel bands. But
when Captain v. Koppy left for Raman's Drift with Second Lieutenant
Schmidt and four men on 23 November, and a patrol under Second
Lieutenant v. Heydebreck had advanced to the region of Hom's Drift
on the Orange, cattle were again stolen near Warmbad on the 25th.
Presumably the cattle thieves believed that the undermanned garrison
at Warmbad, limited in its freedom of movement by having to guard
the captured Bondels, could undertake nothing against them. Perhaps
they wished to lure more soldiers from the station, so that they could
storm it more easily. Lieutenant Count Kageneck, who was in command at Warmbad during Captain v. Koppy's absence, did in fact send

two patrols with twenty-three men after the cattle thieves in the direction of Alurisfontein on the afternoon of the 25th.

While one patrol returned that same evening without having encountered the enemy, the other, led by Corporal Nickel, came under heavy fire near Alurisfontein and dug in on a hill just north of the town. They were now under the leadership of Corporal Wannemacher, who had taken over command from Nickel, who was severely wounded. A trooper named Schulz rode directly through the Hottentots to deliver news of the battle to Warmbad.

Upon hearing this, Count Kageneck set out that same evening for Alurisfontein with thirty-five men and a cannon. They had almost safely reached the redoubt of Corporal Wannemacher when intense and rapid fire was trained on them from all sides in the darkness. They had ridden right into the midst of a far superior force, well concealed and firmly established in the surrounding cliffs. It was later discovered that the Hottentots had gathered almost 300 rifles. Since the German detachment faced an opponent with several times their own firepower, the situation was critical from the outset. They were forced to draw up around the cannon in the middle of the Hom riverbed and, shielded only by a few bushes, found themselves in an even worse position than the ten men of the patrol holding out in their small stone redoubt. Communication between the two detachments could be established only sporadically.

As if that weren't enough, the Hottentots managed yet another successful stroke south of Alurisfontein. Second Lieutenant Schmidt and v. Heydebreck made their way back from Raman's Drift on the evening of the 25th with fourteen men. With both officers far in the lead, the patrol was riding through the twilight toward Alurisfontein when shots erupted. Second Lieutenant Schmidt was killed immediately. Second Lieutenant v. Heydebreck and his patrol raced to the top of a hill and dug in as best they could. Three troopers who were cut off managed to break through toward Raman's Drift.

The three separate German units, already weakened, had thus lost all contact with each other and were surrounded by a superior enemy force. At daybreak gunfire broke out with new intensity from all directions. Losses mounted quickly. Heydebreck's patrol was in the worst position, with the Hottentots, contrary to their normal practice, actively launching attacks. One by one the following men fell: the courageous leader, Lieutenant v. Heydebreck, pierced by five bullets, then Corporal Gerber, Lance Corporal Hübner and troopers Markwardt and Backhaus. Toward noon the three surviving soldiers tried to break through, but only one of them, left wounded on the field, was able to make his way later to Warmbad.

Kageneck's unit was also in dire straits, primarily due to the exhaustion of the troops, rendered almost helpless by hours on the burning sand with no water. The plight of the wounded was particularly distressing, no matter how diligently the medical officer, Dr. Otto, attended to them, ignoring enemy fire. Every horse in the detachment was shot down. Fortunately in this case the Hottentots decided not to attack. Morenga later told Captain v. Koppy that he thought there was no chance that the remaining troops in Warmbad would leave their base to relieve Kageneck's unit. Since they would soon die of thirst anyway, he declined to attack, avoiding unnecessary losses.

Meanwhile unexpected aid soon reached the hard-pressed German detachment. In the morning hours of the 26th, Captain v. Koppy, returning from Raman's Drift accompanied only by Corporal Schütze, entered the general area of Alurisfontein. Suddenly he heard shots, saw a group of men and horses that he assumed was Schmidt's patrol, and was about to gallop toward them when his companion called out: "Those are Hottentots, they'll be firing on us soon." In the same instant they were met with lively rifle fire and were forced to whirl their horses about and retreat. Luck was on their side: swinging eastward, they reached Warmbad at 9 o'clock in the morning, where Lieutenant v. Rosenthal, who had remained there, reported the events of the 25th to his company commander. Captain v. Koppy immediately gathered the remaining natives at the old station and had the buildings in which they were locked mined with dynamite. Six troopers remained behind with them, in addition to the white inhabitants, with instructions in case of emergency to blow up the buildings along with the prisoners. Captain v. Koppy then advanced toward Alurisfontein with the remaining men— twenty-eight of them altogether—and a cannon. He learned en route that the situation of Count Kageneck's detachment was desperate and that his men were nearly dying of thirst. Speed was of the essence.

Captain v. Koppy rode out ahead of his troopers and encountered the enemy in position four kilometers north of Alurisfontein. He deployed his detachment for battle, but shortly after the cannon commenced firing, the Hottentots withdrew; they had apparently been assigned to intercept the rapidly advancing German reinforcements. From the heights abandoned by the enemy, Captain v. Koppy could view the entire field of battle and recognized the critically dangerous situation of the nearby detachments under Kageneck and Wannemacher; at the same time he observed an enemy force of approximately thirty men galloping toward the now almost totally exposed Warmbad. The cannon promptly fired a few well aimed shots in that direction, and the troopers scattered. Several riderless horses showed the shells had taken their toll. Koppy's unit now entered the fray with Kageneck and Wannemacher, occupying a crest of land to the east. They also managed to transport the cannon from Kageneck's unit, for which Captain von Koppy had brought fresh ammunition, to high ground. Both cannons began a lively bombardment of the enemy positions surrounding Wannemacher's unit, while the riflemen fired on the Hottentots dug in between the crest and the Hom River.

An intense firefight ensued. The enemy gradually trained more and more of their weapons on v. Koppy's unit, allowing the latter's hard-pressed comrades to catch their breath. It was not until evening, however, that the Germans managed to get the upper hand, largely due to the effect of their artillery, and as darkness fell the Hottentots began disappearing, singly at first, and then in groups, in the direction of Kinderzit. Now Count Kageneck and Corporal Wannemacher's half-dead men could join v. Koppy's unit and the wounded could be cared for. At midnight the troops set out for Warmbad. Count Kageneck's men, unable to march, were carried on horses from Captain v. Koppy's unit, while the wounded were placed on wagons. Just after two in the morning, without further encounter, the company reached Warmbad.

The battle near Alurisfontein had severely tested the resolution and stamina of the German troopers. It was thanks to the level-headed and energetic intervention of Captain v. Koppy that disaster had been avoided, allowing the Germans to leave the field of battle undefeated. The battle had resulted in substantial losses for the under-manned company. However their ranks were reduced by ten dead, ten wounded and two missing; two-fifths of the officers and twenty-three soldiers were rendered unfit for further combat.

In Warmbad, where the garrison now consisted of fewer than a hundred men including a detachment of Boers and two cannons, Captain v. Koppy immediately set about strengthening the defenses, expecting a new attack. He had not misread his opponent: on the evening of 27 November Warmbad was fired upon from all sides, al-though without success. The enemy pressed forward to within two hundred meters of the buildings, but were driven back with heavy losses. On the 28th there was a second attack; then Morenga, who had cut Warmbad off from the outside world, tried without success to enter into negotiations. Finally, on 2 December, he drove off a few more of the company's pack animals and disappeared northward a few days later by way of Draihoek. Thus Warmbad was saved, al-though several rebel groups, particularly the two Bastard bands under Morris, kept the area south of Warmbad in a constant state of unrest, and harassed all communication with Raman's Drift.

The successful defense of Warmbad not only saved valuable Ger-man lives and property from the murderous onslaughts of the Hot-tentots, but also preserved a crucial supply line with the Cape Colony for German troops, while warding off a potentially serious blow to German prestige in Africa.

DISTANT FIRE

On 17 January, Gottschalk received orders to join a patrol the following morning and attempt (the word actually used) to reach Warmbad.

The General Staff of the southern division felt that a veterinarian was urgently needed there. Most of the supplies for the troops operating in the south would be passing through Warmbad in the future.

Apart from Lieutenant von Rheinbaben, who was leading the patrol, only Corporal Rattenhuber had joined voluntarily. They would be riding through nearly 300 kilometers of enemy territory controlled by rebels led by Morenga and Morris.

Gottschalk's diary,
19 January 1905
(rest break on the way to Warmbad)

Dreamed I had lost my way in the desert. The strange thing was that as I was wandering about, I didn't know I'd lost my way, but at the same time I knew, from the outside as it were, that I didn't know it. So I walked on without worrying, but dead tired, climbing sand dunes that stretched away like waves into the interior of the country. Only after seeing a rider in the distance, and then seeing him again drawing nearer, did I realize I'd lost my way. I felt the sand trickling down into my boots, filling in tightly around my feet, and it was harder and harder to walk. Suddenly, crossing the crest of a dune, I stood before the rider, who wore a German Colonial Guard uniform. I asked him the way, but my questions bounced off him like a wall. Finally he lifted his head. Nothing can be seen beneath the shadowy brim of his hat but a scar: no eyes, no nose, no mouth. A faceless face. On his hat, in place of the black, white, and red cockade, he wears a white marguerite. The horse replies in Nama, but in a dialect I can't understand.

The patrol reached Warmbad on 25 January 1905. As they rode in around noon, none of the chained Bondels looked up, but soldiers came running, ragged figures, asking if they had rum and tobacco and whether any mail had arrived.

In six days of hard riding, the patrol had seen no one. All they encountered were horse tracks, fresh ones, as Corporal Rattenhuber determined from the droppings. The Lieutenant strengthened the forward post and sent troopers southward on a sweep. Gottschalk kept tight hold of his holstered gun until nightfall. The next day his arm ached.

That night several fires could be seen on the distant hills of the Karas Mountains, where Morenga's men were encamped. There was something comforting to Gottschalk in the thought that the rebels were sitting kilometers away around their campfires. Rheinhaben, however, maintained that there was no one around the fires, the rebels were crouching somewhere in the dark on the paths leading to them. The fires were meant to lure the patrol. Rattenhuber agreed that no one was encamped by the fires. The patrol's every movement had been watched by spies during the march. Gottschalk found it unsettling to be watched for hours on end as they rode through the deserted landscape and to see no one; yet somewhere eyes saw him, followed his every movement. Out there the howl of a hyena was not necessarily a hyena, but a call, a signal, that one could hear but not understand. Gottschalk couldn't read on the march. (What a ridiculous plan.) He stinted on feed in his saddlebags to save room to stash away his Kropotkin, which he felt each night as he reached in for a handful of feed for his horse. He would lie awake at night, although he was dead tired, listening in the darkness. He could tell from the way Dr. Haring was breathing that he was awake too. When Gottschalk mentioned to Rheinhaben how much he admired the latter's calm demeanor, without a sign of nerves, and how that must be what was meant by courage or bravery, Rheinhaben replied that in his case it was simply a matter of low blood pressure. Dr. Haring offered to test his blood pressure, and said he had medicine for that in his kit.

Rattenhuber only had to say Psst once during the six-day march, when Gottschalk called Haring's attention to a particularly impressive shooting star.

Compared with this, the march with Wenstrup and Schwinebelly had been a celebration with the boys at the club.

The morning Wenstrup left Keetmanshoop, he'd said farewell to Gottschalk. There was nothing unusual about that. But now he'd been away for two or three weeks.

They shook hands and wished each other well. That was all. Now Gottschalk tried to call to mind every detail of this parting. How had Wenstrup offered his hand? Did he smile? What did he say, and in what tone of voice? Nothing remained but his handshake, a smile, yes, and the easy phrase: Good luck.

Sometimes he asked himself what Wenstrup thought of him. Gottschalk had taken leave of his language teacher, Jakobus, convinced he would see him again soon. He had been trying to find a Nama grammar in Keetmanshoop, but none was available in the entire village, not even in the mission school. The only way to get a textbook was through the Rhenish Mission. It would have to be ordered from Germany and would take at least three months to arrive in Warmbad.

How can we expect to colonize a land if we don't take the trouble to understand the natives, Gottschalk once asked in Keetmanshoop.

With the aid of an interpreter and a hippo-hide whip, Lieutenant Schwanebach replied, an internationally recognized language. Gottschalk found this unusually quick-witted on Schwinebelly's part, not realizing it was an old soldiers' joke.

• • •

In Warmbad Gottschalk was ordered by the District Officer, Lieutenant Count Kageneck, to inspect the few horses Morenga's men had not already driven off and get them back on their feet as soon as possible. Cavalrymen stationed in Warmbad were having to scout the surrounding territory on foot.

The horses were emaciated, most were lame, a few had mange, others had been ridden to the point of exhaustion, and almost all had festering wounds where bullets had grazed them or the soldiers had dug in their spurs. Gottschalk extracted a lead bullet from the thigh of one gelding. He had two horses shot. A few oxen, looking equally miserable, had not been immunized against rinderpest, and no vaccine was available locally. Gottschalk wrote up a detailed feeding plan, since there were only a few sacks of corn and oats in the village, and the fields around Warmbad had been grazed bare. It was impossible to tell when supply trains might make it through, since the Cape authorities had closed off the borders, and the route to the Orange, the frontier river, was constantly disrupted by the Morris brothers and their men.

Three weeks after his arrival in Warmbad, Gottschalk was unexpectedly ordered to report to Lieutenant Count Kageneck in field dress uniform, which Gottschalk had not even taken along on the march. A somewhat unreasonable demand on Kageneck's part, who was well thought of by most of his men because he ran Warmbad in a relatively easygoing fashion. Kageneck, whose reputation as a notorious drinker and morphine addict extended far beyond the borders of the district (occasioning one of those silly soldiers' rhymes: Kageneck spills more they say, than most men drink on an average day) enjoyed a reputation as one of the most effective negotiators with disgruntled Hottentot captains. He could drink any man under the table (and these men were no pushovers when it came to alcohol) without resorting to unfair measures or tricks (lift the glass, happy days, and toss it over the shoulder). The more he drank the more sensitive he became to the Hottentots' problems, and generally wound up swearing brotherhood with them. Since he tended to reach this stage of intoxication around four in the afternoon, a large number of petitioners made a habit of crowding into his somewhat barren brick office building each day at that hour. Sometimes the district office secretary, Gustav Fett, had to force the Hottentots to relinquish the promises made to them by threatening them with a whipping on the following day. For example when, as dawn broke after a night of drinking, Kageneck promised to return land now owned by the German Colonial Company to a Hottentot chief and his tribe. On another occasion, during the Bondel uprising of 1903, at an advanced hour of the night, he ordered a sentry to sever the bonds of a Bondel prisoner scheduled to be executed the following day and give the poor fellow, in just those words, something to eat and drink, after which the sentry was instructed to turn two blind eyes. Kageneck actually said turn two blind eyes. The sentry followed his orders and the Bondel disappeared into the night.

The next morning, stone sober, Kageneck wanted the sentry shot for gross dereliction of duty and for aiding and abetting a prisoner's escape. Only the intervention of a second lieutenant who swore that the sentry had simply been following Kageneck's orders saved the man.

When Gottschalk entered the district office he found Kageneck sitting in a darkened room in a tin bathtub full of water in which floated various-shaped bottles: Flat, rectangular whiskey bottles, a nice round bottle of Jamaican rum, an earthenware bottle of Oldenburg Steinhager, and finally, the triune star of Warmbad, a potbellied bottle of French cognac.

Kageneck enquired briskly as to Wenstrup's present location, and when Gottschalk said all he knew was that Wenstrup had been reported missing, Kageneck informed him that Wenstrup had taken leave of his regiment without permission, or more precisely and in plain German, had deserted, and had done so along with some young Hottentot boy named Jakobus. And what, Kageneck wanted to know, did Gottschalk, who was supposedly Wenstrup's friend, have to say about that? The report had come from the Cape police, from Upington. Now unfortunately, he was forced to interrogate Gottschalk with regard to the affair, after all, the military criminal code included a paragraph concerning failure to report desertion. Since it was already nearing four in the afternoon, Kageneck invited Gottschalk to have a drink with him. Gottschalk allowed himself this liberty and let Kageneck pour him a French cognac.

As the imperial government files reveal, Wenstrup deserted on 2 January 1905; they include only rumors concerning his subsequent whereabouts. It's said that after Wenstrup fled to the Cape Colony, he went to Argentina and was shot in the chest while attempting to rob a government bank in Mar del Plata. Not long thereafter he supposedly died in a provincial backwoods village named Madariaga. According to a second rumor he joined an anarchist cell in Paris and earned his living playing chess for money in cafés and clubs (Gottschalk had never seen him playing chess). And finally, someone claimed to have spotted him on the island of St. Helena, where he had taken up a veterinary practice near Longwood, the village where Napoleon was once interned.

That evening Gottschalk was so lively and talkative that Kageneck was reduced to silence.

The next day the district commander reported that he had totally misjudged the veterinarian. It turned out he wasn't a sad sack at all. Kageneck attributed this realization to the quality of his cognac.

An incident. Wenstrup was sitting on a block of stone, following the skirmish near Naris, his head in his hands, as if concentrating on something. When Gottschalk spoke to him he raised his head; it was evident he had been crying. Wenstrup said it was nothing, an attack of fatigue.
But Gottschalk hadn't pressed the matter.

A veteran trooper standing nearby said that happened a lot

with new arrivals. It was the effect of the climate and the height. The heart had to work harder.

Gottschalk could no longer recall whether that had happened immediately after the prisoner had been executed.

Another incident concerning Wenstrup is a matter of official record as of 14 May 1914, and may be found in the files of the Intendance of the Colonial Guard, in the archives at Windhoek.

If Wenstrup had been a source of annoyance to his superiors during his period of duty, his disappearance seems to have kept whole departments and units of the Colonial Guard and the Imperial Colonial Office in suspense over a nearly insoluble problem that was fought out over a period of nine years, with copious memoranda, legal opinions, reports, and judicial statements, until the outbreak of the First World War brought this bureaucratic battle to an abrupt end.

What brought all this about? The veterinarian had been promoted to Lieutenant on 7 November 1904, effective from 1 February of that same year. (He should not, therefore, have been required to salute Gottschalk first while on board the *Gertrude Woermann* according to the Regulations for Saluting. But in any case he should have received back pay for the difference between the salary of an N.C.O. Veterinarian and that of a Lieutenant). Since at the time of his appointment Wenstrup was already on march in the south, and given the inadequate lines of communication and general confusion of the troops at the outbreak of the rebellion, the news never reached him. But the possibility cannot be ruled out that someone, probably an officer, intentionally withheld notification.

After Wenstrup's desertion, as noted in a Colonial Guard report of 1 February 1905, in accordance with § 911 of the Civil Code, a trustee in absentia was appointed, to whom Wenstrup's salary as a Lieutenant and N.C.O. Veterinarian in the amount of 1508.33 marks was paid. The Imperial Colonial Office had then, after reviewing the figures, issued instructions on 20 November 1913, No. M.2718.13F, ordering the recovery of this sum, having come to the conclusion that the appointment had not had the force of law. The guardianship judge in Keetmanshoop ruled in response that the payment on the part of the Administration Accounts Office of the secondary benefit had been correct, citing Laband's *Constitution of the German Empire*, § 45.4, footnote 4, stating that the effect of a promotion begins with the reception of the appointment decree, and thus the salary had to be paid.

The Intendance of the Colonial Guard appealed, also citing Laband (§ 45.1, p. 421,4, in the 1901 edition), pointing out that the declared intent of the party in question was lacking, and thus it could not be presumed that the appointment would actually have gone into effect. It was conceivable that the appointee might have refused the promotion. The contradiction could only be solved, in the opinion of the Intendance, if the man appointed trustee in absentia would voluntarily refuse the pay differential he had received, failing which the government would have to block the amount in question from leaving the protectorate and sue for restitution, which action would naturally raise the question as to when the appointment had taken effect, and to what extent an appointment was possible in which there was indeed an appointee (existent as an expressed intention of the state), but also a non-appointee (existent as person), which would raise in turn the question of whether the creation of a new post was dependent on the will of the state, or upon the highly contingent existence or non-existence of an individual, or indeed even upon the acceptance or refusal of that individual. The invasion of troops from South Africa and especially the blockade of the protectorate by sea as the First World War broke out had the unfortunate consequence of preventing a decisive judicial clarification of the Wenstrup affair (his desertion was dealt with quickly: fifteen years in prison in absentia), which stood a good chance of setting a precedent on the basis of which later cases of a similar nature could have been more easily decided.

HOW GORTH PREACHED THE GOSPEL,
SPOKE WITH OXEN
AND STRAYED FROM THE TRUE PATH

In the Year of Peace, as the Hereros called 1852, because for once they were not at war with the Hottentots, a covered wagon crossed the Orange River, entering their land. Twenty choice oxen were yoked before it, guided by a wagon master known throughout the south by the nickname Ox-Friend. His tongue clicked more loudly than the crack of any whip. He was Petrus Matroos, a Hottentot baptized almost fifteen years earlier by an English missionary. This missionary, named Rumbottle, had been an able-bodied seaman on a sailing vessel until, tumbling from the rigging, he heard a voice call out as he struck the deck: Be my fisher of souls! He signed off the ship and settled near the Orange River in South Africa, where he spent time trying to drink the heathens under the table. Anyone he managed to baptize was christened Petrus. The spirits finally departed from Rumbottle's earthly vessel after eight years of missionary work, as he sat in an easy chair before a bucket of water holding three half-full bottles of rum.

At the Warmbad missionary station, where fifty years later the veterinarian Gottschalk would sit across from Count Kageneck, the Hottentots had been waiting days for this wagon, said to be coming from the south. Scores of natives had arrived from distant villages, bringing along children, dogs, and goats, and were squatting now on the sandy square, staring southward. At long last the wagon appeared on the horizon, visible as a small plume of sand dust. Anyone who could walk set out toward the wagon, driven by a curiosity against which even the noonday sun was powerless. Finally the man could be seen with the naked eye, preceding the wagon on foot. What threw the crowd into a great state of unbridled excitement was not the pallor of the stranger's skin (although many of them were seeing a white man for the first time), nor the strange sandals strapped on the man's bare feet (after all, the region was swarming with scorpions and snakes), nor was their mesmerized astonishment due to the fact that he was on foot (the white men they had seen up to then had to be tied tight to their wagons even at the break of day, lest they tumble beneath the heavy wheels in their drunken stupor). No, the almost unbearable tension of the crowd was focused on the face of the stranger, who, in an armless black jerkin, a long stick in his hand, was trudging along a good thirty paces ahead of his team of oxen. Dark-haired, with an equally dark beard ringing his chin and mouth, a set of metal frames with glittering lenses on his nose, the trained eyes of the nomads immediately recognized his resemblance to a sheep. And not just any sheep, but, as the rumors flying about the country for weeks had suggested, a fleecy Merino, which was still rare in this region. Was it his long chin, or the narrow bright eyes, or his slightly wavy, crinkly hair? As the stranger greeted the waiting Hottentots with a gentle smile, his face became even more markedly sheep-like. At this, a wave of enthusiastic jubilation washed over them. Forgotten now were all the hardships of the past days, the long wait, the doubts whether the tales were true. And to this enthusiasm was added admiration for the steadfastness of this stranger, who in spite of his pale face marched without a hat beneath the scorching noonday sun, openly revealing his resemblance to a friendly and undemanding animal.

Those who walk beneath God's heaven should bare their heads—this was Missionary Gorth's motto, one he had followed steadfastly even at the missionary school in Barmen and to which he remained true in the tropics. The Almighty created the heavens as his throne and the earth as his footstool, Gorth was wont to say. He regarded the tumultuous enthusiasm which greeted him from all sides as a sign from God. His missionary work, which was taking him to Bethany under the auspices of the Rhenish Mission, seemed to stand beneath a favorable star.

The oxen, spurred on by Petrus's tongue, drew slowly into Warmbad, followed by a large crowd of people. Standing before the missionary house, Mrs. Priestley greeted Gorth with the words: Hosannas today, the cross tomorrow.

The English Missionary Priestley was away on a trip, thank the Lord, so he at least was not forced to witness the enthusiastic welcome accorded his German colleague. At a signal from Mrs. Priestley, the missionary school children, who were arranged in rows by height, sang "God Save the Queen." Gorth tried to indicate his displeasure by repeatedly clearing his throat; after all this land still belonged to the Bondelswarts and not the English crown. The children were still singing out of tune in an English interspersed with tongue clicks, when strange squeals began to issue from the covered wagon. The bemused crowd immediately surrounded the wagon, while the choir began to die away, in spite of poisonous stares from Mrs. Priestley, and finally fell silent. Gorth waved some of the gaping men forward and had them crawl inside the wagon along with Petrus Matroos. A large, blackly-gleaming box appeared and was lowered to the ground by six groaning men and then hauled onto the veranda of the house. It was the second piano ever to enter this land. The first had been carried off on a rainy Friday twenty-five years earlier after a raid on the missionary station by Jager Africans. They had carefully taken it apart so that each member of the tribe could have a share. But the pieces produced no sound.

Following the piano, a loudly squealing pig was lifted to the ground, followed by six piglets that immediately crowded up to the sow. None of the Bondelswarts had ever seen such a fat and fleshy animal, spared the discomfort of a coat of hair, but helplessly exposed to the danger of sunburn.

The missionary society had refused to pay passage for the sow, who had her litter on the crossing. In the end, Missionary Gorth paid for her transportation himself. He had read about the upswing of Islamic missionary activity in Africa and intended to counter this development in a timely fashion by introducing the Hottentots, who already raised cattle and sheep, to the pleasures of pork.

Gorth stepped into the cool interior of the stone house along with the missionary's wife. Outside in the heat, the crowd waited with the sow and the piglets. The subject of their conversation within the house remained a mystery. After half an hour Missionary Gorth emerged onto the veranda, followed by Mrs. Priestley, her hands folded before her. Gorth sat down on a stool and accompanying himself on the piano sang: "A Mighty Fortress is our God." The crowd stood in awed silence. Only the sow, grunting and rooting about in the sandy soil, remained unmoved.

Later Missionary Gorth sat on the veranda, the star-studded heavens above him, and wrote by candlelight to his fiancée, who planned to follow him from Hamburg. She should come now, he wrote, this was a barren land, but the people were friendly and God's hand would soon set everything right.

Should they tie this man up and dump him on the far bank of the Orange River, as some leaders in the Bondelswarts tribal council advised? Or should they opt for the definitive solution already successfully tested on a few of Gorth's predecessors and send him back to his all-powerful patron with the help of an arrow? Saanes, an elder whose voice weighed heavily in the council, warned: He is merely the first of many. The traders will follow and then the soldiers. They will take our land and our cattle, like the Boers did in the south. But this gently smiling stranger, so sheep-like in appearance, didn't seem interested in anyone's land or cattle. Old Saanes. Hadn't he predicted a devastating cattle epidemic this year? And the cattle were healthier than ever. And wasn't the southern part of the sky supposed to tumble down three years ago? They had stared south all year.

Nothing had happened. They had ruined their eyes. Old Saanes was a pessimist. And last but not least the missionary had been summoned by the tribe in Bethany, so it was their affair. A brave man, this stranger, who passed through their land with his head bare and his feet in sandals.

The next morning, taking advantage of his stay, Gorth began planting a vegetable garden near the mission station. The English missionary didn't seem to be tackling his work energetically enough; the station looked neglected. Gorth reported this in writing to the missionary society. Sheep-Face showed the puzzled natives how to water a garden patch. Mrs. Priestley maintained a stony silence. There was plenty of water in the region, some of it even steaming. The time had clearly come for Warmbad to be governed by the Rhenish Mission. When, after a refreshing morning prayer, Sheep-Face glanced out his window the following day, he saw the villagers of Warmbad gathered around the vegetable patch. Pleased by their interest, Gorth went out without eating breakfast. As he drew near, he saw that the beds he had watered were white. For a moment he thought it had snowed. But even at this early hour of the morning it was already hot. Everyone stared at him expectantly. After licking a finger he knew what the white substance on the beds was: salt.

All right then, he said, if we can't grow vegetables, we'll have a saltwater spa some day.

He had already noted that many of the Hottentots, who ate mostly meat, suffered from gout. God's hand would set everything right.

Little Gorth had first expressed his desire to become a missionary at the age of nine. His father, a teacher at Heppenheim in Hesse, was one of many contributing members of the Rhenish Mission. Each year, to the day of her death, his mother crocheted twenty-seven woolen caps, which were sent to the missionary stations in Greenland and South Africa. The only thing little Gorth couldn't decide was whether he should go to Greenland or South Africa. A drawing reproduced in the missionary

newspaper had moved him deeply: three naked little black children were sitting around a nest containing three ostrich eggs.
One of the little blacks was crying. The caption read: Happy
Easter. The final and decisive impetus to become a missionary,
however, came a few years later through a strange incident of
which he spoke only once to his fiancée. On a Whitsunday he returned to church in the afternoon. At the sermon that morning
the preacher had pounded his fist on the pulpit till it fairly rang:
Well you may say unto to yourselves, today or tomorrow we will
go to this or that city and spend a year there and do business and
make a profit—you who do not know what tomorrow will bring.
For what is the span of life? You are but vapor that tarries a moment and then disappears. At the entrance to the church stood a
small metal statue of a nodding black boy, with a slot for coins
in his head, appealing for donations for missionary work. This
time, as little Gorth left the church, the little black boy nodded
directly to him, staring him right in the eye with a serious and
demanding air. God will bless you!

One evening Lukas appeared in Warmbad.

Clad in a long, linen shirt, a shroud that Gorth's predecessor,
Knudsen, had brought along for himself. Knudsen had wanted to
be buried in Bethany in this shroud when the time came. Just
two years ago he had departed for his hometown in Norway,
worn down and discouraged by his nine-year struggle to save the
souls of the Hottentots. But on the very day of his departure he
was involved in a brawl in which he lost two front teeth. There
were various versions of the origins of this fight. One was that
Knudsen had tried to take along the silver cross that the congregation had purchased. Almost to a man, the entire congregation
had given him a good reminder, since he was always railing
against cattle theft and threatening them with the fires of Hell.
At any rate Knudsen came out of it with another black eye, this
one clearly visible. He left his handwoven linen shroud behind
at the mission house. At least the shroud would bear witness to
his work in Bethany. Five months after this incident the chief,
following the advice of his council, sent a messenger to Cape

Town to ask the Missionary Society to send another missionary to Bethany with a remedy for the venereal disease that had broken out while Knudsen was there and was now spreading throughout the tribe. As a result a small box of quicksilver salve was included in Gorth's baggage. Of course the supply had already been substantially reduced on the voyage itself, after word of the existence of this miraculous box spread among the officers and crew.

When Lukas entered the room, Sheep-Face was transfigured. This tall, serious young man in his long robe seemed sent from God. This was the man Gorth had been looking for since crossing the Orange River. Europe had never seen a real Hottentot. It was Gorth's secret desire to show them one, and now the future presented itself to him, as always, in vivid images:

He is on board a sailing vessel bound for Europe, heading home on leave after five years of missionary work. Beside him at the railing stands a good-looking young Hottentot, dressed in European clothes, but with a few native accessories. At his missionary school in Barmen, Gorth had once attended a lecture by an English missionary who was accompanied by a tall, good-looking Somali. The room was overflowing. Many members of the audience had to stand outside in the hall. After the missionary had spoken, the Somali stood up and said in English: My brothers and sisters and I, we say thank you very much for your help. The room went wild. That evening they took in 468 marks. A huge sum. All the greater, then, had been Gorth's disappointment when he saw these stunted Hottentots with their strangely woven locks of hair, and the women with their enormous bottoms, upon which they could sit like stools on the ground. In old age their faces shriveled up like baked apples Gorth was not, God knows, an aesthete, he would never have used the word ugly, or even thought it, not because he knew how relative our concepts of beauty and ugliness are, but because it would have seemed presumptuous, for after all, the Hottentots were also part of God's creation. But at the same time he looked on with the demanding eyes of the members of the Missionary Society, who wanted to know to whom their money, their used greatcoats, and their laboriously crocheted nightcaps were going. And seen from this perspective, none of the Hottentots had measured up in Gorth's eyes until this young man entered the room: tall and well built, with a high, broad forehead, and a calm, direct gaze. This figure demonstrated, so Gorth felt, the ennobling and formative effect of Christianity, how it could turn a savage into an upright human being. With a Lukas like this, he could tour German cities and missionary societies.

Gorth gives a short introduction, in which he emphasizes the general aspects of missionary work in southern Africa. Lukas meanwhile sits modestly and quietly beside him at the table. After brief applause Lukas rises and reports in error-free German on the suffering of his as yet unsaved tribesmen, still living without faith in a terrible darkness, in fear of the never-ending night in which these poor souls moved, constantly threatened by malicious demons, with chaos in their heads and hearts by day, their nights ruled by the spirits of the dead, by restless fiends and vampires. Jesus Christ alone can bring light and love into this darkness. The audience sits in deeply moved silence. A collection is being taken at the entrance for missionary work in Namaland. Many members of the audience add their names to the list of contributing members. Inspired young people spontaneously decide to become missionaries. A school can be built in Bethany.

Speaking in Nama, Sheep-Face asked young Lukas, who was a church elder, how things stood in Bethany. But Lukas merely shook his head, not understanding the question, and when he spoke it was with the same strange clicks that Gorth at first had thought a special trait of the Bondelswarts: as if urging on a horse, or the cluck of amazement an old granny might make upon hearing some terrible news, at times like the pop of a cork being pulled from a bottle. The tongues that spoke this language seemed to glow. From Missionary Gorth's mouth, on the other hand, dull, flat sounds crawled forth like tortoises. The author of the textbook on the Nama language, with the help of which, over a three-year course of self-instruction, Gorth thought he was learning the Hottentot language, had reproduced all the clicks, insofar as they were described to him by a traveler, by means of consonants. A new language was created, spoken only by Gorth and a student in the missionary school in Basel. In order to perfect their ability, the two had even corresponded in the language.

Lukas spoke German, thank God. His grammar was a bit shaky, but he had a rich vocabulary. Of course it was going to be necessary to inform Lukas of the meaning of the terrible oaths that he kept weaving into his tales in total innocence. This was particularly painful for Gorth to hear, since he was always picturing an audience listening in rapt silence.

Father, did you bring a cure for the sickness with you, fuck the Virgin Mary if you didn't.

Gorth would probably need to start work all over again. He didn't want to lose a minute, no use sitting around, he was ready to leave that evening for Bethany, the site of his future efforts.

He called for Petrus, who arrived drunk as a hoot owl and declared: the oxen won't pull in the rain, and it's going to rain tomorrow. Petrus, when he wasn't driving his oxen, was always tipsy, in addition to which he lay around all day with a slattern who wasn't at all shy about carrying her breasts before her, large as pumpkins. Gorth strongly suspected these pumpkins were the real reason that Petrus didn't want to leave, and not the rain. So Gorth told Petrus to get a move on.

And so the clicking of Petrus's tongue was heard that very night, although it was slow and sluggish. This time Petrus was even forced to resort to his whip to rouse the twenty oxen from their cud-chewing doze and drive them to their wagon traces. Gorth wanted to trek in the cool of the morning and rest longer at midday. The Warmbad villagers were up at once, chasing after the squealing piglets, wrestling the sow into the wagon, then the piano, pinching the piglets one last time. Mrs. Priestley stood once more on the veranda of the mission house, her hands folded before her, the children's choir behind her, singing "God

Save the King." Petrus gave a sharp click of his tongue, the ox-boys drove the lead oxen forward, Sheep-Face led the way for the team, with Lukas beside him, the villagers accompanied him for a short way, cast a last glance after him, and the ox train disappeared in a cloud of dust.

After the ox-wagon had been underway four hours, Ox-Friend called them to a halt. This was a good spot to set up camp before the storm broke. Sheep-Face wanted to go on. They were barely eight kilometers from Warmbad. It was ridiculous to set up camp so early in the morning, there wasn't a cloud in the sky. But Petrus pointed to his arm where a bullet from a Herero rifle had lodged eight years ago, a spot that acted up whenever it was going to rain. They set out again. By afternoon a bank of black clouds rose in the west, and a few minutes later rain started to pour down if the heavens had been torn apart. The oxen came to an abrupt halt. Petrus unharnessed them. Pitching the tent proved impossible. Gorth crawled beneath the wagon canvas with Petrus and Lukas while the three ox-boys squatted under the wagon. Petrus pulled a bottle from his camp bag. Lukas lighted up a little pipe that exuded a fragrance like incense. The rain beat down upon the canvas.

Why did Knudsen leave you, Sheep-Face inquired. He was tired, Father, Lucas responded, we wore him out, the way a horse with a rough gait wears out a rider.

And does the false prophet still rule in Bethany?

Yes.

But when Gorth tried to ask Lukas more about this Hottentot prophet, Lukas had already floated far from the conversation on a blue cloud of dagga. Petrus wandered in a dream across a blue sea of rotgut. It seemed as if the heavens had fallen to earth. But it was pure rotgut. Suddenly he sank into it and was about to drown. His cries for help echoed away into emptiness. Then his powerful lead ox appeared, Big-Red, and held out its tail to him. Grabbing hold of the tuft, Petrus was pulled out.

Gorth attempted to write to his fiancée, but the candle was repeatedly blown out by the wind that lifted the sopping wet canvas. Then he knelt before the black piano as if it were an altar and prayed. The sow grunted. The piglets sucked away noisily. Petrus groaned in his sleep. Lukas appeared to be smiling in his transported state, a smile that struck Gorth as malicious. Gorth had prayed for strength and courage to approach the false prophet steadfastly and drive him from Bethany in the name of the true faith. It was this false prophet who had worn down the rugged Knudsen.

One day a Hottentot from the south had turned up in Bethany who amazed Knudsen by reading aloud from the Bible and reciting entire passages by heart. Knudsen's initial joy at finding a potential native deacon for the church was soon replaced by a tormenting anxiety, for Knudsen discovered that this man believed in a dangerous heresy, which he supported with numerous Biblical quotations. This false prophet proclaimed that it was the man of action, not the man of faith living in peace and humility, who found favor in the eyes of God. When Knudsen asked him where he got this foolishness, the false prophet replied: the Bible, and quoted from the letter of Jakobus, the Epistle of James: Ye see then how that by works a man is justified, and not by faith only. Knudsen laughed. But the members of the congregation looked at him inquiringly, and that evening he looked up the Epistle of James in the Bible and found the passage the Hottentot had quoted.

The following Sunday, after the service, a full-blown debate arose between Knudsen and the false prophet, in the course of which Knudsen threatened several times to strike the Hottentot prophet because the latter had gone so far as to suggest that evil might come from good. And when Knudsen roared for an example, the false prophet provided one for both him and the congregation: If you steal a steer from the Hereros, who have thousands of them on rich meadows, more cattle than they can ever eat themselves, cattle that die of old age, if you steal one of those steers and slaughter it and feed the children of your tribe with the meat, many of whom are dying of hunger, but who could live if they had stolen meat, then good has come from evil.

But if God permits children to die just so the cattle of the rich can go on living, then Knudsen's God is the almighty God of cattle, but not of the Hottentots and certainly not a good God. The gathered members of the congregation clicked their tongues approvingly. The tribe, which had previously lived by stealing cattle—the land where they lived was stony and had few springs—had been converted to Christianity by Knudsen, and Schmelen before him, then had been convinced by them that theft was an evil for which they would be damned after death. Knudsen didn't know what to say. The congregation sat in silence, awaiting his response. For years he had been preaching that stealing cattle was wrong. He couldn't say now that if it kept children alive, it was justified. For a moment he thought back with bitterness on his instructors at missionary school, who always said that natives couldn't think logically. Knudsen replied unto them: Even if it allows children to live, it is a sin against God. The congregation immediately divided. Almost all of them sided with the false prophet.

Knudsen, a burly man with the chest of a mature elk, lost weight, and lying awake at night this straight-thinking man began to brood. When he spoke to the five remaining members of his congregation he often tangled his words, and then, interrupting his sermon, would stare wordlessly into space, starting in fright when he was spoken to. This Knudsen was reminiscent of the old Knudsen only at a distance, and even then one could see his figure was bowed. The foundation upon which Knudsen himself said he built was one of patience and faith, and that had not been undermined by his disappointment in the congregation who followed the false prophet, but by the nagging feeling that this prophet might after all be right. Knudsen wrote of his doubts and afflictions and asked the Missionary Society for clarification and advice from an academically-trained theologian on how to present his case. Since no answer could be expected for at least six months, he had to live on with his doubt and his home-brewed liquor. In the end he decided to visit his English colleague in Pella, unloading upon him all the doubts that assailed his heart. The Englishman, called Rumbottle, said he was well familiar with this problem, and it was a constantly recurring one: natives, once they could read the holy scriptures, always picked out those passages that were aimed against the rich, the authorities, and in the end against even the missionary church itself. So sects kept arising. The only way to avoid this problem was not to teach the natives to read and write in the first place. And this in fact was Rumbottle's approach.

Unsatisfied, Knudsen returned to Bethany. Before he was in sight of the village, the smell of roasted meat wafted toward him on the evening breeze. The entire tribe was present, only the faithful few from Knudsen's congregation held back hungrily. That evening the missionary received a thorough beating for the first time, when he tried to make his usual visit to one of his young congregation members. And one week later, before the expert opinion of a professor from Tübingen could reach him, he departed for Norway.

Gorth had not only studied how to write such expert opinions in Germany, but had also been prepared for a confrontation with the false prophet by several debates with a professor of theology.

For three days it rained. For three days Gorth, Petrus, and Lukas sat beneath the canvas of the wagon, while the three ox-boys sat under it, their chatter sometimes reaching Gorth in the night. On the fourth day a south wind arose and wiped the heavens clean. When Gorth flung open the canvas he was greeted by an entirely new landscape. The gray-brown, scorched plain had been swallowed by a silvery green. Water gurgled in the sandy riverbeds, and the fragrance of new grass was in the air.

The Garden of Eden, Gorth said, and urged them to depart.

This land is like a stone, and people die here of hunger and thirst.

Therefore be patient, dear brethren, and await the day of the Lord's arrival. Behold, the husbandman awaits the priceless fruit of the earth in patience, until the earth has welcomed both the early and the late rains. Be thou also patient and gird thy heart, for the Lord will soon come.

But why wait for rain when you can make rain, asked Lukas, his dagga pipe in his hand.

When sober, Lukas was a quiet and reasonable man, one of those young Hottentots Gorth could imagine in Germany standing in a lecture hall before a curious audience. But no sooner would he light his dagga pipe than a strange transformation took place, as if a foreign, unknown being had taken possession of his body. Petrus, on the other hand, who drank his own home-brewed rotgut, always remained Petrus, even when, pulled to the ground with full force, he could no longer coax the tiniest click from his powerful tongue and finally snored away with open mouth. If Lukas had smoked his entire pipe, he might begin singing and dancing in a frenzy of enthusiasm, and when Gorth asked what language Lukas was speaking, he replied: That's the language of my hands, here, and my feet, see, the language of my nose, my ears, a head language, listen, a heart language, a gut language, a language the cattle understand, the fat-tailed sheep, the jackal, the antelope, the sand viper, the wait-a-bit thorn bush. Missionary Gorth was not superstitious, after all, he had come to carry the light of the knowledge of the Lord and Savior into the darkness of superstition, but when he heard Lukas talk like that a strange, eerie feeling came over him, mingled with a touch of curiosity.

After six weeks they had reached the Lion River, which in this strong rainy season was so high that Petrus couldn't find the ford. So he suggested they trek to a compound three days eastward and wait there until the river fell. Gorth, however, insisted on heading west, in the direction of Bethany, thinking of the Hottentot woman in Warmbad between whose breasts Petrus had burrowed his head for days on end. But when Petrus said this particular Hottentot compound had never been visited by a missionary, and had probably never even seen a white man, he agreed.

They stayed in the compound for two weeks. The water had long since run off.

He wrote a letter from this compound and gave it to one of the ox-boys who was returning to Warmbad. Nearly two months later it was delivered to Gorth's fiancée, Erdmute, in Cape Town, where she had arrived following a stormy journey by brig. In this letter, Gorth asked his bride to wait in Cape Town until he sent her word from Bethany to continue on. Nevertheless in her concern she decided to set out for Bethany immediately. The letter consisted only of a few words of greeting, the assurance that things were going splendidly for him (he actually used the word, splendidly), and a detailed description, extending over several pages, of daily life and activities in the Hottentot compound. The people here were poor, he wrote, quite poor in fact. After a drought that had lasted for years—not until this year had rain been plentiful and heavy—almost all their cattle had perished. The children lacked milk. When they wanted something sweet, they caught honeybees and pulled off their honey-filled abdomens and sucked them dry. But if a family ever had a lot to eat, an antelope or a hornbill, they shared it generously with others. In spite of their poverty, they were cheerful and friendly, not just toward him, the stranger, but among themselves as well. Women were not subordinate to men. If a man or child wanted something, they asked for it politely and received it. Children got away with almost anything. Even when they occasionally broke a calabash, no one ever thought of striking them. The children helped each other. It was wonderful to watch them dancing, a boundless vivacity, which could of course take on alarming traits of ecstasy at times. At the same time the strictest morality ruled in the pondoks, stricter than he had encountered in the missionary station in Warmbad. On the other hand the Hottentot considered steady work an imposition: He doesn't look toward the future for himself or his family, he eats and drinks in order to live, he lives in order to eat and drink. And he shewed me a pure river of water of life, clear as crystal, John writes. The most amazing thing, however, was the serenity with which these people faced death, which held no terror for them. He himself was busily practicing tongue clicks. It wasn't even necessary to use the lungs, those bellows. When he pressed his tongue against his alveoli and then drew it down sharply, he produced a cloudless blue, just as he used to like to cry "whooo, whooo" and night would arrive.

Whether it these final lines, or the fact that neither the Almighty nor even the Savior had been mentioned throughout the long letter, at any rate Erdmute—who after all had known her Gorth for nine years now—decided to join her fiancé immediately. A resolute young woman, she took the next ox-wagon heading north toward Pella.

When Gorth finally decided to move on, the tribe planned a departure feast. This time it wasn't so much Gorth's resemblance to a sheep that had awakened the admiration of the inhabitants (the tribe raised cattle and goats) as it was his matches. They had observed with astonishment that the stranger carried his fire with him in his pocket and, whenever he wanted, could start a second fire. It had nothing to do with magic, for Gorth had quickly explained the mechanism involved, which even the oldest woman in the tribe had finally understood. They also admired the iron pots and pans he carried with him, in which one could quickly and easily cook and fry things, and of course most of all his shotgun. It's true the tribe possessed two ancient, rusty flintlocks, which were held in highest respect and scarcely ever fired (powder and bullets could rarely be traded for with other tribes), but what were these thunder guns, which had to be lugged within ten meters of an antelope to have any hope of hitting one, compared with Gorth's shotgun with its rifled double barrels, from one of which a shell could be fired. With the help of this gun Gorth filled the pots of the entire tribe for two weeks. Was it any surprise that not only children and old folk, but also mature and experienced men from the council begged Gorth to stay on? And Gorth indeed stayed on day after day, until the bullet in Petrus's arm said that there would be rain before long. Before that happened, Gorth meant to have at least crossed the river.

On the eve of his departure, two goats were slaughtered. The sow grunted and the piglets squeaked for mercy, but Gorth hardened his heart and let them slit the throats of three piglets. On that warm December night, even Gorth danced, although he had never had a lesson. He smoked a small pipe of dagga that the tribal chief passed to him and which, he said, it would have been impolite to reject. Afterwards he witnessed tonal fireworks: the dentalis hissed across the ground like a snake of fire, the cerebralis exploded into rays of blue and gold, the lateralis sprang rattling across trees and shrubs. Gorth's legs sprang as if freed from chains. He danced with Lukas. Only once, briefly, did he think of his bride: she stood at the railing of a sailing ship, heading into a southwester, she cried out against the squalls, calling orders up to the masts, where sailors sat straddling the yardarms.

Strangely enough, this was all Gorth could recall the next morning, with the sun already standing fairly high in the sky. His head sat mutely on his shoulders, wooden and splintered.

The only remedy is a pipe, said Lukas.

The tribal council assembled and petitioned Gorth, who stood ready before his team of oxen, to at least send them a missionary of their own if he couldn't stay. Then Petrus clicked his tongue and the train set out, accompanied by everyone who could walk, even if they had to limp. Petrus drove the wagon carefully down the shrub-covered bank of the river (where the inhabitants of the compound stopped and stood clapping rhythmically), crossed the sandy riverbed with its scattered puddles of water, and spurred on by the clicks of Petrus's tongue, the oxen, panting laboriously, slowly drew the heavy wagon up the far riverbank. So on they drove into the stony, hilly landscape, the blue-green silhouette of the Karas Mountains behind them, before them a sky in which clouds drifted like sailing ships. Gorth preceded the ox-team as usual, but today he was elated, in his right hand his corncob pipe, in his left his walking stick, not using it with each step like a bishop's staff, but flinging it upward from time to time like a tambourine major and twirling it over his head. Behind him panted the oxen, while Lukas skipped along beside him. Petrus was sleeping off his euphoria on the coach-box. The lead oxen chose their own path.

Gorth was overjoyed that the tribe was asking to hear God's word. Thus would they find the true path and eternal life, said Gorth.

It's your pocket fire they want, panted the left lead ox, whose name was Big-Red, and your tin pans. Who wants to lay snares and struggle to catch the hornbill when you can shoot once into the air and twenty fall from the sky. You're worse than Hurt-Knee. Long, long ago, panted Big-Red, the broad plains belonged to the cattle, they went where they wished, from spring to spring, from river to river, wherever the rain fell and the grass grew tall. Whoever wanted their flesh merely followed them, and since they had plenty, they gave plentifully as well. Hurt-Knee followed them too, the ancestor of all Hottentots, struggling along, limping because his knee hurt. And because he was often unable to follow when they changed pastures, he thought up a trick. He crept up to a cow that was groaning with pain because she had a thorn in her hoof. Then he pulled the thorn from the hoof and asked her to give him milk for it. The cow, called Dotsy, from whom all of us now in the yoke have descended, said to herself: It's good to have someone who can pull a thorn from my hoof, and so she agreed. And so she let Hurt-Knee milk her and wipe the dust from her coat with tufts of grass. But the calf soon found there was no more milk in her udder and had to eat grass. One day the herd gathered in a tall meadow. The bulls discovered the bright white cow with her brown spots and followed her. The herd followed the bulls, the bulls followed the cow, and the white cow followed the limping Hurt-Knee from spring to spring, from river to river, wherever Hurt-Knee chose to go. One day Hurt-Knee caught a young bull, that had once been the cow's calf, and bit off its balls. He tied him to a tree, struck him with a whip and called out, Ox, until he responded to that name and stood quietly while Hurt-Knee sat on his back. Then Hurt-Knee rode off on the ox, while Dotsy followed the ox, the bulls followed Dotsy, and the herd followed the bulls. Before long they couldn't find the springs any longer without Hurt-Knee, they forgot their directions and how to smell the rain. Cattle who had lost their way stood on the plains and lowed in fear. Thus we came under the yoke, Big-Red panted, and nineteen other draft oxen panted with him.

What surprised Gorth most was that it hadn't shocked him to hear an ox speak. He slowed down a little, finally drawing up alongside the panting Big-Red so he wouldn't have to speak so loudly. When Big-Red finished his story, Gorth tried to console him by quoting from the book of Luke: Are not five sparrows sold for two farthings, and not one of them is forgotten before God? Big-Red, leaning heavily into the harness again, answered with a deep groan: For months we pulled a missionary who quoted the lines right after those to the Hottentots: But even the very hairs of your head are all numbered. Fear not therefore: ye are of more value than many sparrows. Animals have no place in your heaven. Big-Red then fell silent, but at the same time all twenty oxen had to pull harder, since they were ascending a steep rocky slope furrowed with eroded channels. Petrus awoke and began snapping his tongue like a hippo-hide whip.

Long after Gorth was dead, letters that had been underway for months reached his fiancée, often with strange contents, and in one of the last he claimed he'd finally learned the language of the oxen.

There were those in the Missionary Society who later maintained that Gorth's confused state of mind was due to his stubborn insistence on running around without a hat in the scorching heat of the burning sun. Others said, in strictest confidence of course, that Gorth smoked dagga toward the end. The dangerous effect of the drug was well known. Many natives had lost their reason after overindulging in the hemp-induced euphoria, indeed it was even known to have had fatal results on occasion. The cultivation and use of dagga had to be strongly resisted by the missionaries. Of course they had to be of strong enough character not to fall pray to the addiction themselves.

On a hot, dusty Tuesday Gorth's fiancée arrived in Pella. It was there that his last letter reached her. A letter she immediately burned after reading. Nothing is known of its contents. She insisted on traveling on the following day, however. Since there were no wagon trains leaving for Warmbad anytime in the next three weeks, she had to mount an ox herself, and at dawn the next morning, accompanied by a Hottentot guide, she set out. A woman like a man, the English missionary is said to have remarked to his German colleague as Gorth's fiancée took her leave and rode forth from the missionary station, her dress draped over the neck and back of the ox like a saddle-blanket. Beneath her dress she wore high-heeled, buttoned, patent-leather boots. On her head a dark-blue velvet hat stitched with two cloth daisies. Since a strong southwester was blowing long plumes of sand before her, she had fastened the hat to her piled dark-blond hair with a hat-pin.

Near Raman's Drift the Hottentot was about to take her across the Orange River when the trader Morris met them and said he had heard in Warmbad that Gorth was dead.

At that they turned around and rode back toward Pella. The missionaries sent a trustworthy courier to Warmbad to learn the precise details. The courier met the wagon master Petrus, who told him that Gorth had died in the field of a mysterious fever, a regional fever, as the missionaries later wrote. The missionary never saw Bethany, although he, Petrus, and a member of the Bethany community by the name of Lukas, had sewn the dead missionary up in an ox skin and taken him to Bethany, where he now lay buried.

Gorth's fiancée decided to return to Cape Town as soon as possible, and take the first available ship back to Germany. Nor did she allow herself to be detained by the English missionary, who asked her to stay in Pella, and after a suitable period of mourning, to become his wife.

During the return journey on the four-master *Erna*, she met a laboratory technician named Schröder who had worked four years in Cape Town for the English governor. The two were married a year later in Coburg, Schröder's hometown, where he had started a business and was mounting trophies for the Duke of Coburg. His wife never talked about Africa, even when her children and later her grandchildren pressed her to, saying only that there wasn't much to tell, it was a barren, empty place.

The second day after leaving the settlement Gorth had the strange feeling that his skull had become too small for this land. This painful expanse no longer seemed to fit inside it. For the first time since his departure he felt listless and at times even dizzy. He blamed that on the heat and the relentless sun, which caused the very cliffs to groan. Since Gorth didn't carry a hat in his luggage, he knotted a small hood for himself from a large white handkerchief. So, after Lukas had gathered up courage to ask if he could ride on the wagon, Gorth plodded on alone, in front of the team, the white hanky like a bandage about his head.

That evening they reached a water-hole. The oxen, who had gone without water for two days, strained forward toward the warm puddle. After they had drunk their fill and their bellies were like barrels, they grazed beside the fire Petrus had started. The three men sat about it in silence, smoking and drinking. Later Gorth went over to Big-Red, who was lying off to the side in the grass chewing his cud with his legs crooked under. Gorth lay down beside him.

Long, long ago, Big-Red began, grinding his teeth in a circular motion, white men came from Holland to Africa, down south where the land comes to an end, and they used great firesticks to kill and drive off the Nama who lived there, for they had only iron assegais. So the Namas moved north across the deeply-flowing Orange, and used their iron assegais to kill and drive off the local Bushmen, who had only stone knives. But since the land conquered by the Namas had little rain and few springs, they couldn't keep large herds. So they moved farther north, where the friends of cattle, the Herero, lived with their great herds, in thick meadows flowing with water. They are the

friends of cattle, they honor us and take of our flesh only what
they need. There cattle die peacefully of old age. But there are
some that none dare touch, they are the holy cattle that stand
beside the ancestral fire. White-Mouth, my own ancestress,
stood beside that fire too, and this is how it came about: One
day the young chief Zeraua decided it was important for his
tribe to have a gun. So he set off to see an English trader named
Lewis and traded eighteen oxen for a gun, including bullets and
powder. The trader explained how a gun is fired. On the way
back to his kraal he spotted a large vulture sitting on a dead cow.
So he loaded his gun, fired at the bird, and hit him with the first
shot. In his joy, he cut off one of the dead bird's claws, tied it to a
calabash in his hut, and declared that only he and his friends
could drink milk from this calabash. He then selected a cow
from his herd whose milk would be destined for this calabash.
He named this cow White-Mouth. So White-Mouth joined the
untouchable herd beside the sacred ancestral fire. There she remained and was milked until the Year of the Wounded Arm.
Jonker Afrikaner injured his arm on a lion hunt and could no
longer use it properly. That year Jonker Afrikaner stole the
Herero herd because he had to pay off a debt to an English trader
by the name of Morris. So the sacred herd came into the hands
of the trader, and with it the daughter of White-Mouth, called
Long-Tuft. Morris drove the herd to the slaughterhouse in Cape
Town. On the way, however, he gave Long-Tuft to the chief of
Rehoboth, so that the herd could graze its fill in the tribal meadows for the long journey. Then the chief of Rehoboth traded
Long-Tuft to old Saans, who sits in the Bondelswarts council, for
a handful of gunpowder, and old Saans traded the son of Long-
Tuft to the wagon master Petrus for a bottle of honey beer. And
that's how I wound up in the yoke.

That night Gorth dreamed he was riding a cow across a treeless plain, swaying pleasantly above a landscape ribbed like a
riverbed. Then he entered a ravine. The cliffs towered on both
sides toward the sky, the sun a black disk above him. Suddenly
he saw a figure approaching through the deep pass. The path was

now so narrow that his legs brushed the rocks. The figure was dressed in a black mantle and wore a black hat. Gorth didn't know how he would get around the figure. As the figure stood before him, he leaned from the cow to peer under the hat brim, then recoiled in shock: he was looking into his own face.

The next morning Petrus asked if they could make a small detour to a nearby village, where his brother's sister lived. Gorth agreed at once, without asking how far it was. He was even more willing when Lukas reported that a missionary had stayed in the village before and that it was visited regularly by white traders.

When the ox-wagon reached the village three days later, the inhabitants were already waiting by the wayside. But how the disappointment spread when the stranger approached at last and they could see his face. The rumors had been shameless exaggerations. Only with the best of wills could the face beneath this strange four-cornered white bandage be said to even distantly resemble a sheep. Nevertheless they were warmly welcomed. Of course it didn't escape Gorth's notice that he was not met with the same effusive, indeed fervent enthusiasm he had encountered on previous occasions. They had scarcely reached the first pondok when Gorth was surrounded by begging children: Licorice, please, God bless you. They repeated this one sentence in a flat monotone German unrelated to the sense of the words.

The missionary who had spent two months in this compound a year ago had been nicknamed the Likrish Apostle. He had brought a case containing licorice with him from Germany after reading that Hottentot children loved it. By high noon the case held a black, viscous porridge; the next morning, after a cold night, it was transformed into a small, hard block of tar. Each morning the Likrish Apostle would chip small pieces from the licorice block with a knife and distribute them among the children.

The men of the tribal council asked Gorth, who sat apathetically in the wagon's shade, to send a missionary or at least a teacher to their compound, so that they could read the IOU's the traders made them sign.

There was a steady drone in Gorth's head. The drone persisted even when he tried to immerse himself in prayer.

After two days, urged on by Lukas, they started on their way again. The members of the compound bid them a fond farewell. At the midday rest stop Gorth discovered that they had stolen his hunting rifle. Two pots were also missing, and a small sack of bean seeds.

Petrus wanted to go back and demand that the tribe return the stolen items. But Gorth just lifted his hand and let it fall.

On 22 December a bank of black clouds rolled heavily across the plains. Around noon a curtain of water cascaded from the heavens.

They set up camp on a gently sloping hill. On a bare hill opposite them stood a single tree. A thick smooth trunk and two correspondingly thick, leafless branches. At the tips stood lonely clumps of blossoms. A Half-Man, Lukas said.

Gorth sweated and froze at the same time. He felt suffocated beneath the mass of water, although he lay protected from the rain in his tent.

Rain fell for three days.

On Christmas Eve the droning in Gorth's head diminished to a hum. He asked Petrus and Lukas to hoist the piano from the wagon for a carol service. The two of them managed to lift the heavy case, but couldn't get it down without dropping it. So Gorth preached from the wagon: And this shall be a sign unto you; ye shall find the babe wrapped in swaddling clothes, lying in a manger. And suddenly there was with the angel a multitude of the heavenly host praising God, and saying, Glory to God in the highest, and on earth peace, good will toward men!

Petrus and Lukas knelt in the rain beside the wagon.

Gorth sat down at the piano. He sang: Lo, how a rose ere blooming. He made mistakes, and couldn't carry a tune. Petrus belched.

That night they sat outside the tent. A southwest wind had swept the clouds away. The moon looked like a Harzorroler type of cheese roll Gorth loved as a child. He smoked his pipe and practiced his tongue clicks. His forehead glowed. He would have liked to place apples on it. It's not really Christmas Eve without baked apples. The Half-Man stood blackly in the moonlight, like the crucified Christ.

On Christmas Day they set out again, Gorth in the lead as always. The stones groaned in the sun. By the time Petrus halted the oxen for the midday break, Gorth had fallen far behind. The next day he sat on the coach-box beside Petrus. Lukas offered to brew herbal tea for Gorth, to combat the fever. But Gorth declined.

By New Year's Day he could no longer sit upright. Petrus made up a bed of blankets on boxes in the wagon, beside the piano and the pigs.

On the third of January, Gorth began to hallucinate. He spoke loudly and clearly: Why is there no place for oxen in heaven? Did not the ox and the donkey stand beside the Christ child in the manger? Who deceived them? So far I've only thought of oxen as food. All this eating and being eaten, tell me Lord, is it necessary? For good can come from evil. Isn't there a tiny spark of God in evil too? Even cattle theft is good, if the cattle are willing to be eaten. Is God's breath in every word we say, but not in the click of tongues? Those clicks are made by men. And we must preach God's word to the Half-Men who stand night and day on the hill, not turn them into something less than human. I want to learn the language of the Half-Men, but I have no wish to teach them how to write just so they can sign their IOU's. I was deaf as a stone that one strikes with a stick. For that which befalleth the sons of men befalleth beasts; even one thing befalleth them: as the one dieth, so dieth the other; yea, they have all one breath; so that a man hath no preeminence above a beast: for all is vanity. The clouds bore only rain, now I see that they are cushions upon which the wind rests.

In the night of 4 January a brief, intense thunderstorm crossed the plain. Gorth recovered his senses. He lay beside the grunting sow. The smell sickened him. For the first time he realized that the piglets had grown into small pigs in the course of the journey. But they still pressed eagerly against the teats of the sow. Before Gorth sat the piano, dragged thousands of kilometers into this barren landscape. He asked how far it was to Bethany. Petrus estimated six days, Lukas five. It was the first time in weeks that Gorth had mentioned Bethany. He asked Lukas to bring him paper, pen, and an inkwell. Leaning against a crate, he wrote a letter to his fiancée and gave it to one of the two remaining ox-boys to take to Warmbad in exchange for a good sum of pocket money.

Gorth drank a mug of tea and slept soundly that night. He had only a slight fever.

On the morning of 5 January he tried to rise, but couldn't stand. So he sat on the back apron of the wagon, leaning back against the piano, and saw, jostled back and forth by the rocking and bumping of the wagon, a valley bare of all trees and bushes, like an immense dry riverbed, bordered on both sides by steep banks of mountains. Between them, silvery-green, the blooming grass, set in waves like a river by the wind.

They had been underway for almost three hours when Petrus and Lukas heard a tortured, choking groan, like nothing they had ever heard. They thought it might be coming from the sow, possibly crushed beneath the heavy black case of the piano. They crawled into the wagon and saw that the groans were coming from Gorth. And with each groan he choked up a blackish-green fluid.

Something swelled within Gorth's skull, growing and growing, stretching it taut, as if air were being forced in with bellows. He concentrated all his strength on keeping his head from bursting. Then he lost consciousness.

It was hotter that afternoon than Lukas could ever remember. The oxen bellowed with thirst. Petrus was going to unharness them and let them rest, but Lukas asked him to press on. Perhaps the missionary would recover in Bethany.

Later that afternoon thunderclouds appeared. The rain drew a thick gray curtain across the valley, and behind it the dark blue evening sky glowed once more.

Around seven that evening Gorth regained his senses. His head felt on fire. He asked them to lay him in the grass, he couldn't stand that stupid black piano any longer.

They started to spread blankets on the damp earth, but Gorth wouldn't have it. So they laid him directly on the ground.

The fire in his head went out. A pleasant shiver ran through his limbs. He was only bothered at times by how loudly his teeth chattered.

He saw the darkness creep forth gradually from the valley, and heard the oxen pulling at the grass. Lukas was leaning back against a wagon wheel. Petrus was already asleep.

Gorth lay stretched out in the fragrant grass. Above him the stars, the eyes of the night.

CONCERNING THE MILDER, MORE
HUMANE, YET MORE LASTING
PEDAGOGICAL EFFECT
OF THE ROPE

From the Archives of the Government of German South West Africa, p. 694

The Imperial District Officer
Windhoek, 16 January 1908

Re: Flogging.

I beg to report to the Imperial Government that since the first of October of the past year no penalty by flogging in excess of ten strokes has been imposed. I regard any further restrictions on flogging as unfeasible under the present circumstances.

Flogging is the only punishment that the native experiences as such. It accords with his intuitive and rational faculties and his customs. It is the sole deterrent he recognizes. Imprisonment—even in chains—is scarcely punishment for the native; on the contrary, as we unfortunately see all too often, those sentenced to prison are pleased.

Fines are equally ineffective. The native does not yet realize and appreciate the value of money. As hard as it is often is for him to earn it, he squanders it with equal abandon.

In light of our experience, we respectfully recommend that for the present the imposition of further restrictions on flogging, as advocated by the Secretary of State in his decree of 12 July 1907, be withdrawn from consideration.

(signed)

Foreign Office. Colonial Division.
Berlin, 26 February 1907

In compliance with the order of 31 October 1905 C.D. 10 497 conveyed in the order above, my predecessor in this office issued instructions that the sjambok, or kibo, be henceforth employed in the flogging of natives in all African protectorates. These instructions met with resistance from the governments of Cameroon and Togo, who, based on alleged incidents of serious injury inflicted by its use, recommended the retention or reinstatement of the rope. Some of our own advisors concurred in this opinion. I enclose copies of the reports of the aforementioned governments, as well as the relevant exchange of memos, for your private perusal and kind consideration.

Since the sjambok (kibo) has been in use in those protectorates for many years, I would like to request that the Imperial Government provide me with the favor of a reply as to whether on the basis of this experience the concerns raised by opponents of the sjambok seem justified, and in particular whether injuries of the sort described by the Station Commander in Atakpame have been commonly observed. At the same time, I would like to request a report on the nature and manufacture of the sjambok, as well as the method of its employment in punishment.

Dernburg

To the Imperial Government in Windhoek

Atakpame Station
Atakpame, 9 August 1906

I wish, in confidence, to suggest considering whether it might not be deemed appropriate to approach the Colonial Division of the Foreign Office with a suggestion to the effect that the hippo-hide whip be replaced as a means of punishment by a return to our traditional rope.

Although I know well, as an advocate of flogging, that severe corporal punishment is deemed desirable as a deterrent, I have nevertheless become convinced over the past four months in which the hippo-hide whip has been in use, that this form of flogging represents a level of cruelty beyond our intention. The blows of a hippo-hide whip almost inevitably tear gashes in the skin, and precisely in an area which is hardest for others to see, and particularly difficult to see for the injured man. It is therefore extremely difficult for the man who has been flogged to care for himself, it is difficult to keep the wounds clean, the injured man requires his posterior for sitting, the wounds get dirty, fester, and the man can't work for weeks.

I do not believe that this was the Colonial Division's intention when they introduced the hippo-hide whip.

Flogging with a rope is a far different matter. The culprit fears it just as much as a flogging with the kiboko. But the consequences aren't nearly so severe, they are milder, more humane and yet of more lasting pedagogical effect. The pain is intense, it burns and smarts, but the skin is seldom damaged, and the "epidermal loss" which was once the departure point of all sorts of protests almost never occurs. The rope seems to me the ideal tool for flogging in disciplinary cases, for runaways, shirkers, refusal to obey orders, gross dereliction of duty and the like. Flogging with the thicker hide whip seems to me too severe for such cases, one uses it gladly only for serious crimes, and so the value of flogging is reduced: it loses its character as a disciplinary method.

(signed) von Doering

I am convinced that the rope previously employed in Togo is a more humane instrument of punishment than the sjambok or kiboko. I believe it may be gathered from my report of 18.4.05 that a change in the instrument of punishment then in use was not desired. The sjambok was introduced (cf. the training manual of 10.1.1906, submitted with our report of 21.1.06), because we were specifically instructed to do so in the order of 31.10.05.

(signed) Count Zech, 21.6.

• • •

I too consider the rope, the maximum length and thickness of which must be set, a more humane method of flogging than the hippo or elephant whip. A further argument for the former is that it can be delivered in a uniform size throughout the entire protectorate, while no two hippo whips, which are made without exception abroad, ever seem to be alike. The whip is cut from skin that is several centimeters thick and gradually shrinks to a fraction of its original size. It is dried by the fire or in the sun. Variations in thickness and sharp edges, which only wear off after use, are unavoidable. A new hippo-hide whip that has not yet lost its sharp edges and stiffness must generally be considered a dangerous tool.

The intention of the order of 31 October of the past year was to effect a moderation in the administration of floggings. Since, according to the government report, the order has had the opposite effect, we should, in my opinion, no longer insist upon its implementation.

Perhaps it would even be advisable to cancel the order for Togo.

Inc: additional ref.

Berlin, 21.6.

Ref. 12.

J.V. (signed) Meyer

Admittedly, the rope spares the skin and leaves fewer slightly bloody welts and direct lacerations than a kiboko, and in this sense one can regard the rope as a more humane instrument. But the rope results more easily in deeper injuries—and the thicker the rope the greater the effect—and it is highly likely that the cases of sudden death that have followed corporal punishment are the result of injuries to internal organs, and particularly to the liver. Cases of sudden death could also be avoided using the rope if the blows could be confined with certainty to the posterior and upper thighs. In spite of all regulations to this effect, however, the extraordinary flexibility of the rope and the difficulty in controlling it make it impossible to avoid blows that wrap around the body. If, therefore, one wishes to avoid cases of sudden death following corporal punishment, or at least avoid as many as possible—and in my opinion that is the issue—no other course remains but to replace the rope with an instrument like the kiboko, which due to its lighter weight does not lead to deep injuries as does the rope, even if, with regard to its effect on the skin, it is less "humane."

(signed) Dr. Steudel, 23.6

GETTING ONE'S HANDS DIRTY

What drives someone to climb the Chimborazo? To fly over the North Pole in a hot-air balloon? To cross the Gobi Desert?

Gottschalk rode through a landscape without trees or shrubs, bare as a vast quarry. Rocky hills shattered in the frosty night after a day of roaring heat, as if struck by cannon fire. Air that slowly melted by noon, the distant mountain chain a blur. Yet air so dry that fingernails broke and lips split.

What had he lost in this stony desert?

He had volunteered for this patrol, which was supposed to secure the road to the Orange, the only river in the southern part of the protectorate that flowed all year. Down here, near Raman's Drift, Sheep-Face had arrived sixty years earlier, bare-headed, wearing his Jesus sandals, enthusiastically welcomed by the Hottentots because he resembled a Merino sheep.

Now they rode with their hands on their carbines, and stared with squinting eyes at every boulder along the road, at every hill behind which the Morris brothers might be lying in wait with their gang.

So why had Gottschalk come along? He wanted to see the Orange. He wanted to finally see a river. It seemed that simple to him, and yet it was something more, a longing for something new which seemed to rise from his childhood, for something far away; a curiosity that burst through everyday habits, through the numbness, a curiosity in which one found oneself, suddenly and surprisingly, another person, in which the boldest daydreams took on terrifying life, ordinary things suddenly shed their skin, turning strange and mysterious. The fragrance of cinnamon from his father's shop. At times Gottschalk could not understand how he had put up with the oppressive narrowness of the barracks for the past year, that dirty-red brick building that resembled a city prison. Here, on the other hand, he had space and not just elbow room. He now understood Count Kageneck, who had broken off his last home leave and returned to Warmbad, that miserable dump, to the battery of schnapps in his darkened office, his kingdom. (The count was later transferred to Windhoek at the instigation of his family, who wanted to gradually re-accustom him to European ways before bringing him back to the Reich.) Of course it was true that Gottschalk had pictured a neat and trim future with red and white checkered curtains at the windows of his farmhouse, with less alcohol, and above all with musical evenings at home, which he saw from the outside, the illuminated windows and in the stillness of the night (even the cicadas had fallen silent) the *La Buscha* sonata. Independent and free, a calm, comfortable life, thoroughly industrious. As one can see from the sketches in his diary, the huts of his native workers had moved right up beside his farmhouse. There was even a small school in which his own children received instruction along with the native children. The garden would be planted with various deciduous trees, whose seeds Gottschalk would import from Europe, but also with a few palm trees. With the help of water pumps driven by a windmill, he would create a leafy green island in the middle of the sun-baked, stone-gray landscape. Here, near constantly splashing water, among the shady branches, song birds would also nest. It was Gottschalk's dream to introduce the nightingale to this songless land. Once he had found the right place, and saved enough money, he would have two or three pairs of nightingales sent to him in a large cage.

What disturbed Gottschalk's daydreams were silly sentences like: Property is theft, or: War on palaces, peace to the cottages.

Wenstrup had left him these and other such phrases as glosses and marginal notes in Kropotkin's *Mutual Aid: A Factor of Evolution.*

Gottschalk always carried this book with him, wrapped in a page of the *Vossische News,* a somber memory of Wenstrup. Whenever he left his room in Warmbad, he stuck the book in the pocket of his uniform. Lieutenant Haring, his roommate, once said: I didn't know you were so religious. He thought the book was a Bible. Gottschalk didn't correct him. He merely leafed through the book, so that he could put it away calmly. Gottschalk thought that only if someone were concentrating hard and seemed caught up in his reading would anyone ask what it was. So Gottschalk read only Wenstrup's notes and a few passages he had underlined in varying colors: red, blue, and green. Each color apparently had a special meaning, but since Gottschalk hadn't read the book, he had no idea what that meaning was. The marginal notes were written by Wenstrup in a small but clearly legible hand in block letters, with a sharp pencil. During the long journey Gottschalk had often seen Wenstrup reading, and as he now believed, reading this very book, but he had never seen Wenstrup sharpening a pencil.

Marginalia from Wenstrup in *Mutual Aid: A Factor of Evolution,* by Kropotkin.

The only good Herero is not a dead Herero (the butcher Trotha is mistaken there), but one who works for free.

The goal of native policy is a well-nourished slave. First iron around the neck, then—a most elegant solution—through the head. The final goal: a slave who affirms his slavery.

Experience teaches us, says the famous Belgian statistician Quetelet, that society is constantly preparing for crime and that criminals are the necessary tools with which society carries out that crime!

The Prussian code of honor: one cannot shoot women and children. Therefore they are driven into the desert to die of thirst.

The German colonial claim: a place in the sun will warm up the German worker too.

The Social Democrat gentlemen in the Reichstag: cosmetics on a stinking corpse. (A sentence Gottschalk could never decipher, in spite of worrying over it a long time. What corpse was he talking about, the rebel Hereros and Hottentots? Or was the sentence meant more symbolically? Did it refer to the state and middle-class society?)

Man is truly free only among free men, and since he is only characteristically human when he is free, the subjugation of a single human being on earth is an injury to the principle of humanity itself, and a negation of the freedom of all men. Bakunin.

An attempt at social pacification (if I were Krupp):

a) Sufficient bread and butter, as well as smoked sausage and cheese rolls. Good food and a roof over one's head satisfies a man. No shortage of tobacco, schnapps and beer!

b) The cost of the above can be easily compensated for by a higher rate of productivity. (One can also make money on tobacco and schnapps.) A man who comes home after a twelve-hour workday asks himself who profits from his labor, and tends toward rebellion. But a man who does the same or more work in eight hours will think it's his weak stomach that's causing the pain in his belly, and his own delicate system seems responsible for his nervous condition.

c) Involve paid functionaries in governmental decisions, especially unpopular ones. Ideally be a union functionary as Minister for Social Issues.

d) Transfer the brutal, unaesthetic type of exploitation to the "savages" in the south. Import cheap raw materials. Export finished products at a high profit. The German worker will be doing fine compared with his black, brown, and yellow colleagues. He will be joining in the meal, even if he is only sitting at the kids' table, his feet in slippers, shuddering as he reads about the rebellions in Africa, Asia, and Latin America in the *Daily Progressive*.

The Wahehe Rebellion, the Boxer Rebellion, the Herero and Hottentot Rebellion. Anyone still sleeping has to be shaken awake—with a bang if necessary.

There is only one fast-acting cure for paralysis: dynamite!

(Are these quotations or Wenstrup's own formulation?)

On 21 February the patrol reached the Orange River near Raman's Drift. Gottschalk was disappointed. A dirty brown slush flowed slowly by, divided by a few islands of gravel. Rocky bare cliffs rose along the banks. In the river bed were round, white rocks, like mighty primeval eggs. On the English side a small stone house could be made out with a Union Jack waving above it: the English border police station. The supplies for the southern division came across at this ford, but so did weapons and ammunition for the rebels. The arms trade flourished.

The patrol rode upstream. Late that afternoon the lead rider spotted a crouched figure running away through the thorn bushes, apparently trying to reach the river. Lieutenant Wolf sent two troopers after him, who soon returned with a Hottentot bleeding from the head. Since the man either couldn't or wouldn't give them any information about Morris and his men, Wolf had him shot. Then the patrol turned away from the river and headed back toward Warmbad.

Gottschalk's diary,
21 February 1905

Around midnight we reach the ruins of the Hartmann farm near Skunberg's Spring. Here the path descends into a riverbed. An icy breeze receives us. At least it feels icy after the furnace of the day and the hot air of the high plains. We dismount, I reach for my rifle, and the Pelham bit slips from the horse's mouth. A trooper descends into the two-meter-deep chalk hole and passes up buckets of water. I and three other troopers hold back the horses, who press forward thirstily.

At last the horses are watered. After a good hour we remount and follow the path, which soon takes us back to the high west bank. One can see for miles in all directions. Silence surrounds us. If it weren't for the occasional cry of a hen we've started, or the howl of some wild beast echoing through the stillness, one would think we were riding through a world that had died long ago.

It wasn't until the following day that Gottschalk experienced shock: shock at himself. He sat on a crate at a table on which a splinter of broken mirror leaned against an empty wine bottle. Gottschalk had shaved. He gazed at his smooth cheeks, the skin still reddened by the razor. A stranger stared at him from the splinter of mirror. The patrol had returned to Warmbad without incident. He threw himself on the cot and slept soundly well into the next afternoon. Then he had a drink of water, ate something, and shaved.

He recalled the crouching man, the one he'd thought no more about since they'd chased him through the thorn bushes, knocked him down, questioned him, and finally shot him. Gottschalk recalled staring intently at the surrounding hills as it happened, afraid that gunfire would break out any moment from the rocks and bushes.

He saw his horse crumple to the ground, shot, saw himself leaping just in time from the saddle, yanking his rifle from its holster and scrambling for cover behind a rock as dark shapes flitted toward him from every side.

But there had been no ambush.

They shot a man, and all I thought was, I hope no one hears it.

What's happened to you, thought Gottschalk, still staring into the mirror shard. Dried lather clung to his upper lip. Perhaps it was the strange faces he made as he shaved the stubble from his upper lip, chin, and neck that made him suddenly seem so alien to himself, although he made those faces daily. A cold feeling of alienation submerged everything in a clear, bright light: his shock of feeling nothing when he thought about the incident. Shock at his own failure to be shocked, at an indifference that should not be indifferent. As he walked over to the kraal, he kept thinking, one must do something. He noticed he kept thinking of himself as another person, referring to himself as "one" and "he." He inspected the mouths of the horses seized from the Hottentots. Not old nags, but good young horseflesh, some having already changed masters twice and answering to Hans or Lotte. The thought that Morenga might have been sitting on an East Prussian horse made him laugh.

There is a hell for animals, created and maintained by human society and institutions. Horses were trained to suppress their natural response to gunfire so they could serve as cannon fodder. A Hottentot rebel's horse has nothing in common with a policeman's nag in Berlin, but neither can chose sides freely. Wenstrup had written these lines in the upper margin of a page in the Kropotkin book, and beneath it an even stranger sentence: Freedom of choice and freedom of opportunity for animals too!

That afternoon Dr. Haring, coming from the typhoid quarantine tent, noticed Gottschalk fumbling at the birth canal of one of the four cows that had been given to the natives for their own use. Gottschalk was maneuvering with his arm in the uterus of the groaning cow, trying to turn a calf that was lying crosswise. Unable to do so, he decided to saw the calf apart in the mother's womb, a bold procedure developed shortly before he left Germany, carried out with a curved saw blade. Gottschalk thrust his arm back through the cow's slit into the womb, felt about, placed the blade on the calf's body and began to saw, while a steadily growing number of curious soldiers, civilians, and Hottentots gathered about to watch the operation. The saw blade slipped several times. Finally, Gottschalk drew a bloody piece of flesh from the cow that proved upon closer inspection to be a shoulder, then a front leg, sections of the ribs, a regular farm yard picnic someone remarked, then the other front leg appeared, part of the ribs with a hind leg, finally a head with glassy eyes covered in film. Everyone stood watching the sweating Gottschalk. A medic gathered up the parts of the calf, saying they should certainly be tender, and carried them aside to be roasted.

What's the point of all this bloody mess, Lieutenant Haring asked as Gottschalk withdrew the saw from the cow's womb. Why not just let the cow die?

Gottschalk made his way through the circle of curious onlookers over to a water barrel, where he washed his arms, face, and upper body. Dr. Haring stood alongside and remarked that as a medical experiment the procedure was quite interesting. It wasn't an experiment, Gottschalk said, he'd just done it. A Hottentot boy had come for help, that was all, the cow couldn't have its calf, it was going to die, and everyone would lose the milk. Gottschalk asked him to repeat the cow's name, a melodic name with several clicks, which meant Soft-Mouth in German. A cow with strikingly long, shadowy lashes, light brown coat, and high withers. Soft-Mouth was a descendant of White-Mouth, who had once stood among the sacred herd beside the ancestral fire of the Herero chief Zeraas, and whose daughter Long-Tuft had been stolen by Jonker Afrikaners' people and thus passed into the hands of the Hottentots in Warmbad. But Gottschalk heard only a mooing cow. He understood nothing. Otherwise he could have heard all about Big-Red, who pulled Missionary Gorth's wagon into this land, or of Christopherus, who had brought Klügge's mighty brandy barrel to thirsty Bethany, or of the most famous pathfinder of all draft oxen, Fork-Horn, who pulled the surveyor Treptow safely and surely through the plains and deserts. Of these prodigious feats Gottschalk knew nothing.

The cow would have died, was all Gottschalk would say as he lay on his cot afterward in his room, leafing through Kropotkin, when Lieutenant Haring asked again why one would want to dirty his hands with a cow in this country.

That same evening one of the bambuses who worked in the field kitchen, a Hottentot by the name of Rolf, came and asked him to explain the procedure with the cow.

Laziness and curiosity are reciprocally related in these people, said Haring as he pulled on his gym shirt, which hung loosely about him, his body having lost its fleshy fullness over the past four months of enforced diet, as he called the insufficient rations offered to the troops. Now tanned and sinewy, he seemed ten years younger and had already sent a good dozen postcard-sized photographs to his wife and friends back home. As a student in Heidelberg, Dr. Haring had belonged to a university gymnastics club and on Sundays he wore his colored sash over his uniform. Soon after arriving in Warmbad, he started a gymnastics team. Based on his sketches a tar barrel was transformed into a pommel horse and parallel bars were fashioned from what were once two wagon axles.

The tar barrel was upholstered with sackcloth, enclosed in leather, and sewn tight. The parallel bars were carved to the right size over several days by a trooper who had studied carpentry. Haring insisted that the fine finishing, as he called it, be carried out with a shard of bottle glass. One false slip with a knife and the bar would be ruined and cause blisters. At first Haring had managed to talk Gottschalk into joining the gymnastic exercises (mens sana in corpore sano). But Gottschalk, who had led gymnastics in school, felt like he was in a traveling circus, since every leap over the pommel horse and every forward roll on the parallel bars was greeted with applause by the half-starved Hottentot prisoners.

Johannes Christian, the chief of the Bondelswarts, was being held prisoner in Warmbad at the time. He had been incarcerated along with most of his men before the revolt, but was later released, then promptly justified his captors' fears by waging guerrilla war against them. He was thought to have been released by mistake. According to rumor he and his men were freed shortly before midnight, when the compassion of the district officer, Count Kageneck, generally reached its high point.

Kageneck participated in Haring's gymnastic exercises occasionally, when he was able to stand. But one day he suffered severe contusions and a cut on his head when he missed his hold on the bars.

It was Dr. Haring's goal, once the rebellion was put down (and he never doubted it would soon collapse), to hold a gymnastic competition in the protectorate in which the victors would receive a simple oak wreath in place of the usual medals and cups.

Dr. Haring observed with some concern the strange alteration in his roommate Gottschalk in the days following his return from the patrol, which he described to Lieutenant Wolf as a personality defect. Gottschalk was putting aside half his ration of army bread and then, when he thought no one was looking, passing it through the barbed wire to the Hottentots. One couldn't help noticing a certain neglect of his appearance as well. He wore a red and white checked shirt under his half-buttoned khaki uniform, and at times a black slouch hat. He had not shaved with the mirror since that shock of realization; this wasn't unusual in itself, many men didn't shave, simply because it was easier, or water was scarce, or they liked the bold look it gave them. Most striking, however, was that Gottschalk was spending more time with brown riffraff, talking with the kitchen hands and ox-boys. A strange bird, Haring said in the mess hall, after Gottschalk had resumed his language lessons and could be seen evenings by the stone wall with the bambuse Rolf, perfecting his clicks. For a while Haring was worried Gottschalk might be homosexual, a thought that bothered him, since he was going to be sharing a room with him. But then Gottschalk was seen several times with a Hottentot named Katharina, who was a kitchen cook at the missionary station. That was always the first sign someone was going native, Lieutenant Wolf said in the mess hall; good breeding and true character were revealed precisely in the ability to resist the lure of blackness. District Officer Kageneck, who thought the reference was to him, ordered Lieutenant Wolf (it was only two in the afternoon at the time) to scout the Pella Drift area with a patrol the following day. Morris and his band were known to be holed up there.

Two days after that memorable event when for the first time in history in South West Africa an embryotomy was performed, Dr. Haring found Gottschalk sitting in the evening in a circle of Hottentots, drawing something in the sand with a stick and giving explanations that were translated into Nama by the Hottentot Katharina. How milk is produced: First the cow must eat her fill. Her digestion is unusual in that she chews her cud. She gathers grass with her tongue, molds it into a small bundle, then seizes it with her front teeth and tears it off. After a brief sideways chew the food slides into the stomachs: the bonnet and the rumen, also called the *saccus ruminus*. (With this the first Latin phrase was introduced into Nama, which was retained for decades in the area around Warmbad.) After the cow eats enough, she will lie down to belch up the food. This time it is properly chewed and well mixed with saliva. The resulting pulp is not swallowed back into the *saccus ruminus*, but now enters instead the manyplies, or third stomach. The manyplies is filled with something like rags (Gottschalk drew a cross section of the stomach in the sand), that stand upright like the pages of a book, they knew the Bible, this way then, and taking the Kropotkin from his pocket he flipped the pages with his thumb. The pulp is rubbed between these leaves. From the manyplies the pulp then slides into the maw, or fourth stomach, where the actual digestion process begins. The body produces various chemical fluids, each of which extracts a particular nutrient from the pulp. In the adjacent small intestine further separations are effected by the gallbladder and the pancreas, which also advance the process of digestion. Gottschalk drew a gallbladder and liver in the sand. Once the nutrients have been processed, they are absorbed into the blood through the wall of the intestine. The indigestible portion is passed on to the large intestine. And the final results are those nice cow pats.

Around this time, Gottschalk started thinking about founding a veterinary school in Warmbad. He outlined the idea to Dr. Haring and asked if he might be willing to give a brief lecture now and then on the pharmacological aspects of human medicine. Haring said he would be happy to. Gottschalk maintained that such a transfer of technical and cultural knowledge was the true function and responsibility of a cultured nation with respect to a population which had fallen behind in terms of its development. One might possibly learn something from these people as well. And when Dr. Haring asked what, Gottschalk replied, nobleness of heart.

Soon even men from the lower ranks were openly tapping their heads when Gottschalk walked by. Lieutenant Wolf maintained that such scandalous behavior was tolerated because of the equally scandalous behavior of District Officer Kageneck. It was high time for a fresh wind. Exemplary models were needed in the south, ones that were steadfast.

Gottschalk's diary,
3 March 1905 (Warmbad)

Cows lacking front teeth will die, even if they are otherwise healthy. A substitute has to be devised, a set of iron or, even better, steel teeth that can be fastened to the jaw by means of a clamp.

Happily enough, competition is not the rule either in the animal world or in mankind. It is limited among animals to exceptional periods, and natural selection finds better fields for its activity. Better conditions are created by the *elimination of competition* by means of mutual aid. (Kropotkin)

Gottschalk must have begun a systematic reading of Kropotkin's *Mutual Aid* around this time. It's true that Dr. Haring never found Gottschalk reading the book in their room. Gottschalk must have read it outside, not for fear of being caught reading it (by this time he was already viewed as an eccentric), but because he enjoyed sitting out under the open sky when it cooled off in the evening. In the course of the day he could often be seen in the blacksmith's shop where a trooper named Zeisse worked, a trained craftsman who knew how to forge horseshoes out of nails and old iron wheel rims. But most of Zeisse's time was spent making a stately iron railing for the veranda of District Officer Kageneck. Zeisse worked with expensive iron bars that could have provided horseshoes for an entire squadron of troopers, forging railings from the end of which blossomed stylized oak leaves, heraldic lilies, and large lumpish shapes, whether buds or acorns no one could say. To be added later at regular intervals between these bars of flourishing iron vegetation were bars with lance tips, symbols of battle readiness.

Zeisse, the son of a farm worker from Bardowick, wanted to be a metal worker, but unable to find an apprenticeship, even in Lüneberg, he hired out to a blacksmith. After completing his apprenticeship there and receiving his journeyman's diploma, he went to Hamburg. He said he wanted to let the wind blow about his nose a bit. But he couldn't find work as a blacksmith in Hamburg and after a long search he was finally hired at the shipyards of Blohm and Voss to heat rivets. He stood at a small portable iron oven fueled with charcoal. The rivets were heated until they were red-hot, then Zeisse would seize one with a long pair of tongs and toss it to one of the riveters, who would catch it in his asbestos gloves, place it in a pair of tongs, and hold it over the rivet hole while the other man pounded it into the iron plate with a heavy hammer. All this took place at dizzying speed. At first Zeisse didn't throw the glowing rivet far enough and it would fall hissing into the slushy snow. Then the riveters would curse because they had to stand around and wait for Zeisse to carry the rivet back to the oven and throw them another one. Later Zeisse became a riveter himself. The noise, the roar gradually filled his head as if it were an empty cavern, the vibration traveled through his arms and upper body, his back grew strained, and a numbness gradually crept through his body, gripping his legs, arms, chest, and neck, making them feel leaden. It seemed as if something were draining out of him into the rivets and bolts, into the rust-brown iron plates, hardening there, until by evening there was nothing left inside but the roaring in his head. Outside the metal parts gradually assembled according to some mysterious plan, becoming hulls, ribs, the walls of a ship, decks, railings, smokestacks. Some mornings, beneath a cloud-covered sky or one of blue, Zeisse would recall the huge plow horses he used to shoe in Bardowick, who had to be soothed and positioned until they stood calmly and their hooves could be lifted. The hissing breath of the bellows at the forge, the smell of burned hoof. In the beginning, standing at the rivet oven, Zeisse would try to imagine where the ships they built would journey one day. Four months later he thought of nothing at all while he worked. When he received his call-up papers, he reported to the military engineers. He was sent to barracks in Altona. Back on leave in Bardowick, he said it was an easy assignment.

When Colonial Guard volunteers were sought to put down the Herero rebellion, he reported at once. It was said the kaffirs had risen up and killed German men, women, and children, showing no mercy. But the reason he volunteered was not for revenge or to defend German soil, but because his period of service would have ended in three months. A few days before he shipped out he put on his Colonial Guard uniform and visited a former foreman who had introduced him to riveter slang. At first the man didn't even want to let him in, then they sat silently in the gloomy kitchen while the children crawled between their legs on the floor. Zeisse wondered why he had come in the first place. He just wanted to say good-bye. He simply wanted to see Jan Lemke, to whom he had been tossing glowing rivets for months, one last time. Zeisse knew from the other recruits that the Social Democrats were opposed to the war down there. But that couldn't be the sole reason for his hostile silence. Lemke just left him sitting dry-throated at the table, fiddled with his chewed-off pipe and stared past him. Zeisse tried to start a conversation by explaining why he'd volunteered for the Colonial Guard. He wanted to let the wind blow about his nose while he was still young. That was a phrase his former master blacksmith in Bardowick used in stories about his *wanderjahre* as a blacksmith's apprentice in Belgium and Holland: You have to let the wind blow about your nose while you're still young.

But Lemke merely replied, rubbish, and asked Zeisse if he'd read what August Bebel had to say in the *Daily Progressive*: it was a war for the junkers and the industrial barons and a great injustice to the blacks. Whose side air ye on? Then they sat in silence at the kitchen table amid the screaming children. Until one of the children started playing with the tassel that hung down from the sidearm that Zeisse wore on his belt. Lemke told the child to stop, and even slapped his hand when the boy was slow in obeying. Then he stood up, turned to Zeisse and merely said: Well, then.

At the apartment door Lemke didn't even shake Zeisse's hand in farewell. Feeling his way down the gloomy stairwell, Zeisse said to himself: You don't need what you don't want.

I feel good here, Zeisse replied once, when Gottschalk asked why he had volunteered. No working my fingers to the bone like I did at Blohm and Voss.

REGIONAL STUDIES 2
KLÜGGE, A TOP HAT IN PÈRE LACHAISE
AND THE END OF OSTRICHES
IN THE BETHANY AREA
OR: THE BARREL

One noon, when no one sane person would emerge from the shade and the valley flickered with heat, three men mounted the fastest horses in Bethany and rode out into the countryside. What were they up to?

From time immemorial the ostrich, with its reddish neck and small, pop-eyed head, had roamed unmolested, grazing peacefully among the cattle herds. Until the day a rider appeared on the horizon and, galloping toward it with yells and whip cracks, got it running, though it had no desire to flee. He chased it across the burning plain until a second rider galloped in from the side and the ostrich veered off in another direction, stretching its neck, only to be confronted by a third rider, forcing it to double back over stones and bushes, the snorting horses on all sides, the men yelling and the whips cracking. And so they chased it until it dropped dead. Why didn't they simply shoot this docile bird? As far as they were concerned, it wasn't worth the powder.

The riders dismounted from the foam-flecked horses and pulled the tail feathers from the ostrich. They left the body lying. Why was this bird, living peacefully and nourished solely on hydrous plants, forced to sacrifice its feathers?

Seven months earlier, on a sunny but cool April morning in the year 1859, there appeared in Père Lachaise cemetery among the procession of mourners following the coffin of Leon de Lafargue, who had died tragically, a top hat that immediately attracted the attention of those present, indeed for a moment occasioned a highly undignified whispering: necks were craned, elbows were shoved into the sides of those who still gazed fixedly at the ground as if a mute remonstrance from the dearly departed might be heard to issue from it, directed toward the coachman who had run him down, and it was thanks only the alert intervention of a pallbearer that the priest didn't plunge into the open grave, as in the act of blessing the burial place, the aspergillum raised in one hand, he turned his head and stepped off into space. For the top hat of the Count de Boncour displayed not the usual mourning band, a white strip of cloth called a *pleureuse*, but instead an elegant white feathered strip that shimmered into blue-gray, and the whispered word spread: an ostrich feather.

Not two days later, on the occasion of the funeral of a member of the French Academy, a novelist and astronomer, two similarly adorned top hats could be admired, and scarcely seven weeks thereafter passersby in Berlin Unter den Linden were straining their necks to see emerging from a carriage another top hat decorated with an ostrich feather, by now a common sight on the streets of Paris. The Paris milliners stormed the two available wholesalers for decorative feathers. A craze set in the like of which had not been seen since the *les merveilleuses* and the hats and helmets under Napoleon. The price of feathers rose from week to week. Then the day arrived on which not a single ostrich feather was to be found for sale in all of Paris. Even the two ostriches housed in a small open-air enclosure in the Jardin des Plantes strutted back and forth naked before the visitors one morning. Someone (presumably a milliner) had climbed the fence at night, entered the enclosure, and cut off their tail feathers. A bottleneck in the import business, customers were told, due to the tedious and complex logistics involved in transportation and heavy demand for the product. The customers' impatience was understandable; after all, when someone died they couldn't wait long, they had to don their *pleureuses* by the day of the funeral at the latest, and who wanted to show up at a social event like that with a cheap scrap of cloth on his top hat? The customers had to be consoled with promises that larger shipments would soon arrive from Arabia, Argentina, and South Africa.

In Bethany, meanwhile, thousands of ostrich feathers had been gathered under the energetic guidance of chief David Christian and were now awaiting one of the traders who passed through once or twice a year. It soon become obvious, of course, that it was becoming more and more difficult to obtain feathers. The birds, which had always been docile, had turned shy, and there was even some danger that they would be totally exterminated in the Bethany area. The tribal council gathered. The church elder Lukas suggested that from then on ostriches should not be chased to death, but instead lassoed and their tail feathers plucked, so that, it was hoped, they could grow back again.

One day, almost ten years earlier, as chief David Christian awakened from a rotgut spree, he had found Bethany abandoned by missionary Knudsen, and his successor Gorth, who arrived at the village dead, already buried. (His grave can still be seen today.) While rising he managed to accidentally kick over his small keg of brandy; for a moment the intoxicating smell hung in the air, then nothing remained but a dark, damp spot in the sand. The earth swayed beneath David Christian's feet. He took that as a bad sign and swore never to touch alcohol again. When Missionary Kreft arrived in Bethany from Wallenbruck in Westphalia, he found a teetotaler as chieftain, who had just passed a law forbidding spirits of any kind, including brandy, liquor, beer, or wine. Traders who passed through had to lock up any and all alcohol under threat of punishment. Within the year, David Christian, nomen est omen (Missionary Kreft was a humanist), had managed to dry out the tribe in Bethany, which had been famous among the traders for drinking even denatured alcohol. Even in Knudsen's time the tribe had begun to revert to its nomadic ways, so Kreft immediately set out to build a stone church. Kreft, an architect manqué, drew up plans for the building and sent them to Germany, since the German donors needed to know what the building they were helping to finance would look like. One morning the slightly-built but energetic Kreft was seen in the garden, dripping with sweat, pulling up dagga plants. Evil must be pulled out by the roots, was his watchword. In order to wean the tribe from unchristian cattle stealing, Kreft had become a vegetarian, and tried to convince everyone of the advantages of lacto-vegetarianism. The intestines of humans, as well as their teeth, were indeed characteristic of an omnivore, but one with a clear inclination toward plant food. It was a matter of developing this inclination fully, so that Man might become himself in the matter of nourishment as well. Apart from his own family, the only person Kreft won over to this diet was a two-hundred-and-twelve-year-old woman, whose age was attested to by the tribe. In order to make the menu more varied and thus more attractive, Kreft set out to discover new kinds of vegetables. He soon found a plant that resembled kohlrabi, and in spite of insistent warnings, even pleading, from his flock, he prepared a meal from it, and to their chagrin proceeded to eat it in front of his cottage (he was an admirer of Frederick the Great). Two hours later he was rolling on the ground, screaming in pain as a stinking sludge oozed from his bowels and the pores of his skin exuded a dark slime. The sun first turned black, then doubled, then disappeared. Petrus Swart is your only hope, they told the missionary's wife, who, although trained in first aid, could only wring her hands in horror. Swart came and poured a mysterious liquid into the unconscious man. Two weeks later Kreft took his first step or two, and in the end he recovered fully. He was forced to renounce lacto-vegetarianism to avoid future problems. But they admired his courage, and when he was well again, they sent their children to his missionary school.

Kreft, who had been nicknamed the Terrier since childhood,

managed to eradicate tribal cattle theft almost entirely over the next few years with his dogged faith and the energetic support of the ascetic David Christian. Aside from the occasional small foray, there were hardly any large-scale, well-planned raids against the Herero. Keeping the seventh commandment was made easier by the facts that the Hereros had armed themselves with guns in the meantime and that the demand for ostrich feathers had increased markedly. These feathers ran around right in front of the pondoks, and it was easier to grab them then a Herero cattle herd, which involved a long trek and a bloody battle. The natives in Bethany had been waiting three months for a trader, not just to unload their hoard of ostrich feathers, which was threatened by moths and termites, but because with the onset of the cold season they needed blankets, and powder and bullets, not to mention other goods like knives, saws, thread, and needles. David Christian also hoped to restore peace in the family by purchasing a large copper kettle so meals could be prepared in a single pot, thus ending the constant quarrel among the children and old folk as to which pot held the largest piece of meat, and allowing him to consider the future of his tribe in peace. He had great plans, including constructing a stone house for himself and his family, and a second house for the tribal council.

What worried him and everyone else were the tales making the rounds about this trader who had never been to Bethany. While he was still on the other side of the Orange, rumor had it his ox-wagon wasn't a wagon at all, but a huge egg on wheels that would hatch in the warm sand of the Namib, and from this egg a mighty bird would emerge that could darken the sun with a beat of its wing. Then someone arrived from Warmbad who had talked to someone else who had worked as a blubber cooker in Cape Town and claimed the egg wasn't an egg at all, but a whale which could be tapped for lamp oil. The stench of blubber and carrion could be smelled for miles when the wind was right, before the wagon had even come into sight. He hadn't actually seen the wagon, but he'd smelled it, and it was the familiar smell of blubber, he knew it well. A few days' journey from

Bethany, on the Lion River, a mountain Damara claimed to have seen the wagon with his own eyes. It was an ordinary ox-wagon, but it carried a huge tree trunk the size of the church. A trader named Klügge was dragging it across the plains because the nights were turning cold, and Klügge was known to suffer terribly from the cold, even wrapped in two blankets.

On Thursday the team appeared on the horizon. But when it drew slowly into Bethany, the Hottentots and the missionary's family stood staring open-mouthed. Twenty-two oxen were pulling a heavy wagon holding nothing but a huge barrel. A barrel in which fifty men could fit comfortably. The biggest barrel ever dragged through the steppes and deserts of South West Africa. And to the eager questions of the missionary and the chief as to the barrel's contents, Klügge replied: Brandy.

Klügge considered himself a good judge of men (the most important requirement for a successful trader), and the best judge of Hottentots anywhere (I can smell business deals, he liked to say, pointing to his fleshy nose and sniffing demonstratively). Klügge interpreted the suddenly stony face of the chief David Christian as a clever attempt to hide his enthusiasm with Missionary Kreft standing there, a busy little fellow with a hostile, anti-business look on his face. Even the steadily smiling eyes of the missionary's wife darkened at the word brandy. Enquiries about powder, lead, knives, thread, and above all a copper kettle were met with a shrug of Klügge's broad shoulders; he said he didn't deal in odds and ends, he wasn't operating a junk shop. What he could offer were several hectoliters of high-quality brandy, entirely unadulterated he hardly need add. He guaranteed a pleasant tipsiness, no headaches the next day and no loss of sight.

When David Christian announced to him that he had passed a law outlawing the sale of brandy anywhere in the district of Bethany, Klügge thought he was joking, until he noticed the smile of schadenfreude on the missionary's face. It appeared he had transported his barrel over hundred of kilometers through the desert sands and burning heat only to encounter a tribe of teetotalers, and a chief whose face, when one looked more closely, bore a trace of asceticism: those two severe furrows between his eyes, the sunken cheeks, the fanatic gaze—yet there was something sensual in the lower part of the jaw, albeit held in check by the tightly-pinched corners of the mouth. It was a repressed and buried penchant for pleasure, Klügge could see that, one that just needed to be laid bare.

Klügge asked permission to stay in Bethany a few days to rest his oxen. Then he would head further north.

This was granted on condition that he sell no brandy. Kreft invited Klügge to stay in the mission house. Klügge did not decline. He pulled the barrel in front of the house, where he could keep an eye on it. There it stood, visible far and wide, a monument to bygone days of pleasure. The inhabitants of Bethany crowded about the giant barrel till darkness fell, admiring the stout oxen, including apple-gray Christopherus from the tribe of Dotsy, the strongest trekker in the south, who was unfortunately moonstruck. When there was a full moon, he had to be unharnessed, since he bellowed all night and was worn out by daytime.

Even David Christian ran his hand over the massive wooden barrel.

Klügge gave orders that no one was to shave even a knife-sliver from the unknown wood, a solid, heavy oak that Klügge had imported from France well seasoned. In the great coopery of Cape Town he had ordered the barrel constructed according to his own figures, with precise details as to its height, width, and various diameters. He then personally supervised the bending of the thick, pre-greased staves and their assembly. The success of this bold, far-reaching project, which Klügge had been planning for over fifteen years, since he first arrived in Cape Town, was critically dependent on making the barrel so tight that not a drop of the alcohol would escape.

Since the barrel would be exposed to the direct rays of the sun during its long transport, he had an additional frame constructed consisting of four long wooden lathes attached with hinges to the wagon on which the barrel lay. This frame had an awning stretched over it that could be adjusted to the various positions of the sun: thus the barrel lay in shadow. As for the construction of the tap located at the bottom of the barrel, Klügge had been brooding about it for months as he traveled and traded throughout southern Africa. The tap had to be secured by some sort of lock to prevent a stranger's hand from drawing brandy when no one was looking. Klügge had therefore invented a steel trap with sharp, jagged edges, which, by means of a spring placed under tension, snapped closed if anyone attempted to open the tap.

To the frightened consternation of the natives the tap now rested in the steel jaws of a beast of prey.

With the aid of a key, one could either open the tap to draw brandy or set the steel spring for the trap. In addition a seal had been placed behind the tap, which could be secured with a bolt reinforced in turn by a padlock, so that even if one were to risk one's hand, it still wouldn't draw. Klügge wore the two keys needed to operate this safety mechanism around his neck on a cord made of twisted elephant tail hair, where they could be seen when he washed his upper body. Klügge made a habit of granting himself the extraordinary luxury, even in the waterless steppes, of washing himself twice daily. Thus at the preordained hour, morning and night, the ox-boys and bambuses would arrive with their tin cans and pots and gather around Klügge, who was standing in a tin washtub. Since even the thirstiest ox wouldn't drink soapy water, the drivers made their coffee with it. It must have been around this time that the rumor arose that in addition to brandy, Hottentots drank soapy water, a statement that also appears in a few early travel journals and was repeated for several years in the scholarly literature. Klügge not only enjoyed a reputation for wasting water, he also had the pleasure of a nickname: the white giant. Klügge, a heavy man over six foot tall, always dressed entirely in black, including his shirt, waistcoat, and corduroy trousers, which had the extra wide legs worn by carpenters in Hamburg. He towered over the undersized Hottentots by a good four heads. He always had to lean forward during business deals; at any rate he had the strange habit of leaning as he walked, as if something were pulling him over.

Klügge came from Hörde, a village near Dortmund. His father was a self-employed carpenter and sent his eldest son to high school in Dortmund. Klügge was considered an average student, noticeable only for his unusual size. Later he wrote poetry, something not in itself unusual, since most of his classmates did too, although it must be said that for one such effort he was expelled from school. The poem had been passed on to the principal of the high school by the literary editor of the city newspaper, to whom Klügge had submitted it. In his accompanying letter, the editor termed a few lines of the poem perverse: Rosy, shimmering towards me, faintly pulsing / Vulva / And a trembling never felt before rewards me.

At a hastily called conference, the German teacher criticized the clumsy meter and unusual rhyme scheme, which offered clear evidence in themselves of the student's moral turpitude. Klügge's immediate *abeundi* from school was unanimously recommended, not because of the pornographic nature of the text— it was common knowledge that uncensored passages from Ovid circulated regularly in Latin classes—but rather the poem's accuracy of detail, a realism, as the minutes put it, that could not have been drawn from any known literary source. It had to be based on first-hand experience.

Klügge's father sent him to Düsseldorf where, through the good offices of an acquaintance, he undertook a business apprenticeship in an export-import firm. In the gloomy accounting office, Klügge stood at a high desk entering orders for cloth and thread, while secretly writing poems between business letters, long, sensual poems, in which ship keels thrust through the foaming furrows of the sea, juices dripped from thick, flesh-colored jungle leaves, orchid pistils ejaculated, a black panther— its eyes glimmering like opals—clawed the white breast of a woman, and the air was redolent of carrion and freighted with the sweet scent of seed.

One year after completing his apprenticeship, on 20 January 1842, Klügge boarded a ship in Rotterdam and sailed for Cape Town. There he worked for a year in a business specializing in the import of buttons, belt buckles, and tortoiseshell combs. The skills he had developed in his apprenticeship lay fallow, since the entire correspondence, accounting, and commercial orders were handled by the proprietor Aron Silbermacher. Klügge minded the shop with Frau Silbermacher and sold buttons wholesale and retail. His large size stood him in good stead in the process. He didn't need to carry the ladder back and forth among the high wall cupboards to pull out the little drawers in search of various sizes of mother-of-pearl buttons, horn, glass, silver, and brass buttons, or gold-plated naval ones; if he stood on his toes he could dip his hand into the highest drawer.

Sometime during this period, moving between the shop counter and the tall cases lined with small button-filled drawers, while fog horns wailed through the rainy twilight and ship bells clanged, Klügge decided he wanted to be rich. He would earn money, and plenty of it. The strange thing was, he had no idea what he would do with the money. He didn't imagine himself owning one of those white homes in the classical style that stood on the coast, with palm trees in the garden, and an orangerie protected from the wind to one side, but instead focused his vision entirely on how he would earn money, how to buy goods at a favorable price and resell them at the highest possible profit. The prices in Cape Town, aside from a few minor fluctuations when the market was favorable, were pretty well set, but in bartering everything depended on the skill of the trader, for money was still unknown in the interior. He saw himself building a mighty business out of nothing. He would cast his trader's net far beyond the frontier, his ox-wagons would ply the northern territories of Africa and carry with them the white man's civilization. Sundays he would sit in his room and figure out various ways to spend the money he was saving, on buttons, combs, and buckles, while keeping in mind the restricted demand for combs among the Hottentots, given their short, kinky hair. In May 1843, having searched out the middlemen for buttons, whose names Aron Silbermacher kept to himself to ensure his monopoly on buttons in Cape Town, Klügge went independent. He bought a small wagon and a pair of mules and settled in Bitterfontein, where he could make trips to the neighboring native compounds. He specialized in buttons, pots, and pans, trading them for cattle, goats, and sheep, some of which he sold to white farmers living on their own, driving the rest once a year to the slaughterhouses in Cape Town.

Klügge was disappointed by the impertinence of the natives where business matters where concerned. He had hoped to find unspoiled savages. Instead he was confronted by Hottentots who, even in rags, wore European clothes. Nowhere on his travels was he greeted with the warm generosity generally imputed to these people, but instead by unconcealed mistrust and cunning duplicity. It soon became evident that the value of a goat, a sheep, or a cow was common knowledge everywhere. Many traders passed through this area heading north. Once he had hoped to trade a dozen solid horn buttons for a well-nourished cow; now he learned he couldn't even get a skinny sheep for them. Indeed on more than one occasion he was shamelessly taken in, for example when he bought a cow that soon started losing weight in spite of being well fed, and finally died. When it was slaughtered an eighteen-meter-long tapeworm was found in its bowels. The world seemed topsy-turvy. Only the supple, relaxed movements of the young women retained some remnant of the wild beauty he had once dreamed of in his accounting office in Düsseldorf.

One day Klügge felt a small hardening on his lower lip, a little lump he couldn't press flat. He'd already become accustomed to it, had even stopped gnawing at it, when suddenly it opened into a small, dark-red running sore with rough edges. The lymph nodes on his lower jaw swelled, he probed the rounded cartilage with his fingertips, a habit he retained until his dying day. Whenever he was thinking something over, he would seize his lower jaw with his forefinger and his thumb as if he were trying to choke himself. Thus he was often seen, his hand at his throat, deep in thought.

During a stay in Cape Town—the sore had almost closed completely by then—Klügge consulted a physician, who confirmed that it was syphilis and prescribed a quicksilver salve.

Klügge made an accounting. The trade in buttons, pots, and pans (he had also added knives and axes to his wares) was not as profitable as he had hoped. It would be years, if not decades, before he would earn the necessary capital for his more grandiose plans. This was due in part to the poverty of the population, but also to a certain characteristic tightfistedness and a corresponding cleverness in which Klügge felt he recognized something Jewish, which was not so surprising, since after all the Hottentots were Semitic in origin, as a Swedish professor in Cape Town had explained to him. But the decisive factor damaging his business was the unbelievable durability of the goods he sold. He hadn't realized that before. But now, returning to a native compound after a year, the natives exhibited the pots and pans they had traded for with beaming satisfaction. A few dents and scratches, that was all. Klügge could see that the next generation would still be using them. The buttons too showed scarcely any wear. On rare occasions one would break, and then, with absolutely no sense for symmetry, another button of a different size and color would be sewn on. Added to this was the annoying tendency of the natives to search for any button they had lost—and they were constantly losing them—until they found it. Old men and women would join in the search, children too, even the dogs. It could take hours or even days, it didn't matter, it became a form of public entertainment, turned into a sort of small-scale festival, until the button was found. This willingness to waste time made any long-term business plans impossible. All the natives wanted were the bare necessities and then they would laze away the day.

Klügge was forced to realize that all his calculations had proved false. He dealt in items that, as far as one could see, could be sold to the same person just once or twice in a lifetime.

There was no great business in that. Gunpowder or brandy was something else again. You could fire a flintlock just once, for example, whether or not you hit anything. (It was better of course, if you missed). The pan had to be refilled with powder, a new bullet had to placed in the barrel. Even better: brandy. The Hottentots would buy the cheapest stuff they could find to get drunk on. But the next day the effect had worn off, and they saw everything as it was once more, that is, soberly, and were understandably upset. That could only be remedied by a new binge, which was necessarily followed once more by sobriety. This thirst was of a higher sort than ordinary thirst, Klügge sensed, although he drank only occasionally. Once you peeled away its metaphysical mist, this thirst had a hard, economic core. Ideally, sale and consumption occurred almost simultaneously, and with brandy thirst was quenched in a way that produced an even greater thirst afterward, so that the disparity between drink and thirst grew increasingly greater, and the intervals of sobriety increasingly shorter, supply and demand driving each other constantly upward. Here was an economic impulse of compelling and therefore beautiful logic.

It was a matter of setting this mechanism in motion.

If Klügge meant to carry out his plan to build a giant barrel, he had to raise money, and with this in mind he turned to Morris, an English businessman in Cape Town. Morris was thought to know southern Africa better than anyone else. He had studied economics and styled himself a disciple of Adam Smith. For two years he had been contemplating extending his business into the region between the Orange and the Kuene. This area was, he told a fascinated Klügge, who sat on the edge of his chair, pressing a handkerchief to the sore on his lip, an economic no-man's-land, a blank spot between the Portuguese commercial interests in Angola and those of the English in the Cape Colony. Only now and then did an elephant hunter or a few traders enter the area. But that was where truly enormous profits were to be had. The plan with the barrel was a bold one, and well thought out, but a little one-sided, for how were the natives who were practically starving to death going to pay for the brandy? And Morris had moral objections. Continued development in an economic sense was not possible from the sale of brandy alone. He spoke of the responsibility of the white race, how one had to first teach the savages how to think in economic terms. The Hereros in the north, for example, kept huge herds of cattle that constantly increased in size because the cattle were part of a cult of ancestor worship. Only if they grew hungry for meat, or needed something, was a cow ever traded. The animals grew older and tougher and finally died a natural death. But, Morris said, an ox that died a natural death had missed its calling. The first thing to do, then, was to awaken new interests and needs among the natives, who had lived a self-sufficient life up to now, and to break through the internal circle of their economic forms of production, which were practically in a state of slumber. The market had to be awakened with a kiss, said Morris, in what struck Klügge as an embarrassing flight of fancy. The missionaries at the Rhenish Mission were already doing their part, said Morris, continuing the thread of his argument; Christianity's battle against the cattle cult was underway, but at the same time it was necessary, and here he cited Adam Smith, to introduce a more highly-developed form of labor. Then, with the resulting division of labor, the market would develop in turn. Klügge shifted his weight from the left to the right cheek of his buttocks. But where does the first division of labor occur in a nomadic people who still trail after their herds, where the division of labor is dependent on cows and steers?

Klügge dabbed cautiously at his sore with his handkerchief, which lent him a thoughtful air. But Morris had not addressed the question to him, for he immediately answered it himself: In theft, and more specifically in cattle theft. Some people raise the cattle and some people steal them. The Hottentot tribes had to be convinced to move from stealing when forced to for food, to systematic cattle theft on economic principles.

Klügge squeezed the swollen lymph nodes under his lower jaw between his forefinger and thumb in deep thought.

It was necessary, then, to awake the Hottentot's self-interest, to create new needs; they were a people capable of pleasures, the wares would have to be given to them on credit to begin with, the payment would come later in the form of cattle, which, since they had so few themselves, would have to be stolen from the Hereros, for which they would in turn need powder and lead and guns, for which they would also have to pay in cattle. The arms trade, which up to then had been more or less hit-and-miss, would take on a certain necessity. Everything was in place, but how were these tired limbs to be set dancing? Brandy, said Klügge, taking his hand from his throat.

Exactly, said Morris, brandy will awaken the slumbering market.

Morris invited Klügge to accompany him on his trading trip to Windhoek, as his right-hand man, so to speak, for there was something forceful and energetic about his plan, and that's what was needed for this great project. Morris would let him share in the profits. Klügge had just one question: Where would they take the cattle?

Wherever meat was needed, to the mines of Kimberley and Johannesburg, to the slaughterhouses of a hungry Cape Town, but primarily to St. Helena. That's where the highest profits could be made.

As a young businessman, Morris had spent almost five years on St. Helena, and had seen Napoleon of several occasions in Longwood, where he once nodded *bon soir* to him. According to Morris, Napoleon annoyed the English governor Sir Hudson Lowe by claiming the only dish he liked was ox tongue in Madeira sauce, obtainable only at great effort and expense. Of course the death of the emperor shortly thereafter proved he hadn't said this just to annoy him. Napoleon died of stomach cancer. This genius, and Morris emphasized he used the word quite deliberately as an English patriot, had given him the idea, even in the throes of death, of exporting Herero cattle to the island in large numbers. Most of the ships sailing to India and Australia put in at St. Helena to take on fresh water anyway;

why shouldn't they buy fresh meat too? Juicy steaks reduced the danger of mutiny and scurvy. In honor of this genius and as a sign of appreciation he later leased the Longwood property and opened an office in Napoleon's study. In closing—Klügge could finally rise from the hard edge of the chair, with its upholstery nails—Morris offered his hand and said: You see, Mister Klügge, in the end an invisible hand will create humanistic acts out of even the most selfish motives.

Klügge pondered this sentence as he returned to his lodgings. Strictly speaking, he was now an employee of Morris, for that was evident in the phrase right-hand man. On the other hand, he told himself, he could learn a good deal from him about carrying out business plans. And his plan went beyond Morris's. He wasn't just interested in awaking a slumbering market, or in elevating trade from a chance operation to a necessity, he intended, in consort with the tribal chiefs, to build a monopoly in brandy. Klügge saw the trip to Windhoek as a chance to gain experience and make contacts. The phrase about the invisible hand, and it was clearly God's hand at work, pleased him. That afternoon, in a darkened room, massaging his throat, Klügge again put his hand to poetry. Coming back he had passed an orange tree in bloom. But the rhyme for bloom that immediately occurred to him, room, and the lines he worked out and said aloud to himself, For every orange tree in bloom, the house of trade will add a room, seemed less and less in harmony with what he had felt on his way home. Finally he could only repeat bloom and room, until they gradually lost all meaning, along with the poem he intended to write, and the attempt to do so merely struck him as odd. On a blank piece of paper he began to add up all his receivables and his obligations. Then he compiled a list of those goods he thought would contribute to increased trade with the natives in Windhoek. In addition to ten barrels of brandy and a large stock of guns, bullets, and powder, he noted sizable quantities of various glass beads, marbles, and sackcloth, entering the latter under clothing material.

When he went over the list with Morris a few days later, the

Englishman replied: no glass beads, no sackcloth, and no cheap trinkets of any kind. Klügge should buy French parasols, mother-of-pearl opera glasses, Japanese silk, Sumatran cigars, Jamaican rum, plugs of Brazilian tobacco of the thickest, sweetest sort, and Italian laced boots for the women, all of the highest quality. He wasn't trying to get the best of the savages, he wanted to awaken their business sense. They had to develop their taste first. While articles of daily use were good, it wasn't just a matter of awakening their sense of utility, but their sense of beauty as well. Those who learned to appreciate only utilitarian objects always ran the danger of turning modest in their ways, even ascetic, and that, from an economic point of view, was a drawback. A point one sought in vain in Adam Smith, the importance of which first struck him here in Africa. There had to be some pleasure in things or the market would never fully develop. Offering fine wares also prevented competition from small-time traders, who appeared along with their pots, sacks, and horse blankets like flies on carrion wherever they smelled a chance to do some business. As if the stench of putrification were already in the air, Morris wrinkled his nose in disgust.

Three months later, on Easter Sunday, the wife of the native chief Jonker Afrikaner could be observed, a parasol in her right hand, gathering up her ruffled dress in her left hand and springing daintily in her elegant laced boots across the puddles left standing after a recent shower

Two overgrown oxen were just dissolving in a blue-gray haze. Jonker's hand held one of the six Sumatra cigars from the small wooden box that stood beside him on a little table. Jonker's great aunt marched past, enveloped in a fragrant cloud of French rose oil, kicking in vain to fend off the goats in hot pursuit.

By early afternoon the well-trained bass of Bill Thompson could be heard, starting up a dance on his accordion, while Morris sold brandy on credit. Klügge suddenly understood for the first time why Morris had taken Thompson of all people along as a clerk, when he could barely count to three. Thompson played: A bi-ba-boogeyman dances all day long, to a diddle-di, daddle-di, doodle-di song. It was soon the tribe's favorite tune. They danced and drank and sang into the night.

The grumpy, carping missionary Kleinschmidt, who now called Windhoek "Little Paris," left a few days later without saying good-bye to his compatriot Klügge. The missionary work was taken over by Missionary Haddy from the Wesleyan Society, whom Morris had brought along. Haddy, nicknamed Ruddy-Nose, was an experienced square dancer who taught the young girls the various changes to the sound of Thompson's accordion, his hand beneath their breasts. Trade and traffic, Haddy preached on Easter Sunday, are pleasing in the eyes of God, the commandments of Moses must be interpreted thus: true scales, true pounds, true scoops, true canisters shall be with you. Wealth comes when God looks with favor on your life. Have dominion over the earth. Jonker and his men related this to the Herero meadowlands.

Morris had thought of everything: Haddy was worth his weight in gold. Two months after his arrival, Morris sent the first eight hundred cattle off to Kimberly, fourteen days later, six hundred headed for Walvis Bay, where they were loaded onto a ship bound for St. Helena. Klügge, who kept the main account book for Morris, registered a profit of over 2000%, even after subtracting the cost of transportation. The account book is the trader's Bible, Klügge explained to the ever-curious Jonker.

It was during this period that Klügge's appearance began to change. Although he had always been unusually thin, he now broadened out, his shoulders seemed to grow, his head, the sore now healed, turned pear-shaped, but what was particularly noticeable was his barrel-like bottom, while his gait, once floppy, now turned into a plod, and he began leaning from the waist as he walked, a trait that became increasingly pronounced as the years passed. Klügge, who had formerly lived modestly, even ascetically, now indulged in Cuban cigars and real Scotch whiskey, not all that often of course, since Morris demanded the same outrageous prices from him that he did from the Hottentots.

Klügge's palate confirmed the accuracy of Morris' theory, as did all of Windhoek; the sins of Babel, as Missionary Klein-schmidt carped, rapidly increased. Morris had brought along a blacksmith who repaired guns gratis for the natives and showed them how to cast lead bullets. Haddy's wife, who had trained in London as a nurse, cared for those wounded in raids on the Herero herds, and Haddy accompanied the fallen to their final rest, while Thompson played bi-ba-boogeyman. Jonker wished to create a great Hottentot empire by uniting the numerous small tribes, and thus strengthened, conquer the Hereros and seize their fertile grazing lands. Morris, who supported his plans, named him The Brown Napoleon.

The important thing was to prevent traders from visiting the Hereros and providing them with guns. A Boer caught trying to do this had his entire stock and wagon confiscated and was forced to walk barefoot back to Cape Colony. There was no word if he made it.

And then came the memorable day on which strips of white cloth fluttered from all the wild currant bushes around Wind-hoek. An unwitting Herero, wishing as usual to pluck a few of the white berries that taste like currants, was caught in the act by Jonker's men, bound, and dragged to Windhoek, where he was flogged in public. Up to that point the wild currants, nourished by the stony soil, and watered only by rare showers, were available to man, antelope, or sparrow; but suddenly the bushes were confiscated and marked with white strips. Unwitting mountain Damara, fetching the honey of wild bees as usual from hollow trees, found the trees patrolled by guards oiling their weapons. A Damara who crept up in the night and tried to smoke out a swarm of bees was stood up against a tree and shot.

Haddy had developed a process for brewing a smooth, strong beer from a mixture of honey and sugar, with a dash of wild currants. It soon became clear that given the length of time it took to transport brandy, supply was falling far short of demand. There were days, and even weeks, when all of Windhoek was stone cold sober in a most unsettling way. It had reached the point of violence. As Thompson innocently plied his accordion to the tune of bi-ba-boogeyman, a black scorpion crawled from its innards. During church service, objections were raised while Haddy was reading a passage from Romans: Let us walk honestly, as in the day; not in rioting and drunkenness, not in chambering and wantonness, not in strife and envying. He endured questions as to why, precisely now, when there was no brandy to be had, he had chosen this passage, why now of all times he preached against rioting and drunkenness, and what he meant by strife and envying, whether that was a reference to stealing cattle. And to top it off, Jonker appeared before Morris in an equally unhappy state of sobriety and said: I'm paying you more for your stuff than it's worth!

I don't understand, Morris harrumphed. What do you mean?

Bring sixteen pairs of trousers from your shop, said Jonker.

An ox-wagon stood before the house. The draft oxen had been driven to the outskirts of the village to graze. On the ground, arranged along the shafts, were long, woven leather harnesses and eight yokes, so that the oxen could easily find their accustomed places for the coming journey. Jonker gave orders to place a pair of trousers to the left and right of the harnesses behind each yoke, until they reached the front oxen, who were led on a rope. Then Jonker himself took up a whip, called out to the trousers to take off, and cracked his heavy whip down on each in turn. He yelled louder, cracked his whip harder, and grimaced like the wagon master did whenever the panting oxen foundered. Finally he handed the whip to a stunned Morris and said with contempt: See, there are your trousers, and each one costs one ox. They can't pull a wagon. The oxen you receive for them can pull your wagon down the bay road all the way to Walvis Bay and back again, and they can work a long time for you, longer than your trousers. And when they cannot work, you can slaughter them, and they are of value to you yet again.

In the council of elders someone suggested they simply drive Morris and his men from their land and distribute his wares to the tribe. Then one morning Ruddy-Nose made his way into the gloomy sobriety of the village so drunk he could hardly stand, and in his hand he held a mug, a mug filled with honey beer that quickly brought even the most hardened drinker to his knees. The day was saved. Morris immediately set up several breweries in the village, delivered sugar, and exchanged Haddy's brewing formula for oxen and sheep. The brewing process, however, was so simple it was easily learned and imitated, so that black-market breweries abounded, which Jonker, under pressure of a threatened sugar boycott from Morris, forbade. But hidden away in many a pondok stood a calabash in which Haddy beer was being brewed. An even more serious consequence was that word of the brewing process spread among the Hereros too, and Jonker's men increasingly encountered wild currant bushes that had been picked bare, in spite of their white cloth strips. The footprints around the bushes were not those of the Nama, their size showed tall Hereros were the thieves. The impossibility of placing a sentry beside every currant bush inspired Jonker to exemplary punishments. Although personally innocent, the headman of the Hereros, who had to work for Jonker, Samuel Maharero, who later became chief, was strapped to a wagon wheel as a proxy, where he spent days upright in the burning sun and freezing nights. Another Herero, caught with a handful of wild currants, suffered a burning stick held to his bottom, just as a burning branch was sometimes held beneath the buttocks of a weary ox to bring it to its feet.

A certain brutalization began to spread, to which the Haddy beer contributed. The worst rotgut produced nothing to match this hangover. After a night of carousal with Haddy beer, Klügge experienced a shrinking skull and swelling wooden brain, swallowing repeatedly to relieve the pressure on his eardrums with reassuring pops.

The old bustle resumed, more dancing and drinking, and the natives with a gift for language sang: A bi-ba-boogeyman dances all day long, to a diddle-di, daddle-di, doodle-di song, embellishing the text with a variety of clicks. But fights broke out with increasing frequency among the singers, suddenly and irrationally,

in which the whole of the village took part, women and children
included. There seemed to be no particular sides in these battles;
as if secretly signaled, they struck out at each other, regardless
of who happened to be next to them, Morris's men not excluded.
In one such fight, as Thompson played to calm their spirits, a
bucket of sticky honey beer was dumped on his accordion.

Then one night, when Klügge entered his cottage as usual
with his young woman and unbuttoned his trousers, she refused
to lift her skirt and mount him like the bold rider of old, but de
manded a handful of sugar first. Klügge jokingly demurred, o
course my sweet, and reached for her firm breasts, but she
pushed his hand away and asked again for sugar. When in his as
tonishment he asked her why, she replied, I give you, so you give
me.

Didn't she enjoy it?

Not any more, she said, it hurts. At this Klügge kicked her in
the backside and roared out drunkenly: get out of here you
whore!

To his surprise he found that none of the women, normally
so friendly and open, would sleep with him unless they go
sugar. Only then did Klügge learn that for weeks all the whites
had been forced to pay their women in sugar, in fact three days
ago the amount demanded had gone up. Until then a woman had
cost one tablespoon of sugar for the night. Now all that got you
was a hand in your trousers and a quick jerk.

A month later, having at first withdrawn in stubborn disap
pointment, Klügge asked Morris to charge a few kilos of sugar
against his profits receivable. The price was outrageous, as
Klügge angrily pointed out to Morris. Morris lifted his hand
helplessly, saying that demand had risen sharply in the recent
past, and after all he was the one risking his capital in this ven
ture. Klügge vowed to himself to take a look at the works of
Adam Smith as soon as they were back in Cape Town.

At this period two letters arrived for Morris, carried by mes
senger in the cleft of a long stick. Morris examined the letters.
The seals were unbroken. Morris withdrew to his house, while

outside, in spite of the heat of the midday sun, the entire village assembled. Hours passed. When Morris finally emerged, Klügge thought he detected a slight change in Morris's expression. A trace of smiling determination had entered that round, freckled face. Everyone stared expectantly at Morris, but he walked silently to the fire and burned both letters, then obliterated the paper ashes with a twist of his boot. Disappointed, the crowd dispersed. One letter, it had been learned, came from Cape Town, the other from the island of St. Helena.

That evening word went around that the governor of Cape Town intended to occupy the land. Soldiers would cross the Orange River bringing a large cannon, alcohol would be outlawed, a large ship with sugar was on its way from the island to Walvis Bay, the gunpowder trade would be controlled and the traders punished.

The next morning Morris called Klügge in and ordered him to total up all accounts due from Jonker and his tribe. Klügge worked all day and through the night, and by the first streak of dawn he had tallied up the orders. Early that morning Morris visited Jonker, who was sitting up in bed, having just awakened, as one could see from his trembling hands, which always settled down after three glasses of brandy. Early to bed and early to rise, makes a man healthy, wealthy, and wise, Morris declaimed in English, in the roaring good mood he always exhibited early in the morning. Morris demanded the immediate payment of all tribal debts, which, as he showed Jonker on paper, amounted to a good three thousand cattle. He needed the cattle at once, for the *Flower of Yarrow* was expected any moment in Walvis Bay and was due to sail for St. Helena with eight hundred cattle, and the remaining cattle he needed to drive to Cape Town to settle accounts there.

The tribe had never owned that many cattle, Jonker replied.

Unmoved, Morris suggested he look to the vast Herero cattle herds. They would have to attack one of the headmen, not just raid the smaller herds.

So the great cattle war began. Jonker attacked the rich Herero

chieftain Kahena, shot the herdsmen and guards, and drove off
over four thousand head of cattle. Eight hundred were immediately separated out and driven to Walvis Bay, while over a thousand were driven off to Cape Town. Morris told his unsuspecting
men that he was closing up his shop and warehouse and returning to Cape Town; anyone who wished to do so could remain.
When Klügge asked him in private why he was leaving now,
when business was going so splendidly, Morris replied that the
pavement was getting a little too hot. The Hereros and Hottentots would soon kill each other off.

It was only later, in Cape Town, that Klügge learned the true
reason for Morris's rapid departure. Morris had received a tip
from a business associate: the Cape government, under pressure
from constant protests on the part of white farmers, intended to
stop the influx of cheap cattle from Namaland, using as a pre-
text newspaper reports of warlike conditions in the land, for
which he, Morris, was to blame. But a major breeding project
with Herero cattle was already underway on St. Helena. Morris
was financially involved in this project too.

After receiving his share of the profits, less a considerable
sum for luxury items, in particular several hundredweights of
sugar, Klügge again became independent, and set out the following year through southern Africa as a trader in an ox-wagon, a
junk shop, as Morris referred to it with contempt. Klügge rigorously saved his money until he had enough to build the barrel,
and when it was finally finished, he could stand tall, as if freed
of a burden.

For days the barrel stood beneath its sailcloth awning in front
of the mission house. Klügge passed time by playing checkers
with the missionary's wife and by washing himself several times
a day. Klügge made a show of going to the barrel a few times, un-
locking the spring trap with the first key, and the seal with the
second, then slowly drawing a cup of brandy, which he proceeded to drink with obvious pleasure before the assembled
thirsty eyes. But at such moments Kreft, the wife, or the ascetic
chief David Christian always seemed to appear. Klügge knew

these people were thirsty, it was simply a matter of who took the first swallow of deliverance. If Klügge offered a cup to one of the natives standing about, he would draw back immediately with a quick shy glance at the missionary, as if Klügge were Old Nick himself.

Klügge thought of moving on, but he'd heard there were already many traders among the tribes to the north, and moreover there were thousands of ostrich feathers warehoused here, which at the moment were bringing top prices in Cape Town. There was no turning back. He had to do business here in Bethany. But no matter what he tried—he played the accordion every evening (he had taken lessons)—nothing seemed to loosen this stiff and joyless tribe.

Kreft went away for several days to visit a settlement near Bethany that was under his pastoral care. On the evening following his departure, Klügge sat in the living room of the mission house with the missionary's wife, playing checkers as the icy cold of night crept slowly across the hardened clay floor. Sabine Kreft, wrapped in a thick woolen shawl, her cheeks glowing and a moist gleam in her eyes, sat bent over the checkerboard. For two days she'd had a cold and fever. Klügge was telling stories about his travels to the interior. How an old elephant had attacked him once, and he'd managed to save himself by scrambling up a tree. The bull elephant had then knocked over his ox-wagon and trampled the pots, pans, clothing, and guns, while Klügge looked on helplessly from the tree. Next the elephant tried to knock down the tree, fortunately without success. How once during a truly old-Testament storm a lightning bolt had struck the horns of one of the lead oxen, then traveled along the yoke chain like a serpent of fire and leaped over to the drag chain, at which the oxen to both left and right fell dead. The glowing bolt then disappeared beneath his feet through the shafts and sprang to the heavy iron rim of the right wheel, which melted and fell to the ground as the wheel broke and the wagon tipped forward and came to a complete stop. Before him, in neat rows, lay twenty dead oxen in harness. Sabine Kreft kept her

constantly smiling and now feverish eyes trained on Klügge saying, yes, yes, ah yes, until a shiver ran through her. Klügge rose
to fetch a bottle of Jamaica rum (white). This will help, he said, a
grog will drive off the fever. For God's sake just don't say anything to my husband, said Sabine Kreft, wrapping her hands
around the hot glass of grog, he thinks alcohol comes from the
devil. Klügge laughed his gurgling laugh, and by this point—they
were on their third glass—the missionary's wife was laughing at
the phrase too, covering her mouth with her hand each time for
no apparent reason (her teeth were even): My husband thinks
alcohol comes from the devil. What a funny sentence. From
the devil. She was feeling so warm, she said. The only thing
to do was dance. One could only survive in this desolate land by
dancing.

Then something happened that night for which various explanations may be found, but which remains incomprehensible
even so. Certainly the decades-long monotony of life in Bethany
played a role, and a certain marital weariness with Kreft, who in
his own small and busy way was indeed brave and honorable
(the terrier), but whose pious integrity had something boring and
burdensome about it. Then there was the added fact that the
Krefts had been living in a state of abstinence, not simply due
to Kreft's Christian convictions (the flesh is weak!), but also to
his narrow adherence to a lacto-vegetarian diet and the debility
that followed his severe poisoning by the kohlrabi-like bulbs
Of course Klügge played an indispensable role too, this broad
shouldered giant with his wild tales. The alcohol—three glasses
of grog—was not decisive, though the missionary later tried to
convince his wife it had been. Those three glasses (Klügge hadn't
even thought of them as an aid to seduction) at most smoothed
the way for what occurred. In any case in that clear, icily quiet
night, one could suddenly hear a penetrating sigh and then
moans, as if someone were gasping for breath while running
followed by a deeper-toned voice smacking and groaning. As
the high-pitched panting that evidently came from a woman's
mouth grew faster, the deeper groans slowly caught up, drew

even and passed them, but, while the inhabitants of Bethany, drawn from their pondoks by this unheard-of race, crept closer and closer to the gasps until they were standing directly before the mission house in which the contest was being waged, the small, high-pitched panting suddenly grew faster and faster, and gradually began to overtake in turn the deeper groans which had hurried ahead, until the bemused crowd standing before the house heard them both roar out in release as they reached the finish line in tandem. That, the missionary's wife was heard to declare, was something new. The grinning crowd listened as a sound like a cork being withdrawn from a bottle emerged from the otherwise silent house, then Klügge's gurgling laugh, the shrill giggle of the missionary's wife, then Klügge's voice: Now turn around, no, like this, and draw up your legs, and they were off to the races again with renewed groans and rapid panting. Outside the crowd nodded appreciatively. Soon thereafter a satisfied-looking Klügge stepped from the house, a tin bowl in his hand, surprised to see the silent audience, while the missionary's wife could be heard singing inside: When all the springs are flowing, a man can naught but drink, if I can't call my love aloud, at least I still can wink. It was astonishing how much surface area this slender woman had offered him, how nimbly she held his testicles in her small soft hands, then pushed a finger gently up his rectum. For a moment Klügge wondered if she were really as innocent as he thought, but then he gazed into the amazed faces of the Hottentots standing silently and realized that all of them, including the woman in the mission house, had been thirsty for years. Then Klügge walked over to the barrel, which arched massively into the starry sky, drew a cup of brandy after carefully releasing the trap and seal, and, in an effusive mood, without the slightest ulterior business motive, invited the entire village to drink: the brandy was on him.

When Missionary Kreft returned to Bethany two days later, on a Friday afternoon, he could hear the shouts long before he reached the village. His heart stood still; he thought the Hereros were taking delayed revenge for all the cattle they had lost. But then he heard an accordion and the harmonium that only his wife could play. He was pleased, for he thought they were practicing a hymn for the coming Sunday, the Jubilate. But as he drew nearer, he saw people dancing, and could hear what they were playing and singing: A bi-ba-boogeyman dances all day long, and he saw with horror that they were dancing around the huge barrel as if it were the golden calf. As he leapt into the circle, shouting and admonishing the dancers, the song died away, his wife rose unsteadily from the harmonium, which had been carried out of the church into the open air, and only the stocky giant, Klügge, continued unflustered on the accordion, tapping his foot in time to the music. They stood silently, staring at the enraged missionary. A few of them, now that they were no longer dancing, couldn't stand, and collapsed to the ground. Among them Kreft discovered even the truest of the true, Lukas, the church elder, who once accompanied Kreft's predecessor Gorth to Bethany, and who, when Gorth passed on, fulfilled an oath by sewing his corpse up in animal hide and carrying it to Bethany. Now he sat grinning impudently. And when Kreft turned with a roar to the tribal chief, David Christian, who was swaying on his feet and struggling to suppress a bout of the hiccups that was shaking his entire frame, demanding to know the meaning of all this, this relapse into heathenism, this barbarism, David Christian grinned and said: We been thirsty ten years, that's long enough.

In the meantime Klügge had stopped playing. He carefully mounted his stool, stood quietly, then puffed out his cheeks a few times and spoke slowly and hesitantly: It must be God's will to see people happy, otherwise he wasn't a good God. And part of happiness was enjoying life, and that meant dancing, and dancing meant singing, and singing of course meant brandy. Everyone clicked their tongues approvingly, and Klügge played "Rolling Home" on the accordion. But the former mood could not be restored, they danced no longer, scarcely a voice was raised in song, they simply drank. (One glass of brandy for one large ostrich feather). Kreft (the terrier!) barked at his wife and dragged her into the mission house. No one knows what was said there; Sabine Kreft never told Klügge. She emerged staggering from the house in tears a short while later, her breath heavy with alcohol. Her husband had cursed her in the name of the Almighty in a most unchristian manner and driven her from their home. So Klügge, whom Kreft had forbidden to cross the mission house threshold, set up a tent beside the barrel that evening and the two of them crawled into it. They lay pressed up against one another on a narrow mattress on the ice-cold ground. They tried to play a game of checkers by candlelight, but their fingers were so numb they couldn't pick up the pieces. So they warmed themselves up with brandy and crept under the covers.

The sounds to which Kreft was forced to listen in that otherwise quiet night were appalling: a bubbling smacking of the lips, delirious moans, lascivious cries, and all coming from the mouth of his wife, as if the devil himself were riding her, sounds he had never heard before, and pressing his hands to his ears he kept mentally repeating one word: Jungle.

The next morning an empty ox-wagon that also belonged to Klügge drew into Bethany. All the goods Klügge had received in exchange for brandy, mainly ostrich feathers, were to be loaded onto this wagon and taken to Port Nolloth in order to reach the European milliners as quickly as possible. Klügge loaded almost six thousand ostrich feathers, the entire yield of the previous six months. In the next few days he intended to head further north, for there was nothing more to be gained here, the tribe had drunk up everything they had. Sabine Kreft would be going with him. He was finally doing good business, two more trips with this barrel and he would have enough capital saved to buy a farm, or if she preferred, to return to Germany and open a small trading company there. It was the first time, even in private, that Klügge had thought about what he might do with his money. But he didn't feel personally involved in the plans, they were simply the sort of wishes he'd often heard from other traders. Thinking of the future, seeking a place for both of them in it, he became less and less certain that he actually wanted to stay with her. But we seem well matched, he said, and although it wasn't a formal declaration, it was still taken as an offer of marriage.

Sabine said yes. But. The thought of traveling across this barren desert with that giant barrel was oppressive. And Klügge too, whom she now saw at times with other eyes, seemed threatening in his massiveness. There was something cumbersome about the man, as if he were taking after the huge barrel, and she was overcome by shameful embarrassment when she thought of all the things she had done with this elephant. But she said yes.

Not long thereafter David Christian appeared in his Sunday suit, a cast-off diplomat's coat and tails. The disturbing news had reached him that Klügge was going to drag the barrel away to another tribe in a few days, and in fact to the Habobes, who were enemies, since they had stolen sheep from Bethany on several occasions. They of all people would be sucking their fill from the brandy barrel while those in Bethany would left high and dry. That had to be stopped at all costs. But when Klügge asked him what he had to offer, David Christian had nothing. In less than seven weeks however, he could offer cattle: Herero cattle. They would steal them from the Hereros, at some risk of course, since the Hereros had armed themselves in the meantime.

Klügge rejected this offer. Meat prices had fallen to almost nothing in the Cape Colony. Heavy rains over the past year had resulted in a higher than average increase in the herds, which were well nourished. Droves of bellowing oxen were pressing at the doors of the slaughterhouses. There wasn't even a market for dried meat. On the other hand there was heavy demand for ostrich feathers. And Klügge was no longer willing to give out brandy on credit.

The tribal council was called into session. Soberly and thoughtfully they considered how best to keep the barrel in the village.

They decided to chase every last ostrich in the region to

death. Church elder Lukas's suggestion that they catch the
birds and pluck their tail feathers couldn't be implemented because the riders selected were not yet skilled enough with the
lasso.

Two weeks later the last ostrich in the region around
Bethany was killed and robbed of its tail feathers. The vultures
circled in the sky.

Now Klügge was determined to leave.

The evening before his departure Sabine Kreft entered the mission house in which she had lived for over five years. She intended to demand that her husband at least return a treadle-
driven sewing machine given to her by a great uncle as a wedding
present. Klügge lay alone and freezing in his tent. Hour after hour
passed. The voices of Kreft and Sabine could be heard in the
house. They hadn't exchanged a word since the day the missionary returned to Bethany and threw his wife out of the house.
Klügge crept from the tent. His joints ached. Recently he felt that
all the sand he had swallowed during his years in the desert had
settled in them. He waited impatiently. He'd asked her what was
so special about a sewing machine, and said he would buy her the
latest model in Cape Town. But she had insisted on taking the
wedding gift with her, she didn't want a hypocritical, unimagina-
tive man like Kreft to have it. The voices inside the house grew
louder, Klügge clearly heard the woman give a little cry, he was
about to rush into the house when he heard a moan, now, and
then the groans of the missionary.

Klügge lay down under the spigot of the barrel, filled himself,
and slowly said aloud what he was thinking: That fucking little
missionary terrier. That Christian bitch in heat. The phrases al-
ternated in his mind, endlessly circling.

When he awoke at noon the next day from a death-like torpor
he saw the barrel on the wagon above him, but at an angle.
Something seemed to have gone wrong with his brain. But then,
as he pulled himself up on the axle, he saw that someone had removed a front wheel in the night. He walked around looking for
it. In vain. Once he saw the missionary's wife in the window, at

a distance and only briefly. That afternoon Kreft, appearing doubled, came to Klügge, who was lying under the spigot, and said
as through a fog: I forgive thee too, my brother.

What's he calling me brother for, thought Klügge.

David Christian had the wheel taken off the wagon in the
night, Kreft explained, to delay Klügge's departure. On condition
that Klügge leave the village the following day and never return,
Kreft was willing to show him the hiding place. Klügge promised, but he was in no shape to walk. He sent a driver.

Though it was still early in the evening, Klügge heard, as if
through cotton wool, yet clearly enough, renewed moans and
groans from the mission house. As he had almost four weeks
earlier, Klügge invited the whole tribe for a round of drinks. He
wanted to have a going-away party he said, with dancing, drinking, and singing. But even through the drunken roar one could
still hear the lewd panting from the mission house. You've given
us all a great deal, David Christian said to Klügge with a malicious grin, including the missionary.

The following morning, with the sun floating in the early
mist, the barrel pulled out from Bethany. A single old woman
appeared and cursed at Klügge, who, still lost in thought, his
hand at his throat, walked along beside the barrel. The curse was
in German with a Norwegian accent. Behind the twenty-two
oxen pulling the barrel, came a team of oxen pulling a wagon
with six thousand three hundred and fifty-nine ostrich feathers
packed in three large bundles. No one appeared at the window of
the mission house, although Klügge didn't turn to look back.
The barrel had just reached the last hut in the village when a
shot rang out. Startled from his thoughts, Klügge reached for his
heart, but the bullet had struck some distance behind him,
splintering the barrel instead, and Klügge realized it had hit its
target. He stared in horror at the spot from which a stream of
brandy would soon pour out. But it turned out the bullet had not
penetrated the thick oak staves. Klügge pried the bullet out of
the wood with his knife. Although deformed by the impact, one

could still see the cross carved in the lead. For four days the oxen dragged the barrel through the sunburned steppes. Klügge, who thought that exercise would do his painful joints good, walked alongside. He felt that more sand had settled into his knees and ankles, and at times, when he was walking ahead of the barrel, in a silence that stretched to the horizon, with only the panting of the oxen far behind him, he even thought he could hear the sand grinding in his knees. But a driver forced to walk bent over beside Klügge for some distance, with his ear near Klügge's knee, claimed to hear nothing. Yet there was a grinding in Klügge's head.

On 15 June, at noon, they spotted a cloud of dust on the horizon. That evening, as they drew near, they were greeted by the doctor and elephant hunter Dominicus, a squat man with a thick blond mustache. Dominicus had a legendary reputation as a brandy drinker, but Klügge could scarcely hide his disappointment when he learned that Dominicus, who was coming from the Cape, was only now embarking on the hunt, and so as yet had no ivory in his wagon. Dr. Dominicus walked around Klügge's barrel several times, rapped on it (that deep full tone), scratched at the splintery depression the bullet had made and finally pronounced it the eighth wonder of the world. An inspiration of true genius, to bring so much brandy into a desert. The doctor had to swallow. Then he asked Klügge where he was headed. Klügge said he was going to Geiaub, and his fears were confirmed when Dominicus immediately replied that that was good because he was headed the same way.

That evening by the campfire, Klügge told the doctor, whom he had treated to a cup of brandy, about the pain in his joints, as if sand had settled in them, and about the strange grinding sound he heard when he walked. Dominicus asked Klügge to stand up and move away from the fire, in which cow pats were crackling. He told him to roll his head around. Klügge look at him in surprise, than began to rotate his head. Dr. Dominicus held his ear to Klügge's throat. It's the neck vertebrae, he said.

No, it wasn't that cracking, said Klügge, it was a grinding sound. Calcification, said Dominicus in a friendly tone, do your fingers ever go to sleep?

Klügge confirmed that he sometimes awoke with a feeling of numbness in his lower left arm.

Rotate your head five times a day, twenty times to the left and twenty to the right.

While Dominicus was examining his knees, Klügge rotated his head to the point of dizziness.

Have you ever had syphilis, the doctor wanted to know.

Yes.

Dr. Dominicus said only, I see.

For this consultation he demanded £2 or three liters of brandy. That same night he drank almost a full liter of the stuff, which Klügge had bucked up with pure alcohol. Each time that Dominicus bent over the campfire to light up a new pipe, Klügge involuntarily leaned back for fear the doctor would explode. The amazing thing was that Dominicus could still speak, albeit in fugal retrograde. He described to Klügge the elephant gun he had constructed himself. A small portable cannon loaded from behind with a flintlock that fired a small grenade with a diameter of 2.5 cm. This grenade had a steel center and a steel tip, both of which guaranteed better penetration, explained Dominicus, who intended to take a patent out on his model once he had solved the problem of the weapon's one disadvantage. The gun had such a strong kick (Dominicus showed his thickly cushioned shoulder-pad) that it knocked you over even if you were kneeling when you fired it, and it was usually impossible to fire lying down because of the tall grass. It the shot struck home, said Dominicus, even the strongest bull elephant would fall. You just had to be careful not to miss, because then you were flat on the ground yourself with no time to reload. A year later Dr. Dominicus missed a young elephant. An unsuspecting Bushman raised his hand to warn Dominicus about the elephant, unintentionally diverting the man's attention. Dominicus didn't have time to reload his blunderbuss and was trampled to death.

Klügge stared at the high-penetration elephant gun. That same night he started carving a wooden plug three centimeters in diameter. To run into this drunkard of all people in an otherwise unpopulated land. Klügge and Dominicus trekked westward for five days. Why does he want to head west, thought Klügge, everyone knows there aren't any elephants there any more.

On the sixth day Dominicus asked to buy a demijohn of brandy from Klügge on credit. He would pay later, when he returned with the tusks. Klügge thought less about the kick that knocked you over with the Dominicus gun, and more about the creditors from whom Dominicus had fled, leaving Berlin in the night, it was said, to arrive in Cape Town by way of America. There he set up a medical practice, but after only seven months, having accumulated huge gambling debts, he had to climb out his bedroom window to escape an angry crowd of his creditors gathered before his front door. His flight took him to Namaland, where, having shot nothing but a few pheasants with a friend in the Spandau forest, he was now hunting elephants.

Klügge said it was a matter of principle with him never to sell on credit. An old salesman's adage: Never loan money to a friend or you will lose both. Dr. Dominicus told Klügge he should have a thorough liver and heart exam. A white man's liver was at particular risk in this arid region. Klügge declined. He didn't even want a free examination, which led Dominicus, who considered Klügge a hypochondriac, to suspect he was hiding something under his shirt near his waist, possibly a moneybelt filled with gold coins that contributed to his strange stoop. (Klügge never removed his shirt completely during his extended daily ablutions, but merely pulled his shirt out and allowed it to hang over his waistband.)

The next morning, before harnessing up the oxen, Klügge checked the tap on the barrel as usual. To his astonishment he found the steel trap snapped shut around the spigot. He came closer and discovered a severed hand inside. Startled by his scream, Dominicus came running and pulled the hand, to which individual tendons and scraps of skin still hung, from the trap, turned it back and forth and said: Small and delicate. Probably a Hottentot hand. You see, the man must have cut through the tendons that were still attached with a knife. He held out the hand to Klügge. Klügge threw up.

When the oxen were driven to the traces, Dominicus discovered that his lead boy was missing. They called for him. They looked for him. He was nowhere to be found.

That evening, when they had set up camp and eaten, Dominicus pulled a deck of cards from his coat pocket and suggested they pass the time by playing a little poker. They could play for a glass of rum. Although it was well known that the doctor almost always lost at poker, Klügge declined. He sat in silence, drawn up near the campfire, his hand at his throat, staring at the flickering shadows. After a time, when Dominicus tried to start a conversation by asking Klügge what he missed most here, the latter replied: The cry of the cuckoo and elderberry bushes. Back home in Hörde they had two elderberry bushes in the garden. In summer they had elderberry soup, with semolina dumplings. The dumplings were spoon-shaped, since they were scooped out with a spoon. He would gladly exchange his brandy for a bowl of that soup now. If he could be a child again as he ate it, of course.

Later, when Dominicus arrived at Walvis Bay and met the missionary there, a Finn called Rautanen, he said Klügge struck him as strange from the day they met. There was something apathetic about him, a peculiar brooding manner, signs of a progressive paralysis.

Klügge continued to stare at the fire in silence, making no reply to questions. Later he stood up, checked the barrel, pulled the steel trap open around the spigot, set the spring, and then lay down, wrapped in three blankets, near the slowly fading fire. He lay awake a long time, shivering. The glow from the burned-out logs died away. He dreamed he had been shut inside his barrel. In the course of building it, they had forgotten he was inspecting the interior and had fitted the last stave in place. Exhausted, he swims about in the three-fourths-full barrel. It's pitch-black inside. He hears and feels the brandy lapping against the round wooden sides. The barrel is evidently being pulled along a bumpy road. Outside he hears the voices of the drivers, but his own as well, and the panting and snorting of the oxen. Then everything is still once more, it must be night outside. He swims back and forth from one end of the barrel to the other. His cries, his blows remain unheard. His hope is concentrated solely on the spigot, that someone will turn the cock and draw some brandy. That familiar gurgle outside when the brandy flows.

A sound makes him jump. Confused, he finally realizes it was a shot. It's nighttime and the embers have turned to ash. He springs up, feels for the wooden plug he's been carrying for days now in his pocket, and runs over to the barrel. Even as he's running he hears a splashing sound, as if a spring has suddenly emerged from this sandy plain, a pipe burst, a faucet left on, and he sees the famous brandy hound Dr. Dominicus standing at the barrel, holding a bucket, with a knot of drivers pressing about him on the ground, catching stray drops in their open hands and lapping them up. He beats his way through the bodies, cursing and striking at them, the plug in his hand, and thrusts it through the thick stream of brandy into the hole, but the plug flies right out again, so Klügge tears off his shirt, stuffs part of it into the hole, beneath him, between his feet, a greedy slurping and smacking. Finally he manages to stuff the plug into the hole. Now it only dribbles.

Exhausted he turns and stares into the grinning face of Dr. Dominicus. A silly accident, he says, he was cleaning his gun, it could just have easily struck him, Klügge. Lucky in a way. And he holds the weapon before him, its barrel trained on Klügge.

The sun had not yet risen when Dominicus had the draft oxen brought before his wagon. He wished Klügge much success. The hole in the barrel could surely be made watertight.

Klügge examined the bullet's entry hole by daylight. It was in the side of the barrel, near the middle, but unfortunately quite low. He carved a wooden plug with an even larger diameter.

Nevertheless, since the bullet hole was splintered, it had to be sealed watertight with something. As he changed plugs, the drivers, still drunk, crowded forward with greedy faces. Klügge placed a bucket under the hole and quickly pulled out the one plug; a thick stream of brandy immediately shot forth. He drove the new wood stopper into the hole with a few hammer blows. Then he harnessed up the oxen and drove on. He watched with concern the narrow but steady stream that ran down the side of the barrel and trickled into the sand. Twice he caught a driver running low beneath the barrel, panting, his head twisted upward, catching the drops of brandy on his tongue. A disgusting sight, in Klügge's opinion.

He saw the greedy glances that were constantly aimed at the plug, sitting undefended in the barrel. In the days that followed, Klügge tried to sleep for the shortest possible intervals. But several times he was overpowered by a profound slumber, then awoke to find the plug indeed still in the barrel, but the drivers lying dead drunk in the shade. Four days after Dr. Dominicus' departure Klügge was unable to raise one driver even by kicking him. The man lay directly under the hole in the barrel. He must have pushed the plug back in, then collapsed right there. Toward noon the man died.

Klügge headed west with his two teams. He sat on the coachbox again, brooding, his hand at his throat. His joints ached. And he no longer kept up the breakneck pace.

One evening he told the wagon master, Hermanus Zeul, of a small but significant error in his plan. He was still convinced it was better and more rational to transport one large barrel than several smaller ones. The smaller ones would require more space, due to their shape, and would be easier to steal. But he had overlooked the fact that a large barrel was quite vulnerable. One would have to construct a barrel with transverse and lateral bulkheads, like the ones they were building into ships these days so they wouldn't immediately fill with water if they sprung a leak. With such a barrel a hole in the side would empty just one section.

Over the next few days, during which the wagon advanced slowly with its drunken drivers—at times even the oxen appeared tipsy—Klügge worked on a sketch for the barrel's construction. A gigantic barrel with an overall length of 63 meters and a base diameter of 6.7 meters. The barrel had six transverse bulkheads and four lateral bulkheads in which smaller trapdoors were built to be interconnected by cords running through tubes. All these cords, which were numbered, came together at the top in a regulator attached to the barrel. An individual compartment could be opened by pulling on the corresponding cord. The wagon upon which it was mounted was truly amazing. In a sense it was a bold forerunner of the railway low loader, which was developed decades later.

The wagon sported sixteen wheels all together, two sets of four at both front and back, with the axles fastened on revolving disks. These allowed a smaller turning radius. It may be that Klügge based this construction on the railroad axles being built at the time in the Cape Colony. The wagon was to be pulled by forty-two oxen, arranged in ten rows of four, with two lead oxen at the head. From the sketch of the shaft and draft rope assembly it may be inferred that Klügge also considered elephants as draft animals. There seems no other explanation for the huge harnesses that bear a faint resemblance to suspenders for lederhosen. Albeit a rough diagram, it includes precise indications of size.

These construction sketches subsequently arrived in Port Nolloth with the wagonload of tail feathers of all the ostriches that once lived in the Bethany area. The wagon master, the Bastard Hermanus Zeul, traded the sketches for a plug of Cuban tobacco to Shelton, an Englishman of independent means from London who was hoping to find a cure for his ailing lungs on the dry highlands of Juib. It is not known through whose hands the two sketches passed over the past century. They resurfaced in a used bookstore in Eimsbüttel, a suburb of Hamburg, not one of the finer rare books establishments but a second-hand shop. The owner could no longer recall who had sold him the construction sketches, which were rolled and tied with red cord, presumably part of an inheritance.

The wagon master Hermanus Zeul reported in Port Holloth that Klügge experimented with numerous materials, including melted wax, in order to make the hole watertight. But to no avail. The brandy dripped to the ground slowly but steadily, faster by day beneath the rays of the sun, somewhat more slowly by night with ground frost. Each time the wagon stopped, a dark damp spot formed in the sand directly related in size to the length of the stop. The lead man of the freight wagon asked Klügge if he could sleep under the hole with his mouth open at night, so he could at least be filled while he slept. Brandy was too good to waste on the stupid sand. But Klügge wouldn't allow it.

Klügge claimed the grinding in his joints was getting louder. And now a grinding in his head with every thought. So the sand must have settled there too. It hurt to think.

Hermanus Zeul, who had to put his ear to the back of Klügge's head, claimed he couldn't hear a thing.

If Nature would just hold its breath a moment, the whole world would hear the terrible grinding in my head, Klügge said.

One day Klügge woke and found to his surprise that both the drivers and the wagon master were sober. He went over to the barrel and examined the hole. The leak had stopped. It turned out that brandy dripped out only if the wagon was tipped at an angle when it stopped, which the wagon master had managed each evening of course. That night the first heavy frost arrived. Klügge found the cold unbearable. He was freezing from the inside out.

The next morning the oxen were driven to the traces as usual. The men took their time. Klügge sat silently, wrapped in blankets, on a large stone, his hand at his throat. When the oxen were finally yoked and the wagon master called out Christopherus! to the lead ox and struck him smartly with the whip to get him moving, Klügge threw himself protectively across the animal and cried out: This is God's creature.

Drivers, lead boy and wagon master stood at a loss as Klügge clung to the ox and tearfully caressed him.

The oxen had to be unharnessed again, since they wouldn't pull the wagon unless they felt the whip. But Klügge wouldn't allow it to be used. He sat all day beneath a camelthorn tree, wrapped in a blanket, in spite of the noonday heat. Camelthorn can't be right, he kept saying, camels don't have thorns. He wished he had a coat as soft as theirs. And he would never try to pass through the eye of a needle.

When darkness fell, bringing with it a sharp night frost, a painful sigh escaped from Klügge. He felt his lungs icing up with every breath. He could hardly breathe for fear of bursting inside. Something strange seemed to have reached his heart, everything below it was frozen. They brought extra blankets and laid more sticks on the fire, but Klügge claimed it would take a mighty conflagration glowing to the horizon to melt the ice inside him. After sitting for a long time by the fire as if paralyzed, emitting a stream of sighs that had something inhuman about them, he bolted upright, grabbed a burning stick from the fire, walked over to the barrel, drew out the plug and held the flame to the trickle of brandy. The pure alcohol Klügge had added to the brandy was still strong and with a puff a small blue flame snaked along the brandy track, gnawed slowly and hesitantly at the dry oak, which crackled and popped, then caught fire. Shortly thereafter gigantic flames shot into the night sky. The barrel was on fire. The glow of the fire could be seen as far as Geiaub, over fifty kilometers away, where Klügge had planned to take the barrel. It was the largest fire ever seen in the region. Many years passed before Morenga's men were to start an even greater one.

Standing before the crackling flames and popping wood, Klügge warmed his hands. Twice his drivers beat him with blankets when his clothes caught fire. The next day the Scottish cart was lifted out of the freight wagon and Klügge was ready to start a new business, one of a higher sort of course. Adam Smith wrote that new interests must be developed for mankind to evolve. He would look for an elderberry bush. A bowl of elder-berry soup would be worth its weight in pure gold.

When Zeul asked what he was supposed to do with the six thousand ostrich feathers, Klügge replied it was all the same to him, Zeul could stick them on his hat for all he cared.

Shoving the cart before him, Klügge tramped off through the sand with his singed beard and hair.

He was later seen in various native compounds, where he was given food and drink. But he could no longer make himself understood. What he spoke was neither German nor English nor Dutch. It was a strange language, never heard before. He was last seen in Otjizeva. It was Corpus Christi, a Thursday, when he left the village. For a long time, it was later said, they could see him far out on the plain, pushing his cart, growing smaller and smaller until he disappeared in the distance.

BATTLE REPORT 3
COLONEL DEIMLING'S OFFENSIVE AGAINST MORENGA
IN THE GREAT KARAS MOUNTAINS
MARCH 1905

When Colonel Deimling failed to defeat (smash) the Witboois near Naris at the close of 1904, he found himself in an awkward situation, both as commander of the southern division, and with regard to his military operations. Morenga and his rebels were camped at the southernmost point of the Great Karas Mountains, threatening supply lines from Cape Colony and from the harbor at Lüderitz. To the northeast the Witboois had disappeared into the endless steppes, but remained a constant threat to supply lines back to Windhoek. The southern division was in a tight spot. Something had to be done. In mid-January Deimling moved his quarters to Keetmanshoop in the south. Since it was impossible to determine where the Witboois were, and since he was reluctant to lead larger forces of men into a waterless region again after the debacle at Aob, Deimling decided to attack the rebels in the Karas Mountains.

Morenga had been quiet from December to March. It was later learned from prisoners that he lacked munitions.

In order to conduct a concentrated offensive against Morenga, Deimling had to first solve the problem of supplies. Water-holes were certainly more numerous in the mountains than in the Aob, but the steep and rocky terrain was inaccessible to ox wagons.

Major Buchholz of the general staff worked out possible solutions: a railroad across the dunes near Lüderitz, increased use of mules in the mountainous terrain, and the experimental introduction of camels, a hundred to start with, whose performance could be tested by veterinarians.

The planned offensive against Morenga led to sharp disagreements between Colonel Deimling, commander of the southern division, and his superior, General von Trotha, commanding officer of the Colonial Guard. Deimling submitted reports outlining the reasons why Morenga should be attacked immediately. (Firstly, the possibility that Morenga and Witbooi might join forces, for which there was hard evidence; secondly, Morenga's now legendary reputation of invincibility). Trotha, on the other hand, demanded that Witbooi be attacked first and destroyed. Trotha and his staff were worried about the logistical situation. In Trotha's opinion, German troop strength, which had risen to ten thousand men, was still not sufficient to wipe out the rebels. A larger fighting force in the south would increase supply problems: The northern supply line from Windhoek was already under constant attack by the Witboois. The English border was closed for the time being, because the Bastard Morris was endangering the region, and the equally long and difficult bay road to Lüderitz was threatened by Bethany Hottentots led by Cornelius. General Trotha and his staff anxiously awaited financial approval from the Reichstag for a railway line from Lüderitz to Keetmanshoop.

Were there other non-military considerations?

General Trotha found himself in an awkward position as well. Not only was he being attacked in the international press for his blood and sword policy—particularly in England—and at home by the Social Democrats (that was no problem), but others had joined the chase and were stirring the pot: missionaries (they had no choice), settlers in South West Africa (no longer a factor), freethinkers (?), and a few people from the liberal rags. More seriously, a certain circle at court seemed to have gained the ear of His Majesty. These people, mostly financial advisors and bankers with filthy lucre in mind, warned that if Trotha were given a free hand his pacification system would leave the colony without a labor force. To Trotha's surprise, Count Schlieffen, Chief of General Staff, gradually came to share this view. What Trotha needed was a victory that would allow him an elegant exit from the South West. One such possibility was a victory over Hendrik Witbooi, whose name was now internationally known, whereas no one had any real idea who this Morenga or Morengo was, some vagabond mine-worker with no real status as a chieftain.

And Deimling?

Colonel Deimling had to patch things up after the debacle at Great Nabas. This lost skirmish (Deimling, who liked to refer to everything as a battle, deliberately played down the encounter in this case) might prove a hindrance to his imminent promotion to the rank of general.

Berthold Deimling was a daredevil of sorts. He considered himself athletic, yet calm and collected, decisive, cool, and calculating. What pained him was his lack of a hereditary title and its attendant dignity. But he was by no means an old war-horse. He lacked the requisite backslapping manner. He was reserved in conversation, seldom drank, was an excellent horseman, wore well-cut, neatly tailored corduroy uniforms even in the field. Military in thought and deed, he was an excellent representative of the military position in political situations. And because he represented that position so often, he became more famous in political affairs than in military ones.

Invited in 1906 to report to the Reichstag on the military situation in South West Africa, he affronted them by demanding that the Kaiser be given control over the budget, upon which a supplementary budget for the government in South West Africa was defeated by the Social Democrats and the Center party. This gave Chancellor von Bülow the chance to call for new elections, the so-called Hottentot elections. In 1911, Berthold von Deimling, to whom the Kaiser had awarded a hereditary peerage in

1905, was prominently involved in the Zabern Affair as Commander General in Strasbourg. After the First World War, Deimling made an unusual wheeling maneuver, to use a military term, and took over temporary command of the Social Democratic banner.

An undated photograph shows him—just after the rebellion had been put down—in the uniform of a major general. The collar and cuffs of the jacket are heavily embroidered with gold oak leaves, and even a few small acorns may be seen among them. There is something strangely obscene about the picture. Perhaps it's the dagger that Deimling, who is sitting on a stool, holds between his legs. But it may also be the display of overlapping decorations, medals and crosses, adorned with eagles, crowns, and swords. Gazing slightly upward past the camera, he sits as if ready to spring. His mustachioed face, particularly his attentive, alert gaze, bears a certain resemblance to a pointer.

General Trotha forbade Deimling to undertake extensive operations against Morenga and gave him explicit orders to concentrate his attacks on Hendrik Witbooi and destroy him. This order was issued to Deimling again in writing on 17 February 1905. At that time Colonel Deimling (line Colonel) was preparing an offensive against Morenga. Deimling hoped to make this order moot by means of a victory. (Personal rivalries between Deimling and von Trotha played a role of course.) "The available supplies," Deimling later wrote in official justification, "were sufficient, in my estimation, to enable me to attack, since we could count on capturing numerous cattle in the Karas Mountains. In my professional opinion as local commander, conditions were optimal by the end of February for a quick and decisive blow."

Deimling decided that detachments should advance from all four sides toward the Naruda Ravine where Morenga had set up camp. The attack column (over a thousand men, with fifteen cannon) would set out on the preliminary phase from 1–3 March and reach the Naruda area on 11 March. A focused operation based on the principle of marching separately and attacking in unison.

Morenga was immediately informed of the advance of the four detachments by his spies; he probably knew of the preparations, since many African drivers, lead boys, and wagon masters, though not themselves Nama, still sympathized with the rebels. Morenga gathered information about the individual columns through scouts sent out to estimate their strength, then when he learned the precise direction of their march, developed his plan of attack. A plan so good it could have come straight from General Headquarters in Berlin, a few staff officers later joked, a bit better than that in fact.

Morenga divided his troops, which couldn't have totaled more than three hundred men at that time, into three groups. Morris was supposed to take a hundred men and engage Koppy's oncoming detachment near Garub, thus slowing its progress.

The Bondelswart headman Stürmann (not the prophet) was to occupy Krai Gap with fifty men. The major unit led by Kamptz would have to pass through this ravine in the Karas Mountains, since it was the only accessible entrance to the east-west axis of the foothills. Stürmann was to defend the ravine as long as possible and then withdraw to the Naruda Ravine at the western egress of the mountains.

Morenga intended to use his strongest group, which may have numbered as many as one hundred and ten men, to attack the weakest German unit, led by Kirchner and approaching from the north. At a valley near Aob through which the detachment would have to march, where two chains of hills narrowed like a funnel and the valley was almost entirely blocked by a high lateral range, he set up emplacements and had his men dig in. After defeating the German unit he intended to ride back that same night to Naruda and join with Morris's slowly withdrawing men, taking up positions in the steep ravine, where he intended to defeat Koppy's unit of over three hundred men. Following which Stürmann's group would combine with those of Morenga and Morris, and at full strength they would ambush Kamptz's largest division, under the command of Deimling, at the western entrance to the ravine. The plan for this operation was based on the rebels' advantage: their knowledge of the terrain, their precise awareness of their enemy's plans, and their greater mobility.

The implacable logic of Morenga's battle plan was that the weakest German division would be defeated first by a rebel band of equal strength, in alliance so to speak with the natural terrain, upon which the rebel groups led by Morenga and Morris would unite and move against the next strongest German division. The Germans would thus grow steadily weaker, while the rebels grew stronger from battle to battle.

The success of this plan was crucially dependent on the skill and steadfastness of both subordinate captains, Morris and Stürmann, would show in holding off the German detachments as long as possible, so that Morenga and his group could cover the sixty-kilometer-long stretch from Aob to Naruda and take up positions for the second battle at the proper time.

The preliminary march of the German division started according to plan and without incident.

Around three in the afternoon of 10 March, the head of Kirchner's column comes under fire in a valley basin. Captain Kirchner immediately orders his men to dismount and form a line. But nothing can be seen of the enemy, which makes everyone uneasy. The German troopers approach the enemy positions without major losses. Both cannons fire randomly in the direction of the rebel shots. But nothing is visible. One of riflemen manages to advance by rushes to within a few hundred meters of the elevation that lies athwart the valley. During the next rush a lively and focused fire breaks out from the heights to the right and left. There are immediate and substantial losses on the German side. Captain Kirchner orders both cannons and the two machine guns forward. A firefight develops that intensifies minute by minute on the side of the still invisible enemy. The large section of the unit, including the artillery, is in danger of being surrounded. At this point Captain Kirchner decides to storm the enemy position. I'm going in, he says, even if it makes us both cry. The German troopers storm the slope with fixed bayonets and hurrahs. The attack appears to succeed, for the rebels quickly abandon their positions, but only to settle firmly into new ones they have already prepared a hundred meters further up. The Germans, winded by the long run during the attack, enter an increasingly narrow cul-de-sac and are shot down from ahead and both sides. The attack collapses. Captain Kirchner falls. Those who can, retreat to the cannons. But the cannons are out of shells. Around six that evening the rebels attempt to storm the Germans, something they seldom do, but are repelled with the help of the two machine guns. Ammunition is running short. Out on open ground the wounded lie screaming. The water has run out. In the words of the official General Staff report, the situation is desperate.

Around one in the morning, Lieutenant Baron Grote attempts to break through with the remaining men. The thirty soldiers who can still fight lead the way. To their surprise they encounter no resistance. With the exception of a few observers, the rebels had withdrawn that night. The survivors of the defeated unit head back to Keetmanshoop.

Morenga rides a distance of sixty kilometers in darkness through mountainous terrain, later drawing praise from the German military for an outstanding accomplishment.

On the previous day Morris had taken up a position on favorable terrain near Garub as planned.

On 10 March, the advance guard of Koppy's detachment came under fire. Captain Koppy, a veteran Colonial Guard officer, convinced that the cliff emplacements could not be taken by storm, gave orders to make a wide swing to the West around the rebel position and roll it up from the rear. When Morris noticed the encircling maneuver, he ceased fighting and withdrew to a prepared position in the Naruda Ravine. If Morris had held his ground another hour, Morenga's plan would probably have succeeded. But as it was, Koppy's division reached the waterhole on schedule, bivouacked there that night in battle readiness, and marched on unopposed the next morning toward the Naruda Ravine. They had almost reached the southern entrance to the ravine when they observed a column or riders to the North advancing rapidly toward the ravine. It was presumably Kirchner's detachment.

Lieutenant von Gersdorff was sent out to make contact with Captain Kirchner. Through the field glasses they saw a rider break from the group and head toward Gersdorff. But before the two met, both Gersdorff and the other rider whirled around and galloped back to their respective units.

What had happened?

Gersdorff reported it wasn't Captain Kirchner, but Morenga and his men. Morenga himself had ridden out and at a hundred meters Gersdorff had recognized him; he was in his blue coat, wearing a white armband, with a Colonial Guard hat on his head.

Morenga must have thought he was approaching Morris and his men, who were of course withdrawing to just this position in the Naruda Ravine. By the time he was close enough to hail him, he must have realized it wasn't a rebel in a German uniform riding toward him, but a real German officer. Now a race began to see which group would reach the entrance to the ravine first; a steep slope which, occupied in sufficient force, would be as impregnable as a bastion. The Germans had a slight lead and managed to occupy a foothill the rebels had to pass to reach the ravine. The rebel horses raced into the rattling fire of the German detachment. Morenga leapt from his horse and, taking cover behind rocky outcrops and large boulders, led his men in a series of short rushes toward the ravine, the left side of which was already occupied by Morris. Ten or twenty minutes decided this skirmish, the battle, and perhaps the whole future of the protectorate. Morenga had not yet given up the fight. He took up position on a slight incline that offered scant cover. Captain Koppy immediately brought up his artillery and opened fire on the rebels' left flank. Around noon he ordered the infantry to advance. Under the concentrated fire of the artillery and infantry rifles, the first Hottentots abandoned the flank. Morenga attempted to stop his fleeing men and lead them forward again. The officers followed his blue coat with their field glasses as he made his way through a firestorm of grenade and stone splinters, with clods of earth from bursting shells raining down about him. His courage and personal bravery were singled out for special mention in the German General Staff report.

Perhaps Morenga might have established a second position further to the rear, in a more favorable terrain, and together with Morris's men, managed to close off the ravine and the water-hole. But in the early afternoon cannon fire was suddenly heard from the rear, and fleeing Hottentots reported that the major part of the German troops were approaching, the head of the column having almost reached the camp and the herds. For some unknown reason, Stürmann had arrived late and found Kai Gap, the western entrance to the Great Karas Mountains, already occupied. The rebels thus found it impossible to close off the entrance to the Great Karas Mountains, and Morenga's plan to defeat the Germans' entire southern division collapsed. While Kamptz's detachment began dismantling the cannons and machine guns to be carried by mule and donkey to the high plains, Stürmann gave orders to set fire to the dry grass of the steppes. This was intended to slow the advance of the German troops. The wind, however, soon changed direction and drove the fire toward the southeast. A wall of flame a meter high raced across the steppes. The following night the entire southeast horizon was still glowing red. The Germans pushed forward into the high mountain plains toward the Naruda Ravine, until they heard the thunder of cannons. Two companies were sent forward at quick march. When the report arrived that the Germans had appeared from the rear and they were in danger of being surrounded by a superior force, a number of the rebels attempted to move their women, children, and cattle northward to safety. Captain von Koppy, who could tell from the cannon fire in the east that the division under Kamptz was advancing on that side, ordered an attack around four that afternoon. The Hottentots slowly withdrew, with Morenga constantly pausing in the rocky terrain and offering stubborn resistance so the cattle, whose lowing echoed from the ravine, could be driven off. The flight turned to panic as the artillery from Kamptz's division opened fire on the ravine from the north. Yet the rebels managed to escape, although they lost the major part of their livestock. Fifty horses, seven hundred cattle, and seven thousand small stock were captured by the Germans.

The offensive in the Great Karas Mountains was over: the rebels were driven out, but not, as General von Trotha had ordered, destroyed.

The experience when the Witbois were driven from their homes was now repeated: with the loss of their cattle and compounds, the rebels became more mobile, more independent, and fought in smaller groups. Deimling discovered this on his way back to Keetmanshoop; his troops were attacked on several occasions by small bands of guerillas, leaving numerous dead and wounded on the German side. Morenga himself was shot in the hip and seriously wounded during one of these skirmishes.

Colonel Deimling was relieved of duty immediately upon his return to Keetmanshoop and was already on his way home by 2 April. The defeat of Kirchner's detachment precluded any reference to victory with regard to the offensive, and upon later reflection it became clear that Deimling's success in driving out the rebels was due not to his strategic skill, or to the strength of the German troops, but to chance timing. The entire southern division had barely avoided a military catastrophe.

There were colonial officers who maintained that Morenga had studied Clausewitz. It was at least conceivable. In addition to Nama, Herero, Afrikaans, and English, Morenga also spoke fluent German.

There is a photograph that shows him with his lieutenants. We don't know when it was taken, possibly just prior to the major German offensive in the Great Karas Mountains. The photo is, regrettably, of poor quality, blurred and overexposed. It is reminiscent of those photos of Che Guevara in the Bolivian jungle, with their harsh contrasts of black and white. The group is standing in a row on the steppes. Four men to Morenga's right and four to his left, he's a head taller than any of them. As far as one can judge, all of them are gazing into the camera with serious expressions from beneath their broad-brimmed hats. They are captured Colonial Guard hats. In addition they are wearing what was called in military jargon outlaw gear: jackets, under them—at least in Morenga's case—a vest, and white shirts (probably from German officers' kits). A few have tied scarves around their necks. One of them is wearing a German officer's jacket. As is apparent from the sleeves, it's much too big for him. They've propped their guns on the ground, modern army rifles, 88's, captured in battle. For ammunition belts they're wearing the usual Colonial Guard belts with shell pauches.

The group stands ready for the souvenir photo. Morenga has a pipe in his mouth. His trousers have a tear in the left knee.

Did an English journalist from the *Cape Times* take this photo? The newspaper reported at length on affairs in the German colony and was sympathetic toward the rebels. Did a reporter meet Morenga on the English border or visit him in secret in the rebel area? Or was it an amateur photo? Perhaps a rebel found the camera in the baggage from Kirchner's division, and a man who once had to carry his white master's camera took the picture.

In a chest found among the equipment left strewn over the battlefield by Kirchner's division, the rebels discovered the diary of the fallen Lieutenant, Edward Fürbringer. Morenga continued this diary in English, from his own perspective. An uneven, distinctive script in pencil, entirely without punctuation. At times there are breaks in the lines, as if they are being written on horseback.

10th [1905]

Arrived at the Klipdam on the 10th the Bondels fired a few shots as a salute slaughtered an ox brought me coffee with salt and milk served me meat in a lid of a billycan

another patrol arrived at Klipdam with Commandant Hendrick behind I saw this day how a man can make substitutes they pulled out
nails from the doors and boards in the house and filed them and shod
the horses with them and they answered the purpose very well the
Bondles are busy making Veltschoons

13.2. 1905

a patrol sent out to Witkrance captured Boer and cattle belonging to a
man named Jekner the man Jekner fled over the line with his rifle the
Bondles said he murdered women and children at Kactchanas in cold
blood they got ammunition from the Boer which he burried there was
also a man named Esau with his family there at the time

Kactchanas 10.3.05

the Bondels fought the germans at Kactchanas the bondels meant to
fight on a narrow pass but they delayed to long and allowed the germans to come to the level country but laid and waited the germans
ride up one was in advance the Bondels fired on the man then the germans stormed but was driven back with heavy loss by a book which
was captured there from a German 110 one hundred and ten was
killed besides the wounded the bondles captured a maxim the Germans fled that night

Morenga's diary was confiscated by the Cape police when he
crossed the English frontier. It was later passed on to Lieutenant
Fürbringer's father in his son's memory. Unfortunately the diary
itself has disappeared. Only a few pages reproduced photographi-
cally in 1910 have come down to us.

The unusual thing about these notes is that Morenga describes only the Bondels fighting, not himself or others. But the
few reports and documents we have today speak only of
Morenga's fate and that of a few rebel leaders. The others remain
anonymous, and appear in the reports merely as numbers, except for a rare name, a verdict.

Morenga, whose name is mentioned for the first time with

regard to the Bondels revolt of 1903, seems to have worked previously in the copper mines of O'okiep. He must have gained his
advanced level of education, so admired by the Germans, at a
missionary school. It's said that he was taken along to Europe by
a missionary, and to Germany. Perhaps he stood at the railing of
a steamer as Missionary Gorth envisioned it fifty years earlier:
tall, calm, and self-confident.

Try to imagine it: Morenga standing before the staging of a
shipyard, or watching the pioneers drill in Altona.

After Colonel Deimling's military offensive had failed, General
von Trotha tried in early April to quell the rebellion in the far
south by negotiation. Captain von Koppy's parliamentary report
not only describes the rebel situation, but also relates details of
a remarkable meeting between a titled German officer and a
rebel Kaffir:

> "On the morning of 24 April 1905, accompanied by Father Mali-
> nowski, Sergeant Schütze, and my native servant Omar, I set out for the
> Hottentot camp, after Father Malinowski's native boy had informed
> Morenga that we were on our way. At Omar's request, I had abandoned
> my original intention to arm myself for the visit, which proved fortu-
> nate, since the Hottentots at the camp told Omar they would have shot
> us had we arrived armed. While still some distance from the Hottentot
> camp a patrol of natives joined us as escorts. When we arrived at
> Morenga's camp I was able to confirm Malinowski's report on the
> enemy's situation and ascertain that the Hottentots were armed with
> modern breechloaders and apparently had a large store of ammunition.
> We left our horses and followed a fairly difficult footpath past several
> emplacements to the camp. Morenga, who has a difficult time walking
> because of his wound, came riding toward me, while the armed Hot-
> tentots pressed closely around us, some of them begging for tobacco.
> Without paying any further attention to the Hottentots I seated myself
> and remained intentionally seated as Morenga, who quickly dispersed
> those crowding about, approached. It was not until he greeted me and I
> saw it was clearly difficult for him to stand that I permitted him to seat

himself, then informed him of the purpose of my visit and the pro-
posed conditions headquarters had indicated for his surrender. Once
Morenga had heard me out, he replied that he understood, but that for
a decision of this magnitude he must first confer with his lieutenants
and Hans Hendrik, the Habobe who had been staying with him since
Hendrik's defeat at the hands of Major von Lengerke. Within twenty-
four hours he would send the messenger I had dispatched from Warmbad back to Major von Kamptz's camp with news of the results of the
conference.

I explained to Morenga he must realize the Hottentots would be
defeated in the long run, and that further resistance would only
worsen their situation, to which Morenga replied that he knew perfectly well the Hottentots would perish in the struggle, but the decision to continue fighting was not his alone, since he was not captain
of the Bondels. I had the impression Morenga no longer retained the
full respect of his people, nor his power over them. Not only has his
fame in battle, and the Hottentots' faith that all undertakings under
his leadership would be successful, been shaken by the events of last
March, but his weakened physical condition has damaged his standing
with the Hottentots. All questions of success aside, Morenga's spiritual superiority over other native leaders in this colonial war is evident
in the unique fact that, in spite of their boundless disregard for other
natives, they willingly submit to the leadership of a Damara Bastard.
Such power, which only hereditary chiefs have otherwise, is shaken
the moment his followers begin to lose their unconditional faith in
their leader's lucky star and the certainty of victory is undermined.

I sensed that Hendrik April, the leader of Bondels living in the
Karas Mountains, had gained considerable influence in Morenga's
camp. The cattle lost at Naruda directly affected Morenga and his
men, whereas April's family still had considerable livestock, so it was
only natural that Hendrik April and his followers were the major opponents of unconditional surrender.

At the conclusion of our negotiations I set out for Major von
Kamptz's camp. I must admit it was not easy to pass calmly through
armed Hottentots I felt had no intention of surrendering, but I rode
off slowly without looking back. There seemed little danger Morenga

would break faith, but it seemed all too likely that someone opposed to surrender might put an end to further negotiations by accidentally discharging a gun. The messenger I had dispatched from Warmbad arrived at Major von Kamptz's camp the following day and reported that the Hottentots had conferred for several hours, then broken camp and withdrawn to an unknown destination."

DOCTOR OTTO HAS TO TELL JOKES

Gottschalk arrived at Kalkfontein on foot.

The day after Koppy's detachment left Warmbad Captain Koppy had personally ordered Gottschalk to turn his horse over to a sergeant: veterinarians should keep horses in good spirits and spare them unnecessary burdens.

Although urged to do so, Gottschalk had not volunteered for a squad saddling up to capture and interrogate a few Hottentot women who fled when they saw the column.

After all, you've had some intercourse with them in the past, Koppy said wittily.

Gottschalk was marching in Lieutenant Hunger's infantry division along with military bakers, cartwrights, orderlies, and staff trumpeters. The men handled their guns gingerly, as if they might go off at any moment. They were going to attack Morenga with full force. He and his band would be surrounded and destroyed.

While still in Warmbad, Captain Koppy said to Gottschalk, now you can show what you're made of, and blinked at him with his little drunken tapir eyes. Gottschalk couldn't see what was so funny about this, but it made all the officers standing around break into whinnies of laughter.

Gottschalk had followed the advice of a veteran infantry sergeant and purchased two baby diapers in Germany to use as foot pads in case he ever had to march. Nevertheless, by the time the column reached Kalkfontein, his feet were raw.

We'll soon bend you back into shape, Lieutenant von Gersdorff said as he ordered Gottschalk to report to him each evening in

field uniform. So Gottschalk stood at attention in a brushed uniform and necktie as Gersdorff droned: Well, we're getting there,
although he continued to complain about Gottschalk's termite-
chewed coattails. Gottschalk struggled for composure, thinking,
I can't stand any more, I can't stand any more, while the rage
built, the hate, so that sometimes it seemed there was no room
left for it. And less than an arm's length away this face, the disproportionately small head on the disproportionately long body,
the long legs, arms, everything had turned out too long, except
the head, everything about the head had turned out too small, the
narrow nose, the mouth, the ears seemingly made of paper, glued
to the thin brownish hair.

Gersdorff inquired whether a veterinarian could be chained
to a wagon in disciplinary cases like an ordinary soldier. Since
no legal counsel was available, Koppy decided this should only
be in cases involving assault on a superior officer.

Gottschalk's diary,
4 March 1905

On the gestures of masters and the facial expressions of power.
In this country they are seen most clearly at their extremes. The most
primitive form: the kick in the backside. But one doesn't like to dirty
one's boots. That's left to N.C.O.s.

Finer, sublimated forms one no longer notices back home, because one is used to them: How one gestures with the right hand
while holding the riding crop loosely in the left. Instead of looking
subordinates in the eye, one glances at the cap rim, up and slightly
past it.

What kept Gottschalk from some rash act like smashing his fist
against the little mouth in Lieutenant von Gersdorff's little face,
was that he knew why Gersdorff was dressing him down. Not
because he had refused to hunt down Hottentot women for interrogation, but because Gersdorff suspected he might have preferred the company of Hottentots to the officers' mess in Warmbad. But there he had been under the drunken protection of

Count Kageneck, who, as Gersdorff put it, kept a few such whores himself, while here they would show him what it meant to get involved with brown riffraff. (Gersdorff: So, how are the Hottentots doing these days?)

Once, after explaining the principle of vaccination to prisoners, Gottschalk had gone for a walk outside the village with a young Nama woman named Katharina. Piles of black stones lay scattered about the slightly hilly landscape like huge mounds of coal. Further on they sat down in the dry steppe grass. The strange thing was that when he put his arm around Katharina on an impulse, he thought of Captain Moll, who raved about the Hottentot women and their wild fucking. Gottschalk tried to push the memory aside and concentrate on something else, but there was that word tittyfuck in his head again, and suddenly he was disgusted with himself and turned abruptly from the girl. Then Katharina put her arm around him and whispered his favorite sentence in Nama in his ear: The midnight-mouse flies through the steppes of red clouds.

Katharina exuded a smell that Gottschalk seemed to remember from childhood, returning home as a boy in the evening, the smell of earth, sun, and wind. The smell of dirt, his mother said, but she had no sense of smell. Dirt, Gottschalk now felt, was just a prejudice of those who never quite succeeded in life.

Katharina and Gottschalk often walked out to the hill after that. And Gottschalk no longer thought of Captain Moll. But each time they lay down in the grass, a strange sense of unease came over him. He couldn't help thinking about the scorpions that often hid under rocks in this region, and he saw them creep out, stirred up by the disturbance, their terrible stingers curved forward to strike.

There is only one reference to Katharina in Gottschalk's diary.

Gottschalk's diary,
28 February 1905

Rain this morning. Around noon the sun broke through. The valley was steaming. I'm going to the hill. It strikes me as odd that she asks to smoke my pipe.

She told me her dream from the night before: she lay fast asleep beneath a wild currant bush. The sun was shining. Then a small desert fox came and drank from her breast. That woke her and she was happy, but cried.

The palmcrist is in bloom.

Around this time Gottschalk began brooding over a question that he knew he couldn't answer solely by thinking about it, but only by doing something; but what that action should be tormented him.

He no longer asked himself if the war was unjust. He was now convinced it was, and there were times when he felt it like a physical pain. In his diary he called the war a terrible injustice. Whenever a native was flogged (a task they enjoyed assigning him to oversee as a veterinarian) his stomach lurched with the urge to vomit. He could only watch if he'd had a few drinks. A veteran troop doctor tried to console him: It's all just a matter of getting used to it. But the thought of getting used to it some day was what frightened him.

Gottschalk's diary,
(undated)

A crust of army bread saves only one person. The art of vaccination is taught to those who will be shot through the head tomorrow. The wonderful symmetry of the brain, where friendliness and experience are stored, is destroyed by the path of a bullet. What stops us (me) from opposing such destruction.

One cannot half decide.

Gottschalk was familiar with the debate over what should be done with the native rebels after the victory. There were suggestions to export them and their families to East Africa, where they could work on plantations. In any case they would relocate the tribes within the protectorate, and the women and men would be used for forced labor. It gradually became clear to Gottschalk that these people were fighting for their survival as human beings.

Wenstrup's marginal notation in Kropotkin's *Mutual Aid: A Factor of Evolution*.

German philistines are wrong in thinking that morality is based on good intentions; it is based instead on living conditions.

One evening Gottschalk asked Dr. Haring, who was pulling on gym tights, if he didn't agree that what was happening in this country was a terrible injustice. Haring stood in the room headless, a striped sack, until his head popped into view. Isn't what we're doing unchristian? (Haring was a practicing Protestant). What a question, Haring said, whipping his bent arms back. But then, after lacing up his soft goat-leather gym shoes, with the veterinarian so far out of step, and seeming odder all the time, he tried to set him straight. Who started the war? Who murdered the soldiers, missionaries, farmers, and women? One thing must be kept clearly in mind: the other side didn't share Gottschalk's scruples—even if he had to admit he did himself at times—the rebels had no such scruples. That was precisely their strength. This lack of pity, this desperate courage, yes desperate, for that was the central fact in this war, that these people, as human beings, yes he used the term deliberately, as human beings, couldn't help but see that the Germans were superior to them, that hard work, knowledge, and careful preparations resulted in more and more land falling into the hands of the German settlers, even without the use of military force. You could see it in this Hottentot economy. The very phrase was a joke.

They considered laziness a virtue. And what was happening now in this struggle was totally natural, yes, that's right, natural. The law of the survival of the fittest could be seen everywhere. Kill or be killed. From the native point of view the revolt probably made sense. Of course that very revolt, and this was the paradox of history, was speeding their final decline. The weak die off so the strong will have more room and light. That was the only way things could evolve onward and upward. The struggle for existence was the basic law of life.

On this occasion, Gottschalk brought the Russian prince and anarchist Kropotkin into the conversation, not by name, which would have meant nothing to Haring, but by referring to mutual aid as an additional principle of Nature. The struggle for existence was not the only important factor, mutual aid within the species was equally important. Exactly, responded Haring, within the species, and twirled his arms about like windmills.

There were examples, Gottschalk said, in which mutual aid extended beyond a particular species. He once read of a case in which a Greek sailor tumbled into the sea from a yardarm. After swimming for several hours, the man felt his strength failing and would have sunk, had he not suddenly felt something rough yet soft against him, and all at once he was lifted up and the smell of fish hit him. He was surrounded by a school of dolphins, who carried him in turns on their backs, lifting him above the water as they did to their own kind when they were tired and having difficulty breathing. For hours he was borne through the Mediterranean in this manner, until an English yachtsman noticed him and pulled him on board.

How odd, said Haring, dusting his palms with talcum powder. And yet he was convinced one law was valid: you're either the anvil or the hammer. It was a universal law: the will to power. Everything else was philanthropy. But that accomplished nothing.

Gottschalk raced after Haring to justify himself, of course he wasn't in favor of a ceasefire, on the contrary. But Haring had already leaped onto the horizontal bar and was revolving about, straight as a candle, wheeling in a giant circle against the setting sun.

On the morning of 6 March, Koppy's division set out from Kalkfontein. They were headed straight into battle. Gottschalk marched with aching feet in the division's dust, his tongue furry, and wondered for the first time why he'd never thought of taking off. (He used this somewhat indirect phrase instead of desertion). But the thought seemed as absurd as it was risky. Where would he go? To South Africa? To America or Argentina? All he had to do was go behind a bush for a piss and he could escape from the troops. They might not even bother to look for him. But then what? He'd be alone in a waterless land, a moving target for the rebels.

That evening, after reporting to Gersdorff, Gottschalk crouched beside the bivouac fire mumbling to himself. One would have thought he'd finally cracked up. But in fact he was trying to work out how to ask the way to the English frontier in Nama. Not that he was seriously considering taking off. Instead he was playing with the possibility, even though he told himself it was farfetched. As he did so it became clear for the first time that he'd been learning the wrong phrases in Nama the past few weeks, bombastic words and sentences larded with clicks that made him a linguistic acrobat, but which couldn't even get him to the English border. The tea rose jackal smokes his black Havana in a cave of dreams!

When they marched into Kalkfontein, Gottschalk thought he saw Jakobus among the prisoners. The boy hopped his way forward. His feet and hands had been bound with a rope, and a noose had been tied neatly around his neck with the end. A bowline hitch as good as any Gottschalk's grandfather could have fashioned. Gottschalk almost called out hello. He would have liked to know what Wenstrup was doing, and whether he'd reached the English border.

He looks funny, like a frog, someone commented.

Zeisse sat down beside Gottschalk. Zeisse was riding Gottschalk's horse now. They gave it to him when he volunteered for the patrol, he said apologetically. Too bad he couldn't finish the gate for the district office. It was still missing a few bars with heraldic lilies. The thought of catching a Hottentot bullet now, of biting the grass before he'd finished the gate, bothered him more than anything.

An old German saying, but it doesn't make much sense here, Gottschalk thought, biting the grass, in a land with nothing but sand and stones.

In Warmbad, Gottschalk brooded over the fact that one's thoughts and words often failed to match the landscape, like pieces of luggage that proved impractical once they had been dragged along. For a time Gottschalk had the crazy idea of learning a new thought form from the landscape and the natives, one that would help him see everything differently, more profoundly, more clearly.

Zeisse explained his plan. He wanted to sign up again, become a sergeant and put his money on the shelf long enough to become a master smith and open a blacksmith's shop near Bardowick.

When Zeisse talked, the sentences crept from his mouth like toads, not because he spoke so little, for he was indeed rather talkative, but because the words came forth so slowly and hesitantly.

Gottschalk rolled up in his horse blanket. Above him hung the moon, like a fat round cheese. His rifle was within easy reach beside him, with the safety off. Two nights earlier, a lance corporal had thrashed about in his sleep during a dream and set off his rifle, shattering his right ankle. Any suspicion of self-mutilation was rejected by Dr. Haring once he amputated the foot, since experience showed almost all self-mutilations were flesh wounds that wouldn't cause permanent damage.

In Windhoek Gottschalk once asked Wenstrup if he thought it made sense to try to plan one's life. Wenstrup didn't think so, at least as far as he was concerned. Plans ran the danger of being too rigid. They killed all spontaneity and led too quickly toward old age. He hardly thought about the future at all and had no idea what would become of him. The thought of already knowing that one day he would be married with three children, returning home with a briefcase, repelled him. Gottschalk felt exposed. For a moment he thought Wenstrup had been reading his diary. But then he told himself that wasn't Wenstrup's style.

Now Gottschalk sometimes felt like he'd wandered into someone else's story.

Gottschalk's diary,
8 March 1905

> I dreamed I was clinging to an empty herring barrel, floating in an icy North Sea. A huge seagull with steel eyes sat on the bobbing barrel, pecking at my hands. I had to keep jerking my hands away then immediately grab hold of the barrel again as it revolved in the water. I was afraid the seagull might think my fingers were fish. And when I looked, my fingers actually were fish.

Gottschalk was disappointed by the battle at Garub. Over the last few days, as he marched along through the sand, his feet smarting, Gottschalk constantly imagined shots suddenly ringing out at the head of the column, shots that would abruptly end the strain and harassment he had been suffering.

After all, Gersdorff made a splendid target on his tall dun. All they had to do was let him get within a hundred yards and they couldn't miss. His narrow nose would bury itself in the mud, the hat he wore cocked so jauntily over his right ear would fly in a great arc to the ground.

The path led through a valley. Two crests pressed toward each other, intersected by the now dry riverbed. Shots suddenly rang out ahead. Koppy had his men dismount and form a line. The artillery was brought up. A cavalry troop with a mountain gun were sent to outflank the Hottentots on their right. Soon thereafter the rebels evacuated the hill. Only once, high up on the hill, Gottschalk saw a small figure, just for a moment, which then disappeared between the rocks. A final shot rang out. Then nothing. No deaths, no injuries. Gersdorff galloped by. Gottschalk was, as noted above, disappointed in Morenga, who had simply cleared off without a fight.

Captain von Koppy was convinced it was only an advance guard. The thick end of the stick was yet to come. He gave out instructions for the next day. They would break camp while it was still dark the next morning and head for the Naruda Ravine, where Morenga's men had set up camp. They would smoke them out of their lair. Three further detachments under Colonel Deimling would also advance against them. A concentric action, surround and destroy. The officers sat hunched over the maps. There were complicated logistical problems to solve, distances to be estimated, salient geographical features on the maps to be compared, sketched in by hand. In the end all four detachments would arrive simultaneously at the ravine. Unaffected by the hectic atmosphere, Koppy lay on a blanket, leaning back against a boulder, drinking the first-class rum he had brought along. He knew this region almost as well as Morenga, whom he held to be a man of honor.

The following day, on the morning of 11 March 1905, a battle ensued in the Naruda Ravine. There is only one reference to it in Gottschalk's diary, entered two days later:

Gottschalk's diary,
13 March 1905
(in the Great Karas Mountains)

Morenga on a white horse. Almost everyone saw him. Then the assault on the ravine. Lieutenant von Eberstein called it a baptism by fire. In such a baptism stone splinters are more dangerous than the bullets. When the first wounded arrived, I was ordered to report to the dressing station, where doctors Otto, Haring, and Clemm were already busily at work. I held the chloroform mask. They carried in a man from the railway battalion who'd been shot in the lower abdomen and was trying to push his intestines back in with his hands. Vultures circling overhead. Someone on morphine raving about cyclamen. Otto and Haring: good, quick craftsmen. Otto, a medical captain, but very unmilitary, told jokes to the wounded. Haring attempted to comfort a trooper whose right leg was going to be amputated by saying the Fatherland would look after its heroes. It still took two medics to hold him down. I pushed the chloroform mask down on his face.

Even such harsh animals as the rats, which continually fight in our cellars, are sufficiently intelligent not to quarrel when they plunder our larders, but to aid one another in their plundering expeditions and migrations, and even to feed their invalids. (Kropotkin)

While the rebels withdrew northward into the Great Karas Mountains, leaving behind their cattle and huts, while the two detachments under Koppy and Kamptz met as planned at the western outlet of the Naruda Ravine, while Captain Koppy, drunk and exhausted, dismounted to report to a sober but bitter Colonel Deimling, while troopers searched for hidden rebels, poking about with their bayonets among the pondoks, and in fact finding two youngsters with their poking, while the troops spread out and searched the surrounding countryside, while four men raped a Hottentot woman behind a thorn bush, while the heavens turned orange as they usually did at that time of day, when Lieutenant Haring at last managed to lay down his scalpel, Captain Otto told his last joke, Gersdorff took a swig from his bottle, Zeisse filled his pipe, after all this had happened, Gottschalk decided to give some sign, to take some action against this human torture, to do something to break through this indifference, this internal frost in the midst of the singeing heat, in himself, but in the others too, something that might restore the balance that had been lost. For a moment Gottschalk considered shooting the colonel with his bird-dog face; madness, he told himself at once, since nothing would change. Someone else would take his place immediately, probably Major von Kamptz, who also resembled an animal, Gottschalk couldn't think which one. Nothing would change. There was a steady drumming in his skull that he told himself came from running up hills at this altitude. Then he realized it must be the cannons. Once he thought he saw Katharina among those fleeing through the valley. He longed to take off, join those fleeing in the valley below, still being fired on with shrapnel: women, men, children, cattle, goats, and sheep, a confused melee. He had no idea what he could possibly do down there at that moment, but joining the enemy, who had dug in further back to protect those who were fleeing, seemed a way to expunge all the humiliations and wounds. His mind was filled with turmoil, and he ran aimlessly about the terrain.

That stuck in his memory, and above all, an image of the gun crews with open mouths and their fingers in their ears, as if they wanted to scream or sing but not hear what they were singing. In the valley small puffs of smoke could be seen where the shells were exploding in the air, raining down shrapnel on the fleeing.

Later Gottschalk was ordered to report to headquarters.

An officer on Deimling's staff asked how a Veterinary Lieutenant came to be hoofing it through the countryside. Gottschalk had no answer to this, but none was expected. He and another veterinarian were assigned to look after captured livestock. If the military operation had failed, and Morenga had escaped with the rebels, at least the cattle could be driven back to Keetmanshoop. Gottschalk was ordered to choose one of the captured horses and saddle up.

At the kraal where the Hottentot horses had been rounded up, Gottschalk met Captain Tresckow, with a fine chestnut gelding which had been caught and brought to him, one he claimed belonged to the fallen Major von Nollendorf. Tresckow slapped Gottschalk on the back in a friendly manner and said he'd see him later, he had to get back to the front. In spite of the general rush and brevity, Gottschalk noticed that Tresckow was missing something: his riding crop.

Tresckow had indeed lost his hand-woven leather crop with the lighter in the handle during a skirmish on patrol three weeks earlier. More precisely, he had tossed it down after his horse had been shot out from under him and the riding crop was slowing him up as he fled. He ran from the enemy, something he never thought he would do, darting back and forth like a rabbit. And he had no scruples about doing so—another thing he had considered unthinkable up to now. Everything about this Hottentot war was topsy-turvy: ancient and honorable rules, valid, time-honored conventions, good manners, even the Prussian code of honor, were rendered null and void. Unlike any conceivable war in Europe, this was a revolt against time-honored values. And when, disheveled and exhausted, Tresckow finally made his way back to the troops, he wondered aloud why anyone would let himself be shot by this brown riff-raff for the sake of honor, when these chaps spat on such notions.

Of course the thought of some Hottentot lout now comfortably lighting a pipe with his gold lighter, while he himself had to rummage around in his pocket for a light if he wanted to smoke a Rose of Hildesheim with its famous Sumatra wrap and Java interior, rankled him no end.

Gottschalk picked out a white horse from among those wheeling anxiously about in the kraal, powerful and well-built, with a sword brand Gottschalk had never seen before. The horse still wore a German army saddle and had belonged to Lieutenant Schmidt, who had fallen at Alurisfontein. The saddlebags contained two plugs of tobacco, a short-stemmed pipe and a bar of soap.

What's a Hottentot doing with soap, asked the sergeant who searched the saddlebags. The horse must have broken away from the rebels and run back and forth between the front lines until we captured it.

The woebegone Deimling would have claimed this horse for himself at once had he known that Morenga had been sitting on it a few hours earlier. As orders were being issued, Deimling was brooding over whether to go on immediate leave, after all he had sprained his left arm falling from his horse. Or should he wait to see what the general staff in Berlin said about the offensive? Perhaps Morenga would run straight into Kirchner's guns. Although it was strange, even disturbing, that nothing had been seen of

Kirchner. He must know the old military rule of thumb, especially as an artillery officer, head toward the thunder of cannon. If
Kirchner had arrived on time, he could have surrounded Morenga
and finished him off. The operation that seemed so bold to Deimling would have been a major military victory. But the thought
that Kirchner had been ambushed didn't bear thinking about.
Deimling decided to apply for leave immediately upon reaching
Keetmanshoop. He gave orders to break off the pursuit of
Morenga. The rebels had disappeared again without a trace in the
vast landscape. Surrounded by his staff, Deimling saw a veterinarian swing onto a white horse and gallop off in the direction of
the ravine, where the Hottentot cattle were milling about. A fine
animal, that white horse, Deimling said. It's ridiculous, thought
Deimling, so much effort, cost, and energy—and in the end one
leaves with a herd of sheep and cattle. Deimling knew how
Napoleon must felt with Moscow burning around him.

Gottschalk christened the white horse, who was nervously
champing at the bit, Ear-Cloud.

Lieutenant Haring had volunteered for Erckert's detachment,
which was ordered to head north and find Kirchner. Haring had
been keeping a daily diary since he left Germany, making entries with tireless zeal, even on days when he spent fourteen
hours at the operating table, extracting bullets from flesh, ampu-
tating feet, legs, and arms. In addition he wrote daily postcards
and letters to former fellow students, professors, colleagues,
aunts, uncles, brothers-in-law, sisters-in-law, but mostly to his
wife, constantly reminding her to be sure and keep all his letters, since they were after all documents of an era, going so
far as to warn her that any given letter might be his last, since
these rebels showed no respect, even for the Red Cross. Haring
felt he was bearing witness to important historical events.
He comforted the wounded with Goethe's phrase: *Später könnt
ihr sagen, ihr seid debeigewesen*—Later you can say you were
there.

Doctor Haring's letter to his wife, 25 March 1905

Dearest!

On the nineteenth of this month we arrived at the spot where Kirchner's detachment was attacked. It was clear even from a distance that something had happened, for vultures and other birds of carrion circled overhead. When we drew near, we beheld a gruesome sight. A dead comrade lies half covered with dirt, another poorly buried, a hand, its flesh eaten away, thrusts up from the earth, not far off lie chewed limbs and the bodies of the fallen, dug up by the jackals. A few of the dead, stripped of their uniforms by the natives, apparently couldn't be buried due to enemy fire. They lay where they fell. On the side of a hill we find the brave Captain Kirchner, who was not robbed of his uniform, no doubt less out of respect for the enemy than because the uniform was soaked with blood. He was a tall, heavy-set man (shot in the stomach). Dead mules, horses, and oxen lie scattered about. Broken boxes of meal, rum bottles with their necks simply knocked off. Letters and newspapers strewn over the battlefield. Birds of carrion perch on the surrounding cliffs, waiting for the opportunity to continue their meal. In the air a sickening odor of decay. The scene fills us with horror, and we carry out our sad duty in silence, preparing a final resting place for the dead.

The noose is finally tightening around Morenga and his band, and once we have them, peace and tranquility will return to this land.

By night I lie beneath the open sky, the Southern Cross above me, and think of you, dearest, and the children.

Warmest greetings to you all!

The captured livestock were to be driven to Keetmanshoop by Kamptz's detachment. They departed on 18 March. Gottschalk had given orders to divide the animals into smaller herds, to be watched by natives, who in turn would be watched by German troopers. Gottschalk requested that Zeisse, a farm worker's son and blacksmith accustomed to handling animals, be assigned to him personally, and Captain von Koppy agreed.

Word soon got around that Captain von Tresckow had slapped Gottschalk on the back and conversed with the veterinarian in a comradely fashion, had been almost friendly in fact. And the Colonel had praised Gottschalk's horse. Perhaps there were relationships and associations no one had suspected. When Gottschalk took leave of Captain Koppy, the latter blinked at him with his tapir eyes and said that Gottschalk had fought valiantly, and that he would recommend him for a medal.

Eight weeks later, Gottschalk found out he hadn't been joking. In Keetmanshoop he received news one day that His Majesty the Kaiser had awarded him the military medal, 2nd class.

Major Maercker, who delivered the medal and certificate to a nonplussed Gottschalk that morning, was not of course prepared to take both back later that afternoon. Maercker thought Gottschalk was just being overly modest, but when Gottschalk insisted he not only didn't want the medal, but wished to have the award itself retracted, the Major turned gruff. He couldn't take back a medal simply on the whim of the person decorated. What reason could he give? Gottschalk said he hadn't earned the medal and therefore rejected it on principle. Maercker dismissed Gottschalk with the remark that he was being refractory. Gottschalk thought of Wenstrup. He had also been called refractory. He decided to sleep on it and reconsider his action carefully.

The next evening, returning from duty, he turned up the wick on the oil lamp and composed a petition addressed to the commander of the Colonial Guard requesting that the award of the military medal, 2nd class, be retracted.

No one in Windhoek felt this was within his jurisdiction. Once awarded, was it actually possible to retract a medal? Gottschalk, who eventually returned his medal and certificate to the General Headquarters of the Colonial Guard in Berlin, received both back by registered mail four months later, with a preprinted form: Complaints with regard to decorations, etc. etc., should be submitted to the Battalion Commander.

At that point he gave up.

• • •

The captured livestock being driven to Keetmanshoop lacked both water and sufficient food. The few water-holes were emptied by the first hundred animals. The others milled about lowing thirstily. Major von Kamptz pushed on, wanted to clear out of the blind passage through the Karas Mountains as quickly as possible. Gottschalk worried that this would endanger the livestock captured by Colonel Deimling. At that pace, scarcely half would arrive alive in Keetmanshoop. Kamptz, involved in a personal feud with Deimling, said let them die, better a dead ox than a dead trooper. (Deimling had dressed him down once in front of the entire staff: Your detachment has fallen behind again, get them back up front, damn it, or do you have some problem, etc.)

Riding along beside the herd, the horizon crowded with bellowing, bleating, mooing, lowing creatures, Gottschalk felt like a cowboy and sometimes like a cattle rustler. He caught himself whistling, once he even broke into song. The memory of the battle caused him to fall silent again each time like a prick of conscience, the brief moment when he'd had the mad notion of joining the enemy. Now he considered that a fantasy of his overheated imagination. But that didn't make the memory any less disturbing.

A rift had opened between his actions and his thoughts. At times he felt that the person spurring his horse, giving orders, overseeing the drivers, was different from the one observing and reflecting on it all. What comforted him, what bound the two parts of his being together, was that for the moment one thing remained: his duty. But then he recalled that he was helping maintain the circulatory system of force and terror, for the natives lived on the flesh and milk of these animals, and would now fight with even greater desperation.

And in fact the detachment was attacked several times by smaller bands of rebels. There were deaths and injuries, and Doctor Otto had to tell jokes again.

Tresckow and Gottschalk would talk now and then as they rode along. Tresckow said he had pictured the war down here quite differently. He thought they were defending the Fatherland, but in point of fact it was the Hottentots who were defending their Fatherland. Sometimes he asked himself what he was doing here. What sort of campaign is chasing off the enemy's oxen, shooting their women and children, and burning their homes?

After the column emerged from the mountains into softly rolling hills, Gottschalk finally had time to mentally concoct a set of cow dentures. There is nothing in his diary at this period that points toward desertion; instead there are increasingly numerous sketches of various sorts of devices a dentist could clamp firmly and painlessly to the cow's jaw.

That evening, when the troops had bivouacked, Gottschalk sat in the saddle enjoying the grilled meat now readily available, and told Zeisse his idea for dentures. There was no good reason to slaughter a healthy cow that gave good milk just because it had lost a tooth, although he realized this hectic pace was killing more cows than had been lost in the last ten years due to broken teeth.

Zeisse pointed out that iron would rust easily, particularly in a cow's mouth; steel would work better for dentures, stainless steel would be best, but you wouldn't find any down here. Whereas you could get high-quality steel. All you had to do was find a fragment from a cannon barrel that had backfired and exploded. Then you could file it down into a tooth. It would be a long and tedious job, but there was plenty of time. You'd need a steel saw and a vise.

Around this time Gottschalk felt pressure in his stomach after meals, at times even nausea, but was unable to vomit. At first he thought he had eaten something toxic, then reminded himself that steaks were cut fresh from the ribs of the slaughtered oxen and grilled immediately. Three days later he went to Otto, the staff doctor. Gottschalk took off his jacket and shirt and stretched out on the ground. Otto felt along his ribs with the tips of his fingers, pressing on his stomach, and said, take a deep breath. Do you know the difference between a Hottentot and an Austrian, he asked, then broke off the joke and said: Gastritis, perhaps an ulcer. You'd best eat gruel. And don't get so worked up. After all, those aren't your cattle you're driving.

Later Gottschalk recalled how he lay on the stony ground with Dr. Otto beside him, pressing the tips of his fingers into his stomach, and the sharp pain he felt when he inhaled.

He could have simply put himself on the sick list and gone home. But strangely enough the easy way out was not possible for him; the mere thought of it seemed shameful, to run off like that. Gottschalk felt a certain pride that prevented him from making compromises. But what is pride? In any case Gottschalk firmly rejected the possibility.

He rode through a landscape that only a few weeks ago had inspired him, but now left him cold. He was thinking how to get gruel in Keetmanshoop.

Once, when he turned in the saddle and looked back, he saw the violet peak of Karas Mountain on the horizon. It seemed like a stage set that could be folded and put away at any moment.

That night, before reaching Keetmanshoop, an artillery officer rushed up to the doctor, who was sitting by the fire with Gottschalk, and reported breathlessly that some crazy fellow was sawing at the defective barrel of a cannon with a very small saw claiming that he needed the pieces to file false teeth for cows. He said he was acting on orders from Gottschalk, the veterinarian.

> Professional statement of the staff physician, Dr. Otto, Imperial Colonial Guard Headquarters, 3 May 05.
>
> Lieutenant Gottschalk definitely does not suffer from what is called jungle fever. Any suspicion of mental disturbance may also be ruled out. One can characterize his behavior at most as eccentric, evi-

denced by an exaggerated interest in the Hottentots, and in his attempt to learn the highly complex Nama language. It explains as well
his excessive compassion for the fate of this tribe. On the basis of my
examination—undertaken in the field and therefore lacking any claim
to clinical thoroughness—I diagnosed irritation of the stomach lining.
His reflexes were normal.

On the way to Keetmanshoop, Tresckow asked what book
Gottschalk had been reading even on horseback.

Kropotkin, Sir, said Gottschalk, *Mutual Aid: A Factor of
Evolution.*

His interest aroused, Tresckow asked, with lots of misal-
liances and powerful cabals?

No, said Gottschalk, quite the opposite in fact, but still
interesting.

Tresckow told him that when he had a chance to put his feet
up again, he'd like to borrow it.

One can't say reading Kropotkin was a revelation for Gottschalk. His curiosity and involvement with the book may have
come more from the fact that he often recognized ideas that had
occurred spontaneously, if somewhat unclearly, in his own
mind: helpfulness, solidarity, and friendship, even in the animal
world. Kropotkin supported his theory with numerous examples
from zoology and human society. Yet the book's insights were
not so powerful that Gottschalk would have read it a second
time. His continuing interest focused instead on how his predecessor had read the book, on Wenstrup's marginalia and the passages he had underlined in various colors. Gottschalk tried to
decipher the meaning of the different colors. Thus, leafing
through the book, he continued to follow Wenstrup's trail.

> A passage from Kropotkin's *Mutual Aid: A Factor of Evolution* under-
> lined in red by Wenstrup:
>
> > One of the greatest pleasures of the Hottentots certainly lies in
> > their gifts and good offices to one another. The integrity of the Hot-

tentots, their strictness and celerity in the exercise of justice, and their
chastity, are things in which they surpass all or most nations in the
world.

Even though he was a trained metal worker and blacksmith,
Zeisse was amazed by the incredible hardness of Krupp steel.
After hours of intensive saw work, the groove in the cannon bar-
rel wasn't half a centimeter deep.

One evening, while he was puttering about with his saddlery
(he was the only person in the entire southern division who
oiled his leather on a regular basis), Zeisse told Gottschalk about
the stone roller. Zeisse's father worked on a farm in Heber, a village on the heath. The farmer's name was König. In the farmyard stood the huge roller, chiseled from an erratic boulder, with
a hole bored through the middle where a tree trunk was shoved
through as an axle. The roller was still used occasionally when
lawns were seeded. It took two powerful plough horses to budge
it. Napoleon's road menders had left it behind in their hasty retreat. Both the farmer and Zeisse's father threatened to roll
young Zeisse flat if he didn't do as he was told. After that, he
wouldn't play in the farmyard any more. He was thirteen years
old before he was as tall as the stone roller. Not long afterwards
he took up an apprenticeship with a blacksmith in Bardowick.
And for the first time he climbed up on the roller.

Sawing away on the cannon barrel, Zeisse kept thinking of
that roller, chiseled from a mighty boulder.

Gottschalk's diary,
30 March 1905

Those who come after us will trace our passage through this land
for years to come: the skeletons of dead animals, and the graves of
those who have fallen, will serve as milestones along the way.

REGIONAL STUDIES 3
THEODOLITE
OR THE USEFULNESS OF SARDINE OIL

I n the beginning was the pop of a champagne cork.

On 5 April 1885, around five in the afternoon in a notary's office on Unter den Linden in Berlin, an assistant opened a bottle of Kupferberg to celebrate a contract which had just been signed by a group of distinguished gentlemen and witnessed by a notary public. The German Colonial Company for South West Africa was thus officially established. The men, who proceeded to drink to the future success and good fortune of the Company, included a leading businessman named Hansemann, the equally distinguished banker and businessman Bleichröder, the Duke of Ujest, Count Henckel von Donnersmarck, various directors of the Discount Society, the Deutsche Bank, the Bank of Dell-brück, Leo & Co., the Dresden Bank, and the bank of the house of Sal. Oppenheim jun. & Co., as well as a person of private means named von Zü., who was unable to contribute any capital to the newly founded company, but who brought with him inti-mate connections with the Imperial Chancellor.

In his toast, Bleichröder expressed what all present felt at that moment, that by establishing this company, the economic sector had finally lived up to its patriotic duty to civilize an un-derdeveloped and backward land. This task was even more pressing since up to that point only the English had been active in this area. It was, however, one of the noblest tasks of the country of poets and thinkers to civilize the savages. It was to this end, and to a successful business venture, that he now raised his glass.

The financial risk, as those involved in the preliminary negotiations quickly agreed, was minimal, since the planned undertaking required a relatively small capital investment of 800,000 marks, intended for the purchase of a few tin pots, rifles, glass beads, and larger quantities of brandy. This start-up capital was necessary to acquire land, with, they hoped, the beneficial mediation of the German missionaries. Since a land company is not labor-intensive, the fixed costs would be low: salaries for a Director, a few surveyors, geologists, and their assistants. The purchasing agents would work on commission.

The country was said to be rich in natural resources. Copper lay exposed to the light of day in some places in great quantities, and it had been rumored for decades that there were regions where one could simply pick diamonds off the ground.

The men knew full well they would not have the pleasure of bending over and plucking diamonds from the sand personally, but they hoped to create the conditions under which others could do it for them as quickly as possible. (In fact, however, it was twenty years before a lineman named Strauch, who worked on the Lüderitz railroad, stuffed his pockets with diamonds valued at 70,000 marks one night when the moonlight gleamed back from the stones.) The worth of the now worthless land would, the gentlemen agreed, increase substantially upon exploitation of its mineral riches, combined with its settlement by Germans (or other Europeans).

Neither the inhabitants of Bethany, nor the three Germans who rode into the village two years later, were aware of these transactions or the nature of the agreement. They were accompanied by two ox-wagons bearing the mysterious tin chests that had arrived in the country some months earlier by way of the English port at Walvis Bay. At the head of the draft oxen stood Fork-Horn, a great-uncle of Soft-Mouth. Fork-Horn eventually reached the legendary ox-age of thirty-four, and was thus one of the few witnesses to those events still living at the time of the great rebellion. Fork-Horn had managed to escape the butcher's knife because he possessed the ability, rarely found in an ox, to find the smoothest path through the roughest land, an ability which grew as he increased in age, and more than compensated for the onset of a certain shortness of breath. Fork-Horn saved any wagon master who hitched him up the trouble of hiring a lead boy.

On this day too, Fork-Horn pulled the wagon safely along the easiest route to the mission house in which Sabine Kreft had once held her panting contest with the hulking Klügge. The very next morning a few instruments unpacked from the tin chests were available for the admiration of the villagers, and among them was one the curious onlookers thought they recognized. Under the direction of an unusually tall and thin man, who held himself so stiffly erect that it seemed he feared an invisible burden might otherwise slip from his shoulders, a small, tube-like apparatus was mounted on three legs, through which, having shoved his pith helmet back on his head, he then took a trial look. This instrument was apparently a smaller version of the bulky photographic apparatus that a delicate man of melancholy mien by the name of Schultz, from Königsberg, had dragged here over a year earlier.

Compared to any other white man ever seen, the man was small in stature, with a positively Hottentot-like delicacy of limb. Schulz, like his subject Richard Wagner, wore a dark-brown velvet beret.

Before the respectful and astonished inhabitants of Bethany, who stood rooted to the spot, he disappeared beneath a black cloth, which he draped over himself and his apparatus. He soon reappeared with a pleased smile. He had captured the frozen figures on a photographic plate. That night he developed the plates in his traveling laboratory. The next morning he showed a few of them to the amazed villagers, who could recognize everyone in the picture but themselves. There was always one stranger among the familiar faces, and that person was, as each onlooker learned from the others, the onlooker himself. They seemed to see their everyday world for the first time: the church, the distant hills, the plains. A piece of frozen time, lacking smell or sound. Schulz explained his apparatus in detail to the curious natives, and had some trouble convincing them that it wasn't simply a self-recognition tool. The tribe asked him to stay, along with this useful device that showed each person who he was. In exchange they would gladly send the missionary and his Biblical proverbs into the desert, and he could see how far his sayings took him.

That evening Missionary Bam, trying to hide his disappointment, told Schultz: their faith is like a thin coat of ice after the first frost. Schultz intended to publish a picture book of the newly acquired protectorate of South West Africa. He had been commissioned to do so by the Colonial Society, who felt that such a book, showing the land and people, would further the colonial spirit among a wide segment of the population. The heavy apparatus was carried by three carefully selected men, while Schulz rode along with a melancholy gaze, then chose some spot, set up the apparatus and disappeared under the black cloth: in front of the mission church, in front of the pondoks, outside the cemetery, and again and again before the Half-Men, those strange trees that he photographed from the widest possible variety of perspectives and under the most widely varying light conditions (Schulz said light was the alpha and omega of his art, and always referred to his profession as enlightened). He finally produced the unique shot that shows a Half-Man in the twilight and—subtly—reveals something of the distant sorrow that Schulz had discovered not only in faces, but in the landscape as well, traces of decay and decline long before the cold damp deadly nights on Shark Island. Schultz photographed the broadly grinning trader, a dog whip in his hand, beside his ragged servant, who is holding a pair of brightly polished shoes up to the camera; a long-bearded Catholic Father among a crowd of Ovambo children, dressed like paper dolls in frilly white communion dresses; an ostrich (slightly out of focus), with plucked tail feathers; a Hottentot woman with three syphilitic children. Schultz asked her to gather her children around her before he photographed her, although he took her face only. When Bam asked why he hadn't taken a separate picture of the sick children, Schultz replied that the horror must be conveyed in the woman's face. The direct presentation of their terrible state would only repel the viewer. And finally the photo that was widely disseminated in numerous ethnological and lexical works: Old man from Bethany. It shows a deeply lined, infinitely wrinkled face, dried up like the landscape in which it was taken, eyes squinting into the harsh sunlight, two slits, as if the characteristic fold of the lids had formed as protection against the merciless light, the sparse, grayly-crinkled hair lacking all color. The karstic face conveys a certain weary dignity, a relaxed calm, even before the curious eye of the camera and a man hidden beneath black cloth. Thus Lukas, whom Gorth once wanted to take on a lecture tour of German missionary societies, made it to Europe after all, if only for the moment in which he waited for a sign from Schultz that he could breathe again.

But the picture book was never to appear. After looking through the photographs, the board of directors of the Colonial Society were of the opinion that the pictures were tinged with resignation, even sadness, and were therefore ill suited to promote the cause of colonialism.

The photographs thus disappeared into the archives of Hermann Schultz in Königsberg and after his death were stored in shoeboxes in his attic, where, in April of 1945, they were burned along with the house when it was struck by artillery. Only four of the 724 photographs survived: the pictures of Lukas (Old Man from Bethany), of the Half-Man, of the Catholic missionary with the communion children, and a seemingly innocuous image in which a cow is licking the hand of a Hottentot boy. Schultz had presented it to the tribe upon his departure from Bethany. He laid out all his photos for the villagers and let them select whichever one they wished as a gift. Men, women and children crowded into the mission house, peered at the display of photos, conferred, and to Schultz's surprise, chose the photo showing a well-nourished cow with a young boy.

They talked until the outbreak of the great rebellion about this melancholy white man with his funny beret, searching slowly through the village, accepting nothing and asking nothing of anyone, except to hold still a moment while he stood behind his camera.

But the man now peering through his instrument with a pith helmet shoved back on his head waved away the children and elders of Bethany, all dressed in their Sunday best, clearing them from his line of sight so he could take a bearing on the red and white rod with black lines. The surveyor passed the church without a glance, saw the Half-Men and found them merely odd, and when the villagers said they could lead him to a massive pile of ashes that was once the giant barrel of a brandy trader, he simply laughed. The florid imagination of these people, Treptow told his assistant Bansemer, stood in inverse proportion to the sterility of the land. Treptow, standing behind the theodolite, called out various numbers to his assistant, who entered them in tables, while the Hottentot boy holding the rod stood still and held his breath. Treptow explained that he wasn't taking photographs, so he didn't have to stand stock-still, he was only surveying land the company had purchased.

When Treptow read in the *Vossische News* that the Land Company was seeking a surveyor for South West Africa, he had immediately applied. He had received his diploma with honors two years earlier from the Technical University in Berlin-Charlottenburg and then worked two years near Niebüll on land reclamation projects. For weeks he trudged across the mud flats at low tide with his trouser legs rolled up, accompanied by taciturn North Friesians who held the rods and gazed into the distance with blue eyes. He had chosen this job among the many offered to him after his exams because something entirely new was being created, a bold project, it seemed to him as a native Berliner, wresting the land away from the sea. Where there was water, fields would be plowed, homes would be built, livestock

and people would live. Knowing he was a pioneer gave him energy and pleasure, even standing in mud in the freezing northeast, with no feeling in his feet, his fingers numb, surrounded by
the stubbornly silent Friesians, so that he too, contrary to his
nature, became in the end a man of few words. As the project at
Koog drew to a close, he began to search for new work. He could
have helped survey a military training ground near Münster on
the Lüneberger Heide, a good offer financially, but he opted for
the Land Company in South West Africa instead. While still a
student he'd decided to work a few years in a foreign country, if
possible in Africa or South America. He had fairly precise ideas
about his future and the life he wanted to live; for example, not
to marry before he was thirty, and to see the world. That was
important for his professional future as well. His strongest drive,
however, was to create something where nothing had existed before. Treptow was convinced of the animating power of technology. If nature still showed imperfections, they would be elimi-
nated sooner or later by technical means. Deserts would be
irrigated, rivers that flooded vast stretches of land would be controlled, dammed, or rechanneled. Anything could be accomplished with technology, in a way that would serve mankind.
Treptow is a techno-fanatic, his professor once said. When
he was ten years old, knowing nothing of James Watt, he re-
invented the steam engine. His father, a mustached bartender
from Kreuzberg, watched in befuddlement as his son disassem-
bled and reassembled alarm clocks, barrel organs, and orchestri-
ons, in the process of which some part was usually left over, a
few screws, nuts, or bolts. But the devices functioned as well as
before, which meant there was something superfluous inside
each one. After Treptow completed his final exams, he intended
to study architecture, but was advised against this because he
was color-blind. So he went into statistics and measurements,
studying construction und underground engineering, with particular emphasis on the construction of tunnels and dams. During his studies he mused over various projects, all of which went
beyond mere sketches and involved an array of geological and

technical data, ordnance maps, geographical maps, and compu-
tations. The first was an irrigation project for the Sahara Desert
in which the Nile would be rerouted to the Kattara Valley by
means of underground tunnels. He hoped that this newly created inland sea would result in a change of climate that would
be beneficial to other areas of the Sahara. Then he intended to
empty the Caspian Sea. The Volga would be rerouted at Tsarit-
syn, later Stalingrad, now Volgograd, into the Black Sea. Treptow had computed the total evaporation of the Caspian Sea and
subtracted from this his interpolation of the remaining waters
still entering. According to these figures, the sea would be completely dry by 1978. Finally, while surveying in North Friesland
he worked on a tropical car. This was a locomotive on moveable
wheels with an engine fueled by coal or wood. The latter was
particularly economical in tropical forests, where the engineer
and the stoker could stop to cut wood as needed. This tropical
car would pull four or five wagons. This would save the labor of
hundreds of native bearers and pack animals.

Treptow's manic energy got on his co-workers' nerves. Although he was quite thin, he displaced the air of any room he
entered, driving out delicate souls. In the final weeks before his
departure, he talked about nothing but South West Africa, as if
he had lived there already for ten years. He had read every relevant travel and exploration report available, practiced arms and
horsemanship, since he had no experience in the military service, and worked out a series of regular morning exercises. After
thirty-five pushups, he would do fifteen squat jumps onto the
table, then ten deep knee-bends on each leg, and finish with fifteen minutes of barbells. He meant to be fit when he started his
job in South West Africa, a land that strained the heart and circulatory system due to its high elevation and extreme shifts in
temperature.

Thus Treptow could be seen in Bethany emerging brightly
from the missionary station each morning, swinging his arms
about, bobbing at the waist, and placing his hands flat on the
ground with locked knees. Then he would shave with a small

razor, the latest invention from England, and wash in the open air. After breakfast he would mount his horse, urging on his assistants and aides, pressuring them to look sharp. And when, on those cool but sunny early mornings, he rode forth from the village, he appeared to be breathing deeply, ready to break into song.

Meanwhile his geologist colleague Hartmann wandered brooding through the countryside with his eyes to the ground, holding a hammer in his right hand and striking a stone now and then so that sparks flew. When Treptow asked why he didn't ride, Hartmann replied he had to be in direct contact with the stone and rock when he worked. In the evening he would inspect the rock samples carried home by an aide. Later, when he had finished writing his report, he sat in the twilight outside his door, smoking a meerschaum pipe. He was believed to be immersed in profound thoughts, but in fact he was dozing. Although Hartmann had just turned twenty-eight, he seemed much older. This was due to his subdued, deliberate gestures and speech, reinforced by an air of brooding reflection. He never expressed an opinion without immediately qualifying it, emphasizing as he did so that things were never that simple. Treptow thought Hartmann, who was an excellent geologist, always looked sleepy, which made his success at finding rich veins of ore in America an even greater mystery. Treptow thought it must be the intuition and sure step of the sleepwalker.

A few days after his arrival, Treptow claimed that one could judge a culture by its use of soap. There were in fact villagers in Bethany who hadn't bathed in over ten years, despite the missionary's powers of persuasion. Hartmann pulled the pipe from his mouth for a moment and said: Ah well, you know, I think you're overrating soap. The use of a pipe is surely more indicative of culture, although it too provides only a limited perspective. But it takes a cultivated and refined taste to smoke properly, and pipe smoking, when correctly conducted, is a complex matter. In that respect one can say the Hottentots have a highly-developed culture. Hartmann shoved his pipe back between his teeth and added: soaping oneself on the other hand is relatively simple. (It was this 'Ah well,' with which Hartman was in the habit of opening his remarks, that struck Treptow as obtrusively know-it-all. Even his drawn-out intonation had something grandfatherly and dull about it.) Pipe smoking seemed to bind Hartmann to the Bethany villagers in some unspoken way. Sometimes in the evening he would join a circle of old and young Hottentots, smoking, and for the most part silent. Now and then one of the elders would tell of a giant barrel that once passed through the village, a barrel with steel jaws around its tap, or of Missionary Gorth, who was carried to Bethany sewn up in an ox-skin, already beginning to smell, and with his corpse came the first sow and the first piano to enter the village. Treptow could see this ragged club of tobacco smokers from his room, where he sat working with figures and sketching regional maps. The way Hartmann sat, wearily facing the setting sun, was how Treptow pictured the twilight years of his own life. But Hartmann, as noted, had just turned twenty-eight. Treptow found the behavior of Hartmann's assistant Bansemer, a former Saxon artillery lieutenant, even more embarrassing. Bansemer had been forced to resign due to gambling debts and bad credit and had become a land surveyor. If you're off target from time to time because you've figured the angle wrong, at least it isn't noticed right away, Bansemer said when Treptow asked him why he had chosen to be a surveyor. What else could he do, at most he could have been a barman. At first Treptow thought that was an allusion to his father, to his own background. But since Treptow had never mentioned his father's profession, there was no way Bansemer could have known that. Bansemer sat squatting in front of the pondoks almost every night drinking brandy with the Hottentots. One night when he returned to the missionary station drunk as a pig and found Treptow still at work on his sketches, he started to rave about the tit-fucks with these massive Hottentot women. At this Treptow, who was by no means a prude, cut him off: go ahead and act like a pig if you want, but I don't want to hear about it. Later he was annoyed he hadn't thought to say: if you want to play the pig, you should be grunting. Treptow had a harder time than usual falling asleep that night, because he kept thinking up new and more trenchant rebukes.

Even so, there was nothing at all unusual about Bansemer as far as the Bethany villagers were concerned. They had met many Europeans over the years, and a good number of them were strange, it came with the territory so to speak: the splenetic English scientist Stephenson (a pioneer of Swiss mountain climbing) who wanted to travel the length of Africa, from Cape Town to Cairo, alone and on foot; Gorth who went bareheaded beneath the burning sun wearing Jesus sandals because the earth was God's footstool; the weak-lunged Shelton, an aristocrat who hoped to be cured in the dry climate and taste a moment of eternity, but who longed most of all to pat the behinds of little Hottentot boys in exchange for a few raspberry sweets; the greatest drunkard of all times, the physician and elephant hunter Dr. Dominicus; Klügge, who pulled the largest brandy barrel that Africa had ever seen through the desert; Mick and Mack, two able-bodied seamen from Hamburg, known as the Siamese Twins, who were shipwrecked and built a cottage in lower Swakop, living on yogurt made from cow's milk, growing old together, happy and content like Philemon and Baucis; missionaries, who preached the gospel with the Bible in one hand and a bottle of rum in the other; traders who introduced the villagers to any number of canker sores and volatile, nerve-deadening alcoholic spirits. And more recently, German officials with pince-nez perched on their noses and fingers stained with ink from their rubber stamps, donning their blue sleeve protectors while composing treaties of protectorate, and strutting through the sand on Sundays in richly-embroidered diplomatic uniforms, prominent among them the fat-handed Imperial Commissioner, Doctor Göring, a bird of paradise on show. All of them, with the exception of the melancholy velvet beret from Königsberg, came to do business, to find gold, in search of adventure, or as fishers of souls for the Rhenish Missionary Society. A few, not many, got rich. A good number succumbed to this land, dying strange, unique deaths, worthy of their lives. Trampled to death by elephants, crushed by the heavy wooden wheels of their own ox-wagons while drunk, bitten by sand vipers. They put bullets into their addled heads, some by accident and some with full intent. One had his throat slit in the night by his lead boy. Many lost their way and died of thirst, others expired in a delirium. Those were the normal ways to die.

It wasn't Treptow's furious energy, nor his dizzying zeal for work, that set him apart from other Europeans, the traders, missionaries, and gold prospectors. It was the strange fact that one couldn't deal with him. Not because Treptow was a cold and calculating businessman, but because he had no authority. Treptow established the boundaries of the land purchased from the tribe with his equipment, so like the friendly camera, and did so more precisely than any plow. A line so thin it couldn't be seen, as Treptow himself once explained. The natives had hoped while marking the borders to guide the horses cleverly enough to retain parts of the best pastures for the tribe, and that with cunning they could keep a few good water-holes. But Treptow peered through his theodolite, worked with angles and measuring chains, and even offered to check his work mathematically. Since no one else could, he taught mathematics at the missionary school, where the Hottentots showed a great talent for numbers. (Although it must be noted that Hartmann, without Treptow's knowledge, tutored a few stragglers.) Having drawn up the regional maps, Treptow was the first to notice that the company had pulled the wool over the eyes of the tribal chief. Even when they were buying a stretch along the coast, Lüderitz and Vogelsang, those honorable Hamburg businessmen, intentionally specified the use of the geographical mile in the contract, knowing full well that the Hottentots were familiar only with the English mile and had that in mind when they signed the contract. An English mile, however, is almost six kilometers shorter than a geographical mile.

The new land purchases were so cleverly formulated that the

tribe was literally left high and dry, retaining only barren land
with few water-holes. The agent who closed the deals on the
Land Company contracts now being surveyed must have been a
shrewd customer indeed. Treptow wondered if there were such a
thing as professional confidentiality for surveyors. Since the regional maps would be shown to the tribal council at the latest
once clean copies were produced, Treptow told the missionary
about the unfavorable sales one evening. The next day, as Treptow stepped out onto the veranda with arms outstretched for his
morning exercises, he was beseeched by the chief and members
of the tribal council to turn a blind eye to a water-hole or two
and add them to the tribal lands. Couldn't the border on the
right bank of the river be moved three or four miles to the right,
where the good pasture land was? These attempts to win his
favor, which intensified to the point of attempted bribery, had
something touching about them. Treptow tried to explain that
this was no rough survey measured by eye over a thumb, but a
mathematically precise one, and since specific geographic points
had been noted in the contracts, any high school student who
knew a little trigonometry would discover such irregularities
immediately. They should have paid more attention during the
contract negotiations; now any revisions would require the
agreement of the Company.

But who was the Company?

Treptow spoke of shareholders, shares, and percentages. But
he couldn't say how the shares were divided, and in fact didn't
know the number of shareholders. Nevertheless he came up
with two names: the Deutsche Bank and the Dresdner Bank,
both of which were in turn joint-stock companies. Both the
trustworthy Hartmann and the drunken retired artillery lieutenant confirmed these details. The hotheads in the tribal council were soon convinced that there was no use placing a sand
viper in Treptow's bed, or simply picking him off while he was
out on one of his surveys. They could have recovered the ill-
gotten ostrich feathers from Klügge that way, but they couldn't
shoot the Company. Several of the younger tribal members said

that Klügge should have been shot down like a dog, better yet, the first trader who crossed the Orange. But where to start now? Should they have shot Gorth, that pious and friendly man, who brought a useful animal like the pig to the region, and who looked like a Merino sheep himself, asked old Lukas. Voices were raised to strike now and drive out the whites, especially the Germans. The whites were still weak, but more and more soldiers and cannons were arriving, and they had already built forts in many villages. Did men with good intentions build forts? And the missionaries? Fine, Bam might have been all right. And Kreft, the little yapper, wasn't such a dirty dog. But hadn't the missionaries helped bring the Germans to their country? Was it not through their mediation that many tribes entered into the treaty of protectorate with the German Reich? Now they were supposedly subjects of the German Kaiser, a man who wore an ox-horn beard under his nose. And the eagle on his helmet, did it build its nest in all that steel? Missionary Bam, who hung a picture of the German Kaiser on his wall when the protectorate treaties were signed, removed it without comment one day because the children just wouldn't stop giggling. Some Hottentots made long journeys just to see the picture. They stood before it and grinned, then traveled back the next day.

But there were tribal members who were satisfied with the present situation, and the chief was numbered among them. Hadn't they received a tidy sum for the sale of the land, one that would guarantee them brandy and tobacco for many years at current prices? And the Germans, couldn't they be stirred up against the Hereros? Yet there were a few voices in the council, among them Cornelius, who later led the revolt against the Germans, who questioned everything, the old ways and the new, even the hereditary rank of chief. They claimed the Germans could never be driven out unless all the tribes rose up as one. Before that happened, however, they had to extract everything the Germans had in their heads, and that was no small matter. And without adopting their sweaty brows, that caged animal look, frightened and ready to spring, and those cold, clammy hands.

Cornelius accompanied Treptow on all his surveying trips, took math lessons from him, and became his right-hand man. The right hand was introduced to ballistics in the evenings by the drunken artillery lieutenant.

You would have made a good artillery man, Bansemer said, after Cornelius delivered one direct hit after the other on paper. In the tribal council meanwhile no agreement could be reached on whether to take action against the Land Company, and if so, when. Did it actually exist? After a day of heated debate, the decision was to slaughter two oxen, celebrate with brandy, tobacco, and dance, and do nothing more. A few difficult types wouldn't settle down of course. These raw youths, the most radical in the council, demanded a total ban on the consumption of alcohol, with violators flogged. These ascetic zealots saw alcohol merely as a means to stultify the Africans (they no longer spoke of tribes) and pacify them. Old Lukas, who had switched from smoking dagga to drinking brandy under the influence of the terrier Kreft, then was converted to total abstinence by chief David Christian, then drowned with the rest of the tribe in Klügge's brandy barrel, just shook his head and said that life always repeated itself, people just didn't live long enough to realize it. He recalled the false prophet who forced Missionary Knudsen to his knees and eventual retreat, followed by the militant prohibition under David Christian. The radicals called Lukas an ignorant Soft-Man. Why had the missionaries foamed at the mouth about dagga? Because the plant could be grown locally. Anyone could raise the weed for his pipe in front of his own pondok. So the missionaries pulled it up by hand and opened the way for the brandy trade, damned it from the pulpit, but gladly had a few drinks themselves. It was time to act!

Old Salomon Matroos finally gathered his courage one night and slipped off, leading a fat goat behind him, to Snuffle-Lip, an old woman who lived at the far edge of the village and had thus far refused to be baptized. Her viscous love potions, brewed from roots, herbs, bark, and lizard eyes according to an ancient recipe, were known throughout southern Africa. Now and then, as a

favor, she would dispose of particularly stubborn and trouble-
some rivals by making a doll, casting a spell, and then placing it
on a termite mound. In unusually difficult cases she also stuck a
thorn through the doll. Salomon Matroos didn't have to ask
twice, she was more than ready to kill the Land Company, and
even declined the gift of the goat in return. Over the next few
days she stuffed a pot-bellied Company with her best rags, and
even sewed a little black frock coat for it, like Dr. Göring wore.
She waited three weeks for the most favorable constellation:
clouds billowed, rain fell, a west wind blew, and the moon was a
sickle blade. That night she went to Heiseb's grave, muttered
her curse, pushed a thorn through the chest of the Land Company, and threw it on the termite mound. The voracity of termites is well known. In the course of a few weeks they can de-
molish solid houses and all their contents. There were farmers
who returned from a three-month stay in Europe, only to be
greeted by a pile of sawdust that was once their home. Termites
are able to effortlessly digest even holm oak in the fermentation
cellars of their hindguts. But a week later the terrified old
woman found the Land Company lying untouched on the termite mound. She died four days later, ancient but fit as a
fiddle. A month later the Bethany villagers gaped at a sight
that sent shudders through them: the Land Company in tails,
still without the slightest sign of damage, again lying on the termite mound.

A minor miracle, said Bam worriedly, and referred again to
the thin ice of faith among his parish children. The slightest burden and they broke through.

Treptow didn't believe in miracles. He was convinced that
this unusual phenomenon could be explained.

Thus one evening he was seen approaching the termite
mound with a long stick and fishing out the doll from the
swarm of insects. He examined the doll. It was indeed made entirely of rags. Even under a magnifying glass he found nothing
unusual. He was sorry he didn't have a microscope in his luggage. He placed the doll, which he found charmingly archaic, on

the sideboard and forgot about it. When he returned to Germany, he packed it away in his tropical chest as a souvenir. But the weird thing was, as he told his grandchildren years later, that one day he found that nothing remained of the doll, which had been lying next to an ostrich egg on a shelf, except a few tatters of cloth. It had been devoured by ordinary domestic ants, which had quickly swarmed through the house and just as quickly disappeared. A few days later, in 1918, the Land Company was dissolved. Treptow always maintained this was pure coincidence, but strange all the same.

He never revealed that Bam had begged him to exercise a moderating influence on the Company's agent. One evening in the year 1887, Bam came to him and reported that the land sales were noticeably upsetting his flock, and radicals in the tribe were putting this to their own use. These radicals had long since ceased attending his services, by the way, but now they were stirring up the congregation by quoting one-sided, tendentious passages from the Bible such as: It is easier for a camel to go through the eye of a needle, than for a rich man to enter into the kingdom of God. Bam feared this might lead to a revolt against the Germans. He wasn't raising moral objections, although one must say the tribe was being badly fooled with these sales, he was simply trying as a man of God to ensure peace on earth as well.

Treptow replied that a land surveyor had no influence in business matters. It wasn't his job to buy land, just to survey land already purchased. And there was no fiddling with that, it would be contrary to his professional honor, his work could be checked mathematically. He stood above parties, apart from a certain loyalty to the Company, to which he was contractually obliged. Nevertheless, at Bam's insistence he agreed to talk to the agent, whom he didn't know, at the earliest opportunity.

Was it in any sense morally justifiable to buy land from these people for a few marks, which, he had learned in the meantime, would soon be poured down their throats as brandy? On the other hand, how else could the land be developed? These friendly folks did only the minimum required, and not a stroke more.

Any chance of economic and cultural progress is nipped in the bud, Treptow wrote to his former professor, the one who claimed that Treptow was a techno-fanatic. Like children, they live only for the day, without a care for tomorrow, and make no provision for themselves and their next of kin. According to tradition, a chief provides for his subjects, who in turn stand ready to serve him at any time. They can't earn money working for the tribe, since their basic rule is, we help one another. This produces a chaotic situation and is the main reason these people don't amount to anything. It is this established custom among them (communism) that the missionaries are unable to alter. It has become second nature to them. So perhaps it's just as well that they sell land they are in no position to use properly, and set in motion an evolution that will teach them to work and gradually lead them toward civilization.

After sending this letter to his mentor, Treptow felt better. He saw things clearly again, without the blurriness of the past few days. But he hated having to wait so long for an answer. It took months for a letter to reach Germany, and equally long for a response to arrive. And so by evening the debilitating uneasiness had returned, something totally unfamiliar that he had not experienced even on the cold damp nights in Friesland. A newly-published textbook from England on the transmission of steam power to moveable wheels had been open to the same page on his desk for days, along with untouched figures and data from the bearings taken over the past week or so. Treptow sat at the open window, staring out into the night. The air was like silk. A fat cockroach crawled across his desk and over the map, making a scratching sound. It wandered toward his bed, but he didn't get up to step on it, and was surprised that he felt no disgust when it disappeared under his pillow. He could hear the tobacco club exchanging pleasantries outside with Hartmann, and further beyond, in the distance, singing and a harmonica. Bansemer was celebrating the Kaiser's birthday with the villagers, Hottentit style. Did I say Hottentit, Treptow asked himself in disbelief. He would have liked to go out and sit with Hartmann's tobacco club. Or better yet cross to the village where they clapped rhythmically, probably dancing to the music, the wayward artillery lieutenant among them. This booze-hound had the enviable ability of being able to talk with anyone. Natives who measured the white man with a cold, malicious stare in stubborn silence would swear brotherhood with him by the fourth glass of rum. Treptow failed to see how Bansemer could communicate with the Hottentots, who spoke only Nama, when he didn't speak a word of himself. Bansemer would throw out a mixture of Saxon, French, and English, the natives would nod in response, answer in Nama, and Bansemer would suddenly laugh and slap them on the back as if he'd understood everything, poking them lightly in the chest and saying: Trés bien, formidable, that was good, de Fleescher sachte eenfache nee, vraiment, that's very good. Sometimes Treptow suspected that Bansemer actually did understand Nama, but kept it under his hat. On the other hand that didn't solve the puzzle, since the Hottentots would still have to understand Saxon.

For the past few nights he'd scarcely slept. He lay exhausted on the bed, its legs encased in cans of oil to stem the onslaught of bugs. In the meantime they climbed the walls and crawled across the ceiling until they were over his bed, and then dived down on him. He imagined he could feel the impact of the tiny armored tanks on the sweat-soaked sheet over him. He tossed and turned, scratching, brooding over a question that had nothing to do with his work: why work at all? And all the while he kept thinking: what a stupid, idiotic question. A childish question. A question that can't be answered logically. An illogical question. Strictly speaking, not a question at all. You might as well ask why you live. Why do I live? Surrounded by the high-pitched drone of cicadas, Treptow bored into this question until he disappeared, and no longer saw himself.

Why work—a typical Hottentit question. Then he realized he'd said Hottentit again. In this profound darkness, this stuffy room, he suddenly realized that the painful erections that woke him at night had always been coupled with longing for young Hottentot women. But he'd been too afraid he would catch a dose of the clap.

Treptow had a general fear of filth and dirt, and so for the past several days he had frightened himself. He hadn't bathed in five days (culture reveals itself in the use of soap), and he no longer dislocated his arms and legs mornings on the veranda to the general amusement of all. (Five days ago he couldn't have cared less what the natives thought.) And while they normally saddled up for survey work each morning at precisely six o'clock, it might now be ten or even eleven before the group got moving, Treptow jog-trotting along at the rear, the sour smell of his own night sweat in his nose.

His inner gyroscope has restored his balance, said Bansemer, in human terms. Bansemer's own balance allowed him to stay on his horse even when he was dead drunk.

Treptow stared into the darkness. Somewhere overhead the bugs would be positioning themselves again, ready to fall bloodthirstily upon of him. He scratched his painful bites. Humans only ask questions that can be answered, he told himself. But this maxim, which at first seemed so reasonable, meant less each time he said it, and in the end he might as well have said: humans only raise cauliflowers that can be eaten.

It had started five days ago, when he returned from a survey trip, followed by a worn-out Bansemer and, far to the rear, his assistants. He leapt from his foam-flecked horse, washed in cold water, changed clothes, then went to his room to review the data. Outside his window the tobacco club sat in the twilight, chatting and amiably puffing their pipes. He heard Lukas ask the geologist Hartmann, who was sitting nearby, why this Treptow was slaving away so. Hartmann removed his meerschaum momentarily to respond: There's no easy answer to that one.

Treptow, bent over the table with the maps that left the tribe high and dry, smiled.

But he couldn't get to sleep that night; the same stupid question kept going through his mind. The next morning, during his twenty forward bends on the veranda, he suddenly saw himself through the eyes of those who watched him perform each morning without smile or comment. How comical he was. Standing there, his knees locked, then suddenly bending from the waist, right hand to left toe, quickly up and over again, left hand to right toe, mechanically, like a machine. A jumping jack. He stopped, shaking his legs a little to cool down. He had only done nine bends. The next day he discontinued his gymnastic program.

The week before, the missionary's wife had told him the rumors circulating in the village. The tall German was supposedly chewing some sort of root that made him work incessantly. More specifically: the Company was forcing him to chew the root. Ridiculous, said Treptow, what strange flowers blossom from the imagination of these fine folk. But in fact he now recalled that he'd munched on a carrot or two from the missionary's wife's garden, since he was plagued by those damned roundworms that forced their way out at night, distending in his rectum and itching unbearably. The missionary's wife went on to say that once this rumor made the rounds, carrots were being stolen from her garden, even though the villagers didn't like vegetables. Treptow was flattered.

But he then heard that rejected lovers were putting the finely grated carrots in their rivals' food as an anti-love potion. The root would supposedly set the rival in hectic motion and keep him in a constant state of repulsive sweat before the beloved's eyes.

Treptow nodded, yes, fine, and then without any apparent connection: The Hottentot economy.

A good talk with his mentor, Professor Bernhard, would have helped. He had written him several letters over the past few months, but it seemed senseless to write now, since it would take weeks for the letter to be carried on a stick through the countryside by a messenger to Walvis Bay, lie around waiting for the steamer, and finally rock its way slowly northward. He continued to wander about, brooding and scratching.

Treptow's sudden change had not escaped Hartmann, and he spoke to him one day in his calm and thoughtful way. But Treptow brusquely avoided his cautious questions, saying he couldn't sleep, it was the weather, this damned heat, and to please just leave him alone.

On a Friday in February of 1888 Treptow bought a bottle of whiskey in the only store in the village. That morning, sitting bleary-eyed in a wicker chair on the veranda, he sent Bansemer and his assistants home with the words: it's too hot to work today. His earlier resolve not to drink in the tropics seemed silly. Just a glass before bed, one needn't start boozing like the wayward lieutenant. Treptow hadn't yet opened the bottle when Bam brought in a letter from Germany that had just arrived at the mission, with the messenger still panting out front.

Treptow couldn't say later on what it was in this letter that roused him, what, as he put it, got him moving again. Professor Bernhard's letter from Braunschweig was, if anything, sober and matter-of-fact. He began by stating in detail his reasons for moving from the famous technical university in Berlin to the provinces, as if he felt the need to justify himself to Treptow. The offer included a higher salary, as was customary, but the reason he had relocated, he wrote, was that Braunschweig had established an Institute for Technical Measurement and offered him the position of Director. After thorough consideration he had accepted. Bernhard then enlarged upon an idea which, he said, would revolutionize the field of measurement: to fly over an area that was to be surveyed in a balloon or other flying machine and photograph it. Of course the flying machine in question would have to maintain a constant altitude, which would be difficult, or strictly speaking, impossible, for a free floating balloon. But even now, for example, a captive balloon could be used in otherwise inaccessible regions. He had great hopes that inventions in the area of flight would have a major influence on techniques of measurement. Of course a particularly sophisticated photo-technical process would have to be developed that could clearly differentiate the various tones of gray in a land-scape photo, indicating in turn significant variations in eleva-tion. These would be copied and one would have, as if in layers, the profile of the land. Then Bernhard reported briefly on the successful attempt of a certain Daimler in Augsburg, who, Trep-tow would be interested to hear, had built a gasoline engine on a wooden go-cart and then propelled himself and the cart with it. Bernhard sent Treptow greetings along with those of his wife, and wished him all the best. In a P.S. he added yet another the-sis, as an interested amateur straying beyond his own field, so to speak, that the Sahara Desert might have resulted from some prehistoric natural catastrophe, an enormous whirlwind, or more likely, a vast flood that washed away the plant cover and then the topsoil above the clay. He had discovered a similar the-sis, by the way, developed quite independently, in Humboldt's *Views of Nature*. He asked Treptow, if he got a chance, to take notes on any signs of such a flood in the Namib.

After rereading the letter, Treptow stood up, paced back and forth, and finally approached the mirror. He was startled by the face that stared back at him. The reddened eyelids, the bearded stubble, the hair hanging in strands. He was embarrassed to think that others had seen him that way. Run down. Filthy. To make it seem intentional, he decided to let his beard grow. It would turn into a dark blond, slightly reddish full beard. He went to wash, but there was no water in the pitcher. The wash-bowl contained a dried soapring with hairs clinging to it. How slovenly, Treptow said aloud to himself and called for his bam-buse. After washing and changing clothes, he assembled his con-struction plans. So it was already possible to propel a two-wheeled cart with a small gas engine. For a moment he feared his model, the maneuverable locomotive, had already been over-taken by technical progress, and that if it were ever built it would be a fossil on wheels, a clumsy steaming dinosaur among little rattling two-wheeled sporty models. But then he reminded himself that this wooden go-cart (what was that anyway?)

moved nothing but itself and this Herr Daimler. Whereas his tropicar would pull loads over thousands of kilometers.

The following morning a nonplussed Bansemer, arriving two hours late, found a freshly-washed and raging Treptow roaring at the men carrying the rods: Vacation was over, it was time to get a move on again. Bansemer noticed that Treptow was standing very erect, with his shoulders thrown back, as if an iron cross had been mounted on his back.

That evening after work, Treptow approached the missionary's wife with a request for benzene. When he noticed her hesitation, he assured her it was needed for an experiment. Two months earlier a Swedish trader had tried diluting his rotgut brandy with benzene. It had reduced him to a dried husk. Father Bam read the beautiful verse from Matthew over the Swede's open grave: The light of the body is the eye: if therefore thine eye be single, thy whole body shall be full of light. Since only one small bottle of benzene was to be found in the little medicine chest at the mission, Treptow decided to mix it with lubricating oil, of which there was plenty at the station, to make it go further. He filled a bottle with benzene and lubricating oil, wrapped some gauze around a cork and stopped it. A small amount of this flammable liquid was meant to trickle out through the gauze onto an iron skillet Treptow had borrowed from the mission kitchen. This experimental arrangement was the basis for a burner to be placed beneath the boiler of the tropicar. It could then be fired not only with wood, but also with kerosene and this mixture of benzene and oil.

When he ignited the liquid that had trickled onto the skillet, the flame leapt to the bottle with a puff, and he barely managed to toss it out the window before it exploded. Treptow stared into the night, where the jaws of hell had opened. The members of the tobacco club were flat on the ground, their clothes and hair singed. They crossed themselves. The crackling flames attacked the dry wood of the veranda. Bansemer roared orders. Figures ran in all directions. Finally they managed to extinguish the fire with sand. Bansemer approached with singed beard and eyebrows to congratulate Treptow on the invention of this miracle weapon. Only then did it dawn on Treptow that he had become another Berthold Schwarz.

He told Bansemer how it was made; a procedure combining utmost simplicity with maximum effect: fill a bottle three-fourths full with benzene, top it off with extra-thick lubricating oil, stop up the bottle with gauze or cotton wool, then light the ball of cotton wool and throw the bottle in the right direction.

Treptow and Bansemer agreed that the invention must be kept secret, particularly from Cornelius, who was demonstrating a disturbing interest in all military matters revealed by the Germans. As an army man, Bansemer said, he could easily judge the devastating effect this simple weapon would have in the hands of natives should there be a revolt. It would be easy to set the newly-built forts on fire with it.

That same night Treptow wrote a detailed report for the War Ministry in Berlin, including a small sketch showing how to assemble the bottle-missile. He christened it the Moloch.

Eighty years later in Hamburg, in a basement across from the Philosopher's Tower, a wild-haired fellow named Treptow, a math student, maintained amid roars of laughter from his fellow revolutionaries that his grandfather had invented the Molly they had just decided to toss into the consulate of the Vietnam murderers, following a discussion of the use of force against property, and that the name Molly didn't come from the Molotov Cocktail, but from Moloch, the name his grandfather gave to this racing fuel. The old chauvinist had not revealed the invention to the natives, but offered it instead to the German army. But the closely-meshed interests of the state, capital, and the military were evident even then, for the idea was not pursued by the War Ministry due to interference from the Krupp armaments lobby.

Moreover there was justifiable fear that this weapon, which anyone could produce, might fall into the hands of the oppressed. After all, a Molly a day keeps the fat cats away.

It was only after many years, and submitting many petitions, that old grandpa Treptow finally received an official response. A certain Captain Engel, as equipment and munitions man, reported that the bottle-missile had been thoroughly tested, but had ultimately been rejected as less than optimal. The newly-developed hand grenades were more convenient and posed fewer operational problems in combat. Moreover the effect of shrapnel was greater than the mixture of benzene and oil in the Moloch, which, unless it struck its target directly, merely burned the skin and clothing of its victims without disabling them. Nevertheless they thanked Professor Treptow for his patriotic work and efforts to create a new weapon. Treptow kept this letter within easy reach in his desk drawer.

After fate had bestowed this good fortune upon him as an inventor, Treptow's shadow could be seen bent over his desk into the early hours of the morning, calculating axle pressures and wheel friction. In the end he initiated Bansemer into his nightly work, for the two had drawn closer through Treptow's pyrotechnical invention.

Bansemer was enthused about the plans for a tropicar. He calculated that given Treptow's planned payload of up to 1500 kilograms, the car could transport a good 1400 bottles of the best Scotch whiskey from Walvis Bay to Bethany in less than a week. That would open a door for rapid expansion in the future, he said excitely.

Treptow completed his plans for the tropicar simultaneously with his survey work for the region. Not long afterwards, he was ordered to leave for Windhoek. He passed on the sealed plans and relevant explanatory material to Bansemer, who was heading home, and asked him to send the work to the patent office in Germany.

Treptow also composed a memorandum to the Colonial Of-

fice in which he summed up the utility and value of the tropicar
for the German colonies:

> The tropicar is a steam-driven car with an engine producing
> 15–30 horsepower. Steam power was selected as a propellant because
> combustion engines have the disadvantage, given the small number of
> repair shops in the colonies, of being more complex, while increasing
> the weight of the car significantly. The tropicar's engine has four pairs
> of cast iron cylinders. The valve box consists of four separate com-
> partments, sometimes known as elements; these are rectangular cases,
> each of which may be shut down separately if damaged, while the en-
> gine continues to run.
>
> In line with colonial conditions, the engine is fired by wood,
> which need not be seasoned. The boiler pipes are barely affected by
> wood fire, and operating expenses are cheaper with this fuel; in com-
> parison with gasoline for example, the relationship is 1:10.
>
> The water tank is located in the rear portion of the car, and may
> be easily filled using a bucket. The tank holds enough water for a 20-
> kilometer uphill trip; on level terrain the water supply will last for
> 30–40 kilometers. The boiler is fed by a pump located to the right of
> the driver's seat. Once the car is in motion the pump continues to op-
> erate on its own. The rear axle drives the car. Two chains transfer the
> force, both situated outside the car rather than beneath it, for easy
> access.
>
> The drive assembly is not constructed like a combustion engine
> and not intended for changing speed; therefore it is less delicate in its
> construction. Speed is controlled by the amount of expanding steam
> allowed to enter the cylinders.
>
> There are three available methods of braking: one brake is ap-
> plied to the rear wheels, one affects the engine, a further possible
> method is diverting the steam. As with all self-driven vehicles, the car
> is steered by the driver using a hand-operated wheel fixed to a steering
> column that in turn controls the front axle.
>
> The car can be operated by one man; he must stop every few kilo-
> meters to put wood on the grate of course. To avoid this a boy may be

taken along to undertake the task, so that the driver may devote himself entirely to his car.

The car can also be fired with alcohol, kerosene, or even raw kerosene, simply by placing a burner over the grate and feeding it with fluid under pressure.

The vehicle has an unloaded weight of 10,000 kilograms. The steel-rimmed wheels are constructed of thick leather treads set with steel plates.

The car carries a payload of 10,000–15,000 kilograms, replacing 600 native bearers; it can pull two cars with 10,000 kilograms each, replacing three ox-wagons. Its maximum speed per hour is 15–20 kilometers and it can climb inclines of up to 20 degrees.

The construction diagrams, calculations, and description for the tropicar disappeared in a manner never explained. Almost a year after Bansemer's departure—Treptow stood among his packed luggage, ready to head home—a letter arrived from Chicago. The letter was written in the broadly flowing script of former artillery lieutenant Bansemer. He had emigrated to the New World to seek his fortune, he wrote. He was sorry to report, however, that he had lost his suitcase on the return journey from South Africa, in Southampton in fact, while standing in line at customs, preparing to board a steamer headed for Hamburg. Reading a newspaper, he had shoved his newly-purchased fashionable light-brown suitcase before him with his foot without looking up as the line slowly moved forward. Having reached the customs official, he lifted the suitcase onto the table amid protests from the person in front of him. Upon opening the suitcase, it proved indeed to belong to the person, which Bansemer had at first vehemently denied. Since the suitcase was, as mentioned above, the dernier cri, there were several of the same color and shape, so that it was quite easy to see how a mistake could be made. He immediately went back along the entire line, called for the police, or bobbies as the English say, but the suitcase was nowhere to be found.

For years thereafter Treptow busied himself tracking down

every passenger who had stepped on board the *Midsummer Night's Dream* on that fateful day of 24 April, 1889 (there were one hundred fifty-three of them), visiting them in person, or if they lived in Sidney, Bombay, or Montevideo, writing to ask them, if their suitcase had been accidentally switched, to return the construction plans to him, in exchange of course for a finder's fee. Treptow was aided in his search by the fact that, he was not rerouting the Nile into the Kattara Valley, but instead working as a claims agent for an insurance company dealing with cases of fraudulent land development and improper foreign construction.

The construction plans for the tropicar never resurfaced. Nevertheless, years later, Treptow discovered a photo of his tropicar in the *German Colonial News*, which he read regularly. A serious-looking man with a thick mustache was turning the steering wheel. Next to the picture was a report on the model, developed by Dr. Robert Goldschmidt of Brussels. The report was identical to the one Treptow had written six years earlier in Bethany. Treptow made immediate enquiries, but was unable to discover whether the automobile had been built according to his plans or whether it was one of the many cases of simultaneous invention common in those years. A few of these tropicars were actually built, and one was shipped to German South West Africa at the initiative of a German Lieutenant Troost. Hissing and steaming it pulled two cars from Swakopmund eight kilometers into the countryside, then got stuck in the sand, where it remains as a monument to this day, nicknamed Luther by the locals: Here I stand, I can't do otherwise.

On a June evening, when the first nightly frosts were setting in, Treptow left Bethany in the company of the geologist Hartmann. On the ox-wagon drawn by the pathfinder Fork-Horn, among the tin chests holding the surveying equipment, were several boxes of rock samples Hartmann had chipped off in the Bethany area. He was convinced there were copper and silver deposits in the Trias Mountains.

Once in Windhoek, Treptow immediately sought out the

Company's land agent, Kleinschmidt, who lived in one of the few stone houses in the village. His home lay on a gentle slope amidst a garden of trees and shrubs. A small spring emerged higher up on the hill, with a water pipe leading to the house. His was the first house in South West Africa with indoor plumbing, and several of the officers stationed in Windhoek, driven by homesickness, visited Kleinschmidt just to hear that familiar sound. On hot days Kleinschmidt would sit in a bathtub filled with cold water solving the chess problem from the back page of the *Appenrade News* (Kleinschmidt came from Appenrade). Now and then he would add cold water. Then he would send the solutions to Appenrade, where they always arrived two to three months after the deadline. For this Kleinschmidt would be explicitly mentioned by the editors at year's end: a son of our city, who practices the western art of chess in faraway Africa. Kleinschmidt clipped these references and pasted them into an album. Coming from the northernmost part of the German empire, he also took a lively interest in onion domes which showed striking variations depending on the locale. He enjoyed displaying his engravings of them to visitors and, more recently, his photographs. If the day was particularly hot, he kept all the doors and windows closed. He refused on principle to receive any visitors on these occasions. A servant would point wordlessly from within at the boiling mercury in the thermometer outside the window. Not until evening, when the temperature outside had fallen below the temperature inside (which Kleinschmidt always checked personally) would he allow the doors and windows to be opened.

Treptow had been sent away twice with gestures at the thermometer before he finally found the door open later that afternoon. He was greeted by a tall, heavy-set man whose dark suit exuded authority. Kleinschmidt asked him if he would like a cup of tea. He didn't allow alcohol in his house on principle, he added, preempting any move in that direction by Treptow. He fixed camomile tea for himself. Unfortunately his stomach was extremely sensitive and he had to watch his diet, for his stomach was his capital. Treptow chuckled amiably, but Klein-

schmidt hadn't meant it as a joke. He was feared in society because he lacked a sense of humor, and the strangest rumors were
making the rounds, that Kleinschmidt received a case of sardines in oil each month from Portugal, which was transported
across oceans and deserts and for some inexplicable reason disappeared into his cellar. Yet no one had ever seen Kleinschmidt
eat a sardine, and once he told Governor Leutwein that like
many people who grew up by the sea, he couldn't stand fish. For
a time people said he planned to start a wholesale business in
fish, but then he was seen carrying a case of sardines whenever
he visited a chief to negotiate a land purchase, so they assumed
he must be taking it as a gift.

While they drank tea served with English cheesecake, Treptow discussed his plans for a tropicar. Kleinschmidt immediately insisted the name be more Germanic, Heißzonenselbst-
fahrzeug for example. Foreign influences on the German
language were already disturbingly evident. It was high time societies were established to preserve the purity of the German
language. Treptow nodded thoughtfully and picked at the
cheesecake, which tasted slightly rancid. Kleinschmidt also
chewed in silence. At some point, thought Treptow, he would
have to break the silence, he couldn't sit there saying nothing,
that would be impolite, and so he finally told him about the
missionary's fears in Bethany.

Kleinschmidt polished his pince-nez carefully and clipped
them back on his nose. The sooner they revolt, the better, he
said. This country needs a war. War is the father of all things. It's
the only way to develop the land. Troops will be reinforced, rail-
roads built, there will finally be a market for beef, natives will
be expropriated, a labor force created, and farmers can move in.
Do you know what this country needs, young man, this Sleeping
Beauty? Missionary Knudsen, a far-seeing man, said it over forty
years ago: take the land away from the natives. That's the only
way they will ever be useful members of society. Only hunger
will force them to work. As long as their goats and steers do
their work for them, there will be no economic progress. Only

war can cut the Gordian knot. Treptow nodded. On a birchbark plaque hanging over the display cabinet, he read the wood-burned motto: The industrious shall inherit the earth.

You see, our Governor Leutwein is trying to square the circle if he thinks he can acquire the land from the natives by peaceful means. He's seeking a humane solution, but at the same time he wants to import German settlers. That might work for a while, since these folks are fairly trusting and can generally be pacified with liquor, but at some point they will realize what's going on, and then it's going to be the night of the long knives.

Kleinschmidt rose suddenly from his chair and pushed it back. We ought to calculate the degree of friction produced when a chair is shoved back, he said, and the loss of heat. He sat down in a plush chair, disappearing into it as if sinking into a sandpile, the smoldering Havana stretched forth from his fingers as if he were taking an oath. Then, without transition, he declaimed: What once fell short is here fulfilled, what words can't say has now been willed. Treptow felt obliged to nod again. In the new and lengthy silence that set in he thought he could hear the termites chewing in the beams. The house had been built just four years earlier by the Italian architect Mazzoli, but it already had cracks in the walls, the flowered wallpaper hung in strips, and parts of the stucco work had fallen from the ceiling. Treptow ducked his head involuntarily. Nevertheless, the house was considered one of the most beautiful in the protectorate, with its balconies, gables, and scrolled eaves. Kleinschmidt dismissed him to work on his chess problem. In three days he would be leaving on a business trip and Treptow was to come along and survey the land immediately upon purchase.

It wasn't until they rode off from Windhoek on Friday that Treptow learned the goal of their journey: the region around Walvis Bay. They rode in silence. Kleinschmidt played chess. He'd constructed a wooden tray that could be buckled onto his saddle, and his pegged chess set was clamped securely onto it. Engrossed in a third variant, he was borne across the steppes on his horse Lisa. All Fork-Horn had to do was follow the beaten path from the coast to Windhoek. By the campfire that evening, Kleinschmidt explained the differences between Walliser and Allgäuer onion domes with the aid of sketches in the sand. Indeed there were rare cases of towers with double onion domes.

After seven days, on Thursday, they reached the Topnaars' compound. Kleinschmidt immediately unloaded the wagon. He wanted everyone to see what he was offering for the land: bottles of rum, plugs of tobacco, sacks of sugar, and tins of roasted coffee. Earlier the Land Company had sent hundredweights of glass beads from Gablonz, cheap trinkets, not worth tuppence, that he finally had to give away to the children. People here had come to know the difference between rum and blended rum. Those in charge back home knew little about the wider world, picturing these people as half-savage. It took some time for Kleinschmidt to convince them to send high-quality goods along with plenty of tobacco.

While Treptow was overseeing the unloading of the surveying equipment, he also spotted the mysterious crate of Portuguese sardines in oil. It was carried into Kleinschmidt's tent.

Negotiations were scheduled to begin toward evening the following day—a wet, cold Friday—with Klaas Hendriks, who could hold his liquor with anyone in the land.

That afternoon Kleinschmidt began preparing himself. He ate half a loaf of white bread, tearing off chunk after chunk, chewing slowly and steadily, softening them with saliva and then slowly swallowing the mash. Sitting beside Kleinschmidt, Father Defregger described the charm of the local land owned by the natives, the calm monotony of the desert, the incredible waterless expanses, as Kleinschmidt stuffed another wad of white bread in his mouth, the grass of the steppes doesn't begin until you're north of Swakop, then it's thorn bushes, and finally, almost at the bank of the river, trees, pastures, farmland, waterholes too, even in the dry season. Kleinschmidt swallowed and had them bring six tins of sardines in oil while Defregger, making a slight detour to the east, waxed eloquent over the Valley of

the Moon, a huge, dried-out primeval riverbed valley, then returned to the tribe's valley, noting minor points of interest, here
an unusually tall termite mound, there an ancient petrified
thorn tree, good pasture in between, with Kleinschmidt forking
one sardine after the other from the open tin, chewing with oily
lips, bolting them down, going white around the nose as he finished the fifth tin, then green and finally even blue. Defregger
arrived at a water-hole as sweat poured from Kleinschmidt's
brow, tiny rivulets soaking his eyebrows, dripping down, while
Defregger reached a steep rock formation as Kleinschmidt removed his pince-nez, a rock formation from which fresh springs
flowed that could irrigate the fields, a beautiful area, the reddened rocks reminding Defregger, in the light of the setting sun,
of the rose garden in Bozen. Kleinschmidt meanwhile was slurping up the last of the cloudy, shimmering oil with the tiny bits
of fish from the tins, gagging as he did so, once, twice, but not
vomiting. He breathed deeply, stood up, taking care not to burp,
and then said: all right, now we're oiled for negotiations, and
then proceeded, with knees flexed and rolling lightly on the
balls of his feet to avoid the slightest vibration, to Klaas Hendriks's pondok. They drank for three days. Kleinschmidt had entire batteries of bottles brought in. By night the rapt listeners
could hear the occasional pflop of a rum or brandy cork and in-
termittent belching. Each morning Kleinschmidt would appear
briefly outside the pondok, with an increasingly swollen face,
bags like potato sacks under his eyes, his nose glowing red. He
would step to the side, put a finger down his throat, gag briefly,
and jerk erect as a brownish sludge of oil, alcohol, gastric acid,
undigested fish albumen, and gruel shot forth. Yapping and
growling the village mutts crowded about his feet and lapped up
the puddle. Surrounded by the tangle of dogs, he ordered three
more tins of sardines and told the dumbstruck Treptow that in
three years he was going to retire, not in Appenrade, but in
Gmund on Lake Tegern, where there was a church with a particularly beautiful onion dome. Then he turned around and
coughed up more bits of sardine and oil. Even as a child he hated

fish, he said apologetically, and asked for three new tins, throwing the sardines to the dogs and slurping up the oil. Then back to the pondok. On the evening of the third day Klaas Hendriks collapsed, his face Prussian-blue, and lay on the ground stiff as a board. All attempts to revive him were in vain. Even a bottle of ammoniac smelling salts produced no reaction. But his pulse, though unsteady, was still perceptible.

Shortly before he fell, he placed his three x's on the contract, witnessed by Father Defregger. The southeast portion of the Topnaars' land was transferred to the Land Company in exchange for £210, sixty bottles of brandy (German), twenty bottles of the finest Cuban rum (white), fifteen kilos of tobacco, twenty-five kilos of coffee, and a pair of mother-of-pearl opera glasses. He hadn't wanted to pay more than £190, Kleinschmidt said, but Klaas Hendriks drove a hard bargain and talked him into it just as they were signing the contract. He was still bitter about the extra twenty pounds. Kleinschmidt poked his finger in his neck and said, done! He kicked the mongrels out of his way and had his bambuse cook some unsalted gruel. He sipped a little camomile tea with it and told Treptow to prepare a detailed map of the area with the Land Company's borders marked in red. The fixed points were indicated in the contract, as usual. There was an old, petrified thorn tree he should be careful not to chop down. Then he went to bed and slept until the following day. On Saturday morning Kleinschmidt, wrapped in a lambskin cloak, rode back toward Windhoek, the pegged chess set on the saddle before him.

Klaas Hendriks remained stiff and motionless, but he had twice raised his left eyelid. Early the next morning, Treptow set up the theodolite. The men carrying the survey rods knew it wasn't a camera. The harbor of Walvis Bay lay too near. Slowly the morning fog lifted. Treptow set to work.

DAYS WITHOUT WATER

Gottschalk could never understand how such a bizarre idea gained so a powerful hold on him; strange as it seemed, it became almost an obsession to act on it.

He wore a baggy, soiled linen suit and sipped lukewarm rotgut from a flask. A foreigner, he sat on a veranda, gazing down the street, or rather down the muddy lane where pigs lay grunting in the shade of the huts. No one in the village knew where this stranger with his broken Spanish came from, nor why the vet had chosen to settle in this particular godforsaken part of the world. For some time rumors had been circulating in the village that he was on the run, until these too faded away and were slowly forgotten in the crippling monotony of the heat.

In this disturbing vision there would be no turning back. Gottschalk would have to lead another life. A strange and alien life, frightening yet fascinating.

By the end of March Kamptz's column reached Keetmanshoop with the captured herd of livestock.

Gottschalk rode in amazement through a transformed village. Three months ago there had been only a few tattered soldiers and scores of ragged natives.

Now the village looked like a military garrison in Germany. The officers had been quartered in the few houses made of stone. Tents had been pitched for the soldiers on the outskirts of the village, a sick bay of corrugated tin stood beside the mission house, along with a field bakery. Barrels and crates of ammunition were piled behind a barbed wire fence. In the street, Gottschalk's hand was constantly at the brim of his cap. More than twelve thousand soldiers were in the country now.

A young Hottentot woman minced her way through the sand in dainty laced boots, her powerful breasts poured into a black corset, her mouth painted red like a wound. She called out to Gottschalk in accent-free German: Hello, dearie, how about it, one fifty.

Captain Otto reported that prices had risen dramatically in the eight weeks Gottschalk had been away and would probably climb higher with the arrival of new reinforcements. Otto thought the prostitutes might be in league with the rebels, for a particularly virulent form of venereal disease had broken out and had already infected nearly half the troops in the village.

For a time the Captain considered importing experienced streetwalkers from the Reeperbahn in Hamburg, accredited by the Office of Health and cleared for intercourse, who could practice their profession under the supervision of military doctors. But venereal disease was already so widespread that it was now impossible to stem the tide. They would just have to treat those who were ill, either as outpatients or in sick bay depending on the stage of their infection, and introduce preventive measures for those not yet infected. Captain Otto ordered a large supply of contraceptives from the army store and worked up two lectures on early detection of venereal diseases in women. One of these, ribald, colorful, and ruthless in its detail, was delivered to the soldiers; the other, discreet and couched in generalizations, was for the officers. Within a few days one could observe the first troopers heading for their rendezvous with pocket lamps.

Military court martial specialist Volley studied legal decisions from the Franco-Prussian war of 1870–71 to determine to what extent syphilis or gonorrhea might be considered self-mutilation and punished as such.

Gottschalk was surprised by the Hottentots he saw in Keetmanshoop. In Warmbad they were prisoners, emaciated and wrapped in rags, squatting in the open field behind barbed wire. Here, however, they went about freely, well nourished, wearing cast-off German uniforms that were threadbare but not tattered. Christian Goliath, the chief, had managed to convince his tribe of Berseba Hottentots not to join the revolt. The young native men stood at attention for the soldiers, saluted so crisply they might have been studying the Prussian drill book, and responded to orders with, Yes, Sir! Even older men and women recognized the various ranks by braid, buttons, and epaulettes, and addressed Gottschalk by his full military title, Veterinary Lieutenant, Sir! They even recognized ranks as arcane as that of the Assistant Quartermaster.

This latter fellow, Pfannenschmidt by name, wore pince-nez and large wheeled spurs, and always carried an enormous revolver. He was followed three paces behind wherever he went by his bambuse, who had the same jerky gait and spoke the same Swabian dialect.

Gottschalk was almost physically nauseated by this sight, which embarrassed him to the point of anger. He wondered if the first signs hadn't already been apparent three months ago in Warmbad and he hadn't noticed them. He found himself thinking more and more about Katharina, trying to recall the details of their trysts on the hill. And each time he pushed the images aside, concentrating on something else, the tennis players outside his window, for example.

He'd been assigned a room in the newly-renovated mission school, a private one in fact, although they were normally reserved for staff officers. Probably no one wanted to share a room with him, just as he had initially tried to avoid rooming with Wenstrup. But people steered clear of Wenstrup because he was critical and refractory, while they regarded Gottschalk as simply odd and slightly stubborn. The staff officers might not have wanted the room, for although it was six meters in length, it was just over a meter wide. To get to the window, Gottschalk had to step over his cot, which he had placed half-way down the room for reasons of symmetry. The room had once been a corridor with a window looking out on the tennis courts where the district magistrate and the district medical officer occasionally played a match. In the meantime three new courts had been installed, strewn with brick dust and swept daily. Late in the afternoon, when it cooled off, the officers would play. Gottschalk would sometimes sit at the window and follow the flight of the ball, turning his head back and forth each time, until it seemed too silly. But he found it distracting when he wanted to read or write, and when the wind was from the west his uniform turned red with brick dust. Outside the village, ten native prisoners hammered old bricks into powder.

Since there were four other veterinarians in the village, Gottschalk had very little to do. He no longer sat with the tobacco club, which was still in existence, but lay instead on his cot in the long pipe-like room and followed the progress of the bugs on the walls and ceiling, unnaturally large, bloodthirsty ones, which the villagers swore had increased remarkably in size over the past few months.

Sometimes he woke in the night, imagining Katharina's warm body beside him, her matte brown skin, the smell of the earth. Then an uncontrollable, passionate longing for physical contact, for tenderness, made him pound his head against the wall. Only the knocking from the next room brought him to his senses.

He visited her family in Warmbad only once, at her request. The pondok lay outside the village and was hung with ragged mats. Two goats stood in its shade, children crawling between them, her siblings. Her father sat on a bench, an unlit pipe in his hand. An old man, already frail, who had married late for the third time. Although it was still morning, he was already drunk. He immediately asked Gottschalk for tobacco, which Gottschalk had brought as a gift. The only word he said in German, which he constantly repeated, was: Gehtinordnung—'sfine. Katharina offered Gottschalk some goat's milk. A fat woman appeared, her breasts hanging out of her tattered dress as if these large lumps of flesh did not belong to her. Her backside was the size of a barrel. Everything small and delicate in Katharina was colossally enlarged in this woman. The frightening thing was that Gottschalk saw the mother in the daughter. The father babbled something incomprehensible in Cape Dutch and kept repeating the word 'sfine, the meaning of which Gottschalk only gradually came to understand.

After this visit Gottschalk avoided Katharina. Once, in the night, she crept up to the house where he was sleeping and called out to him in Nama. Doctor Haring wanted to call the guard, but Gottschalk managed to dissuade him.

When Gottschalk received orders two days later to set out for Kalkfontein with Koppy's detachment he was actually glad to be leaving.

Now he wished he were back in Warmbad, though he had no idea what he would do if he were.

What oppressed him about this memory was the feeling of physical intimacy combined with unbridgeable distance.

He awoke nights with a bad taste in his mouth and a gnawing pain in his stomach. He felt raw inside. He brooded over the question of free will. Wasn't everything that one thought and did inevitably determined by a thousand tiny accidents that coalesced into an iron necessity, forcing one to act one way and not another? Were not wishes, too, predetermined by all the small empty spaces in one's life, which one slowly filled, and didn't these wishes in turn predetermine each intended act?

Several diary entries, none of them dated, must also be from this period.

Gottschalk's diary,
(undated)

The word "will" simply describes an empty spot where our views and intentions impel us toward an action we regard as necessary. If one wants to know more, one must take one's wishes apart, ruthlessly, to see if they are stuffed with down or horsehair.

(undated)

This steady roar in my head (day and night). It is time flowing by. And my skull is the time sluice.

(undated)

When the roar breaks off, the sound remains in the heads of others, separating what is deepest within from what is outside, and me from the world.

(undated)

Now, now, now, now, now, now, now, now, now: me.

Notes, numbers, and brief tables follow these entries over the next two months, dated and undated, isolated or out of context. An analysis of these numbers reveals certain recurring figures indicating distances to the English frontier, together with the daily distances covered by the horses. There are also notes indicating areas in which large numbers of shammas are growing. These are a sort of aqueous gourd whose bitter juice the Namas use for weeks at a time to slake their thirst. There are also numbers that can't be deciphered. They may indicate the specific quantities of oats or maize required by the horses.

In Warmbad Gottschalk once told Doctor Haring he didn't want to be complicit in this war's inhumanity. He wouldn't take an active part in fighting or shoot any Hottentots.

So what are you going to do, Haring responded, you're on one side and the Hottentots are on the other, not a hand's breadth away. Everything else is eyewash.

Gottschalk just couldn't accept this either-or. It was either-or for Wenstrup too, but from a different perspective, and he had chosen sides. What was Wenstrup up to now? Was he tending lame horses for the rebels or examining swine for trichina in a

Johannesburg slaughterhouse? Only the first of these was politically consistent, but the second was more consistent than getting horses back on their feet for the Colonial Guard, which was Gottschalk's job.

Wenstrup once called Gottschalk a dreamer.

Sometimes during the day Gottschalk would give a start, tiptoe to the door of his room, and jerk it open. He thought they had locked him in.

Gottschalk's diary,
2 May 1905

> A dream: I was strolling through a pine forest. Large pinecones were dropping from the trees. When they hit the ground they exploded like hand grenades. Captain Otto told a joke, and long white worms crawled out of the cones.

Did Gottschalk see alternatives then? Did he see a possibility (on his part at least) of bringing the two sides together, the Germans and the rebels, or the Germans and all Africans?

In the weeks since they'd returned to Keetmanshoop, Zeisse had taken two steel pieces sawed off the cannon and filed them into teeth, neatly and carefully, following Gottschalk's sketches, then soldered them on the clamp according to Gottschalk's design.

One morning Gottschalk left town with Zeisse and searched the outskirts for a suitable cow skull. They had to stay in sight of the village. Even if Keetmanshoop seemed like a German garrison, a person couldn't go for a piss in the bushes two kilometers away without a rifle.

The rebels often drove off livestock pastured near the village, boldly seeking out the best cattle.

On this occasion, as they walked among the scattered bones of cattle, Gottschalk asked Zeisse what he thought about taking land and livestock from the natives and then killing them or penning them up because they resisted. Did he think that was right?

Well, now, Zeisse replied, I don't know that I'd call it right. And when he was back on his horse: It's probably their own fault. And then as they were re-entering the village: It probably isn't right. But there's nothing to do about it.

Gottschalk had the cattle skull boiled clean. then broke two teeth out of the jaw. He stuck the steel teeth in the gaps. The clamp, fastened to the other teeth and correctly curved, held the false teeth so securely that they didn't wobble even when they were pulled on.

You should have that patented, Sir, said Zeisse.

Gottschalk placed the skull with false teeth on the table in his room. This denture will save the lives of many cows, he thought, and had to laugh at what he'd said. He realized as he laughed how foreign laughter had become to him, and was even more amused.

With its two dully gleaming steel teeth set in white bone the skull gave the impression of a sculpture, bizarre and sinister.

In the officers' mess they talked about the skull with false teeth. The vet's behavior was becoming more and more bizarre. They stopped speaking to Gottschalk, but left him alone.

Gottschalk's diary,
7 May 1905 (Keetmanshoop)

Jumping Bean Tree (*Spirostachys africana*): the tree grows six to nine meters high, its foliage attractively asymmetrical in form, although its bark, rough and black, peels off in regular rectangular strips. The beans, which fall from the tree shortly before Christmas, jump about on the ground for days. When I asked an old native what kind of tree it was, he replied: it's where our wishes grow.

I gathered up a few beans and took them home. The next day,

when the sun came through the window, they jumped about on the table.

I investigated the phenomenon with a scalpel and magnifying glass, and found the larva of an insect inside the bean.

The nights are cool. Baron von Gaisberg snores next door.

9 May 1905

Yesterday a black cloud erupted on the eastern horizon. They were already covering the munitions with tarps to protect them from the rain when they realized it was a huge swarm of grasshoppers, and in no time they were everywhere, bouncing blindly against walls and windows. People slipped on the shiny green carpet. Horses stumbled. Only the chickens raced about nimbly, cackling and snapping up the fattest grasshoppers.

The boiled eggs this morning were green and inedible.

10 May 1905

Language is the bare necessity of our loneliness.

11 May 1905

Even Zeisse has a Hottentot boy as a bambuse, one he shares with three other troopers. For a crust of bread and some tobacco he polishes their boots and leathers, but is useful in other ways too. He fetches customers for his three sisters.

Wenstrup's marginal notation in Kropotkin's *Mutual Aid: A Factor of Evolution*

The man who rides in a wagon will never be friends with the man who walks. (traditional Indian proverb)

Gottschalk considered this proverb false.

When an N.C.O. from the Second Battery saw Zeisse filing away on the steel teeth he asked him: Hey, tell me, has the vet gone soft in the noodle?

Zeisse said no, without looking up.

Captain Otto declared that a person with too much free time came up with odd ideas. At his instigation, Gottschalk was assigned a new area of responsibility. Major Buchholz, the line commander, ordered him to test the feasibility of camels as pack animals in German South West Africa.

On the last Friday in May the first camels arrived in Keetmanshoop. The entire village gathered and gaped in wonder. A Frenchman with a long white neck guard attached to his kepi was mounted on the lead camel. He'd served ten years in the French Foreign Legion in Algeria and had been sent as a riding instructor. The animals ambled along to the stable yard, their lips wobbling up and down at every step, as if the earth's gravity was concentrated upon these poor creatures, pulling their upper lip down over the lower, which hung limply in turn. The animals slouched along as if struggling to pull their legs out of a morass, even their humps flopped over sideways. Gottschalk walked around the animals, who were dully chewing their food, and said: When they're fed properly their humps will straighten up again. They're war-chests for hard times.

Zeisse was disappointed that they didn't require shoeing.

They bring honor to their zoological order, artiodactyla: callused soles, Gottschalk said, who also reported that camels lacked a gallbladder and were the only mammals with egg-shaped blood corpuscles. That was the extent of his knowledge, since he'd seen a dromedary only once before, in a zoo.

When Gottschalk received his orders to test camels as possible mounts and beasts of burden for the Colonial Guard, he was so taken aback he couldn't quite follow Major Buchholz, at whose instigation the first animals had been purchased in the Canary Islands. In a daze he watched his moving lips talk about days without water, kilograms, daily workload, average value, speed. Gottschalk said: Yes, Sir, saluted and left the room.

Stretched out on the cot in his corridor room, his hands folded under his head, he wondered what to do. Up to now he had simply done his duty, peering in the mouths of horses, making compresses, giving enemas. Yes, he'd helped keep the machinery in motion, but now he was being asked to speed it up. The camels were intended to counter the rebels' advantage in the countryside. With these undemanding creatures one could easily cover long distances through arid expanses.

The war was already the subject of malicious ridicule by foreign papers, particularly in England. It seemed so funny that a few hundred Hottentots were leading the greatest military power in the world around by the nose, itinerant cattle thieves putting scratches on the shiny war machine of the swaggering Kaiser. The Imperial General Staff intended to make a clean sweep of things as quickly as possible, and Gottschalk suddenly found himself helping to prepare that strategy. Outside he heard the clop of the tennis balls, and the west wind swept that damned dust into the room. Gottschalk stared at the dusty red cow skull with its steel teeth. Weren't social-democratic laborers helping too? True, a few in the Reichstag railed against the war, but the workers assembled the machine guns and stitched the saddles for the camels all the same. And there were social democrats who said openly that colonies were necessary if Germany was to remain an industrial power. Why should Gottschalk rack his brains over it? But he felt he was just making excuses. It was approximately two hundred fifty kilometers to the border, to Rietmont. A horse could travel seventy kilometers a day, a good camel could cover a hundred kilometers a day without water. A horse needed water by the second day at the latest.

Gottschalk told himself that every innovation brought to this land furthered its development and would benefit the natives one day. And if he refused to carry out the order, what good would it do? If he refused to execute a rebel the troops would see it as a protest, a sign. But to refuse to test camels would be a joke, and camels were always the butt of jokes anyway. The Colonial Guard would just laugh. Some other veterinarian would be more than happy to take over the task. Baron von Gaisberg was snoring next door again. Lieutenant Auer von Herrenkirchen tapped out his evening love note on the water pipes to Lieutenant Schüler, a fellow officer in the signal corps.

Lieutenant Auer called it finger exercises.

The distance from Keetmanshoop to the English settlement at Reitfontein was exactly two hundred thirteen kilometers, a little over two hundred and eight-six kilometers if one chose a path further to the north where there were no German military garrisons.

Gottschalk decided to undertake the experimental program.

Three years later, in 1908, the last rebels were tracked down and defeated in the Kalahari with the help of a German camel corps led by Captain von Erckert.

Gottschalk's diary,

25 May 1905 (Keetmanshoop)

Toward morning I woke from a dream: I lay in one of those zinc coffins used to transport corpses back to Germany. But I was not dead. The coffin was screwed down tight and soldered, as usual, to prevent the lid from warping under the pressure of decomposition gases. When I drummed on the lid, a voice (Tresckow?) said: That's the noise the stomach makes digesting itself. The voyage was entertaining, since I could converse with the inmates of the other coffins. Among them was Lieutenant Schwanebach, who, as he told me, lost his sense of direction and headed bravely into enemy fire. He was the victim of his own stupidity said the voice of an N.C.O. who had lost his way in the Namib and died of thirst. In Hamburg the same band that played *Muß i denn zum Städele hinaus* as I left had now launched into *Ich hatt einen Kameraden.* My coffin was lifted onto a gun carriage, a click of the tongue, and the horses pulled out, broke into a trot, then a gallop, and finally went hell bent for leather. My zinc coffin bounced and clanged about on the gun carriage until it finally crashed to the ground and sprang open. I woke up.

25 May 1905

The wife of the local missionary planted rose trees two years ago. Now, at the end of May, which is autumn here, the roses are blooming.

The next morning Gottschalk noticed a large crowd of people at the edge of the village. He walked over and saw the four camels standing by the thorn bushes, neatly tearing off sprigs and shoving them into their mouths, thumb-length thorns and all. Thorns that would penetrate even the thick soles of a combat boot.

The Frenchman, a stocky fellow, explained to Gottschalk in melodic but flawed German that these weren't really riding camels but pack animals, and poor-quality ones at that. One or the other might have carried an occasional English tourist, but if so it was in baskets hanging at its sides and not in a saddle. Jean Dermigny, who called himself Sergeant, said their performance could never compare to that of good riding camels. He had discovered on the ride there that these particular animals could only do a nine- or ten-hour trek, and covered at most fifty kilometers. Good riding camels on the other hand could go fourteen hours a day and cover over a hundred kilometers. To say nothing of the truly incomparable Bisharin racing camels. He had mounted one of these, a white camel mare, only once. It belonged to a Tuareg prince who wouldn't have sold it for the world, but lent it to the French sergeant as a gesture of hospitality, so the sergeant could deliver an important message across the waterless wastes of Erg to Ben Quinef. In three days the animal covered over five hundred kilometers without a day of rest, and without a single drink. It had been like flying. Horses were dumb, ungainly animals in comparison.

Gottschalk's diary,
27 May 1905

Today a mentally disturbed Hottentot was brought to the native outpatient ward. He claimed he was a zebra finch with an injured leg.

(He was in fact limping.) The orderly challenged him to fly. He warbled and said the clouds were too thick. A medic tried to talk him into jumping off a high wall, since that would make flying easier. Captain Otto showed up and put a stop to it.

280 km, four days by horse, with four stops for water. Two on the riding camel D. raves about, and no need to stop for water.

That morning Gottschalk mounted a camel for the first time in his life, one that had carried tomatoes and melons to market in the Canary Islands and lugged tourists to Pico de Teide.

The animal, which had knelt down on its front legs, rose again immediately once Gottschalk was in the saddle. The trio of Gottschalk, Dermigny, and Zeisse rode through Keetmanshoop followed by the laughter of the natives and soldiers. Gottschalk and Zeisse hopped about like monkeys on the camels' humps. The ambling gait of the camels threw the unpracticed riders about wildly, bouncing them up and down while tossing them from side to side. Their heads rolled and nodded, and by the second time around Zeisse's face was gray-green. As he passed a third time he was hanging sideways from the camel and spewing an irregular stream of half-digested bread, coffee, and four-fruit marmalade down the side of the plodding ship of the desert.

Zeisse gave up, to the catcalls of the curious onlookers, while Gottschalk urged his camel into a trot with sharp blows of his crop. This change in motion reduced the lurching considerably and as he leaned back in the saddle in imitation of Dermigny and braced himself lightly in the stirrups, he could scarcely feel the bumps. The animals trotted around the village at an amazing speed past the gaping Hottentots and soldiers, who now stood in silence.

At the end of May Gottschalk began what he rather pompously referred to as his experimental program, to which three troopers had been detailed, Zeisse among them. Since these camels were not particularly suitable for riding, and he knew of better animals through Dermigny's stories, he petitioned headquarters for the purchase of riding camels from the Esnch stud farm in upper Egypt. Thoroughbreds, so they could eventually set up their own stud farm in South West Africa. Gottschalk thought headquarters would be more likely to purchase these expensive camels if they could save money by raising their own.

Plans for a stud farm to breed top thoroughbred riding camels occupied Gottschalk in the coming days, as can be gathered from sketches and notes in his diary. There is also a special recipe for couscous that apparently came from Dermigny.

Gottschalk tested the four camels as pack animals on the stretch from Keetmanshoop to Gibeon. During the first trek in a troop convoy, which Gottschalk accompanied on horseback, he was surprised to find that the camels, who slouched loosely along, were actually moving faster than a horse at the same gait. And although Gottschalk urged his mount, it couldn't keep up for more than half an hour.

On his Hegira, the flight from Mecca to Medina, Mohammed rode a Bisharin camel mare that covered two hundred kilometers a day according to Dermigny.

At one point on the march to Gibeon, Gottschalk asked Zeisse if he would volunteer for a camel corps. Zeisse said he wasn't interested in camels, he detested their smell, and they didn't need to be shoed. He figured that if he were promoted to N.C.O. by the end of the year, it would take two more years in Africa to save the money he needed. Then he would finish his master craftsman's diploma and take over the blacksmith shop in Bardowick.

When Gottschalk returned to Keetmanshoop three weeks later, you could smell him through a closed door. The camels had a gland on the back of their heads that excreted a disgusting goaty smell. Dogs sniffed after him. He tried to cover the stink with cologne, but the camels reacted violently to it, refusing to stir from the spot. One of them terrified him, biting him on the arm, and the wound had to be treated with iodine and bandaged. Camel bites were often fatal according to Dermigny. During rutting season, when the animals are particularly unruly, a comrade in Mauritania had been bitten so savagely by a male camel that a section was torn from the man's skull, including skin, hair, bone, and part of his brain.

When he returned to his corridor-room, Gottschalk found the cow skull in its accustomed place, but draped with a handkerchief. The captain who occupied the room while Gottschalk was away was laid up in sick bay with a serious intestinal infection.

Each evening Gottschalk sat at his small wooden table writing reports on the endurance and characteristics of the Canary Island dromedaries, adding figures and drawing diagrams. In increasingly urgent petitions to Colonial Guard headquarters he demanded better camels, Bisharin riding camels from East Sudan if possible. He wrote that only quality camels could flush out the rebels once and for all from their lairs in the barren Kalahari. But then, rereading what he had written, he was ashamed of himself and tore it up. At night he slept like a stone, and heard neither the love notes tapped on the water pipes by Lieutenant von Herrenkirchen nor the snores of Baron von Gaisberg. When he awoke he couldn't remember a single dream. At times, in the midst of a statistical comparison of the fodder needed for a mule and a camel, he thought again of those sleepless nights in which he tormented himself with abstract questions of free will and the source of moral authority. An abyss of brooding.

Around this time Gottschalk took on a bambuse, although he loathed the idea of servants. But he wanted to practice his Nama, and the young man, a Hottentot, pushed himself on him: polished the smelly, sweat-soaked boots Gottschalk left standing outside his room, brought him coffee in the morning, and stood outside the house with the heavy camel saddle on his shoulder when Gottschalk left for work. One day, not wanting to seem stingy, Gottschalk gave him a few pennies. Thus began his employer relationship with Simon, who was determined to serve as a bambuse for an officer, since he had been a catechist at the mission school in Berseba and spoke fluent German, and could also write and do figures. Simon had an insatiable desire to learn. He devoured newspapers, magazines, Gottschalk's veterinary and medical textbooks, Kropotkin's *Mutual Aid*, and the only novel Gottschalk had brought with him to South West Africa, Fontane's *Stechlin*. Gottschalk had read the novel in Germany and meant to reread it at leisure on the crossing, but never got to it. Now Simon talked about the Mark Brandenburg area as if he had grown up in a manor house.

Simon, reared from childhood in a mission house where he excelled through his love of learning, traveled to Germany at the age of seventeen with the missionary. Inspired by the paved streets, the stone houses, the gas street lamps, electric trams, shops, all the well-run institutions, the public pissoirs, the policemen on the corners, he was mildly disturbed now and then only by the color of his skin and the crinkly hair on his head.

What were ox-wagons, toiling their way laboriously through the sand, compared with the underground railway, which need not follow a complicated journey through the streets, but instead disappeared beneath the buildings and reappeared elsewhere at its goal? Everything was set up to save time, to shorten the journey.

The same mysterious strength seemed evident in the people he saw walking the streets; they knew their goal, and did not stop to stare or chat about every little thing in their path.

When Gottschalk asked Simon what impressed him most about Germany, he replied: The funeral parlors. The missionary's father died while they were in Germany. A gentleman dressed in black appeared, preprinted forms were filled out, and the deceased disappeared from the home. He wasn't seen again until the burial service, carefully coffined atop a catafalque, then carried by uniformed men to a pre-dug grave. Everything went smoothly and neatly, no smell, no endless hours at a wake. The family members of the deceased went on with their work. Simply fantastic.

Gottschalk spoke in Nama, Simon answered in German. He claimed he no longer spoke Nama correctly. If Gottschalk couldn't find the right word, Simon waited patiently until Gottschalk paraphrased it or said it in German.

One day Simon started to speak in Berlin dialect, pulling thoughtfully at what little beard he had. A habit of Leonhard Brunkhorst, Professor of Ethnology.

Professor Brunkhorst had arrived in Keetmanshoop two weeks earlier. He wore a self-designed traveler's outfit of English cloth, which with its various belts, pockets, and buckles appeared eminently practical. Brunkhorst would often tell the story of how he once met an English professor of botany in the middle of the Kalahari Desert who immediately assumed he was a countryman and said How do you do. Even after a long conversation the man couldn't believe he was German. Brunkhorst had studied two years at Oxford. He collected Nama folktales and was working on a Nama grammar. He soon incurred the displeasure of several officers by constantly singing the praises of their admirable cousins across the channel, who were more cosmopolitan, more diplomatic, more self-controlled, more tactful, more skillful, fairer, finer, fitter, in short, miles ahead of the Germans.

The professor carried a black leather case on his excursions, which he opened whenever he encountered an interesting Hottentot. He would pull out an oversized circular gadget made of chrome-plated steel and fit it over the terrified Hottentot's head, guaranteeing in fluent Nama as he did so that it wouldn't hurt. He measured the heads of the various Nama tribes and after a few months reached the conclusion that based on the skulls of the Hottentots one could not infer a lower level of intelligence, indeed the opposite was more likely.

Professor Brunkhorst came to Keetmanshoop intending to search for the remains of a huge barrel. He wanted to know if there was any truth to a Hottentot tale from the Bethany region that decades ago a white trader had brought a giant barrel with him and then burned it near Geiaub. Brunkhorst found nothing.

Schliemann searching for a Hottentot Troy, quipped the wags in the officers' mess.

Gottschalk's diary,
12 July 1905

The pinched nasal tone of the officers is like the scent gland behind the camel's head: a familiar recognition signal. The camel has his callused soles, the career officer his motto: der Berufsstand zum Tode—our profession unto death.

13 July 1905

In two weeks I leave with a patrol for Heirachabis. The village is a day's ride from the English frontier.

16 August 1905

Gentleness and composure can, as the camel shows, overcome the stickiest defense. The soft lips of the camel manage to break twigs with finger-long thorns and shove them so skillfully into its mouth that it can extract nourishment from the inedible.

(In the night.)

As I reread this, I'm struck by its one-sided point of view. There is nothing friendlier and more self-sufficient than a thorn bush, which grows in sand and whose thorns are only for protection. In the rainy season it blossoms yellow.

17 August 1905

I will try to complete the experiments with the camels here in Keetmanshoop so systematic camel breeding can begin. Distances will shrink. The economic advantage—in peacetime—would be obvious. I would like to see the countryside from above. To fly over the wastelands and savannas in a balloon, over the dried-up riverbeds, the ravines of the Karas Mountains. Balloon flights could also be used for

patrols. (I'll be careful not to talk about this.) One could fly peacefully
over the countryside, in soundless flight, and land near a settlement or
water-hole. As long as the wind is blowing from the west, as it is today.

When Brunkhorst heard that Gottschalk was being dispatched
to the very center of rebel territory, he asked him to look for
rebel skulls and mail them to him collect at his institute in
Greifswald.

Professor Brunkhorst was building an ethnological collection
concentrating on Nama and Bushman cultures. In addition he
collected interesting examples of Hottentot skulls. He asked men
on patrol to watch for fallen rebels. The skulls of the dead were
usually picked to the bone by vultures and jackals, then cleaned
by termites and nicely bleached by the sun. Sadly, the rebels seldom left a dead comrade in the field, except in extreme cases.
They usually dragged them off for burial, even under heavy fire.
So although there were plenty of skulls of natives who had died of
hunger or typhus, mostly women and children, there were very
few from fallen rebels. But these were precisely the ones that interested Professor Brunkhorst as a phrenologist. Did the skull
bulge out noticeably at the point where the will was located?

You see, Brunkhorst once said to Gottschalk, holding a well-
preserved skull in his hand, with all its teeth, but displaying a
small round hole in the forehead, you see, there's no need for such
unsightly blemishes if we could just settle on a reasonable colonial policy. Treat them well, awaken their interest in work, fewer
rifle butts and drinking bouts, and these people could be useful
members of society. Perhaps one should avoid the word colony altogether, since it has a somewhat negative overtone. Protectorate
is a good deal better, although colony seems to be gaining cur-
rency. When it comes to civilizing people, we should keep our
cousins across the channel in mind. We can learn a good deal from
them. Or from the highly interesting experience of the North
Americans, who freed their blacks in the south from slavery. Released from the personal care of the slaveholders, the blacks en-

tered into a free state and therefore into lively competition with each other as workers. The result is an open, dynamic society.

Gottschalk's diary,

3 August 1905 (Keetmanshoop)

For B. everything is perfect, even the future. When I asked him if he feared death, he frowned thoughtfully, then—once again—came up with a fitting answer: Not death, but dying.

But dying is nothing compared to death.

B. researches myths of death and handles skulls, filling them with mustard seeds to determine their volume. Death cannot be measured with mustard seeds.

Gottschalk's diary

24 August 1905

The wind drives billowing clouds across the Kalahari. Soon it will rain. The bushes stand gray and scorched.

I leave K. in two days. Baron von Gaisberg snores next door.

Early in the morning of 26 August a supply train of eight ox-wagons readied for departure for Ukamas. Gottschalk was to join them.

Zeisse had also received marching orders for Ukamas. They wanted to get rid of him too, feeling he'd been infected by the refractory vet. An N.C.O. complained that Zeisse called the treatment of prisoners inhuman. He'd even mentioned August Bebel, the socialist leader.

Upon hearing this, the company commander blocked Zeisse's eagerly-awaited promotion to lance corporal.

During his remaining days in Keetmanshoop, Gottschalk worked on his report regarding the use of camels as pack animals in South West Africa. On 25 August he completed the task.

In the annals of German military history, Captain von Erckert is credited as the creator of the camel corps.

NAMALAND AND THE KALAHARI

eport to the Royal Prussian Academy of Sciences concerning an expedition undertaken by Dr. Leonhardt Brunkhorst, Senior Lecturer at the University of Greifswald, from 1903 to 1905.

The relationship of the Hottentots to other races:

The following is not intended as a history of the Hottentot wars; whoever wishes to write that history must trace in detail how a small vegetable garden belonging to the Dutch West Indies Company grew into the Cape Colony. Our own concern is to show the specific relationship of the Hottentots to the white races, and thereby provide a possible insight into the proper treatment of these natives.

The Hottentots have been in contact with the Boers for centuries, for the most part as slaves kept by the white cultural pioneers of southern Africa. Even today the Boer generally refers to the Hottentot simply as a "schepsel," that is, a creature existing alongside him like any number of other inexplicable or superfluous things in the world. Or he calls the Hottentots "geel goed," yellow goods, that one can harness or handle like livestock. The custom of taking Hottentot children and raising them, "groot maak," is less rewarding now than it was when the lord of the manor still exercised free rein over the life and death of his chattel and could simply shoot those who disobeyed or tried to run off. That this ancient traditional right was taken from him by the culture that followed, supported by the English administration, is the primary reason the average Boer I met in Little Namaland loathes English rule (which in all other matters leaves him as free as he could wish).

The Boers were nonplussed to learn that even in the German area to which they were emigrating, Hottentots still maintained certain rights. As I became more closely acquainted with the Boers, I tried to gain some insight through conversation as to how, in their eyes, the God to whom they knelt three times a day in prayer would regard their concept of brotherly love as it applied to the colored races. I was directed to the Bible. I would not have taken seriously their arguments from the Old Testament if they hadn't advanced them so seriously, and if they had not in fact proved to be the guiding principle behind their actions, here and in their former home: In the ninth chapter of Genesis, Noah curses the son of Ham, Canaan and his descendants, to servitude. The Boers extend this curse to all Hamites, among whom they include the Hottentots, viewing them as natural-born slaves. Now what master did God place over them? What the nation of Israel was in the Old Covenant, Christ is in the New. In the seventh chapter of the fifth book of Moses the destruction of the Canaanites is ordered. As Christian heirs to the Israelites, the Boers have been or-dained by God as Lords over the life and death of the cursed descen-dents of Canaan unto their most recent generation (the natives of southern Africa). This is the Boer's position, and the narrower and more racist they are, the more strongly they hold to it. This type of evangelism appears to free thinkers among the Boers as a cloak that reveals most clearly that which it should conceal: the boundless ego-tism of the Boers, which will soon leave the Hottentots with no other recourse than to conduct a long slow war of attrition with equal ruth-lessness. Whoever has the upper hand in any particular situation, acted and continues to act, whenever not enjoined by law, according to this basic principle.

The Hottentots are regarded quite differently by another group of whites, the representatives of the Christian mission, embodied today by the emissaries of the Rhenish Missionary Society at Barmen. The earlier reports of this society reveal the distance between the cur-rent Nama mission and the one of fifty years earlier. A mission among the Hottentots in this ungoverned land, plagued by conflicts among the natives, was once a sacrifice of the highest order. Without the pro-tection of a government the missionary placed himself at the mercy of the natives, followed the restless tribes on their nomadic journeys, shared their hunger and thirst, and at times went so far as to marry a native, to achieve a deeper and more intimate empathy with them. And many a missionary met a mysterious end, Gorth for example. Others gave up and returned to Europe, convinced that Hottentots could never be turned into civilized Christians.

Not until treaties of protectorate existed with the Reich, strongly promoted by the Missionary Society, were guarantees given for the missionaries' life and property, and their work prospered. In the meantime the Hottentot tribes became sedentary, and the mission houses were the finest buildings in the land, homes not only of vocation, but comfort as well, and, I emphasize with heartfelt gratitude, of gracious hospitality for the traveler.

Only a person blindly opposed to missions could fail to recognize the importance of the bridge for peaceful understanding between two heterogeneous races built by Christianity, and its consequences for the cultural development of this country. But it is equally crystal clear that the mission would become a curse if it too narrowly pursued spiritual goals while losing sight of political and economic well-being. This well-being depends on the extent to which it succeeds in regulating the competing interests of the natives and the invading race according to economic efficiency. But this obvious truth is constantly shoved aside by both utopian humanists and apostles of force. Emotions are of no use here. It can't be a question of slapping the natives on the back and making friends or of simply eradicating them. One must recall the calamities in the Cape Colony, but also those in the protectorate at this very moment, at the time of the Hottentot revolt, to understand what a huge saving of money and blood it would mean if the colonialists' interests could be properly linked with those of the natives. (Even now the government of the protectorate is faced with a serious work shortage trying to build the railroad from Lüderitz to Keetmanshoop.)

An unbiased and detailed knowledge of the living conditions and conceptual world of the natives is crucial to successful economic development. This is a precondition for proper leadership, for motivating native workers. Shooting or hanging, even the sjambok (hippo-hide whip), are far from optimal solutions, leaving aside the issue of whether it is humane. The ideal case for the colonial economy would be to guide the worker in such a manner that he would think he was making his own decisions, so economic demands would be congruent with his own wishes. Herein lies the difficulty, for as older missionaries have confirmed, after a hundred years of missionary work, the Hottentot has yet to be converted into a disciplined worker. The average Hottentot sees in Christianity not least the white man's preference. Just as he thinks more of himself in a white man's jacket and trousers or color print dress than his brother or sister in an animal-skin loincloth, so he sees his membership in the Christian church as a mark of a modern Hottentot. There is a driving impetus behind this, for the Hottentot has an alert instinct for what's new. At the same time, however, he is lazy and cunning; he sees the contradiction between Christian theory and practice in both the social and the private life of the whites too clearly to become the sort of naïve, obedient Christian we sometimes find at home. He takes what suits him from Christianity, and his disputes with missionaries, traders, and officials, referring to the Bible for support, are frequently feared. German colonial officials are seldom prepared for such refined and rapid debates, and driven into a corner, have been all too quick to answer with the whip.

Beyond such utilitarian motivations to accept Christianity, there exist more profound affinities between Christian morality and traditional social norms from their heathen past that have persisted to the present day: brotherly love among the Hottentots in the form of mutual aid, respect for the elderly and for women, their tender affection for children, their abstemiousness with regard to the property of others (although limited to the property of their own tribe)—all these are such autochthonous laws.

But it is precisely these social norms that stand in the way of an evolving civilization. That evolution rests essentially on the principle of competition among individuals. This competition is the driving force behind all economic development and constitutes the foundation upon which the free individual is formed. In the tribal association of the Hottentots, however, competition is negated by the principle of mutual aid. No thought is given to hard times or old age, since each knows that the others, insofar as they have anything, will share it with him. We find in the Hottentots a human type that devotes all its intelligence, which its possesses in abundance, to the single goal of living comfortably, enjoying life and doing as little as possible, a stance that has led some hedonists to see in it a proof that great inventions are motivated only by laziness, because the intelligence mobilizes astonishing powers to uncover the easiest path. At any rate the fertile inventiveness of the Hottentot is highly developed when it is a matter of maintaining his own comfort, sitting around, drinking schnapps, dancing or dreaming away beneath blue clouds of pipe smoke. I myself have met Hottentots who make fun of the zealous activity of the Germans. To this very day the Hottentot has difficulty seeing another person as a competitor. Here centuries of missionary activity have borne no fruit. The name of our Lord, whose life was one great self-sacrifice, can only be claimed by someone who is capable of at least the smallest of sacrifices in the service of his fellow man, namely work. In this sense few Hottentots have become Christians. The systematic training of the natives for work has been demanded often enough for economic reasons. But it seems to me irrefutable that it should be a religious demand of the Christian mission as well. Experience has shown that a primitive people whose economy has gone bad also descends morally, since it will sell any service to the superior race for its daily bread. So the demand that natives learn to work does not entail a secularization of duties contrary to the missionary's agenda, but simply a path toward a solid foundation of his religious duty. The white population for its part will be more thankful for a trained work force than for ninety-nine heavenly applicants who know the Bible forward and backward but are afraid to work.

The efforts of the Catholic and Evangelical missions should also be viewed from this perspective; they should be allowed to compete, instead of the present official interference with the Catholic mission. Only when we know which of the two missions produces the more willing workers, the stronger government supporters from among the native Christians, will a success be clear that extends beyond the missions themselves.

The relationship of the Hottentot to his German master may be characterized as follows: the Hottentot learns our language fairly rapidly, he is a keen observer of foreigners and is clever enough to keep the results to himself. In all these points he differs positively from most of our countrymen. Outside Africa his language is mocked because of its clicks. This might be harmless enough in itself; but a great majority of our countrymen are content to pick out what seems odd, unusual, or comical about the Hottentots, and that is more disturbing. At the same time great contradictions come to light in our intercourse. The same chief who is occasionally invited to the house by officials as a "top man," is offered hospitality by the trader in his own fashion with the words: "How about a brandy, you old dog?" In one case a white man receives a fine for chasing an impudent Hottentot off his farm with a whip, in another an understandably angry official personally wields it. The punishment itself—as long as the Hottentots fail to freely adopt cultural norms—is not what is reprehensible, it is the inconsistency in its administration. One may disapprove of the ruthlessness of the proceedings in individual cases; but the rigorousness with which even the more mildly-inclined Boer, with the total support of his peers, maintains his strict principles with respect to the Hottentots, is the solid core of the Boers' praiseworthy ability to deal with the natives. Not unlike rearing children, to whom it is not entirely unfair to compare the naïve, stubborn, and at times impertinent natives. It's not the punishment that's reprehensible, but the inconsistency of wielding a blow and then immediately apologizing for it in front of the child.

Such uniformity in the treatment of the natives must be the spontaneous result of a congruence between the general character of the native race and the particular situation. In countless cases I've found that a Hottentot who is himself convinced that he deserves punishment expects it. Thus one day Captain Schöpwinkel couldn't find his tobacco. He called his bambuse, a young Hottentot, and asked him where his tobacco was. At this the Hottentot youth, a devout Christian, handed him the sjambok without saying a word. He had stolen something, but he was also prepared to accept the punishment he deserved. In the eyes of a Hottentot it is a sign of weakness or limited intelligence if he is spared punishment, or if it is sugar-coated in any way. He may thank you for your leniency in granting him absolution, deeply moved, and if he is a Christian ask the Lord Jesus to reward you—but anyone who can see behind the backdrop knows that he's laughing at you. He wants to be dealt with rigorously. The claim of justice must be raised in the interest of authority alone, even when the punishment involved is not severe.

Even a man unadorned by any public office must constantly be aware that in this semi-civilized land his personal intercourse with natives is never a purely private matter. Each individual bears a direct portion of responsibility for good or bad relations between the races. The outcome of this confrontation with direct responsibility is the sharpest test of the maturity of a people in international relations. Here we are clearly revealed as amateurs. Within borders too broadly spaced, we waver between a fraternization lacking all authority and official posturing as masters. The middle road: sympathy for foreign qualities joined with a calm, firm preservation of our own superiority, does not appeal to us. Our cousins across the channel are more cosmopolitan in this respect.

We must openly admit that at present the Hottentot knows us better than we know him. Well aware of his own weaknesses, he never loses interest in studying the white invaders. Schooled for generations, and from childhood on, to work with cunning, he allows the white man an insight into the results of his own observations of human interaction in only the rarest of cases.

Thus I encountered one and the same Hottentot working as a deacon with the missionary, speaking with gestures of blessing about brotherly love and how the money changers must be driven from the temple, who within a few weeks was handling the account books for a cattle trader, and four months later was serving as a bambuse with a lieutenant, speaking to his donkey in a pinched nasal tone that sounded like he came from the Berlin garrison of a regimental troop. In all three cases his gestures, facial expressions, and manner of speaking were startlingly similar to his master's, but in all three so exaggerated and almost caricatured one couldn't be sure that he wasn't making fun of all three in secret.

But we need hardly continue piling up examples. Even without them we have blazed a trail for the admission that we have committed a serious error in our relationship with the natives by underestimating the Hottentots both in the details of their daily lives and in the matters that touch the core of their being. We have had to pay for this error with so much precious blood that it is the duty of every witness to point it out, so that in the future it may be avoided.

MEN BEHIND THE SCENES

The *German News*, 1 August 1906

Interesting news has reached us from an old Africa hand concerning English partisans in southern Africa who are endangering our interests, news that sheds new light on secret English sources of support for the South West African rebels.

Scarcely a man living on the border of our South West African protectorate has played such a damaging role, nor promises to cause us so many future difficulties, as George St. Leger-Lennox—Scotty Smith. It seems all the more important, then, to bring this political figure to the attention of the German public, including the world of officialdom, since the connection between Scotty and the Imperial Ministry in Cape Town, as well as with the expansionist De Beers Company in Kimberly, itself so closely tied to the ministry in matters of business, is now beyond all doubt.

The political agenda of this man, an important personality of his kind, emerges clearly from two remarks he made in passing in my presence. In one he declared that it made no sense to divide southern Africa along political and economic lines, since we Germans were incapable of developing the economic potential of South West Africa, which Scotty sees as quite high. We are kept from doing so by the narrow-mindedness both of the colonial government and parliament. Having Germany as a neighbor is a constant military and political threat to the supremacy of the British flag. Scotty attempted to convince me to enlist the aid of the German press in introducing a new business deal: an exchange of South West Africa for British East Africa and Zanzibar.

On another occasion, in the presence of a German doctor in Up-ington, Scotty declared: "If I wish, you'll be at peace tomorrow, and if I wish, the Union Jack will wave over your protectorate, whenever I think the time is right!"

Many considered this remark, which was much discussed in Gordonia, ludicrous self-aggrandizement on Scotty's part. But such doubters fail to realize the power Scotty has managed to achieve in over forty years of hard, single-minded work, even if it has not always been unobjectionable from a moral point of view. This considerable power in the hands of a man who unites the most extreme moral contradictions, a man for whom the end justifies even the worst of means, who controls the arm of the Cape government in spite of nu-merous crimes and even murders, not divested of their nastiness by special circumstances (Scotty considers political assassination accept-able and even necessary in the interest of the state!), a man who has at his disposal the funds of the De Beers Company—power in the hands of such a man carries great weight. No one rates this power more highly than the imperialists in Cape Town, and De Beers. From the very start, Scotty exploited the favorable political and economic circumstances so effectively that Cecil Rhodes once remarked: "He has the upper hand. It's not clear if Scotty is a tool of the govern-ment, or the government a tool of Scotty's." His power and influence have increased even further since the Boer War, in which Scotty knew how to make himself useful to the British. Today he is sixty-three years old, powerfully built and extraordinarily energetic. Six months ago he married a woman who had already presented him with a string of children. Possessed of a positively brilliant mind, the man makes no secret of his anti-German activities, nor of his political and busi-ness connections with Cape Town and Kimberly. True, he wraps his chess moves in a cloak of impenetrable darkness. He lards newspa-pers with clever and well-written articles, he sends messengers with news or advice for the natives in the German protectorate, he organ-izes daring raids, in which he seldom participates personally. In gen-eral he is held to be—and admits it himself, not without a certain tinge of vanity—the secret generalissimo of the rebels.

His influence on Hendrik Witbooi dates from the time of the first

Witbooi orlog and emerged most clearly two years ago. The traitorous role that Hendrik played may be traced primarily to Scotty's influence. Scotty also arranged the sale of the cattle stolen from the murdered farmers, which the Witboois had to turn over to the English.

This influence was also exerted on Morenga. When Morenga was forced by our troops to sue for peace a few months ago—and unfortunately allowed to retain his weapons for "self-defense," and even fed on top of it, while our own troops went hungry!—Scotty worked on this bandit chief so long through his agents that he came to Narogas (Spanenberg's farm) in British territory at the end of September in 1905. Morenga had substantial debts with traders living on the border: as one example among many, he owed a certain Grünblatt £strl. 462. We don't know what deal was struck in Narogas. But it is a fact that a messenger arrived at Grünblatt's with a note from Morenga that the debt would be paid in early November.

Then, at Heirachabis, Morenga issued a new declaration of war, which a German veterinarian who happened to be there and Herr Walser-Ukamas had to write down and then witness, attesting to Morenga's well-known signature. At the end of November the money arrived at Grünblatt's. The debt was paid through a certain Mr. McK . . . (Kinney) from Kimberley, who according to a letter which fell into my hands, also served as an intermediary for the firm of Harris Bros. in Zwartmodder. Hendrik Witbooi's debt, which according to the letter amounted to £strl 400 plus interest, came from this same source.

There is no legal proof that these funds came from the De Beers Company, but it seems obvious, since Scotty's patriotism doesn't extend to the expenditure of such substantial funds himself. It has been shown that he had his hand in the affair, and he has admitted his connection with De Beers. To this one may add news stories that at the beginning of "Germany's little war" openly discussed the "prospects" for the De Beers Company in German South West Africa. It should also be mentioned that the Harris Bros. firm, with whom both Morenga and Hendrik Witbooi had dealings, continues to supply our German troops.

The existence of these debts, the full extent of which it is of course impossible to determine, shows that Morenga was not speaking truthfully in a interview published in the *Cape Times*, presumably provided by Scotty, when he claimed that he lived exclusively on goods taken from German supply trains. This claim is also contradicted by a report in which German troops were said to have found a store of supplies in the Karas Mountains that was not of German origin.

This observation is even more important given the fact that Representative Erzberger has attempted to spread the conventional wisdom stemming from the missionary station at Heirachabis that if the south is abandoned the Hottentots will starve. In doing so Erzberger is at the very least furthering the business aims of the English De Beers Company!

The speed with which Scotty transmits messages to the Hottentots can be gathered from the following example, which is also characteristic of his hostile actions toward Germany:

We captured a native near Witpan who told us that the Hottentots had drawn new courage from the fact that the German Reichstag had refused funds for the continuation of the war. Four days later I was in Upington, where no one had heard this news, although Lieutenant Burges made a remark the import of which became clear only later. A few days thereafter I found a Reuter's telegram in the Cape Town News in which the elimination of certain credits had in fact been used to fabricate the story that all funds for the continuation of the war had been denied. The story had been heliographed by way of Reitfontein to Scotty, who immediately forwarded it to our enemies.

THE JUMPING BEAN TREE

Lieutenant Elschner, the commander of the supply train, was in a bad mood. Why had he of all people had been saddled with this strange bird? He had only seen Gottschalk twice, at a distance: once as he made a few rounds on a camel as if he were in a circus, and again as he was talking with the professor in Nama. But he had heard plenty about him. He had a reputation as an eccentric. Fine, there were plenty of them running all over the place. More to the point, he was said to sympathize with the Kaffirs, and had made several ill-conceived comments in the past few weeks. The man was thoroughly military in his bearing, however. He could easily have made lieutenant. Elschner saw the man's recalcitrance as a result of the discrepancy between his desire to be a lieutenant and his duties as a horse doctor. There were also rumors that the vet had been downright friendly with the colored folk in Warmbad, that he had even had a relationship with a young Hottentot woman. And of course Elschner had heard of the merry patrol ride with Lieutenant von Schwanebach (who had fallen in battle in the meantime). There were even reports of yodeling. Anywhere Gottschalk showed up, there was bound to be trouble. And Elschner hated that. It was hard enough guiding these clumsy, groaning teams of oxen safely through rebel territory with all the cracking whips, shouting drivers, and billowing clouds of dust. He had been given twenty men as an armed escort. That wasn't many. The southeast region of South West Africa was not considered dangerous at the moment, since the Colonial Guard headquarters had arranged a ceasefire with Morenga and were negotiating for peace. But, as Elschner knew, that was only a delaying tactic. This period was being used to quietly prepare an offensive against Morenga. Elschner's wagon train was to bring supplies and munitions to the supply depots in the south. He was worried that Morenga, that sly fox, would see through the German negotiating strategy and resume the struggle. So Elschner urged the wagon train on toward Ukamas at top speed. This war could easily be won, but one could just as easily fall into an abyss.

Sitting high on his camel, served up on a platter, Gottschalk would surely be taken for the convoy leader by rebels waiting in ambush. The camel's hump was like an observation tower. Elschner rode up to him repeatedly to ask what he could see. Gottschalk would take a look around with the field glasses, the camel chewing away beneath him, and say: Nothing in sight. Once he offered to let the lieutenant ride, but Elschner declined, saying he could hardly start learning to ride a camel now, in the middle of enemy territory. Gottschalk, peering out over the wagon train, felt he'd made a mistake taking the best of the four camels out for what he called a test ride.

After Gottschalk's negative reports on the Canary Island camels, Colonial Guard headquarters had ordered another breed, with the order going to the Hamburg firm of Hagenbeck.

Unfortunately well over a thousand Canary Island camels had already been ordered, a majority of which were already loaded and on the high seas.

Gottschalk's diary,
3 September 1905

The road leads along the Geitsaub, far from any human habitation.

Although it hasn't rained for six months, water still stands in the Vley, which is partially overgrown with reeds, a refuge for all living things. We also find repeated traces of Hottentots and Bushmen. But the dust clouds of our troops and the subsequent flights of wildlife announce our coming for miles in advance.

Yesterday we found grass pondoks on the Geitsaub Vley, constructed weeks earlier by a German detachment: great shade-making
beehives. But only a few steps away human bones were scattered
(food for wild animals). I found a shoulder blade, small and delicate.

The thought that Wenstrup might have rested here on his flight,
however, made everything seem familiar.

For the first few days Gottschalk usually sat around the campfire
with Zeisse, talking about mass-producing cow teeth, but on this
evening Elschner had invited him for a glass of arrack. Elschner
wanted to know the story about this strange device that
Gottschalk carried around in his saddlebag. Gottschalk declined
a second glass of arrack. His rebellious stomach was acting up
again. In Keetmanshoop he'd noticed it less toward the end, but
this eternal traveling about didn't seem to agree with him.

From then on Elschner and Gottschalk ate together. Elschner's goal was to serve on the general staff. He said that quite
openly. Troop duty offered variety, and for a short time it was
like a fresh breeze in summer holidays, but in the long run
it proved dull. No wonder most troopers were drunks. Elschner's dream was general staff maps with tiny red and blue flags,
and sickle-sweep attacks that tore open, or more precisely, split
apart, the enemy front (French for the most part). Elschner
had the makings of a great tactician and would probably have
helped develop battle plans for Walküre and Barbarossa thirty-
five years later if a Hottentot bullet hadn't shattered his right
knee in 1906. So he stayed in South West Africa with a stiff leg,
married the daughter of a baker from Swakopmund and farmed
at Schwarzrand. Now, however, sitting on a crate across from
Gottschalk, he criticized the way the Germans were running the
war and, with all due respect, Count Schlieffen, the general chief
of staff, who was still conducting a European-style war against
the Hottentots and was failing to respond to what was new and
revolutionary with equally new military tactics. This minor war
was, like the Spaniards against Napoleon, a guerilla war. Even
back then the French couldn't have their way militarily. Fortu-

284 • Uwe Timm

nately the present situation was far more favorable. He didn't
want to think what it would be like if more people lived here.
But as it was, the troops which had now swollen to over four
thousand men could be spread out rather than march in
columns, and a guard could be placed beside every Hottentot
who was caught, including old men, women, and children. In
fact you would have to do that, since each one was a
potential rebel. But that led quite logically to serious consequences. There were two possibilities for radical pacification of
the land. One was based on General Trotha's motto: The only
good Hottentot is a dead Hottentot. That was the radical solution. Or they could be placed in a camp, which would result in
the mixed form of interment and decimation currently in use. In
the long run, however, that would give rise to a new problem:
those who were kept in the camp couldn't feed themselves, so it
would become necessary to feed the most resistant of them. But
this second alternative was not feasible, since it was impossible
to catch all the Hottentots. The general staff should get down on
their knees and thank the Hottentot rebels, Elschner said. They
can test on a small scale what might be used later in a larger and
more dangerous situation. He was thinking of a guerilla war in a
heavily populated colony, Cameroon or East Africa or, even
more dangerously, a minor war within a larger European context, in France or Russia for example. Up to now they had considered only troop strength and material superiority, without
thinking of possible variations. They hadn't bothered to develop
or test new military equipment here, except for the machine
gun. Admittedly, a man felt aristocratic on a horse, but in fact
the animal was an anachronism, dependent on water, meadow,
and mood, not to speak of such imponderables as the mating
urge. The automobile had no such whims. It's ridiculous the
way we run all over the place with these stubborn oxen. Think
of the possibilities an airplane offers. That's where war will be
waged in the future, in the air. Insight can be gained from above.
Then too, consider our response to the rebels in non-technical
areas. The standard reaction at present is rather crude: burn

down the pondoks, fire randomly on men and women. We need new methods that will elicit the right reactions from those affected. If you're clearing out a Hottentot compound, you don't shoot the men and women down like you're hunting rabbits, then soft-heartedly chase the children into the fields; instead you shoot a child before its parents' eyes, ask where the rebels are hiding, and if you don't get an answer, you shoot two more, then four, eight, and so on, until someone reveals the hiding place. We know how attached they are to their children. One could keep statistics on the various methods of interrogation and discover which works best. If the general staff would just realize how this war could serve as a model, it would completely justify its costs, including those sacrificed on the German side. One could never achieve such meaningful results through war games. By the way, Elschner had nothing personal against the Hottentots, he found them amusing and clever, but personal feelings have no role in war, particularly when it comes to effective methods for future use. In considering a new invention, an engineer can't be guided by how many men will lose their jobs, or their livelihoods, and perhaps their lives as a result.

When Elschner asked about the strange metal device Gottschalk was carrying around in his saddlebag, he replied evasively that it was something he'd found.

It was the objectivity, the apparent absence of all emotion in Elschner's reflections, that shocked Gottschalk, but not until the following day, like a slow fuse, while he was swaying southwestward once more on his desert ship. The evening before Gottschalk had listened with cool interest, observing the way Elschner spoke: that's what he thinks and that's how he says it, brief, curt gestures, a mouth repeatedly exposing an amazing expanse of somewhat irregular front teeth, and now and then a flash of gold from the back. Elschner's arguments made sense. (Elschner himself was thoroughly friendly, a hearty comrade. Zeisse said something he never said otherwise: our lieutenant.)

All you had to do was accept his premise, that the Hottentots were our deadly enemies. Everything else followed with complete consistency. Logically. The Hottentot was out to destroy us, his deadly enemy, therefore we must anticipate him, our deadly enemy, and destroy him.

But even that was a false alternative, one had to seek the causes. Elschner replied that these were material constraints, uninfluenced by individuals. Gottschalk countered that it was precisely the individual who mattered, and he alone.

Only a Don Quixote would try to do battle against material constraints.

That was aimed at Gottschalk, and he reacted at once: Certain developments would change if the individual decided to do what he thought was right. That's tilting against windmills, Elschner said, it's ridiculous. Historical developments can't be influenced by individuals and certainly can't be stopped, just as the invention of the steam engine could not be stopped by destroying it for fear of progress.

Gottschalk was tormented once more by the sharp pain in his stomach. For the most part he sat with loosened belt atop the camel's hump. Gottschalk had downed three more glasses of arrack that evening and announced with a slight slur: You have to imagine something new, something quite different from the way you've been living your life. Can you do that, asked Elschner.

No, said Gottschalk, unfortunately not, but perhaps just wanting to is part of it. Then Elschner talked about Don Quixote again and said Gottschalk reminded him of Quixote, riding on his camel through the countryside.

Grit ground between his teeth. Gottschalk rode next to Zeisse, but they couldn't even think about conversing, given the difference in height. And Gottschalk didn't know what they would have talked about.

The day before he left Germany—Gottschalk was sleeping on board the *Gertrud Woermann*—he went back into Hamburg, where he'd arranged to have supper with a former school friend.

There were no horse cabs in the harbor area. The steward explained that Gottschalk would have to take a launch over to the landing stage. He could take a cab from there.

A narrow gangplank led to the pontoon where the launch would dock. The gusty northwester drove the rain into him, tugged at his coattails. Leaning forward, he pressed his new broad-brimmed Colonial Guard hat tight to his head. It seemed silly to draw the storm strap under his chin now. Dock workers all around him, most with packs over their shoulders, a few holding lunch pails. They stood silently on the swaying pontoon.

As the launch drew near, the men sprang into motion. One who was standing near Gottschalk said something softly in low German, as if speaking to himself: That's a whopping big hat for such a little bean. Best stay home. The man who said this wore a practical small-brimmed cap, while Gottschalk held his hat on with his hand like a woman. Gottschalk pretended he hadn't understood. Nothing more was said.

His father always spoke low German. Only when certain customers entered his colonial goods store, Frau Doktor Hinrichsen, the wife of the physician, or Frau Pastor Jakobsen, for example, did he switch into a slow, awkward high German.

The launch approached the dock and was not yet moored when the first workers sprang over the foaming abyss into the rocking boat, the others pressing forward from behind. Gottschalk received a sharp blow in the lower ribs, as if by accident, and for a moment the wind was knocked out of him; he almost took his hand from his hat. Someone spat a stream of brown tobacco juice near his foot. The pontoon was suddenly empty, and Gottschalk stood there alone, still struggling to get his breath. The ship-boy threw off the ropes, the launch moved off again, the gap between the side of the boat and the pontoon quickly widened, the waves slapped high. Gottschalk decided to jump. Everyone in the launch was staring at him, and later he was sure he had seen an expectant schadenfreude in their eyes. Gottschalk sprang, still holding his hat on his head, with a powerful leap, landed nimbly, flexing his knees to catch himself on the vibrating boat, as he had learned to do as a boy on his grandfather's herring boat in Glückstadt. As he straightened up again and glanced at the faces of the workers, hoping to see admiration or at least disappointment in their eyes, no one was looking his way.

Perhaps here, in the wind and rain, on the vibrating boat, wedged between the Blohm and Voss boiler riveters, his hand on his hat, it may have occurred to Gottschalk how sensible the military manual rule was that officers should always travel first class. Tensions and conflicts could be avoided that couldn't be satisfied by traditional means, since none of the men about him were socially qualified to duel. One would have to fight with them, or choose sticks for weapons, but in any case one would then lose one's officer's commission. Gottschalk was annoyed by his officer's hat (after having first been quite proud of it); its felt brim, soaked with rain, would slowly grow heavy and go limp, until it was hanging in his face. He tried to assuage his anger by telling himself that the hat was not made for European weather, although he had read that there was a rainy season in South West Africa too.

At the landing stage he was the first to disembark, immediately found a cab, settled with relief into the dry cushioned seat and headed for the Uhlenhorster ferry house, where he was to meet his former school friend.

Who's afraid of the big black man: a game he played as a boy in the streets of Glückstadt.

Gottschalk's diary,
7 September 1905

The other, the new: the Jumping Bean Tree. Its exact opposite: clicking your heels. Clack. Standing at attention. The German eagle. The abstract. Asking no questions. Saying yes, sir. The love of law and order. Isn't it telling, after all, that we Germans always say: Geht in Ordnung when we mean that's fine.

8 September 1905

I would translate the Nama word for "order" as "obvious." It rained a bit today, from a single black cloud, not much, but big drops that turned to dusty balls on the ground.

9 September 1905

I asked Zeisse (a dumb question) if he'd still been working for Blohm and Voss last October. If so, we might have been standing together on the launch. Of course he was no longer at the shipyard then.

10 September 1905

Paddidream.

11 September 1905

Is it Nietzsche who says all passionate emotions (love of adventure, lust, triumph, pride, boldness, insight, self-certainty, and happiness itself) have been branded as suspiciously sinful, seductive?

12 September 1905

The other would be a new perception of time, based on a logic of the senses. Not on the logic of ends and means. The properly trimmed hedge of meaning. Elschner logic.

Strange and bizarre rock piles scattered over the landscape, hollowed out by the rain, by rapid changes in temperature.

In mid-September a patrol reached the wagon train with the news that Morenga had broken off negotiations with the German mediators and taken up arms again. On 15 September the cavalry escort of the 12th company at Nochas was attacked and the animals driven off.

Lieutenant Elschner merely said: We're in hot water now. He reinforced the head of the column with three men. When Gottschalk joined Elschner by the fire that evening, his rifle was lying beside him. Elschner gushed as he spoke of Morenga. He had chosen the moment perfectly. The sly fox knew the negotiations were only for show on our side, so we could take care of the Witboois and build up our supply depots here in the south at the same time. Now the whole south is unprotected and he can get whatever he needs with no trouble, while the 12th company makes its way on foot through the steppes. At least that doesn't make as much noise as lumbering through rebel territory with those stupid, bug-eyed, bellowing oxen.

Gottschalk could not help but take Elschner's praise of automobiles and airplanes as a personal rebuke, coupled with his view that any and all pack animal convoys were medieval, strange, comical, prehistoric. Even with the best will in the world, he felt, without Elschner's having ever said so specifically, that his own existence was being called into question in a fundamental and profound way.

The day the news reached the convoy that Morenga had once again declared war on the Germans, Gottschalk ordered Zeisse to stop watering the camel. That evening Zeisse had difficulty holding back the loudly complaining animal from the water (camels are famous for being able to smell water miles away), while the horses and oxen were drinking their fill.

It's an experiment, Gottschalk explained to Lieutenant Elschner when he came to check, alarmed by the animal's roars.

Gottschalk's diary,
16 September 1905

A man who can't learn gets smart when he starts bleeding. (Nama proverb)

On the sixth day, as the runaway Dominican, Father Meisel, rode up, Gottschalk sat so low on the camel's limp hump that he wasn't the first to spot him.

The Father looked like a railway engineer riding a mule through the steppes, dressed in blue fatigues and wearing sturdy high-laced boots. It wasn't until he had removed his leather railway cap that a scholar's head appeared, a bald round dome, a blond halo of hair, the smooth face of a child. He wiped his

brow, bald dome, and neck with a large blue and white handkerchief, introduced himself as Father Meisel, and said to the mule,
who kept stubbornly pulling to the side: settle down, you piece
of shit.

The question as to whether Meisel remained a priest, answered with an unambiguous no by his order, but with a less unambiguous yes by Meisel, had occupied the spiritual community
of the protectorate for some time. Father Malinowsky, who
headed the mission station in Heirachabis and who was said to
have enlightened views, had taken Meisel on as a deacon. Meisel
accompanied Father Malinowsky, who had acted as go-between
for Morenga and the Germans, and set up their meetings. Now
that Morenga had broken off negotiations, Meisel had departed.
Military officers in the southern part of the protectorate were
wary of his pacifism. He bored ruthlessly into the inner life of
his interlocutor with his questions, asking about his life history,
why he had done this and not that, why his response was eva-
sive, whether he had something to hide, why he insisted on hiding it. He insisted on absolute frankness and truth in the belief
that one must remain open before man and God, so that the
light of illumination may enter the darkest chamber of one's
heart. Since he demanded the same of the superiors in his own
order, tensions and frictions were pervasive, particularly when
he suspected half-heartedness or laziness of the heart, let alone
bearing false witness. Four years earlier he has removed his
soutane, replaced it with a simple gray business suit, and exited
through the front entrance of the neo-Gothic cloister in Cologne. He believed that only a genuine heart could become a true
Christian. One must start over from the beginning. Ideally with
those untainted by education. With savages. Strangely enough,
no one knew anything about Meisel's earlier life, except that he
had left his order in Germany. Was it because he was always
asking questions, or was it because others were always so busy
answering that it never occurred to them to question Meisel?
Did Meisel miss those questions?

Meisel rode along beside Gottschalk. After a few hours, Gotts-

chalk felt stripped bare. Meisel's first question, why was Gottschalk riding a camel, drew others in its wake: Why did
Gottschalk want to start a camel farm? Why had he come here?
Why wasn't he married? Why didn't he want to talk about it? Was
he hiding something from himself? Weren't there other reasons,
ones Gottschalk didn't want to admit, even to himself? Why was
he so shy about personal matters? What did he have to hide?

It was an interrogation, and Gottschalk was constantly
forced to justify himself, not only to Meisel, but oddly enough to
himself too. During a pause in the conversation, like coming up
for air, Gottschalk tried to escape the interrogation by saying he
found the countryside charming.

Meisel bristled and said now Gottschalk was just making conversation. If so, they might as well say nothing. Then Meisel
stared straight ahead and fell silent. At first Gottschalk was surprised himself. He was indeed indifferent to the landscape in this
area, which was if anything boring. It had just been an empty remark to extricate himself from the conversation, which, however, held up to him for what it was, took on another, more profound meaning: as something dishonest, almost a lie. The longer
Gottschalk struggled with this idea, and the longer Meisel punished him with his silence, the stronger grew an inner physical
rage that sought expression in some motor action, anger at
Meisel's self-righteous demand for absolute and unrelenting
truth. They rode on in silence, Meisel on the rapidly plodding
mule, trying to keep up with Gottschalk, who rocked back and
forth on the ambling camel. Finally Gottschalk got fed up with
the accusatory silence, urged his camel into a trot, and left the Father behind.

In the two days preceding the attack on the wagon train,
Gottschalk and Meisel didn't speak again. Whenever the convoy
stopped to rest, Gottschalk avoided him, but felt bad about
doing so, which annoyed him. Each time that he saw Meisel
(and he saw him constantly), he felt he should apologize. While
Meisel seemed completely at ease with the other troopers, talk-

ing with everyone except Gottschalk. He was always plying someone with his questions. An N.C.O. busy cleaning his rifle was asked why he would shoot at someone who had never hurt him. A trooper on night duty was asked why he was staring into the dark so anxiously. Did he have something to hide? And a trooper who had just helped extricate a wagon from the sand was asked why he had come to Africa. Was it right to shoot innocent people? Was it right to kill?

Our Wandering Conscience, Lieutenant Elschner joked; later, in bold anticipation of what was to come, he coined the term demoralization of the troops to describe what had happened. In a written report following the attack on his convoy, he maintained that one reason his men put up such a lackluster defense was that the troops had been demoralized by a certain former Dominican named Father Meisel. A military veterinarian had also played a part, not so openly and obviously as the Father of course, and therefore less open to attack. The veterinarian always spoke Nama with the native drivers and lead-boys, which at first occasioned the normal jokes among the German personnel, but later awakened their admiration. To this was added the veterinarian's unmilitary admiration of all things Hottentot, their peaceful nature, their tradition of mutual aid, the precommunist structure of their society.

More than the silly objection on Meisel's part that he had just been making conversation, what bothered Gottschalk was the Father's accusation that he had come to terms with the injustice being done to the Hottentots, and was even aiding the oppressors in their bloody work.

At first Gottschalk denied this, emphasizing that all the results he obtained, whether they dealt with the care of camels or the raising of cattle, would eventually be of use to the local inhabitants. Eventually. Exactly. But when would that be, this eventually?

What disturbed Gottschalk most of all was that he suspected Meisel might be right.

What was it that allowed the strange and bestial to become bearable and finally quite ordinary? Could one live, if one couldn't forget?

Elschner once said to Gottschalk in passing: The individual is nothing.

The individual is everything, Gottschalk replied.

He now finally understood what Wenstrup had written on the title page of Kropotkin's book: There is no solitary battle. He copied it into his diary and added: There is no solitary hope.

Gottschalk's diary,
23 September 1905

The beauty of the village names: Besondermeid, Kinderzit, Greondorn, Zwartmodder, Rosinenbusch.

24 September 1905

Tonight I awakened from a dream, but couldn't remember the details, only that I woke with a start as something calm and indescribably beautiful approached me. Dazed I lay wrapped in the blanket. Around me the sound of snoring. Above me the stars, quite near. Then I was suddenly overcome by fear and hate, and everything seized up inside. I couldn't breathe. I sprang up with the insane desire to shoot everyone lying asleep around me, snoring, stinking of alcohol and sweat. I rose and picked up my rifle. The sentry sat off to the side, smoking a pipe. The smoke, clearly visible in the moonlight, calmed me.

On the afternoon of 25 September, rain clouds appeared. Not long thereafter the first heavy drops fell, then poured, coming down in buckets. Within a few minutes Gottschalk was completely soaked on his camel. He again felt the pressure in his stomach. A queasy feeling of nausea. The brim of his hat slowly softened and hung limply in his face. He recalled the day he left Hamburg and felt a deep longing to run through the streets of Eppendorf. The trees along the lanes would be losing their leaves now, turning color. The notion of starting a farm in this country seemed like someone else's dream, something someone else had talked about. And yet there are sketches and calculations for a farmhouse in his diary, for huts and cottages intended for the farmhands. The last of these sketches (completed in Warmbad) shows a form of agricultural co-op or commune, in which everyone lives in similar housing. Larger complexes bear captions such as: school, reading room, library, gymnasium. An undated entry from this same period includes a few lines that he must have copied from a book of Hölderlin's poetry:

> So come! let us gaze into open spaces,
> Seeking something our own, no matter how far.
> One certainty remains; be it noontide or turning
> Toward midnight, there is one measure
> For us all, yet to each his own is also given,
> Toward which each comes and goes as he can.

Once, as Zeisse was riding along beside him, Gottschalk asked him what he would do if he were wounded in an ambush. Would he give himself up to the rebels? Zeisse thought about it for some time, then said: Nope.

When Gottschalk put the same question to Lieutenant Elschner that evening, wrapped in all sorts of subjunctive and hypothetical phrases, Elschner, instead of answering, rummaged around in his breast pocket and pulled out a small capsule. He held it out to Gottschalk on his open palm. Cyanide. Just in case he ran out of bullets. One doesn't always keep track in the heat of battle. Of course Elschner would enjoy a chance to talk with Morenga about strategic goals. Even though Morenga might have the advantage for the moment, he would surely lose in the end. Did he realize that?

Gottschalk's diary,
25 September 1905

Why do we kill? How can men shoot or hang each other? And how can others look on like they're at a fair? Why this indifference in the midst of terrible hate? Perhaps there's something they hate in themselves, some unlived part of their lives. What kills compassion?

That evening Gottschalk sat beneath a stretched tarpaulin on which the rain was drumming down. He was leafing through Kropotkin. Although he always handled it carefully, the book had become badly tattered. His soaked uniform smelled of camel. The smell was on his body too, and at times he believed that no soap in the world would ever wash it off again. But it was strangely comforting, like the smell of goats when he was a child.

"In short, neither the crushing powers of the centralized State nor the teachings of mutual hatred and pitiless struggle which came, adorned with the attributes of science, from obliging philosophers and sociologists, could weed out the feeling of human solidarity, deeply lodged in men's understanding and heart, because it has been nurtured by all our preceding evolution."

Gottschalk's diary,
26 September 1905 (in the night)

It appears we'll reach Ukamas without any losses. Elschner says it's a three- or four-day march at most. How great must be the injustice done to these people—and how deeply we must suspect it—for us to prefer poison or a bullet to surrender.

Perhaps one day it will be taken for granted that we should help every living creature, the trees, bushes and flowers, yes even the earth, the soil. The Garden of Eden. I lie on soil that sweats, the landscape breathes, warm and moist. Some of the men stripped naked in the rain this evening. One who hanged a captured rebel in Keetmanshoop was fooling around, throwing mud at the others.

On 27 September, the wagon train neared the mission station at Heirachabis. Meisel wanted to ride ahead. Elschner warned him against it, but Meisel claimed he had nothing to fear from the rebels. It rained without pause. Visibility was poor. The countryside was rugged and more thickly covered with shrubs. Elschner reinforced the head of the column. Toward evening he gave orders to halt on a hillside. The hill stood like a bastion in the landscape and offered a good field of fire on all sides. An N.C.O. took up position with six men at the top. The ox-wagons were pulled into a circle. The sentries were doubled. Gottschalk was given a position too. He was determined not to aim when he fired, even in fear.

Later, under the dripping tarp, he ate some dried meat.

Gottschalk's diary,
27 September 1905

The Hottentot dead are more alive than ours. That may be because the living take more time to remember them. Perhaps they find it easier to die knowing they will be preserved by others for a time.

After these downpours, springs and greenery everywhere.

Death: a logic outside us.

That is Gottschalk's last entry in the oilcloth notebook, which was found a year and a half later on one of Morenga's fallen cornets.

A few leaves had been torn at random from the book, probably used as spills for their pipes.

On the following day, 28 September, the rain stopped and Elschner ordered the column to set out at five in the morning. The oxen, their bellies filled with water, strained at the yokes. The earth steamed beneath the rising sun. Elschner gave orders to march nonstop, even at noon, to reach the environs of the military station at Ukamas.

Around four that afternoon, the first shots were fired at the head of the column. Elschner called out orders. The native leadboys and drivers disappeared immediately. The oxen became tangled in the traces. Now the convoy was taking fire from the hills on both sides. Gottschalk's camel fell. Attempting to rise, it rose up as usual on its rear legs, groaning like a man. Its mouth foamed with blood. Then it collapsed and expired. Elschner fired from his horse. Wounded men were screaming. The first crouched figures ran toward the wagons. Several bellowing oxen had been hit. Gottschalk watches the troopers flee. Elschner calls out: Back, everyone back.

Gottschalk sits without moving.

DANCING

V eterinary Lieutenant Gottschalk
  Report to Imperial Colonial Guards Headquarters

In mid-August I received orders to join a convoy that was to proceed
to Ukamas on 30 August. The convoy was under the command of
Second Lieutenant Elschner. At the end of September we reached the
region of Heirachabis. We had been informed by a patrol that
Morenga had again taken up arms. We were joined on the way by Father Meisel, who had accompanied Father Malinowsky. The latter had
served as a middleman, delivering messages between Morenga and
Colonial Guard headquarters. Meisel didn't discuss the negotiations,
but made no secret of his pacifism. On 27 September he rode out
ahead of the column toward Heirachabis. That he might have betrayed the convoy to the rebels by doing so seems highly unlikely,
since the bellowing of the oxen both day and night could be heard for
miles.

On 28 September, around four in the afternoon, we were surprised by fire. My camel fell, struck by several bullets. I hit my head in
the fall and was slightly dazed. As a result I can't recall subsequent
events clearly. Nor can I say whether Second Lieutenant Elschner attempted to establish a line of defense. (Marginal note in an unidenti-
fied hand: Sergeant Feller says yes.) Since my mount lay dead and no
others were available, and four of our men lay wounded, I decided to
stay. I tried not to make any sudden movements, so as not to be shot.
A few of the rebels immediately begged me for tobacco, but otherwise they didn't bother me. On the contrary my subsequent treatment
was courteous and obliging. They asked me who I was. I told them I

was a veterinarian and had stayed behind to treat the wounded. (Marginal note: Was that all?) Shots could be heard now and then in the distance. Then someone I took for an Englishman approached. But it was Morris. It was only later, when he took off his hat, that his Hottentot heritage was revealed, the crinkly hair, though it was reddish-blond. He questioned me in English about the dead camel, which the rebels were staring at. Was it true that such an animal could travel up to three hundred kilometers without water? I confirmed this was true, at least for the riding camels of the Bisharin, since it was not a military secret. Morris said it would be good for the rebels to have such camels. I bandaged up the wounded, none of whom were critically injured. There were no wounded among the Hottentots. They ransacked the wagons and tossed out everything useful. They were particularly delighted by the tobacco, schnapps, and ammunition. Later I was taken to a man standing off to the side by a wagon, leafing through captured files and maps. It was Morenga. He was strikingly tall and wore a civilian coat with an ammunition belt over it. He had placed his rifle beside him. He asked me where the convoy was headed and when Colonel van Semmern would arrive with his troops. (Marginal note: Lieutenant Colonel.) He appeared well informed about our troop movements. I refused to give any information. Morris asked my rank. Morenga said he had once captured an N.C.O., but never an officer. I tried to explain that I wasn't an officer in the true sense, but simply a veterinarian, an animal doctor. Morenga wanted to know why that wasn't ranked higher, since one needed to know more than a normal officer. (Marginal note: ??) He and Morris assured me that they would spare the life of any trooper who gave himself up. They wanted me to pass that message on to headquarters. (Marginal note: classified information, ditto for the veterinary lieutenant!) Then Morenga asked me to examine him, saying a bullet had lodged in his right hip months earlier. The slug had probably shattered in the bone. Small pieces of metal and bone had suppurated from the wound, which had already closed once. I examined him. The wound was badly infected. Walking and riding, which were clearly difficult for him, must have been extremely painful. He was in need of surgery. But I did what I could, painted the wound with iodine, treated it with an antiseptic salve, then bandaged it. (Marginal note: Isn't this aiding and comforting the enemy according to §124a?) I asked Morenga why he didn't make peace with us. He said he wasn't responsible, it was the Germans. I asked his conditions for peace. (Marginal note: Is he crazy?) He said his demands were quite simple: to let them live freely in their own country. When I asked if he thought he could be win against the mighty German empire he simply said: No. But he thought a negotiated peace was possible, since he could inflict heavy losses on the Germans over many years. (Marginal note: !) Help might also come from the outside, from England, or perhaps even from the Germans themselves who opposed injustice and systematic slaughter. (Marginal note: Can he have put it that way?) But Morenga also emphasized that he would keep fighting to the last man. And when I asked why, he offered the surprising answer: So that *you* and *we* can remain human. (Marginal note: native logic!) He ordered for me to be given a cart and mules so I could take the wounded to the mission station at Heirachabis. I decided to leave the next morning. (Marginal note: why not at once?) That evening the rebels celebrated their victory with dancing and singing. (Marginal note: And what did our esteemed veterinarian do?) Several of our draft oxen were roasted. Meanwhile the rebel women and children had arrived. Morenga wanted to take them across the Orange to safety. An old woman danced, to the general amusement of all, in Colonel van Semmern's uniform, which had been found in the convoy.

I estimate the strength of Morenga's troops (Marginal note: band!) at sixty men. Most of them wore Colonial Guard uniforms and were armed with model 88 rifles. The quality of their horses was excellent, probably stock from the 12th Company. The morale of the men was high. I didn't have the impression anyone was being forced to fight. The recognition Morenga received as their leader seemed equally voluntary.

The next morning I received the cart with the mules and was able to carry the four wounded men to Heirachabis.

Two months after the attack on the convoy, Colonel van Semmern having been defeated by Morenga in the meantime at the mouth of the Hartebeest, Gottschalk was interrogated by a staff officer in Warmbad. After initial puzzlement as to why Morenga let the veterinarian go so easily, suspicions had been aroused after the grave losses of the battle. In his search for scapegoats, van Semmern came upon Gottschalk. After all, wasn't it possible that Gottschalk talked too loosely and gave away the plan of attack of the southern division, or even intentionally betrayed them? But this suspicion could be easily refuted, since at that time Gottschalk couldn't possibly have known the plan of operation. On the contrary it was Gottschalk's remarks about Morenga's future intentions that, quite unintentionally on his part, created the impetus for the German plan of attack. The primary reason Colonel van Semmern decided to march along the Orange was the information that Morenga wanted to take the rebel women and children across the Orange into English territory.

Not until his recall had been ordered due to this military debacle did the disturbing thought occur to van Semmern that Morenga might have given this information to Gottschalk fully intending that, in his general state of humanistic befuddlement, the veterinarian would innocently pass it on, and lead van Semmern into an ambush. Van Semmern ordered a further investigation into the matter. The troopers who were wounded in the attack were also to be re-interrogated. Two of the troopers were on sick leave in Germany, a third had died of typhus, so only Lance Corporal Lämmer remained, lying in sick bay with a bullet wound in his knee, who, with van Semmern already back in an autumnal Berlin, put the following on record: He understood nothing of a longer conversation between the Lieutenant and Morenga, even though he had been close enough to hear it, since both of them had spoken in Nama. He had noticed nothing further, except that when taken to Morenga, the veterinarian held out his hand, which the other man simply ignored, which Lämmer found unbelievably impertinent. But he hadn't noticed anything suspicious. The veterinarian had been allowed to keep his personal things, as had all the wounded men. Morenga even instituted a search for Gottschalk's diary, which had disappeared from the saddlebag of his camel during the looting. But in the general confusion, and since many of the natives were already drunk, it could not be found. Such notebooks, indeed books in general, were highly sought after by the Hottentots for use in lighting their pipes.

That evening, after the oxen were roasted, the wounded were carried to the fires and given meat and something to drink. Lämmer drank Kupferberg champagne for the first time in his life, the champagne Bismarck always had for breakfast. The veterinarian was also sitting at the fire, and ate and drank as well. The next morning they were loaded onto a cart. Morenga took leave of them personally and said he wouldn't kill prisoners. We were to spread the word among the troops. He and his men were fighting for their lives. The veterinarian gave Morenga a wire device and said something to him in Nama, which Lämmer didn't understand. He was certain it wasn't a machine gun part; he knew those from using them. When they left, Morenga held out his hand to Gottschalk. Then they traveled to the mission station, where they were received by Father Meisel. He had been struck by the fact that the Father asked the veterinarian why he hadn't stayed there.

Lämmer also expressly recorded his gratitude to the veterinarian, without whose help he would have lost his leg, or perhaps even bled to death.

In the written transcription of Lämmer's statement, next to the passage mentioning a wire device, there is a large question mark in ink. But this one question mark, even if it was made emphatically, was not sufficient cause to summon Gottschalk a second time to Warmbad. Particularly since Lämmer had assured them it was not part of a machine gun or weapon.

With that the file entitled "Re: Contact between Veterinary Lieutenant Gottschalk and the Bandit Leader Morenga" was closed, sewn into a cardboard cover, and stored away in the archives of the district office in Warmbad.

• • •

In the general staff record there is a brief entry concerning this incident: "The Bondels, over whom Morenga, in spite of his dismissal, still seems to maintain a major influence, continued their march southward and on 28 September attacked a supply train of ten wagons near Heirachabis, wounding four Germans. On this occasion Morenga and Morris told a veterinarian who had been left behind to care for the wounded that he had decided to fight to the last man." (*The Battles of the German Troops in South West Africa*, ed. by the Office of the General Staff, vol. 2, p. 232)

Six months after this incident Captain Bech pushed into English territory with his detachment. Morenga had set up camp with his men on the Van Rooisvley. The armed attack caught them by surprise. The Hottentots offered bitter resistance, but were shot to pieces in a short time by the well-concealed Germans. Fire continued to be returned from only three pondoks, as if they held an entire company of special guards. Since losses were being inflicted on the German side, the Captain gave orders to storm the pondoks. The Germans finally rushed the pondoks with fixed bayonets, where to their surprise they found only three men and two women, whom they shot on the spot. Meanwhile an English police corporal on a hill was waving a white sheet on a walking stick and protesting in the name of His Majesty the King of England against this transgression of his borders. Nevertheless the Germans calmly combed the battlefield. Morenga had been shot twice, in the head and neck. He later told a reporter from the *Cape Times* that when he saw two German soldiers coming toward him, he stayed face down and played dead. The first soldier jabbed him in the side with the butt of his rifle and tried to turn him over, but then saw the blood on his head and neck and said: This one's had enough.

Three days later Morenga, starving and exhausted from loss of blood, and accompanied by ten other Hottentots and two Hereros, turned himself in to the English police. He was then interned in Cape Colony. In one of the three pondoks that had to be cleared out with bayonets, Morenga's possessions were also found: two pipes, a few plugs of tobacco and a wire device, whose function no one could explain.

The only person who could have given information on the origin and function of this strange device was Lance Corporal Zeisse, had he not been killed two days earlier, on a burning hot afternoon, shot in the head.

Colonel von Davidson included the item found in Morenga's possession on the list of captured goods with the note: Fertility fetish.

GENERAL SITUATION

On 29 September 1905, Hendrik Witbooi fell during a battle near Fahlgras. Shortly thereafter his two sons surrendered. They had been reduced to seventy-five men, not all of whom were armed. General Trotha could finally begin his return journey to the homeland. Colonel Dame became acting commanding officer of the Colonial Guards.

By mid-September, after Morenga broke off negotiations, Lieutenant-Colonel van Semmern began an offensive against the rebels in the southeastern part of the protectorate.

Van Semmern's troops were supposed to march in two detachments along the Orange River toward the mouth of the Hartebeest, where, it had been learned, Morenga intended to take the women and children across into English territory. Van Semmern intended to destroy the Hottentots with a pincer movement. Koppy's detachment, with the Colonel, was moving from the east along the Orange, Siebert's detachment was to push forward across the Orange Mountains. On 24 September, Koppy's detachment reached the mouth of the Hartebeest, not far from the spot where, over fifty years earlier, missionary Gorth entered the country. In early morning the head of the column came under fire from steep cliffs on the right front flank and from thickly-grown islands in the Orange River. The detachment was routed and withdrew with heavy losses. Siebert's detachment, which was supposed to close in on the Hottentots in the pincer movement, heard cannon fire, but couldn't find a path through the steep mountains. Under the leadership of Morenga and the Bondelswart chief Johannes Christian, the rebels had achieved a

victory over the southern division of the German Colonial
Guard that would secure their position on the Orange for the
next several months. Colonel van Semmern was replaced by an
experienced Colonial Guard officer, v. Estorff. Estorff was considered the most capable man in South West Africa.

He spent several months carefully preparing a new offensive:
he requested and received extensive reinforcements, particularly
in the communications area, including four wireless stations
and eleven cavalry signaling troops. In addition, food, ammunition, and fodder had to be assembled for more then five thousand men and over six thousand horses, and supplies provided
for the upcoming offensive. Once again a major portion of the
fodder and supplies had to be imported from the Cape Colony,
which led to the paradoxical situation that beef cattle were repeatedly being herded across the Orange River, captured and
driven off by the Hottentots, brought back across the Orange,
purchased cheaply by the same traders, and sold back to the Germans, where they finally made it into saucepans for the troops.
Business had never been better for the traders. When rinderpest
broke out and the English government closed the border for a
time, the prices shot up, bottlenecks in supplies developed, and
dissatisfaction grew. The military repeatedly requested the construction of a railroad from Keetmanshoop to Kalkfontein in the
south, into Bondelswart territory.

By February 1906 Estorff had completed his preparations for
the offensive. The advance toward the Hottentot positions near
Kumkum began in early March with thirteen companies at full
battle strength and thirteen cannon, as well as six machine
guns.

More than five thousand men on the German side were faced
by approximately two hundred and sixty armed Hottentots.

Continuing his previous strategy, Morenga tried to lure the
weakest of the German detachments to where they would be at a
disadvantage and defeat them there, then attack the next
strongest detachment. In this way he hoped to stop the advance of
the German troops as he had at the mouth of the Hartebeest and

force them to retreat. But this time the Germans had too great an advantage. Communications among the various detachments by heliograph and the new wireless stations had been substantially improved, so that in case of a rebel attack the detachments could come to one another's aid. There were several skirmishes in the rocky landscape. None of the German detachments could be routed. The German troops finally pushed through to Kumkum, where the rebels had their compounds. In the face of the approaching enemy they moved the compounds with their women and children across the Orange into English territory. The so-called orlogs, the fighting men, broke through the encircling ring of Germans. A few men led by Morris escaped toward the west into the canyon of the Great Fish River. Johannes Christian, chief of the Bondelswarts, broke through with his men and headed northwest toward the Great Karas Mountains, while Morenga went east, crossed the English frontier and set up camp on the Van Rooisvley, where his men could supply themselves with food and ammunition. Here he was surrounded by Captain Bech. The majority of the rebels were killed. Morenga himself was seriously wounded and gave himself up to the English police. He was interned at Prieska in the Cape province, three hundred kilometers from the German border, on condition that he not leave the village. He lived there for the next few months, receiving journalists, guests, and curiosity-seekers who wanted to see the Black Napoleon. It was probably here that the photograph showing him with two Hottentot boys was taken.

After Morenga's departure, the following guerilla leaders still remained at war with the Germans in the southern part of the protectorate: Johannes Christian, chief of the Bondelswarts, with approximately ninety armed men; Lambert, Morris and Fielding, with a total of at most eighty men; and finally, in the rugged backlands of the Kalahari, Simon Kopper with ninety-five men. In addition there were still several small groups of rebels, most consisting of five to seven men, roaming about southern Namaland.

In the period from May 1906 to the end of the year there were three hundred and thirty further encounters, mostly attacks on station garrisons, patrols, water carts, and horse guards. In May Johannes Christian inflicted two further defeats with heavy casualties on the Germans at Dakib and Sperlingspütz.

Colonel v. Deimling, knighted in the meantime, replaced the previous commander, Colonel Dame, in July. He quickly realized that in its present phase, despite overwhelming superiority in troop strength, with six thousand German soldiers facing around two hundred sixty rebels, the war could no longer be won in the traditional sense. The rebel groups, given their mobility and the support of the local population, could carry on the struggle for years. Even though they no longer presented a danger to the larger German detachments, they were nevertheless capable of ambushing smaller convoys, patrols, and sentries, and carrying on a war of attrition. Colonel Deimling thus developed an anti-guerilla strategy: draconian punishments for captured rebels and their sympathizers, immunity for those who turned themselves in and provided information about the rebels. Forced relocations. The tribes were to be placed in so-called reserves (army villages), under the supervision of German officials and officers. Tribes from the south were to be transferred to uninhabited areas in the north. All cattle herds belonging to farmers and troops were to be moved to strongly-protected assembly points in the north, to remove the basic source of nourishment from the rebels. Communications were further strengthened. Small, mobile task forces were formed, with specially selected men, armed with modern weapons, machine guns, and mountain cannons. The task forces formed pursuit columns, which would switch off with each other in pursuit of the enemy and thus stay fresh. The general staff record includes the following comment on Colonel v. Deimling's plan: "He hoped in this way, without brilliant victories, but slowly and surely, to deprive the rebels of their material support and to reduce them to futile attacks on well-secured posts. The ensuing relentless pursuit with constantly refreshed troops would eventually exhaust the opponent and rob him of his powers of resistance."

It turned out, however, that even with these operational means, the war could not be brought to conclusion in the foreseeable future, so that Deimling eventually found himself forced to enter into negotiations with the rebels through Father Malinowsky. They were assured immunity, their lives, and even the right to remain on their tribal lands around Warmbad. In return they were to turn in all their weapons and recognize the authority of the German government.

> The German negotiator, General Staff Captain von dem Hagen, writes concerning the negotiations: "I was constantly delivering messages between Ukamas and Heirachabis. The negotiations were extremely difficult and intense on occasion; it took enormous patience to talk the Bondels out of their myriad reservations. On 21 December I rode over for the last meeting and informed them that the preliminary negotiations were concluded and the final negotiations would take place on the 22nd in Ukamas. And in fact Johannes came to us with five men. Lieutenant-Colonel v. Estorff personally conducted the negotiations, with outstanding composure and skill. His knowledge of the natives, and the high regard in which they held him, were strikingly useful to the German side.
>
> On the evening of the 22nd the chief finally agreed to give up their weapons, but he resisted settlement in the Keetmanshoop area. Under no condition would they allow themselves to be transplanted from their traditional homelands, they would rather fight to their last breath, until the final man had fallen. Lieutenant-Colonel v. Estorff was thus faced with the question: should he give in or insist on the resettlement near Keetmanshoop. In that case the end of the war would be postponed for the foreseeable future. The point under contention seemed too inconsequential for that; and since Colonel v. Deimling replied to his query by directing him not to allow negotiations to break down over the issue, he gave in, and the treaty was signed by us and the Bondels.
>
> That evening Father Malinowsky held services in the little mission church; after three years of waging orlog, all the Bondels sat

there peaceably. The pastor spoke eloquently about the successful peace. It was a strange feeling for me personally to sit in church with all these people who had fought against us for three years. During the service I had all the surrendered weapons quietly loaded onto a cart and drove back to Ukamas at 10 that evening. It was a splendid trip! The prize of victory, for which we had struggled so long, was finally in our hands. How many thoughts passed through my mind on that journey. I recalled in particular all the brave troopers who had met these guns and lost their lives. For they were all our own guns, and each one was linked to the death of a brave trooper. I was in Ukamas early on the 24th. It was the birthday of Second Lieutenant v. Estorff, and I could deliver the guns of the Bondels to him as the best of birthday presents; they were placed on display around the walls of our Christmas barrack, with the Christmas tree in the middle of the room—a unique Christmas celebration!" (*The Battles of the Colonial Guard in South West Africa*, ed. by the Office of the General Staff, vol. 2, pp. 294 ff.)

On 31 March 1907, by order of the Kaiser, the state of war in South West Africa was ended.

The land and livestock of the rebel tribes were confiscated. Laws were passed denying the natives the right to buy land, raise cattle or horses, or keep riding animals. Exceptions were possible only by permission of the governor. No more than ten native families could live together on a single piece of land. The purpose of the regulations was to deprive the Africans of economic power and at the same time force them to work for the whites. In addition, in order to render the deprivation of economic power and the pressure to work more effective, the traditional tribal organization was to be destroyed.

All Africans over the age of eight had to wear a pass token around their necks. Anyone not wearing such a token could be arrested by any white person. In addition there was a so-called work book in which information about the work record of the individual was to be entered. Africans working without contract had no rights and would be punished as vagrants. By this means an indirect form of forced labor was introduced.

In the year 1907 there were six thousand prisoners, either in concentration camps, or consigned to forced labor, primarily building the railroad.

THE WONDERFUL CLOUDS

One Sunday Gottschalk arrived at Ukamas, two months later than planned. He moved into a single room partitioned off with wooden boards inside the sun-dried brick station house. Lieutenant Gerlich, the station chief, slept in a second wooden partition. Between these two partitions twenty-two men were cramped side by side. A double sentry sat on the roof. No one wanted to sleep outside for fear of being shot in a sudden attack. We're smack on the front line, Gerlich liked to say.

Gottschalk lay awake, thinking of Wenstrup, Morenga, and sometimes of Katharina. The stuffy room was filled with the farts and snores of the sleeping men. The next night Gottschalk went outside, wrapped himself in his horse blanket, lay down on the ground beside the station house and slept under the open sky. Gerlich claimed that was sure suicide on a mission like this.

These Kaffirs can smell us miles away. That was Gerlich's theory about rebel victories: When the wind is right they can smell our patrols from miles away.

In February 1906 Gottschalk was ordered to return to Warmbad, where he was again interrogated by a staff officer about Morenga's attack on the wagon train. He was asked if he'd said anything about troop strength or the southern division plans, which Gottschalk denied. Did he think it possible that Morenga intentionally passed on false information about where the rebels were headed, in order to lure the German troops into an ambush?

Gottschalk did not rule out the possibility. What pained him was that his report might have contributed to the destruction of these people; he had only wanted to show that the rebels were guided in their struggle by humane considerations, taking their women and children to safety into English territory. He had intended it as a hidden appeal to the German command to spare the women and children. His replies to the remainder of the interrogating officer's questions were vague and confused.

A sleepwalker, the interrogating major said after dismissing Gottschalk.

Shortly before his return to Ukamas a heliogram arrived at Warmbad with the following news: Veterinary Lieutenant Gottschalk had been promoted to Veterinary Captain for his contribution in establishing a camel corps. Colonel Dame, commander of the Colonial Guard, sent his congratulations.

In Warmbad they were pleased to inform Gottschalk that the lessons he had given the Hottentots in animal hygiene had been extremely useful. The Hottentots knew so much the army was forced to press them into service with the Colonial Guard and farmers in the north. Of course they were still lazy, but very knowledgeable. So they were placed under police guard and rented out to civilians for ten pennies a day. The money went into the government coffers.

Every effort Gottschalk made to intervene in some positive way in this land seemed to turn into its opposite according to some mysterious law. He rode back to Ukamas in troubled thought.

Lieutenant Gerlich's eyes widened when he saw Gottschalk returning alone. Gerlich said Gottschalk must smell like a Hottentot, otherwise he couldn't have passed unharmed through rebel lands. He was dead certain that anyone else would have been shot.

Gottschalk asked about Katharina in Warmbad. But none of the captured Hottentots knew her.

• • •

In Ukamas, Gottschalk prepared a petition requesting his discharge from active service in the Colonial Guard and the army. But he left the petition in a folder. He thought about what he would do after he was discharged from the army. Start up a country practice, or try to enter a university and go into research. But something made him hesitate to hand his petition to a patrol headed toward Warmbad, something he couldn't name, as if he were waiting for something.

There was very little for him to do in the village. Now and then he vaccinated draft oxen passing through from the Cape Colony, or gave a horse an enema, or performed an autopsy on a dead cow to check for anthrax.

Gottschalk often spent the day on the station house veranda in silence. The frayed wicker chair creaked now and then as he moved it to follow the shade. He sat there, unshaven, in a grubby khaki uniform that still bore the insignia of a veterinary lieutenant, as if he hadn't been promoted, and stared over at the cattle kraal. Behind it lay the kraal of the native drivers and bambuses: half-breeds, Bushmen, Hottentots, mountain Damara, and a few Bantus from the Cape Colony. Gerlich maintained that the whole brown and black pack of them were sleeping under one blanket with the rebels. That's where they were getting information about troop strength and the habits of the German leaders. The only way to solve the problem was to import foreign workers, as they had for the railroad, Italians for example. Although they were unreliable too, these eye-ties, as a recent strike had proved.

Next to the station house veranda, also in the shade, lay a sow. She was the first pig Gottschalk had laid his eyes on in the protectorate. As skinny as a racing sow, she had made the long journey from the English territories and had been captured by a sergeant. A metal tag in her right ear betrayed her origin as Pella. A German missionary was said to have first imported a pig over fifty years ago. Since then pigs had been raised at the mission station in Pella. The sergeant who caught the animal, which had reverted to a wild state and bit, accustomed her to the stall again and fattened her up, intending to start a pig farm in Ukamas. What he needed was a boar.

The sergeant came with a delegation of troopers to Gottschalk seeking his professional opinion as to the economic viability of breeding pigs in this region. Gottschalk's opinion would determine whether the pig would head straight for the spit, as the troopers hoped, or if they should actually look around for a boar in line with longer-term plans for producing pork.

Gottschalk looked into the greedy eyes of the delegation and said: The conditions for an extensive pig farm are extremely favorable given the quantity of the dirt and rubbish left behind by the German troops.

The pig wasn't slaughtered and Gottschalk continued to enjoy the familiar grunting from the shadows on those scorching afternoons.

What bothered Lieutenant Gerlich was that the staff veterinarian neither talked, nor read, nor even drank, which would have been perfectly normal. He just sat there squinting out from under the brim of his cap toward the heavens. An eccentric, with nothing comical or oddball about him. No one thought of laughing at him, as they had in Keetmanshoop, where he was constantly lobbying for camels, or earlier in Warmbad, with his Hottentot University. Now and then someone would tap himself on the forehead, not even attempting to hide the gesture. Here in Ukamas he sat silently staring into the distance, surrounded by a cool reserve. It was the loneliness of total apathy, which caused even a joker like Gerlich to pass by without a word. Only once, and completely unexpectedly, was Lieutenant Gerlich witness to a strong, even agitated reaction from the veterinarian, when he received news they had finally caught Morenga. The vet stared at him as if stunned. It was some time before Gerlich could get through to him that the black swine hadn't really been caught, but only shot, put out of action anyway, and was now in an English prison. A German detachment

had simply smoked him out in English territory. Not long thereafter, toward the end of May, Gottschalk handed in his request
for discharge to a wagon train headed for Warmbad.

After losing his diary, Gottschalk began a new one. He made his
entries in a pocket calendar with lined pages. Each page of the
calendar is filled with notes in pencil up to the day of his departure from Ukamas. Strangely enough, however, with three exceptions, these are restricted to meteorological observations, entered daily with great precision: the direction and speed of the
wind (Gottschalk must have either built himself an anemome-
ter or got hold of one), precipitation, sunrise and sunset, cloud
cover and cloud formations. These descriptions fill the pocket
calendar in a small script, and most incredible is the way in
which the clouds are described.

The dry, conventional categories of the meteorologist are enlarged by a highly idiosyncratic language that works with bold
images, even with new coinages, in an attempt to describe the
form of something that itself is steadily arising out of change,
infinitely complex, in constant transformation, yet always the
same: the clouds.

Gottschalk seems to have attempted to develop a descriptive
system that would include movements and varieties without
being rigidly tied to a specific nomenclature.

One example:

12 January 1907

At sunrise, a wooly, pale-rose carpet in the southeast, its fringes frayed
light gray. In the morning the carpet blueshimmies slowly southward.
In the afternoon a wool polo-neck hallmarked steel gray.

In the evening around 17:20: expulsion of driftclouds northward.
Downy featherish.

This and a second pocket calendar of similar format with daily
entries would be a rich source of information for meteorologists,
since they list all significant climatic data in the Ukamas area for

the period March 1906 to May 1907. They represent, moreover, a passionate attempt to restore to a fossilized and desensitized language an element of the spontaneity, diversity, and individuality that Gottschalk seemed to recognize in the formation of clouds.

Of course there is no indication in these diaries how Gottschalk might have conceived of an information system that was not based simply on a constant series of new descriptions, but by means of at least some degree of abstraction might also allow for conceptual generalization. It is precisely this, however, that is required for an intelligible transmittal of meteorological observations. The value of the current meteorological code lies in its fungibility. The Gottschalkian cloud morphology lies at cross-purposes with this.

Only twice during the period in Ukamas do we find something other than the weather mentioned in the diaries.

Once, in the address section of the pocket calendar for 1906, there is a sketch for the construction of a free balloon, steered by means of two dragropes and a balloon sail, a method already known at that time. The balloon pilot, who would be completely at the mercy of the momentary direction of the wind if he were sailing freely, is able to navigate the balloon to some degree by means of the resistance of ropes that drag along the ground. The engineer Andrée, a Swede, tried to fly over the North Pole in such a balloon in 1897. He was lost without a trace. But Gottschalk was probably unaware of this navigational technique, and invented it anew himself. The second occasion is on the page for 30 March 1906, where we find the following note: Learn to understand our inner self as a geological formation. A geology of the soul with its fissures, displacements, sediments, deposits, and erosions.

Not once in either pocket diary is mention made of any individual, Morenga or Meisel, for example, or Lieutenant Gerlich, or even Wenstrup.

Once, at the end of October, Meisel rode over from Heirachabis on his mule. Meisel and Gottschalk sat on the veranda drinking tea. Meisel discussed his intention to make public to the world certain terrible things that were happening to these people. Prisoners were supposed to be transported to camps, but never arrived at their intended destinations. Villages were found with pondoks burned, and vultures circling. The Hottentots who surrendered with Cornelius and the Witbooi sons had been taken to a small rocky island in Lüderitz Bay called Shark Island. Women and children were dying by the hundreds in the cold, wet sea climate. Unfortunately this was part of a systematic plan. Even his Evangelical colleagues from the Rhenish Mission, who scarcely knew the meaning of Protestantism, had been protesting against this treatment with letters and petitions to the government and the Imperial Colonial Office. Here was a letter of 5 October from his Colleague Laaf in Lüderitz:

> "For several weeks now almost all the Hottentots taken prisoner have been here, around one thousand seven hundred souls. So I've been up to my ears in work, since I've begun baptismal instruction with the heathens—how many I'm not sure. The majority of them are ill, mostly with scurvy, and fifteen to twenty die each week. Samuel Isaak, the second in command in the Witboois, who is my interpreter, recently told me that since 4 March, when he gave himself up to the Germans, five hundred and seventeen of his people had died. Today the number is even greater. An equal number of the Hereros have died, so that one can figure that on average fifty die a week. When will this misery cease? They are given enough supplies, both clothing and food, although they can't all eat the latter. But the climate is too unfavorable for them, and if the government doesn't transport them elsewhere, they will eventually suffer a great shortage of native workers, which is already noticeable in other areas. This is itself sufficient reason to make a change, not to mention the purely humane considerations."

Meisel went a step further and described the situation of the natives in letters he sent to socialist newspapers in Germany, Sweden and Switzerland.

One must take some action against this inhumanity, Meisel kept saying. Gottschalk sat in the creaking wicker chair, his boots on a footstool, and said: Yes, you're right, but he thought writing letters was a very modest response compared to the dimensions of the injustice, torture, and death.

But it was something. Better than sitting around and staring at the sky. Better than doing nothing. He'd stayed with the rebels once, voluntarily. Had he wanted to join them, as Meisel thought? He was convinced that was what Gottschalk had intended. That would indeed have been a sign. A signal. An example that others might have followed. Why had Gottschalk backed off? Why not take the final step, face the radical consequences? Fear? Or was the rumor true that Morenga hadn't wanted to take him along? Meisel stared at Gottschalk, who abruptly took his feet off the stool. The wicker chair creaked incessantly. And after a long pause in which Meisel also remained steadfastly silent, Gottschalk said: Have you ever noticed the way we move through this land? And when Meisel indicated by his furrowed brow that he didn't understand the question: We move through this land like the lame and the blind.

But Meisel wanted an answer to his question, not a simile. Similes were always evasions; as an experienced biblical exegete he knew that well.

No, he hadn't spoken with Morenga about whether to stay or not.

He had stayed sitting out of curiosity, but also because he had this idée fixe, for some time, about running away, even joining the other side. When he saw the rebels, he said nothing and postponed his decision. He wasn't sure what he wanted to do. When he observed these people, spoke with them, smelled then, there was a distance he felt could not be bridged, even though he told himself that by taking that step everything would change; things wouldn't be easier, but he would draw closer to himself. Toward evening the great celebration began. Oxen were roasted, the looted wine and champagne were poured. There was eating and drinking, accordions and mouth harps, later there was singing and dancing. He'd never felt so joyful, so relaxed as on that evening, a joy that came from everyone, not just because of alcohol, a joyous release. He recognized his delight in their laughter, a delight in living of which he had been unaware till then. They danced, all the rebels, young and old, women, children, village elders. Imagine our soldiers celebrating in the evening after a long and tiring march, after a victorious battle, you know those dull-witted drinking bouts, but here they were dancing. Imagine our troopers, N.C.O.s, even the officers, dancing. Gottschalk had at first only clapped his hands in time to the music. But then he let himself join in the dance. For a moment he tried to imitate Morenga's movements, who danced somewhat more stiffly due to his wound. But he was unable to. He was too tense. In fact he was downright ridiculous. And even as he tried to dance, and in spite of his sloshed head, it was clear he couldn't stay with them. These people were near to him and yet infinitely distant. Had he remained, he would have had to learn to think and feel differently. Radically change his thinking. Think with his senses. So the next day he left on a cart with the wounded for Heirachabis.

Meisel said it was ridiculous not to take an epoch-making step simply because a dance didn't go well, a great example like Count York von Wartenburg had given at Tauroggen, or even better, like Saul, who persecuted the Christians, yet became Paul. Weren't there other reasons, ones that Gottschalk didn't want to admit to himself, comfort, lethargy of the heart, fear, even cowardice perhaps?

Gottschalk and Meisel argued on this day for the last time. Gottschalk interrupted Meisel's interrogation with the remark that he had reached a decision, and when Meisel wanted to know what it was, since he was simply sitting around staring holes into the sky, Gottschalk replied curtly that he didn't want to talk about it any more, for fear it might turn into mere conversation.

Meisel stood up abruptly and rode off without saying goodbye.

He had actually come to win Gottschalk over to what he called a rebellion of the conscience. Instead he encountered a stubborn vet who talked of radical action in the struggle against injustice, but sat around gazing at the smoke from his pipe and waxing eloquent about the dance of the Hottentots.

Gottschalk continued to spend his days observing the cloud formations (cloudless blue skies bored him to death) and waiting for a response to his request to be discharged.

Sometimes he suspected that his request might be lying in a drawer somewhere unopened. But then he reminded himself that every written piece of paper that entered an office or department was immediately received and registered, then proceeded along its dusty way toward processing. Perhaps at this very moment a departmental advisor was studying his request in Berlin. But in fact it lay in Warmbad, in the desk drawer of Major Treager.

Treager, who knew Gottschalk from Keetmanshoop and considered him an idealist and camel lover, suspected that an oversensitive Prussian sense of honor, severely wounded by the mere suggestion that he might have dealt with the enemy, lay behind his petition for retirement. The veterinarian had asked to retire not because he was sulking, but simply to expunge this ugly suspicion.

Since Treager planned an inspection tour along the eastern border of the protectorate in November of 1906 in connection with the peace negotiations, he decided to take the opportunity to visit the vet in Ukamas and try to talk him into withdrawing his petition. He took Gottschalk's letter along with him on the ride. He wanted it in case—as Treager fully expected—Gottschalk withdrew the petition, so he could simply tear it up. Then the whole thing could be forgotten.

Major Treager and his squad reached Ukamas in mid-November, rode into the station, formed a line and reported to Lieutenant

Gerlich. Treager wondered why Hottentots were lolling about in chairs on station verandas these days. The man sitting there in a frayed wicker chair in greasy trousers, his bare feet up on a stool, a woman's blue hat on his head, a pipe in his hand, didn't even rise when Major Treager reined in his horse in front of him. It wasn't until the seated man lifted his hat like a civilian that Treager recognized him as the veterinarian Gottschalk. Treager, who was said to have a sense of humor, doffed his hat in turn.

Later, after grilled cutlets—the sow, to the sorrow of her captor and lord, the sergeant, had sacrificed her life for this high-ranking visit—Major Treager asked whether this inauspicious request for a discharge might not after all have been a bit precipitous. And when Gottschalk remained silent, unconcernedly picking scraps of the old sow from his teeth with his fingernail, Treager played the jovial comrade: Damn it all, Gottschalk, why?

At this Gottschalk removed his finger from his mouth and said he no longer wished to take part in the slaughter of innocent people.

Lieutenant Gerlich repeated the story later on many occasions, how this horse doctor, this veterinary captain, who had begun to resemble a Hottentot even in the way he smelled, had delivered himself of this declaration about the slaughter of innocent people, at which the major, since the veterinarian refused to leave the table, rose and left the room.

On that same day, when Major Treager returned to Warmbad from his inspection tour, he forwarded Gottschalk's request with a note to grant it as quickly as possible.

At the end of May, 1907, on a cloudless, boring day in Ukamas, Gottschalk received notification that his request had been granted. Corresponding pension rights were being examined. He would not have the right to wear his uniform after leaving the service. He simultaneously received his marching orders for Lüderitz, where he was to board a ship.

On 10 June, the day of his departure, Gottschalk made his last meteorological entry: Radial-blue sky. In the northwest from the horizon: ostrich feathers, harrier-gray, feminine, well-ordered, virtumuli.

Gottschalk was ordered to join a half-battery being transferred to Keetmanshoop.

Arriving there, he heard that Morenga had left his internment village of Prieska. He studied a map of the Cape Colony for a long time to find the place. It was more than three hundred kilometers from the German frontier. For a moment he considered going on leave and riding there, but instead went to the Italian who had settled in the village and opened a barbershop where Caruso sang his arias through a gramophone. Gottschalk regarded himself in the mirror with new eyes after Signor Cevettri had shaved off his beard and trimmed his hair. Afterwards he went to a tailor's shop—also newly opened—and ordered a new uniform. Now he wore the epaulettes of a veterinary captain. Veterinary lieutenants would salute him first.

The village had changed in many ways. It no longer seemed like a barracks square with a few black lackeys; the small shops, bars, and hotels made it seem like a small provincial town with a large garrison. A camel stud farm was underway, and the veterinary captain who was running it, and showed Gottschalk around, explained that this was the only way they would ever get to Simon Kopper, who had withdrawn into the far reaches of the Kalahari. But his honored comrade knew that far better than he did, having done such fine preliminary work in this area.

In the stud farm Gottschalk saw a Bisharin camel for the first time, purchased at his own insistent request for breeding riding camels. A white camel mare of gentle and melancholy mien.

Gottschalk asked permission to take the camel out. Before he resigned from the service, he wanted to write a report on the characteristics of racing camels, and simultaneously seek the remains of the legendary barrel that the professor had never found. He was warned that there were still scattered bands of rebels in the region, but because of his prior service with camel breeding, permission was granted. It wouldn't be any great matter if a Hottentot bullet just happened to hit the balmy vet, but the camel had cost a great deal.

On that evening by the rebel campfire, over the aroma of roasted German oxen and to the dongdididong of the mouth harps, Gottschalk sat down next to Rolfs, the Hottentot he had instructed along with other prisoners in veterinary medicine months earlier in Warmbad. From Rolfs, Gottschalk heard more about Katharina for the first time. Rolfs had heard that Katharina was herself imprisoned in Lüderitz for aiding and abetting the escape of others, but knew of no further details.

Rolfs had been released by mistake in Warmbad, along with Johannes Christian. (It was late in the evening, and Count Kageneck had downed his daily quota.) Rolfs then joined Cornelius and rode with him, and when Cornelius gave himself up, he joined Morenga, and when Morenga, wounded and half-starved, turned himself in to the police, he joined Simon Kopper, and when Kopper in turn made peace with the Germans, Rolfs instigated a rebellion of his own, together with a few men, to fight to the death. He actually managed to capture a few German carts, but in the end couldn't bring himself to shoot the civilians. Instead he merely had the snooty whites whipped with the sjambok, as they had done daily to his brothers and sisters. He was finally caught and died on the gallows in terrible agony, hanged by an inexperienced Bavarian lance corporal. That night the faithful Rolfs, who had absorbed enough from Gottschalk in Warmbad that he could get any lame nag back on its feet, told Gottschalk the story of missionary Gorth, Sheep-Face, of the land surveyor Treptow, and of Klügge, who had a giant barrel of brandy hauled overland by twenty-two oxen. A barrel destroyed by fire before Klügge was swallowed up by the interior. And when Gottschalk scoffed at the stories, Rolfs claimed that the remains of the barrel were still around. Gottschalk laughed and dismissed it as a fairy tale, a professor had searched for weeks for those remains.

Rolfs replied that he could hear the story straight from a cow owned by the Bondelswarts, one they had kept safe to now, in spite of the war, a cow from the tribe of Dotsy. Gottschalk, who had consumed a good deal of the good Jamaica rum and the Kupferberg champagne, decided it wouldn't hurt to go along with the joke and walked out with Rolfs to the herd and a pale-colored cow with long, soft eyelashes. But all he heard was chewing, belchings, and an occasional moo. Gottschalk said the cow was ruminating, but he couldn't understand a thing. At this the drunken Rolfs doubled over with laughter: You call yourself a cattle doctor and can't even understand what they say. The remains of the barrel lie on a small hill, twenty paces south of twin rocks facing a yoke on a plateau to the east.

On the night of Thursday, 29 July, Gottschalk joined a patrol from Keetmanshoop headed toward Geiaub. The camel mare moved more smoothly than the pack camels Gottschalk had ridden up to that point. The swaying and trudging motion of the animal was like a steady, calm swell. When Gottschalk urged the animal into a trot, it seemed to lift from the ground, and what Dermigny described as camel flight began. The patrol tried to keep up at first by urging their horses into a hard gallop, but quickly fell back. The snorting and hoof beats of the horses faded behind, and when he turned they had disappeared into the darkness. Gottschalk rode his racing camel through the night landscape, above him the stars, close overhead, the roe of the night; he started to hum, then to sing, he felt tipsy, and his fear dissolved. From time to time he laughed aloud and recited lines sprinkled with clicks: So come! let us gaze into open spaces, Seeking something our own, no matter how far.

Shouting and singing until he was exhausted and grew calm, Gottschalk later dozed off a few times and nearly fell from the camel, which raced on with no sign of fatigue. Suddenly it cleared in the east and the sun broke free from the earth. Not long after, still in the cool of the morning, he found the face of the plateau with a notch to the east, a sort of glacial valley, the yoke. Gottschalk rode along a few twists and turns until he found the twin rocks, rounded and polished, tall as a man, a pair grown together at one point like Siamese twins. He halted the camel and it immediately began munching on a thorn bush. He walked a few paces to the south and scratched in the sand with the heel of his boot. He was no longer surprised to find brownish-black earth beneath, with bits of wood, rusty hooks, a piece of iron hoop, melted into a bizarre shape at one end, and two screws.

Gottschalk picked up a small piece of charred wood, the grain still visible, polished by the sand, a tiny part of those holm oaks brought from France almost fifty years ago to rouse this sleepy world and set it dancing.

THE PURSUIT

The political situation in 1907 was considered critical and unstable by the General Staff and the Colonial Office. Particularly because, as noted in the General Staff's record, "the longing for freedom is not yet extinguished in the 16,000 prisoners." To this insight was added the knowledge on the German side that they had not held to the agreement for rebel submission and that the prisoners on Shark Island were being allowed to die. The greatest uncertainty, however, was Morenga. The internment of "the Black Napoleon" in the Cape Colony had not damaged his aura. On the contrary, many Africans, and not just in the German protectorate, considered him their liberator and leader in the struggle against white oppression. This slowly brought him into opposition with the English government as well, which at first had generously granted him political asylum.

The Colonial Office in Berlin and the Commander of the Colonial Guard, v. Deimling, corresponded with the German Governor General in Cape Town, v. Humboldt, as to whether they should press the English government to relinquish Morenga, or if they could convince him to endorse the treaty of surrender signed with the Bondelswarts. The German consul advised the latter course of action. In his estimation a request for extradition would not be granted by the English government, and to attempt both at once would be ill-advised, since once a request for extradition had been made Morenga would be suspicious, and with good reason, if he were then to be offered freedom instead of the gallows. But Deimling wanted to go to the root of the problem. A request was made, a case constructed that accused Morenga of having committed murder prior to the up-rising, but without being able to name a single witness. As pre-dicted, the government rejected the German extradition request, in consideration, among other factors, as v. Humboldt notes, of the "local natives." The General Consul was now supposed to deal with the guerilla leader, who was free following the refusal to extradite him, and convince him to return to the protectorate under a guarantee that his life would be protected and he would have his freedom. The meeting between the Imperial General Consul v. Humboldt and the Hottentot leader took place in the office of the British Colonial Secretary on 8 June 1907. (Try to imagine it: Morenga, sitting in an Empire chair across from the General Consul, His Excellency v. Humboldt.) As can be gath-ered from the Consul's reports, Morenga was a skilled negotia-tor. He emphasized his peaceful convictions, but explained that his personal safety did not seem adequately guaranteed. He said he first wished to undertake a journey to Upington, to visit his family and followers there, and discuss the situation with them. Had Morenga already decided even then, sitting across from His Excellency v. Humboldt, to take up arms again?

Morenga must have reached Upington in July. German agents, traders for the most part, kept watch on him. He is said to have thrown a German out of the house. He is reported say-ing, in English, I bring together my lambs. He sent messengers to Johannes Christian, urging them to rise up again against the Germans. An English Lieutenant reports that two messengers from Simon Kopper visited Morenga. A telegram to Colonial Guard headquarters indicated that Morenga left Upington with eight armed men, in the direction of Kaimas, heading toward the German border.

Events are now moving rapidly. The commander of the southern division sends troops to the eastern border. Supplies stations are set up. Batteries move out. Reserves are called up. Captain v. Hagen is sent to Cape Town to press the English po-lice to intervene, but more importantly to coordinate future op-erations between English and German troops. On 9 August,

Morenga's support is said to have grown to thirty men. By mid-August it has reached sixty. Hottentot bambuses working with troops stationed on the border run off in the night. Morenga is said to be somewhere near Kammus, near Zwartmodder, in the Gamsis Ravine, in Aries, in Knidas. He often seems to be in several places at once. Since, contrary to conditions imposed by the police, he had approached the German border, after several notes of protest from the General Consul in Cape Town, an order is issued for his arrest. There is concern in the Cape Colony over high-level political ill-will, since a meeting between the German Kaiser and the King of England was in the offing. Morenga sends another message to Johannes Christian: Better to die standing than crawling on all fours among the rocks. Johannes Christian tires of the struggle. The English report that Morenga wants to make peace with the German government, if he and his men are allowed to enter the Cape Colony and are given 100,000 marks. Other rumors have it that his price is six sheep and the assurance that his life will be spared. In early September the German troops march toward the frontier and the English troops under the command of Major Elliot begin pursuit.

THE MIRACLE BUSH

On Tuesday, 18 September 1907, a longboat brought Veterinary Captain Gottschalk to the steamship *Adolf Woermann*, anchored in the roads of Lüderitz. To the left lay a small rocky island, connected to the mainland by a narrow piled-up dam. Figures could be clearly seen, crouching on the naked rock. Not a tree, no grass, no huts, just the broken rock.

Just short of the island the dam was crossed by a barbed wire fence. They can do almost anything, said a district office secretary heading home on leave, but they can't swim.

In Gottschalk's notebooks, after the meteorological data and descriptions of cloud formations, there is one further undated entry made on his way to Ukamas or on board the steamship:

> Rains are our dreams.
>
> On a bare rock in the desert stands a small bush, like a candle. The Hottentots call it the miracle bush. Its branches are gray. The buds roll up brown in the dry season. It stays like that for years or decades, until it rains, then overnight it blooms in undreamt-of glory, blooms until the water is gone. Then the buds roll up to await the next rain.

Toward noon the steamship weighed anchor.

Gottschalk's last view of the country was of the granite-gray cliffs of the island, and behind them the yellow swells of the dunes, flowing off into the blue sky, saturated by a painfully clear light.

THE END

On board the Imperial Mail Steamship *Admiral* / 2 October 1907 / Report of Captain von Hagen, General Staff of the Colonial Guard, South West Africa.

(From the Governmental Archives for German South West Africa, 2368, vol. 2, p. 251)

On 24 August 1907, I received orders in Windhoek from Lieutenant Colonel von Estorff to travel to Cape Town and inform the Ministry of War and the Chief of the Cape Mounted Police (C. M. P.) of the plans of the German troops for a joint operation against Morenga. I was to travel to Upington to Major Elliot, Commander of the English border troops, to set up communications between German and English troops. I left Windhoek on 26 August and arrived in Cape Town on 1 September.

On 2 September, Baron von Humboldt, the General Consul, accompanied me to the Cape Governor, Sir Walter Helly-Hutchinson, to Prime Minister Dr. Jamson, to the Colonial Secretary, Sir Peter Faure, and to the Chief of the C. M. P., Colonel Robinson. All received me in a spirit of full cooperation. The Cape government seemed to realize that they had made a gross error in allowing Morenga to go to Upington, and this time they appeared seriously intent on cooperating to the best of their ability to settle the Morenga incident. Two factors seemed to have aided in this decision:

1. The Cape government is said to have received a sharply-worded note from London demanding that the Morenga affair be dealt with as quickly as possible.

2. South Africa could no longer be confident with regard to its

own natives. Blacks throughout the south had set their hopes on Morenga, "the Black Napoleon." If he succeeded, a general black uprising might well ensue. The unrest wasn't limited to Upington, but extended as far as Basutoland and Swaziland.

The *manner* in which the Cape government wished to deal with the affair was consistent with the prior approach of the English: not by war, but through peaceful means. The main troops had been reinforced, more to intimidate Morenga and thus encourage him to turn himself in, than to fight. It was even said in Cape Town that the C. M. P. had orders not to shoot.

I left Cape Town on 5 September and arrived in Upington on 10 September. Here I learned that Major Elliot and his troops (about 120 men) had been in Longklip—halfway between Upington and Ukamas—for several days; and furthermore that Morenga had sought to make peace with the German government after the 150 Bondels with him had defected.

I proceeded to Longklip on 12 September and arrived on the evening of the 13th.

I was warmly received by Major Elliot and his officers, but with a certain degree of suspicion; they were quite open about it, feeling I had been sent to keep an eye on them and give instructions. Suspicions eventually eased, and I got along well with all the officers.

Since the weather in Longklip is generally bad, Major Elliot decided on the morning of the 14th to march to Zwartmodder, which offered better weather and reasonable accommodations. There was no reason to object to the move. The following days were uneventful; therefore on 17 September I decided to ride to Ukamas to see Major Baerecke and speak with him personally.

About two hours outside Zwartmodder, I was met by a patrol of English officers led by Second Lieutenant Curris, who reported that Morenga was not far away on the path to Longklip, and told Curris that under no conditions would he make peace with the Germans, and requested a meeting with Major Elliot outside Longklip on the morning of the 18th. I returned to Zwartmodder with Curris.

My assessment of the situation was as follows: Morenga had expressed peaceful intentions to the Germans in the past, but was not negotiating seriously, rather he was seeking time to escape. Now he was repeating the pattern with the English. Morenga had to be prevented from giving himself up to the English, however, for they would simply throw him in prison for a year or two and the same old story would resume. Therefore I suggested to Major Elliot that he march to Longklip that same night *with all his troops*, realizing that Morenga might be frightened off from negotiations. But first of all that wouldn't displease me, and secondly I would be present if Morenga failed to appear for the meeting.

On the 18 September, at 1 o'clock at night, we set out from Zwartmodder and arrived at 6 a.m. in Longklip. Around 8 in the morning Second Lieutenant Curris rode out around 8 kilometers to where Morenga was camped with his men, to escort him in. Since I considered it likely that Morenga would refuse to come to the meeting, I discussed the situation with Major Elliot. I sent a telegram addressed to Major Baerecke informing him that if Morenga wasn't found, or refused to negotiate, Elliot would begin immediate pursuit. Elliot had seen a draft of the telegram and agreed to it, and was thus committed to judging Morenga's failure to appear as *casus belli*, and to immediate all-out pursuit. We watched tensely from the heights of Longklip for Morenga to come into sight.

Around 1 o'clock in the afternoon we saw a cloud of dust in the distance; it was Second Lieutenant Curris arriving, but without Morenga. The signs indicated that Morenga had withdrawn toward the German frontier. Major Elliot immediately ordered his men to take up pursuit—just one squad for now, until the exact direction of his retreat could be more accurately determined.

By 2 that afternoon Second Lieutenant Mander set out with approximately thirty men. Elliot added instructions to fire on Morenga.

At noon on the 19th the first report from Second Lieutenant Mander, dated that morning at Gous in the Molopo district, arrived in Longklip. According to the report, Morenga's trail from the spot approximately 8 kilometers west of Longklip led first toward the German border, then turned north and passing between Zwartmodder and Longklip at Gous, headed east in the direction of Upington. The trail Mander followed was still fresh, since Morenga's lead was slight. At 2:30 on the afternoon of 19 September, Elliot set out from Longklip with the rest of the detachment. We arrived in Gous in the Molopo district at 5 o'clock and stopped for an hour to water the horses.

In Gous we received Mander's second report that Morenga's trail continued eastward toward Upington.

After a two-hour march—from 6:30 to 8:30 that afternoon—we arrived at the major road between Zwartmodder and Upington, approximately one hour west of Kocgockub, and stayed there until midnight.

At twelve midnight we marched on. The trail continued toward Upington. At 1:30 a.m. we watered the horses—for the last time until 21 September—in Middelpütz not far west of Kocgockub. Just beyond Middelpütz Morenga's trail turned sharply north.

No further doubt was possible; Morenga was not heading for Upington, but crossing the Kalahari to Simon Kopper. The sly fox figured that he and the few men in his band—numbering around thirty—could probably cross the waterless Kalahari and feed on shammas, but that troops with animals would shy away from pursuing them into the Kalahari.

But just as he misjudged the pursuit by Bech's detachment in May 1906, when he crossed the frontier into English territory, his flight into the Kalahari was of no avail. As we entered the Kalahari, it was clear that only a ruthless and *uninterrupted pursuit* would achieve our goal. *We had to catch up with Morenga in the course of the 20th* and engage him in battle. If not, we would have to turn around in Morenga's tracks and head back, due to the lack of water. Morenga would then have escaped to safety with Simon Kopper.

Major Elliot and I quickly realized the situation. To his credit it must be said that he demanded the best of his men and gave his best. The troops deserve special recognition for their outstanding stamina and endurance under difficult conditions over a 14-hour chase.

The march lasted from twelve midnight until 2 o'clock in the afternoon—with only a one and a half hour break—in great heat across well over three hundred heavy dunes.

Morenga's trail led first from Kocgockub northward, then northeast across the farms of Harrisdale, Khorkam, Roipart, and Norokei to Eenzaamheid.

Around 1 p.m. we caught up with Lieutenant Mander's squad, who reported that Morenga was not far ahead. Mander had stopped around noon to wait for our arrival. Mander's pause may have caused Morenga to assume that the English troops had called off the chase. It seems Morenga ceased to worry, in any case he rode on for only another hour before he too rested. After joining up with Mander it became imperative than we advance as quickly as possible. At 1:30 p.m. we started on a forty-minute gallop.

Around 2 in the afternoon the landscape altered completely—no longer dunes, but a mountainous countryside with shrubs, offering excellent defensive cover for Morenga.

Elliot ordered the lead squad to dismount at once and deploy for battle—spreading out broadly to outflank the enemy wings.

Our assumption proved true. Morenga had occupied the heights as we expected. The heights abutted the waterless pan of Eenzaamheid.

An extended firefight now ensued. The enemy was so well hidden that for the first hour not a single foe was spotted. Gradually, however, it became clear that a particularly prominent height was the key point in the enemy's position.

Major Elliot agreed with my suggestion to storm the height; I took over command of the right wing—Scouts and Cape Mounted Rifles—while Lieutenant Mander led the left. Proceeding in alternating rushes, we took the height. Major Elliot was with the reserves at this time. Four of the foe were killed at the enemy position, and one wounded; we lost one sergeant, with one man wounded. Once we reached the height, we were fired upon from thick bushes about 400 meters away.

We returned volleys of lively, well-aimed fire in the direction of the bushes, so that the firing from there soon stopped, around 5 in the afternoon.

In the subsequent search of the battlefield we found Morenga lying dead under a tree. He had been shot three times: once through the right temple, exiting behind the left ear; a second bullet had torn away the back of his head, a third had passed through his heart and exited from his back. In addition we found 2 other men dead, 4 women dead, and one man wounded.

The enemy losses were as follows:

Morenga, 6 men and 4 women dead. Among them according to prisoners, a brother, a brother-in-law, and three nephews of Morenga. Two further prisoners were taken, both Simon Kopper's men. 6 rifles and many bullets.

Concluding remarks:

1. The conduct of the English troops during pursuit and the battle was outstanding. The long chase was made easier by fine horses, each receiving 20 pounds of hay during the operation.

The Scouts (native soldiers) proved their worth as trackers. Even by night they followed the trail without hesitation. They were assigned to a special officer.

2. According to prisoners' statements, Morenga sent messengers to Johannes Christian, the Bondel, asking him to break with the German government and join him. Morenga received an unequivocal rejection, a sign that the treaty with the Bondels solidly based and has a good chance to hold firm.

3. The cooperation of German and English troops has become of the greatest *political* importance:

a) It has brought the German and English nations closer in South Africa. There were strong avowals of German-English friendship in Upington after the battle: German flags were raised; enthusiastic speeches were addressed to His Majesty and the troops at various celebrations, etc.

b) The natives of South Africa will now realize they're not fighting the Germans, or the English, or the Dutch, but that *now the entire white race stands united against the black.*

c) The blacks have lost their most important hero, the man they set their hopes on.

EPILOGUE

They have risen from a meadow in Allgäu, after sitting around for three days in an inn playing chess, waiting for favorable wind conditions.

Balloon flight is more than a means of conveyance, balloon flight is an art, a work of art in which the pilot, the balloon, the wind and weather, and the landscape as well, unite. There is no exploitation, except for the fuel. No living creature is tormented or mistreated, the elements merge with consummate ease in drifting flight. The economic factors in balloon flight, aside from the manufacture of balloon silk and the basket, are of no small importance. Nor is the balloon suited for the transportation of goods, since when not traveling in the direction of the wind, it can only be navigated to a limited extent by means of dragropes and steering cords, which trail along the ground.

On a sunny, calm September day the bag was filled with gas; ballast and supplies were carried into the gondola, and the two pilots stepped into the basket. With the help of a small garden trowel enough sand was shoveled from the ballast bag for the balloon to rise a meter or so above the ground. Lüdemann's two assistants simply shoved the basket and the balloon from the hangar into the middle of the meadow. The windsock dangled limply from the mast. Even a narrow strip of silk attached to one of the balloon lines hung motionless. Lüdemann said to his fellow passenger: Balloon flight is like working with precision scales. He took a handful of sand from the ballast bag and, after the holding rope had been tossed back into the basket, let it trickle slowly through his fingers. The balloon immediately rose several meters. Beneath them, small and staring upward, stood one of the assistants, rubbing one eye as he did so.

He's still new, said Lüdemann.

A gentle pull on the valve line and gas escaped with a hiss, for an instant only: the balloon moved downward. A little sand sprinkled through Lüdemann's fingers over the edge like salt and the gondola steadied again approximately one meter above the ground. Then Lüdemann cast seven scoops of sand from the ballast bag with the garden trowel. The hangar grew smaller beneath them, the inn came into view behind a gentle hill, beyond it the village, fields, meadows.

They rose into a cloudless blue sky. At a height of almost 500 meters they were caught in a gentle breeze and driven slowly in a southern direction. Beneath them villages and ponds, people small but clearly recognizable stopped on the streets and stared up at them; the most surprising thing, however, was that every sound could be heard with extreme clarity while floating in total silence: the barking of dogs, the murmur of a brook, the crowing of a cock and, colossally, the ringing of a church bell. They floated over late summer fields, over meadows, over the deep green of the forests, toward the Alps, which rose huge and snow-covered on the horizon.

Lüdemann longed to fly over the Alps in a free air balloon. For many years he had been keeping charts on fall winds and the rise of the Föhn, on the seasonal formation of cumuli and thunderstorms. During the flight Lüdemann and Gottschalk exchanged only a few words. Scoop by scoop Lüdemann let the sand slowly trickle down until the barograph indicated 2500 meters. The earth was a brightly-colored rag rug of gently folding hills and valleys, distant and tranquil beneath them. Their eyes opened to the calm distance, and every sound blossomed with incredible clarity. Lüdemann brought out roast beef and uncorked a bottle of Stein. They drank the wine from small silver cups.

To your health, Professor, said Lüdemann.

When thick cumulus clouds rose in the northeast, Lüdemann

pulled on the valve line a bit longer, and as they descended they entered a stronger current of air that quickly drove them in a southwest direction, slowly sinking, toward the sun.

The wind has picked up, said Lüdemann, pointing down at the rippling waves in the treetops. They sailed over a farmyard at low altitude. People ran out and stared after them. The trees on the country lanes shimmered in the wind. Lüdemann dashed a few more scoops of sand from the balloon, to rise over a small wood. As the basket touched down in the meadow beyond, it was suddenly there again, the rattle of the wind in the ropes, the creaking of the basket. The silk ribbon floated tautly. The basket was pulled a few meters further through the meadow, then Lüdemann pulled the valve line, and slowly, a sky-high flag, the green silk balloon drifted to the ground.